ACCLAIM FOR JUDITH FREEMAN'S

Red Water

"The narrative soars. . . . Freeman's novel makes astute points about the almost indistinguishable similarities between faith and love."   —*The New Yorker*

"Intense, charged with real feeling and electricity. . . . Intelligent, complex prose will give readers a chance to reflect on the deeper meanings of love and faith and endurance."   —*The Oregonian*

"Engrossing. . . . Freeman eschews the tributaries of contemporary domestic life for the deeper and darker lake of the past. . . . Unforgettable."
                    —*St. Louis Post-Dispatch*

"Captures the mayhem of America's westward expansion. . . . An evocative tale of religious brutality and pioneer hardship set against an unforgiving landscape."
                    —*Chicago Tribune*

"A powerful novel whose three narrators engage us so completely that we absorb their intricate history effortlessly."   —*BookPage*

JUDITH FREEMAN

Red Water

Judith Freeman is the author of three
novels—*The Chinchilla Farm, Set for
Life,* and *A Desert of Pure Feeling*—and
of *Family Attractions,* a collection of
stories. She lives in California.

ALSO BY JUDITH FREEMAN

Family Attractions
The Chinchilla Farm
Set for Life
A Desert of Pure Feeling

Red Water

JUDITH FREEMAN

Anchor Books • *A Division of Random House, Inc.* • *New York*

FIRST ANCHOR BOOKS EDITION, APRIL 2003

Copyright © 2002 by Judith Freeman

All rights reserved under International and Pan-American Copyright Conventions.
Published in the United States by Anchor Books, a division of Random House, Inc.,
New York, and simultaneously in Canada by Random House of Canada Limited,
Toronto. Originally published in hardcover in the United States by Pantheon Books,
a division of Random House, Inc., New York, in 2002.

Anchor Books and colophon are registered trademarks of Random House, Inc.

The Library of Congress has catalogued the Pantheon edition as follows:
Freeman, Judith, 1946–
Red water / Judith Freeman
p. cm.
ISBN 0-375-42092-4
1. Mountain Meadows Massacre, 1857—Fiction.   2. Mormons—Fiction.
3. Utah—Fiction.   I. Title
PS3556.R3915 R44 2002
813'.54—dc21
2001033833

Anchor ISBN: 0-385-72069-6

Author photograph © Anthony Hernandez
Book design by Trina Stahl

www.anchorbooks.com

Printed in the United States of America
10 9 8 7 6 5 4 3 2

To Joy

Red is the most joyful and dreadful
thing in the physical universe. It is
the fiercest note, it is the highest light,
it is the place where the walls of this
world of ours wear the thinnest and
something beyond burns through.

—C. K. CHESTERTON

Contents

PART ONE   The Execution · 1

PART TWO   Emma · 13

PART THREE   Ann · 169

PART FOUR   Rachel · 261

The Execution

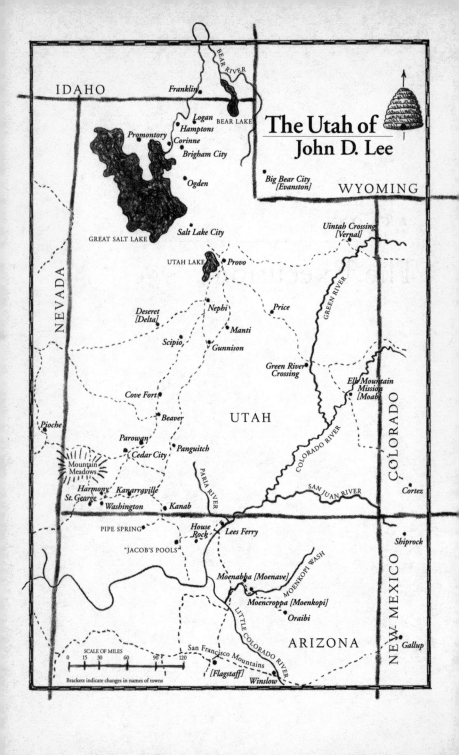

The Utah of
John D. Lee

IDAHO

Franklin

BEAR RIVER

Logan
Hamptons
BEAR LAKE

Promontory
Corinne

Brigham City

Ogden

Big Bear City
[Evanston]

WYOMING

Uintah Crossing
[Vernal]

GREAT SALT LAKE

Salt Lake City

UTAH LAKE   Provo

NEVADA

GREEN RIVER

Deseret
[Delta]

Nephi

Price

Scipio

Manti

Gunnison

Green River
Crossing

Elk Mountain
Mission
[Moab]

Cove Fort

UTAH

Pioche

Beaver

COLORADO RIVER

COLORADO

Parowan
Cedar City

Panguitch

Cortez

Mountain
Meadows

PARIA RIVER

SAN JUAN RIVER

Harmony
St. George   Kanarraville

Washington   Kanab

Shiprock

PIPE SPRING

House
Rock   Lees Ferry

"JACOB'S POOLS"

NEW MEXICO

Moenabba [Moenave]

MOENKOPI WASH

Moencroppa [Moenkopi]

Oraibi

Gallup

ARIZONA

LITTLE COLORADO RIVER

SCALE OF MILES
0   15 30   60   90   120

Brackets indicate changes in names of towns

San Francisco Mountains

[Flagstaff]   Winslow

A WIND WAS blowing that day, old and wintry and mean. It came up in the morning, arriving from the southeast, and by noon it had gained in force and shook the heaviest branches of the trees and caused them to saw back and forth with a low groaning noise. Patches of snow still lay on the hills, old grainy slubs nestled in crevices on the north-facing slopes and thinner white lines running in scallops along the northern ridges.

When he sat on his coffin, the wind ruffled his hair and lifted the flaps of his jacket and they fluttered like the wings of some small black bird clinging to his breast.

Meadowlarks broke into song occasionally, and the wind continued to blow in heavy gusts as more men arrived, riding singly down out of the hills, or coming in groups of two or three, like pale apparitions.

He could hear the sound of the water in the stream.

Where the cows had trod the muddy ground they left hoofprints the size of dinner plates and the earth had now dried and the path was left uneven and hard to walk. The wind made it unpleasant to be out of the shelter of the wagons and many of the men stood with their backs against the running boards or set their shoulders against the warmth of their horses.

In spite of the cold, it felt like spring would soon arrive. All the signs were present—the hopeful notes of the meadowlarks, the grass greening up in the meadow, and the patches of bare earth on the hillsides. There was a feeling some corner had been turned and winter was behind them now, even though the wind still held such bitterness. The sky, though not really overcast, was covered with a white film of clouds, thin and insubstantial, like a layer of gauze stretched over the palest blue eye, and this lent the day a muted feeling. It seemed like a time between seasons—not yet spring, though spring had officially arrived two days earlier, and no longer winter, though something of its recent chill still carried on the air. He noticed the photographer standing downwind of his portable tent and he also noticed how the tent billowed in the surging wind like a living breathing thing.

He could hear a hammering sound of a woodpecker working away at the trunk of a gnarled and misshapen cottonwood tree whose lower branches had grown so thick the main trunk had broken and the heavy limbs now bent to earth. All along the stream the spidery and tangled old cottonwoods had been stunted from drought years and grown more horizontal than vertical, and yet they had managed to hang on to the stream bank, sending out new shoots and new growth each year, shedding the heaviest of limbs to wind and the forces of gravity.

All morning the birds called from the east and the west sides of the stream and the silence seemed magnified by the pale and colorless sky, the dry brown hills, the ridges and north-facing canyons scalloped with the thinning snow. In another month the sedges would green up along the banks of the creek and the snow would be gone and the deer that bedded down here now would leave the meadow and begin working their way back up among the cedar-covered hills.

By June it would be so hot and dry the grasses would begin to dry out and the creek would fall, the once deep water lowering and eddying in pools deep enough to hold fish in the shadows.

They killed him before noon.

The wind was still blowing.

Both spring and winter were on the air.

He had been brought to this spot by the marshal who had befriended him during his long incarceration and who had been helping him maintain his spirits during his first trial, as well as his second.

He arrived about an hour before the actual execution and he appeared to be tired yet calm.

The firing squad was not visible. The five men were hidden behind the canvas cover in the back of a wagon drawn up before the man sitting on his coffin, and they fired their shots through an opening in the canvas.

Before that, however, before the shots were fired, he was allowed to converse with several men who had come to witness the execution.

His photograph was taken by the man who had been pacing near his tent and he asked the photographer to deliver a copy of his likeness to his remaining wives. When that request had been made and agreed to, he rose and said a few last words to the crowd that had assembled to witness his execution.

His voice broke only once and that was when he mentioned his wives and his children who, he said, would be left unprotected in this world.

A minister knelt with him and prayed.

He sat again on his coffin. He took off his coat and handed it to a young man standing nearby with the request that it be given to one of his sons. He said he could see no use in destroying a perfectly good jacket.

He was blindfolded but, at his request, his hands remained unbound.

When the blindfold was in place, he called out to his executioners in a strong and steady voice: Center my heart, boys. Don't mangle my limbs.

Five shots rang out, and then another five coming so close together they sounded like one slightly drawn-out explosion.

He fell back upon his coffin, dead.

Before his death and after, the birds fell silent.

The sun was the same metallic white as the sky, only brighter, far brighter.

The shots had pierced his heart and the blood flowed freely from the wounds in his chest and back. They laid him on the ground and removed the blindfold and someone thought to close his eyes. After a while the blood slowed and it no longer pulsed and gurgled but rather it came in sporadic and weak trickles.

He was placed in his coffin. His hands were crossed over his chest, the big work-reddened knuckles sticking up in hardened knobs. The photographer took one last picture of the dead man lying in the pine box and then the lid was nailed on and the coffin was loaded in a wagon. The wagon, pulled by a pair of white mules and driven by the marshal, lost no time in setting off, much to the disappointment of those in the crowd who would have preferred a longer look at the deceased.

———

THE PHOTOGRAPHER was the last to leave the meadow. When the others had gone he stayed behind and developed his plates and then he packed up his camera and his Carbutt's Portable Developing Box, strapping everything onto his mule with an ease born of much practice. By then the light was falling, raking across the meadow in slatted bands of light and dark, and the wind had almost ceased. He took one last look around him before heading up the trail.

Nothing good ever happened here, he thought.

And nothing good ever will again.

It is a place forever now of death.

He knew that the man had died for his own sins, and he had taken on the sins of those around him and he had died for those too. He had died for a whole people: he had been made the goat, and there wasn't anyone the photographer knew who didn't believe that.

———

THE MARSHAL drove the body to Cedar City and delivered it to the sons, who set out the following morning for Panguitch, where they intended to bury their father. The woman who accompanied them could have been their mother, but she was not, though she had nurtured them often enough in the course of their short lives. They drove an open wagon, the two boys sitting up front on the wagon seat and the woman nestled in back next to the coffin. The wagon was drawn by two red mules that were related by blood as well as temperament. The worn trail rose up through the dense trees once it left the valley floor. There were hills all around. Hills covered in cedars and snow.

To the south the morning light was bright yet overcast. In among the cedars near the road, patches of snow lay clean and white against the red earth and already the sage and rabbitbrush looked a bright green. Where the sage grew up, the snow had receded, creating depressions and dark moist wells, as if the plants themselves, in all their newfound life, had radiated warmth and melted the snow around them.

On the right side of the road, where the bank sloped to the north, the snow clung to the rocks and ravines and in places had drifted to considerable depths.

They came up into the hills, the road a long slow ascending route past the stands of orange and maroon willows, and here the rabbitbrush had grown tall in places, almost as tall as the willows, and through a gap where the hills closed in before opening up again, the vista afforded a view of the wide valley and revealed a settlement. Through this gap the boys could see the farms stretching out from the little cluster of houses and the dark shapes of the animals in the fields. Everything presented such a peaceful scene against the backdrop of red cliffs and the dark cedar-covered mountains, with the snow-clad ridges of the Kolob Range stretching to the south. The clouds had drifted into hard smooth shapes, dense and white, with flat heavy bottoms. They looked like solid domed objects hanging in the sky.

The road crossed over the creek and the boys studied the brownish red water breaking over the rocks beneath the wagon wheels. Everything was red. Red or orange or some shade thereof—the water, the stream banks, the earth, and the rocks that rose up from the fresh greenness and the cedar-dotted slopes. All red, shades of rust and dried blood. Everywhere the snow was melting and trickling down the rich red earth. And everywhere the rock columns rose up and formed towers and pinnacles and other fanciful shapes.

There were ice falls in shadow and water flowing everywhere, red with the burden of the clayey soil.

―――――

THE HIGHER they rose the more the forest thickened. They passed into tall pines. Water oozed out of rock ledges. The snow around them grew deeper and deeper, and they came upon stands of silvery bare aspen and shining dark rocks slick with the water.

The air grew much colder, chilled by the heavy layers of snow now surrounding them. The boy who had charge of the mules said, Whoa there, Sadie, whoa Sam, and drew the animals up, and the other boy sighed and said, Why'd you stop for? The first boy, the older of the two, said that he was cold and he asked his brother to pass him one of the blankets folded in the back and the boy did so. They both wrapped themselves in brightly colored Navajo blankets and then the oldest boy clucked to the mules and they dug in, their hooves gaining purchase against the steep, gravelly road.

Later on they stopped to let the mules rest. The boys got out of the wagon and stood looking up at some spires of red sandstone surrounded by dark pines. Far below them they could see a place where the mountain formed an amphitheater with sheer walls on three sides and out of this great bowl rose dozens of twisted rock spires. The spires stood like figures in a play, wrapped in cloaks of orange and red, all enclosed within a hard stage. Hundreds of crows were flying in circles above the spires.

Look at that, the older boy said to his brother.

I am looking, he replied.

I mean all those black birds.

They're crows not blackbirds.

I know they're crows. I just meant their color.

If you knowed they were crows how come you didn't just say crows?

Give it up, would you? the older boy said and walked away.

During the stop the woman did not leave the wagon but sat with one hand upon the coffin and the other balled into a fist in her lap, her dark eyes looking straight ahead and her mouth drawn into a somber, fixed frown, but as the boys prepared to set off again she asked them to wait and climbed down from the wagon and walked into the woods. She came back shortly and took up her place beside the coffin again and they moved on to the sound of hooves clattering against rock.

The higher they climbed the farther behind them they were able to put the valley they had just left and all its cruel events, and for this they were grateful. When they broke out onto the level at Webster's Flat they let the mules rest again and this time they all left the wagon and sat upon some dry logs and ate the food they'd brought with them.

The sky doesn't get any bluer, the older boy said at one point in order to break the silence. He gazed up through the trees, and his brother and the woman gazed up also, though neither made any comment.

When they had finished eating, the younger boy made a few snowballs and threw them one by one at the stump of a lightning-struck pine, missing it each time, and the older boy, watching from a distance, laughed and told him he was a bad shot just as one of the balls hit its mark.

Up where the pines began to stunt he pulled the mules over again and climbed down to relieve himself. Now the air was very cold. They had almost reached the summit. He stood facing south then turned out of the breeze so the wetness wouldn't blow back upon him. The mountain dropped away sharply. It did not descend at once to the desert floor but rather rolled away in plateaus and ridges, pine covered and falling away from him and the pine and the aspen were intermingled, spread out evenly over the slopes except in the places on the bare ridges and where little meadows created openings in the trees. He could see the line where the snow ended. He could see a butte in the distance, shaped like a house that stood solitary, backed up against the valley, so that what he saw now, what he was seeing, were the backs of the peaks he had looked at driving north yesterday toward Cedar City, when he had left the settlement. No time seemed to have passed since then and yet he was here, with his brother, and with the woman who was not his mother, and with his dead father. That was his father in the box in the wagon, he reminded himself, as if this was something he might have forgotten.

What is the difference between a butte and a mesa? he had once asked his father and his father had said, Now, I believe a mesa has a broader top and otherwise there isn't any difference. Both are solitary, and stand alone in the world.

Back in the wagon once more, he picked up the reins and stropped the long ends against the side of the wagon and at the sharp sound the mules stepped smartly forward.

They camped that night on the summit, sleeping in the wagon box with the great white fields of snow surrounding them, lit up eerily by the light of a half-moon. They slept one on each side of the coffin and one crosswise its end and in the night the youngest boy awoke fearful at lying so close to death and moved his blankets to the ground where he finished out the night next to the wagon wheel.

Coming down into the valley the next morning, the yellow earth matched the color of the greasewood yellowed up from a long winter. At the junction on the valley floor they turned north and headed up a watershed that ran parallel to the one they had left the day before, a green, fertile valley with a well-traveled road winding through the red hills and following a creek.

The road was more beautiful than he remembered. The slow water in the creek the same red color as the earth, and the thick stands of rosy willows. It was a gentle landscape that gave off a warm glow. The earth seemed more golden here. The world a much warmer place.

In Panguitch the boys were met by their aunts and uncles and the brothers and sisters they had not seen for a long time. Behind the little house where their favorite aunt lived, two spotted horses stood in a field and they had never seen these animals before and wondered where they'd come from.

They unloaded the coffin and placed it upon sawhorses set up in the cool dark parlor where it remained for the night.

In the morning the family gathered early for prayers. We ought to get him in the earth, the elder boy said when the prayers were finished. He did not need to tell anyone why. An odor had already begun to issue from the coffin. The women asked the boys to open the coffin and they made as if to raise the body to dress it but it had become necrotic and there was no possibility of disturbing it further without risking unpleasantness and so they laid the clothes over the body. Across his chest they draped a green bandolier made of satin and on his head they placed a white cap shaped like a mushroom. They removed his boots and put white muslin slippers on his feet. Over his lower half they spread a pair of white pants and a green cotton apron sewed in the shape of a fig leaf and when he had been thusly dressed in his temple clothes, they nailed the lid shut once more.

There were few mourners at the cemetery. It stood on a sloping bench south of town. The boy noticed a few other graves with a fresh appearance. Private Riley who had served in the battalion. And several graves of children, all dead before their first year.

The older boys had dug the grave and it looked to be a good job. The sun was warm as they unloaded the coffin. There were more sons than needed to carry it and so the younger boys were given preference, a task to which they applied themselves with unfeigned solemnity. A wind blew from the south and the sound it made as it moved through the thick boughs of the pines sounded like the deep sighing of a dozen anguished souls.

No one spoke as they laid him in the earth. Afterward his son John Alma recited a prayer. The women wept. The boys turned away. Some had set their jaws against emotion, whatever turned in them. The oldest boy, who had driven the coffin from Cedar, fixed his eyes upon the nearby graves of the Sevy children and read the names and dates. Warren Spencer Sevy, born and died the same day in 1865. Mary Malinda Sevy, born and died the same day in 1866. Riley Garner Sevy. Born in

1867 and dead just one year after that. A bad run of luck for that family, he thought. So much death, and them all so young.

Later he headed home in the same wagon drawn by the red mules and this time he traveled faster, with his brother beside him again. The wind sent the tumbleweeds flying in front of him. They rolled across the road and across the flat greening fields and they looked to him like animals scurrying across the ground, some large and dark-colored, and others small and almost bone white, all rushing before the wind.

It's over, he thought. The thing's now done.

He sighed deeply, as if to blow from his being all the rancor and sadness weighing so heavily upon him, and set his homeward course, thinking of his mother, and of what he would say to her when he finally saw her again.

PART TWO

Emma

A STRAIN OF melancholy hangs about me this morning and I am powerless to dispel it.

I have lived at the ragged edge far too long and now the void has finally opened up before me and threatens to draw me in. He is gone, truly gone, and there is no one now left to share my sorrows.

The end has arrived. I have kept a cold hearth here today at the cabin, a wet day with an icy wind blowing down the Paria. Not a soul has come to cross the river and, should anyone show up, Mr. Johnson knows to attend to the ferry himself.

The boys are not about. They have gone north. I do not know when they will return. Perhaps tonight or, at latest, tomorrow or the next day. In any case, I will light no fire today. Nor will I eat any food or break my water fast until the day is done. Not until this black day has passed shall I stir from my silent and melancholy vigil.

The younger children are outside, playing in the orchard. I have given the baby over to the care of the twins. I know she will be safe with them.

I can hear the *tock tock tock* of the blood running in my ears and feel the beating of the pulse in my neck. I can't see anything except for to do this thing, sit here quietly and wait out the day, second by second, minute by minute, and hour by hour. In the wooden chest in the corner I have stored some newly sewed blankets. These I intend to take with me, should the boys return in time. I expect a hard journey. If it is not too late, by morning I will be on the road, traveling northward, in an effort to catch up with the wagon that will carry his coffin.

Do not bury him until I can get there—that was the message I sent with the boys. I am bringing the new coat, the finest coat I ever made. We'll see to it that our husband does not want for a proper funeral.

———

MY LIFE seems extra long to me today.

I was born forty-one years ago, in Uckfield, Sussex County, England, in 1836. My father was Henry Batchelor, my mother Elizabeth Divel. A poor place it was, the place of my birth. Even then the famine had begun to spread throughout the land and the hardships were felt not only by my family but by everyone we knew.

Then the missionaries came. They said we were ripe unto the harvest and the new gospel could take us to a promised land. A free land where the chosen were already gathering. I left my father and mother. They did not believe. But I believed. And so did my friend Elizabeth Summers. We were both touched by the word of God and, when the testimony arose in our breasts with the force of a calling, we went down into the waters of baptism on the same cold afternoon and thus cast our lots with the chosen people.

We left on the last ship to depart from Liverpool that season. My friend Elizabeth Summers and myself. We left our families and our friends behind because they did not believe and we did and there was nothing else we could do but turn our backs on all we knew and on those we loved in order to join the Saints in the great gathering.

The millennium was nigh, and we had been told there was much work yet to be done to prepare for the Second Coming. We would play our part in it, Elizabeth and I. That is what the missionaries promised us. That we should have our part.

I was just nineteen.

Elizabeth was twenty-seven.

We made our plans together and decided to share cooking utensils and supplies in order to save money. What clothes we couldn't buy we made, and in time we were ready for the journey.

We set sail from Liverpool on May 25th, 1855.

The ship was called *The Horizon*. Edward Martin was our captain's name. We had a difficult crossing and many times I felt the storms might have sent us to the bottom of the sea had it not been for our prayers and the intervening hand of our Lord.

We landed at the port of Boston and traveled across country by train, in boxcars fitted out with special seats, reaching Iowa City on July 5th. With the help of the Perpetual Emigrating Fund, which advanced us much-needed money for our journey, we were able to secure a place with the Willy Handcart Company, and although it was late in the year to begin the crossing of the plains, our party was anxious to set out, for nothing less than Zion awaited us in the mountains to the west.

God tempered the wind to the shorn lamb and still the journey was harder than we ever could have imagined. My strength and youth served me well, as did my knowledge of the healing arts in which I had been well schooled. I walked across the plains in the company of Brother Gourley and his family. At Fort Laramie, I delivered Sister Gourley's baby, the first of many children I have since helped come into this world. Many days when others were too weak or sick to be of any help, I pulled the cart myself. I carried the Gourley children across frigid streams. Many in our party lost their feet to frostbite but I did not because I always removed my shoes and stockings before crossing the streams and, once on the other side, rubbed my feet with my woolen scarf until they were warm and dry before putting on my shoes again. This, I believe, saved my feet and allowed me to go on and be of use to others.

But when the storms came, when the heavy snows caught us out on the plains of Wyoming and trapped us in our tents for days, it seemed nothing could save us then. Seventy-eight in our company died in the storms. They perished from freezing and starvation. But I did not die. I lived on to reach the Valley of the Saints. And that is where I met him, a short while after my arrival.

I met him one Sunday in church.

I liked his voice. I liked the way he turned his sentences. He was a man of God, I could tell. He came from the southern colonies. I didn't know that Brother Rollins had invited him to dinner that night and that I would cook for him.

He said my biscuits were like none he had ever tasted.

He said, did I have a partner for the dance the next night? He said, did I want to go with him?

John D. Lee, from Washington County, here in the city attending the legislature, delivering the opening prayer in church.

I didn't know what had already happened, what had transpired just a few months earlier. How could I have known? The events that would later come to haunt my life had already occurred and yet word had not yet reached us in the north. Only the General Authorities had been informed. Later I would gradually come to understand the terrible truth but by then my fate had been sealed.

The hearth is so unnaturally cold today.

I am cold. And I feel such fear for him.

I tell the boys, Your father is a man of God. Do not listen to what others might say.

I have never been sorry—not once—that I became his wife.

Your father is a man of God, I tell them. I knew it the instant I heard him speak that day in church. Bishop Woolley stood and said, Brothers and Sisters . . . Brothers and Sisters, let us begin. It is time to begin our meeting. The opening prayer will be offered by Brother John D. Lee who is here attending the legislature from Washington County.

I liked his looks in general.

The comeliness of his person.

He had a strong face. It was as if he were surrounded by a numinous aura. Some energy flowed outward from the simplicity or unity of his being, and a composure and controlled vitality radiated from him. He possessed both masculine and feminine force in equal measure, and although he was not a tall man, he was broad and strong-looking. He carried himself with an effortless grace. He wore a fine suit of clothes. He held his head up high and his eyes were clear of any blemish. I sensed a godliness in him—something bright shining there in his eyes that bespoke a spiritual force.

Here, I thought, was a man a girl could look up to.

Years later, when my own son waited for me to give birth to my last child, he said, I think Father should be here now. I spoke to him sharply. He would be here if he could get here, I told him. But he could not get here. He was with Rachel, and so I delivered my own child with my son there to help me and I never thought of holding it against him.

I believe I loved him from the moment I saw him.

Such things, I now know, are possible.

We went on our first outing in a fancy buggy drawn by a fine team, all borrowed from Brother Judson Stoddard. We went to the dance held the night after the meeting in church.

I had never encountered a better dancer. He acted as if he really enjoyed the quadrilles and polkas. He showed me dances I had never tried. Before we set out to drive home that night, he tucked the robe about me. He spent a long time tucking it just so, and he kept saying, Are you warm enough, Emma? Are you happy now? He said this as he folded the robe so carefully about my body, tucking it under my thighs and wrapping it snugly about my legs, then drawing the edges over my feet so my boots were covered by the thick wool.

Are you warm now, Emma? Are you happy?

I *was* happy.

Here was a man a girl could look up to.

Now I am not warm, and I am not happy. The fire has all but gone out of me, never, I think, to be rekindled.

I was living with Brother Rollins and his wives at the time, working as a servant to pay off my debt to the Perpetual Emigrating Fund. From Brother Rollins I learned that John D. Lee already had seven wives living with him in the southern colonies. I wanted to become the eighth. I wanted very badly to become the eighth wife of John D. Lee. I did not know then that he had had many more wives than seven. That others had married him and left him over the years. And had I known this it wouldn't have made any difference. My heart had already decided the matter.

He did not take me back to Brother Rollins and his wives the night of the dance. Instead, he took me to the house of his married daughter, Sarah Jane, who was about my age, and I slept in a room with her young daughters.

The next morning, after breakfast, he took us shopping. He let us each—Sarah Jane and me—select a pretty fascinator, a fine shawl to cover our heads. Then he took us to have our pictures taken. Sarah Jane and I had a picture made together, wearing our new shawls. John had his taken alone, in his tall silk hat.

Then he bought us cookies and ice cream.

Later, when we were alone, I expressed my attachment to him. I was afraid that if I didn't speak up he would return to the southern colonies and I would not see him again. So I expressed my desire to him. I said that on first sight he was the object of my choice.

He said he would consult the Prophet the next day on the subject of our marriage and let me know his decision.

I said, Why not do it right now?

I was not afraid to meet the Prophet face-to-face, and I believe John was impressed by my forthright readiness and composure. So we went to see him right away. The Prophet wished to know my history, and he listened carefully to my story of leaving my parents in England, and of my experiences with the handcart company.

After that, he told me to make preparations and he would marry us the following Thursday.

And so, at noon, on January 7, 1858, the Prophet—the Lion of the Lord himself—pronounced John D. Lee and myself man and wife, united for Time and All Eternity. This was done in his own private sealing room, with Sarah Jane as a witness.

———

We set out for the southern colonies the same day. By great coincidence, my friend Elizabeth Summers had also recently married, and she and her husband, Isaac Haight, a colonist from Parowan, were also traveling south, and so we took them to our wagon and journeyed together until our load became too great for the team and we had to part. Elizabeth and her husband went on with a Brother McGavin and his two wives, who had a much more commodious outfit, and although John urged me to join them for comfort's sake, I could not think of leaving him to travel on alone.

A strange honeymoon it was, in the dead of winter. Our wagon was loaded with supplies and the going was slow. But we did not have to camp out. Each night we stayed in a home and were given a bed in settlements along the way.

I was a new bride on the way to my new home.

I was the only English girl he had ever married.

He loved the way I spoke. He found my accent pleasing. He said he had never had a more kindhearted, industrious, and affectionate wife. He saw my strength, my devotion, from the very beginning. When the wagon bogged down, he saw how I did not mind putting my shoulder to the wheel. How I did not hesitate to toil beside him in the mud and freezing sleet. My touch with animals was sure, and this, too, he saw, how I could quiet a team and get them to work in the traces.

I was a virgin, surely it goes without saying, I was a virgin. Not his first. And not his last. Yet I did not care that he had more worldly knowledge than I did for this was the province of men, and in truth I relied on this knowledge to guide me in matters that lay ahead.

I did not know when I lay with him for the first time what I would feel and I was afraid my nervousness might spoil everything, but he took me slowly, he made time with me. He touched me and I felt the knowledge in his touch, how his hands and his body knew how to pleasure a woman—knew the landscape of a woman like one knows the landscape of one's own childhood. I felt that I could trust him to take me past the pain, the first shock of it when I felt my body give way as the membrane rent there at my center and he seemed to break through to the core of me, to a place so deep within me that once discovered I understood that he would always occupy it, that place where he was then, known to no one else but him. I could feel that this was how it would be from then on—*he would occupy me.* He would fill this space that I had never known was empty, and I understood that the pain was part of it, part of the man fitting to the woman, and I discovered that the pain didn't last but turned into something else because when the pain eased I found myself filled with a burning meditated desire and my back arched to him in eagerness as he began moving, moving as if he would drive himself not just into me but through me and then become me, for I felt I was not only myself and separate from him now but had become lost in the union of our bodies. That is when I began to cry out—not in pain but with desire, a desire for more of him, and he was forced to cover my mouth gently with his hand lest our hosts be disturbed. He whispered, *Yes, Emma, now, yes,* and I felt the great shuddering pass through him as his body bucked against me and I did and did not know what was happening then, only that he grew heavy and quiet upon me and in the warmth and wetness came the sudden quiescence of the still unmoving moment of our union, and then he moaned, and breathing heavily, he hefted his weight to his elbows and rolled to one side.

After a few moments his hand moved to me. He said, Now I am going to show you something, Emma, my English bride. I am going to give you something you will always remember and from now on you will know it is I who can give it to you and only I. His fingers began to move against a place I had not known was part of me, a knob of pleasure, a fleshy welt freshly wet from the slickness he had left behind, and I began to feel drawn back and away from myself, as if all of my senses were being gathered up into another realm—yet also cupped there beneath his hand—and I felt somewhere near but not exactly in my body, no longer separated from him but gathered there beneath his fingers into an all-engulfing sensation of such exquisite feeling that rose and rose and rose into an almost unbearable crescendo—and then burst, releasing and carrying me beyond him and beyond myself and far beyond the dark confines of the room where we lay. Everything came in waves then. I pulsed as if carried aloft on waves of light and heat and there was no mind to it, only an escape from the body into pure spirit. I felt transported on the bright and quivering shafts of light. I felt I became the dancing light of distilled spirit, dislocated from any temporal sphere, and I could not stop the little cries from escaping from my lips. He whispered, *Shhhh. Emma, shhhh,* and forced the edge of the blanket against my lips until my shuddering had passed and I'd grown limp against him, though he remained rigid there beside me, his body taut as if he must now hold the shape of our union by himself, lest we both dissolve into utter formlessness.

He let the silence lay between us for a moment, and then he spoke.

Call me Father, he said. From now on you shall call me Father and I will care for you as a father cares for his little ones.

Even then this seemed to me a strange request because no father would touch his child as he'd just touched me but I did not question him. Rather, I tried out the word and whispered, *Father,* and immediately I felt the disappointment fill me, for much of the beauty of the moment dissolved then as the face of my own father floated up and I saw the haggard, drawn countenance of an old man filled with the anger of my abandonment.

For the six nights of our journey south, our coupling was repeated, each time in a strange bed in a different house, and each morning I had to struggle to arrange my countenance and bearing in an effort to conceal the passion that lingered in me long after the sun had risen, in order to meet the day composed and confront the strangers among whom I found myself at breakfast.

By day the traveling was hard, not simply because we encountered storms and unseasonal cold but because there were times when, riding bundled up in blankets beside him on the wagon seat, I could not stop myself from thinking of his touch and there, on that jolting wagon, the tingling would begin again in that place I now knew existed and such feelings rose in me it seemed the thing might happen of its own accord and the reckless urgency of this, the unfettered and uncontrollable force of my desire, obliterated everything else happening around me in the waking and hugely present outer world and all of it, all of these new and urgent longings, frightened me a little.

And then I would remember the Prophet's words, which I had only recently heard delivered from the pulpit in the tabernacle: God Himself is capable of sexual intercourse. In these words I took comfort. I was able to reassure myself that my feelings were indeed a holy part of my purpose here on earth.

At Coal Creek the team broke through the ice while crossing the stream and in the struggle to get out, the wagon tongue was broken and this delayed our journey by a full day while we laid over for repairs.

I wish the delay could have been a month rather than a day, in order to arrest the progress of our journey. For the next evening we reached the rim of the basin and arrived in the tiny settlement of Fort Harmony, where the family awaited us.

They received me kindly.

They were all most cordial, this much I can say. They had not known he had taken another wife until we came through the door of the small log house and he made his announcement, saying simply, My dear wives and children this is Emma, who has been sealed to me and who now takes her place among us.

First I was introduced to his older wives—two sisters, Aggatha and Rachel, who bore a strong resemblance to each other. They seemed about the same age as my mother, and equally stern in appearance, prematurely aged by their harsh lives in the southern climate. Then the other set of sisters, Lavina and Polly, greeted me, a little more stiffly than I would have liked. They were thin, brittle women, less attractive than the first wives, though slightly younger, and in them I also detected a worn-down spirit that I attributed to their harsh circumstances, for although I could see that every effort had been made to convert the humble little cabin into a cozy home, it was a poor place with few feminine touches to soften the sense of a brute and meager existence.

And then Leah stepped forward and took my hand in an icy clasp. She was a large, loosely built matron. I felt a heaviness in her, as if she were standing with reluctant feet on the uninteresting borderland between middle and old age. As she studied my face, the look in her eyes was even colder than the touch of her flesh and I quickly released her fingers and looked away to spare myself the unpleasantness of her gaze.

Last, I met Sarah Caroline and Mary Ann. The former, Sarah Caroline, was a comely girl, close to my own age. The latter, Mary Ann, was a mere child, the girl-wife who had been sealed to him a year earlier when she was only thirteen with the understanding that she should not be required to perform the duties in his marriage bed until she reached the age of sixteen unless she herself desired it, as was the custom with child-brides.

There was no way to know whether she had expressed such desire, but I thought I detected a swelling under her clothes, and I wondered if she was not already with child. If so, her condition gave her a beatific countenance I could only envy.

Of all the wives, I felt most strongly drawn to young Mary Ann, the tall, pretty child-bride. Whereas the others regarded me with a calculating eye, as if trying to judge what sort of threat I might pose to the established order of things, young Mary Ann warmed to me immediately. She came and took my hand and smiled at me—a smile that conveyed such innocence and beauty I felt moved by it—and in this way, wordlessly and yet firmly and openly, she let me know she welcomed me.

There were many children who came forward then, summoned from the sleeping loft and the other cabins within the fort where the various wives kept house. I could not attempt to keep their names straight, or figure out which child belonged to which wife: it would take me days before I could do so. All I knew that first night was that I met twenty-eight children, some of whom were no longer really children but young men and women of my own age, while others still suckled at the breast, and there were many more of differing ages in between, all curious to meet the newest addition to their household.

When the introductions were over, I waited, not knowing what to expect. I felt exhausted and a little overwrought from the strain of the journey and this, combined with the sight of so many people among whom I was now expected to make my place, seemed to elicit a kind of sympathy from the other wives who began to take charge of me.

First I was given a chair before the fire burning in the hearth and told to sit and warm myself, and then Rachel brought me a bowl of soup, which I ate slowly, trying as best I could to answer the questions that were politely put to me by the other wives concerning my accent, my place of birth, the length of time I had lived in the Valley of the Saints and with whom I had lodged and so on and so forth, until I felt myself quite exhausted by their inquiries. All the while I kept stealing glances at my surroundings, wondering how I could possibly live in such a poor place, with so many people sharing such a small space. Everywhere the mounds of bedding had been folded against the walls, awaiting the moment when they'd be laid out for sleep.

The question foremost in my mind was, where shall we sleep? In all my innocence, with all the feeling still fresh in me from our nights of coupling, it did not occur to me that I would not be with him tonight as I had been with him for the last six nights.

When I had finished eating, Father said, We are very tired from our long journey, let us all now retire. And taking a lantern down from its hook, he beckoned to me. Come, let me show you to your room, Emma. Mary Ann will come with us.

These words, simple as they were, filled me with a sudden dread.

It seemed to me that the thing I could not have imagined happening was going to happen and I was startled by this thought. Were

Mary Ann and Father and I to share the same bed? How could I be expected to agree to such an arrangement? And yet how could I refuse? Under the terms of our marriage, I was bound to obey his wishes.

I followed him out into the dark night—so dark that we had to join hands to keep from stumbling—and the three of us, holding on to each other, began to slowly make our way across the uneven earth. The wind was howling with such a terrible force I had to walk with my head bowed to keep my balance. He led the way down a rocky path, the lantern throwing a feeble and wavering light before him and illuminating the white patches of snow laying on the black earth. The night was like an immense void—blacker and vaster than any earthly realm—and were it not for the occasional pale patch of white snow I might have been stumbling through the cosmos, loosed not only from the pull of gravity but from any reality I might heretofore have known. I did not know what I was moving toward. I simply trudged on in the darkness, tugged forward by the clasp of Father's hand and in turn pulling young Mary Ann along behind me, as if we were yoked to one another in a fixed and immutable human chain, until finally we reached the door of a darkened cabin and I was led inside and shown to a small room at the rear of the structure.

There was only one bed in the room, covered with a thick quilt. It was unspeakably cold and I stood there shivering, whether from fear or cold I wasn't sure. Mary Ann stood at my side, not speaking, only smiling, her bright eyes shining there in the lamplight.

He turned and faced us and drew us both to his breast and held us there for a moment. You shall be sister-wives now, he said, and share this dwelling.

He undressed slowly, pulling off his heavy boots and removing his dusty outer clothes until he was left standing in his endowment robes, the pure white garments of our faith, and we did the same, Mary Ann and I, undressing there beside each other, and then we crawled beneath the covers together.

Thus I spent the first night in my new home, curled up against a cold wall, sharing the narrow bed with my new husband and the girl-wife who fell asleep with ease while I lay awake in the darkness, listening to the wind as the cabin creaked and settled with the cold. I could not empty myself for sleep in such a strange place. Nor could I dispel the great heaviness in my heart, for I knew then that the days of sharing had begun.

———

THE LIGHT has fallen here in the canyon. Already the sun has dropped behind the cliffs and the shadows fill the world.

From the window I can see Mr. Johnson. He is toiling down by the river. A party has arrived and commenced to prepare for a crossing. The barge has been readied for the wagons. But the loose oxen are refusing to take to the water and Mr. Johnson is struggling so, lashing the beasts forward with a brute vengeance while others attempt to form lines to keep the cattle from turning back. I can tell the men in the party have little experience in such matters and Mr. Johnson is no help. He is riling the beasts beyond all reason and no good can come of it. Father has told him before, the animals must be coaxed to their purpose calmly if they are to succeed, otherwise fear shall rule and defeat all efforts. If only Father were here, the job would be finished by now.

If only Father were here.

I believe he must be gone by now. The execution was set for noon.

And yet I still feel his presence in this world.

The ravens are calling from the cliffs. Their plaintive cries echo throughout the canyon and fill the evening sky with the sound of loneliness itself. My heart feels like it barely beats in my breast, as if I'm the one whose life is ebbing away.

But this is not so.

I am here, in this room with its cold hearth, in this cabin we built together.

And where is he? This thought fills my mind: *Where is Father now?*

TWO

T HE BOYS STILL have not returned.

A while ago I fed the younger children and put them to bed. As I tucked the quilts around the twins and bent to kiss them, Annie said, Where is father to tell us good night?

He is away, I said.

Away, away, called Dillie in a tiny singsong voice.

Emmie then spoke up and asked, Will we see him tomorrow?

What could I say to them? When I myself no longer know if he still lives and walks on this earth?

Soon, I said. I hope we shall see him soon.

Then I blew out the lantern and returned to the hearth where a low fire now burns, in deference to the comfort of my children.

I have decided to set down this narrative exactly as it comes to me, even if in the telling a somewhat wayward chronology emerges, because I wish for there to be a record of the truth. So many falsehoods have attached themselves to my husband's name, and I feel that I can—that I *must*—be a witness to the events of the past, for if Heaven is the only true reality and the world is but a tale, who but the witness can give it life?

———

IT WAS A strange land to which he brought me as a young bride, fresh from the comforts of the city. Nothing could have prepared me for the world that awaited me in that region far to the south. When I first spied it, it seemed contrived by some scene painter given to employing the most lurid color, so vivid and extreme was the palette of the land-scape spreading out before me.

It was as if the mountains had broken open to reveal their hidden, molten cores. This was the sight that greeted me when I awoke that first morning and took stock of my new surroundings. The peaks of Kolob Mountain rose like the massive prows of four great red ships steaming their way into the valley. Bare of all vegetation, they seemed made of no earthly substance, unless it be fire. I wished very much that Elizabeth were with me then so I could have pointed out the great peaks to her and said, We have come a long way from Uckfield, haven't we, dear friend?

I felt at that moment as if I had arrived at the edge of the known world.

As if I had finally reached the true Zion.

The land of the burning rocks.

———

IMMEDIATELY UPON my arrival, I entered into the business of cook-ing and kitchen work, for this was my specialty. I tried to take hold with a cheerful efficiency, which I believe not only Father but the other wives appreciated.

And yet I found that I had to cut desire into short lengths and feed it to the hungry fires of courage during those first weeks in my new surroundings. It was not easy finding my way in that large house-hold. Nor was it a simple matter sharing my husband with seven other wives.

On the first morning, not until breakfast was over did I venture outside. Mary Ann and I shared the dishwashing and then we went out to look over the area together.

The settlement had been constructed on the plan of a fort. It was enclosed by high adobe walls for protection against the elements as well as the natives who, by and large, Mary Ann informed me, were not to be feared—but neither were they to be trusted. The Pah-Utes, as the local

Indians were called, often carried out predations on the horses and horned stock unless the animals were confined within the fort at night, although the herds had now grown so large that the cattle remained outside the walls, in specially built corrals, with rotating sentries to stand guard.

The double gates of the fort were on the north, and straight across from them stood the meetinghouse, a rectangular building constructed of strong timbers. Father's family quarters—composed of several adjoining cabins made of unbaked adobe bricks and hewn logs—were all on the west side of the fort. The well had been dug in the center, and all the privies were outside the enclosure.

Thirty-two families lived in Fort Harmony, Mary Ann informed me as we strolled toward the gates, passing workers who were putting the finishing touches on Sarah Caroline's new cabin. Mary Ann explained how most of the families lived within the fort although a few more adventuresome settlers had recently built dwellings across the valley, at a new town site that had been laid out at the base of the mountains.

Once outside the enclosure, we stopped and stood looking toward where the cattle were grazing quietly in the fields. Mary Ann began pointing out which herds belonged to Father. Knowing the value of one animal alone, I could not help but be impressed by the great number of cattle he owned and I felt compelled to ask, How did Father come to have so many fine animals?

It was the Indian Depredation, she said. In the aftermath, Father gathered up the cattle left roaming in the hills and claimed them for himself.

I remembered what Father had told me during our long journey south, that there had been an incident involving the local Pah-Utes and a wagon train of emigrants from Arkansas, bound for California. The wagons had been camped in a meadow to the west of this valley when they were besieged by the natives. For three days the natives carried out their depredations. Many people had died, Father said. Many men, women, and children, and it was only through the intervention, during the last minutes of the attack, by a group of local settlers that some of the youngest children had been saved. Father had been one of those who had intervened, and Elizabeth's husband, Isaac, had been there as well. They had managed to rescue seventeen children. These orphaned children had later been brought back to the settlements and adopted into homes.

When he had finished telling me this story, Father warned me there were people, mainly Gentiles and Californians, who were now spreading rumors, trying to suggest that the settlers who had rescued the children had also had a hand in the killing of the white emigrants, but, as Father was quick to point out, our enemies were numerous and they had always spread lies against us. Besides, he said, such talk was to be expected in this time of impending war. He wished only to prepare me, he said, for the stories I would surely hear once we reached the settlements.

———

I ADMIT IT disturbed me, as I stood there with Mary Ann, looking over those fine herds, to think of Father profiting from such a horrible event, but there was something else about the story that troubled me even more. What was to keep the natives from meting out the same fate to us as they had the emigrants? It was a question I put to Mary Ann.

You said the Indians were not to be feared. And yet they carried out a most brutal attack on an innocent party of whites. How do we know that we are safe?

They didn't attack us, she replied calmly. They attacked the emigrants—the Mericats—who I'm told were a wicked and rowdy people and incited the natives to action. Many say they deserved their fate. But that's not for me to judge.

She turned and smiled at me. In any case you needn't worry, she said. The Indians are our friends. They trust us as they trust no others.

I started to ask her another question but we were suddenly interrupted by a boy who strode up to us. Mary Ann quickly introduced me to John Alma, father's oldest son by his third wife, a boy who had not been present when I arrived the night before. He was perhaps fifteen or sixteen, only a few years older than Mary Ann, and extremely comely to gaze upon. He had a fine unblemished complexion and clear blue eyes. Like his father, he possessed an aura of manliness, even at his young age, and it seemed to me that he had also inherited some of the spiritual magnetism of his father. Mary Ann seemed greatly affected by him. She appeared to come to life more fully in his presence.

Would you care to get into the wagon and take a ride up to the big house? John Alma asked us. He had the outfit ready, he said, and he would be pleased to take us for a drive. Father had been called to a meeting with some of the other brethren. The women were all busy with their own affairs. And he would be happy to take us for a ride if the prospect interested us. I had no idea what the "big house" was, but I quickly agreed to the outing.

We set out across the broad expanse of valley, Mary Ann and I sitting on the front seat of the wagon next to young John Alma. The trip was a revelation to me. The daubed color and running shelves of red and pink and white rocks flashed through the cedar-covered slopes. Amid the spreading reaches of the fields, several men could be seen plowing the dark red earth while others toiled to clean out ditches. A smell of burning weeds hung on the air, and a sense of industry, of a colony beset by activity, infused the scene spreading out before me.

But the greatest revelation of all was the big house itself, the stone mansion that occupied a fine site in the new township at the base of the mountain, which was our destination and which, I slowly realized, belonged to Father.

The house, Mary Ann explained as we drew up before it, was not quite finished. I could see for myself that the workers were still engaged with the task of putting on the roof. When it was completed, she explained, the two-story dwelling, already called the "Mansion

House," was to be occupied by Aggatha and Rachel, Father's oldest wives.

Once again a strange feeling came over me, as it had as I gazed at the large herds. How had Father contrived to acquire the means to build such a grand place? I realized my impression of the previous night—the sense of penury and harsh circumstance that pervaded the small cabin and which greeted me upon my arrival—stood in conflict with the sizable herds and the grandeur of this mansion I now beheld. I had believed Father to be a man of no more than ordinary means, and indeed, every impression I had gathered in my short time in the small colony was of a people struggling to survive at the edge of the known world. The children were dressed in little more than rags and some went shoeless. The women wore dresses made of the poorest material. And food seemed to be so scarce that our wagon-load of supplies from the city quickly disappeared into various pantries, whisked away by the wives as if a packet of tea or sugar were the rarest treasures, worthy of being laid up in the most secret of places.

Perhaps one day Father will build you a fine house, too, Mary Ann said.

I made no response to this, for I had lived among the Saints long enough to know that in households where the Principle was practiced, it was the older wives whose needs were met first, who received the treatment of preference. What could be left for the eighth wife?

And yet, looking at the great stone house, I couldn't help but hope that one day I, too, would have a dwelling of my own—not necessarily a house this grand, but merely a simple place, over which I could preside as mistress, in the company of my children.

For it was children that I wanted more than anything else. Many children to call my own, and in whom I might see a perfect likeness of their father.

We continued on, driving up a steep road that led from the new town site to a spot called Lone Pine, where John Alma stopped the horses in order to allow us a view.

The whole valley presently lay before my sight, as well as the magnificent peaks of Kolob Mountain, the four red stone ships bearing down on the little pastoral scene spreading out before me. The wind was blowing from the north, an icy wind that penetrated my clothing and cut to my bones. Later I would come to realize that this wind was a regular feature of this landscape and I would come to despise it, and curse it, and fight it to no avail. But then, on that first day in the valley, I simply drew my shawl around my neck, imagining that this wind was perhaps an exception instead of the rule in the land of the burning rocks.

In spite of the coldness of the wind, the scene inspired me, and I had no wish to leave it yet. From this height I could see more red peaks, gigantic rocks twisted into fantastic shapes such as a person might see when he had the fever in his head, an otherworldly landscape of indescribable beauty.

I said, If Father should ever build me a house, this is where I'd like it, high up here, where there's a running stream and trees and a view of things. And then I blushed at my own boldness, for who was I to command such a house, or even to dream of it?

———

THAT WAS how I spent the first morning in my new home.

I did not lay with Father that night.

Nor the night after.

Nor the one after that.

But on the fourth morning he came to me. He came to the place where I slept with Mary Ann in the little cabin we now shared as sister-wives. She had already left our rooms that morning. Father entered suddenly, without warning. He greeted me fondly, calling me his English bride, his rose of Sussex, his sweet Emma-child. He smelled of a wood fire and I knew he'd come from another's hearth.

He pressed me to him and told me he was pleased with me, much pleased, and he asked if I was happy. He kissed my face, and as he did so, he undid the buttons on my bodice. Give me my little tummies, he murmured, using a word I had never heard him utter before.

And yet instinctively I knew its meaning.

I gave him my breasts, allowing him to take first one, then the other, and he sucked like a hungry child, inspiring in me the most sublime feeling. I wanted him to take me again to that place known to him and only him, and once more I felt myself being taken up by the light, the quivering shafts of light that led to the dancing realm of distilled spirit. And here was a new revelation, a fresh awareness that dawned only at that moment: I understood that there were many paths to the sublime, and Father seemed to know them all, for who could have imagined such pleasures issuing from the breasts?

That is what he called them from then on.

My little tummies.

And this is how he often came to me.

In the morning.

With the first light.

I HAD WITH me only one book, an Encyclopedia of Greek Mythology given to me by my mother for my twelfth birthday. This book had been my companion for so long that I couldn't bear to think of parting with it, nor had I ever contemplated the idea of doing so, until Father spied it one day and objected to a work of such paganism finding space beneath his roof. He suggested I might divest myself of it at the earliest opportunity, proposing that I could barter it for more useful items the next time we had occasion to journey to Cedar City, the settlement fifteen miles to the north of us, where there were several Gentile families who, he said, might find use for such a book.

The wives called it my heathen book and ridiculed me for having carried such a heavy—and to their minds completely useless—object all the way from England, these stories of multiple gods being not only an affront to the idea of the One True Supreme Being but a foolish encumbrance as well. And so, to avoid such criticisms, I took to hiding my book of mythology, and taking it out only when I was certain I wouldn't be discovered leafing through its worn and familiar pages.

———

By watching and listening carefully during those first few weeks in my new surroundings, I discovered many secrets of Father's household.

I learned, for instance, that Sarah Caroline could neither read nor write, though she pretended to be skilled at both.

I learned that Aggatha no longer liked the deed and turned Father from her bed whenever possible, though I noticed he often insisted on taking his turn with her, as he did with all his wives.

I discovered that Rachel was a petty thief and that unless I kept careful watch over my tiny pantry, my coffee and my tea—those precious items I had brought with me from the city—soon began to disappear, spoonful by spoonful.

I came to understand that Polly and Lavina, the sisters whom Father had married ten years earlier, were so cojoined in their movements and sentiments that they had even managed to time their pregnancies so they coincided, a situation I dared not give much thought to for it seemed to me to contain some element of the unnatural. As indeed did the women themselves. They had long thin faces with dark and heavy brows. They often attired themselves in clothes made of the same fabric and they wore their hair alike. Each had three children the same age. And each seemed to require the other to the exclusion of anyone else, except of course, their children, and Father, over whom they fawned like new brides.

I discovered, too, that Leah, the wife of heavy build and stern temperament, was given to swoons and talking in tongues. She seemed to find this a form of evening entertainment. Many times, in the midst of a quiet evening round the fire, she would suddenly fall into a fit and, with her eyes rolling and her tongue lolling from her mouth, begin trembling while the most astonishing gibberish poured forth from her. At such times, the other wives would surround her and support her head and shoulders, giving her nonsensical utterances the greatest attention, as if she were a sibyl capable of delivering a verdict on the future, but it seemed to me these swoons were but staged events, orchestrated by the poor lumbering Leah—a homely and much-fleshed woman—as an attempt to gain attention, for I often glimpsed a flash of cold calculation showing through a fluttering eye, and I refrained from participating in such dramas on the grounds that I did not believe in their authenticity.

I learned also that the small boy named Charley, the child with the sad face and fearful eyes, was not the natural-born offspring of Leah, as I had first assumed, but rather one of the orphans rescued by Father and the other brethren in the wake of the Indian Depredation. The boy's father, a certain Mr. Fancher, had been the leader of the company of Arkansas emigrants who were slaughtered by the Indians. The boy rarely spoke and seemed still to be in a highly disturbed mental state, even five months after the awful affair, and for this I could not blame him. From all accounts, he had seen his parents and his brothers and sisters killed before his very eyes. Who would not fall mute with fear? He now spent much of the time sitting quietly in a corner by the fire, playing with a little wooden horse that Father had carved for him.

I learned also, after only a short while in the settlement, that I was not to ask too many questions about the Indian Depredation. Whatever had happened, whatever they had seen there at the meadow, it had left the brethren in the colonies tight-lipped and anxious. And as for the women, they would not meet my eye when they spoke of the lamentable affair and turned my questions aside with the standard reply, that it was a thing best forgotten, the sooner, the better.

I discovered, too, that a number of Father's wives were with child, although Mary Ann was not among them as I had first imagined. Rachel was due to give birth in February, Leah in the spring, and

Sarah Caroline in the summer, and the idea that I, too, could soon be with child filled my heart with the deepest feelings of wonder and excitement.

Of all my early discoveries, however, the most shocking and at the same time most titillating was the revelation that Mary Ann—my sister-wife, the sweet-natured girl I grew more fond of every day—loved not Father but Father's son, John Alma, the comely lad who had taken us on the drive that first morning I spent in the settlement.

This discovery I made one night when she took me into her confidence, as we lay in our common bed. She confessed that many times since her marriage to Father he had attempted to press himself upon her and that each time she had spurned his advances, protesting that she was not yet ready, that she was too young, that she was frightened of the deed. And she most truthfully *was* young, having only recently celebrated her fourteenth birthday, while Father was entering his forty-seventh year. I had no difficulty whatsoever understanding her wish to be wed to someone nearer her own age, someone with whom she might still enjoy the pleasures of youth, who shared the passions and energies common to the young, and John Alma's charms were certainly manifest. And it seemed that he, too, had fallen in love with her. The attraction, the passionate feelings, were wholly mutual, I was told. But he had made it clear that he feared going against his father in this matter. He did not see how he could reasonably challenge him for Mary Ann's hand without inciting anger, or even banishment, and then where would they be? Unable then even to arrange the stolen moments they now enjoyed? Many nights we lay awake discussing her predicament, until at last Mary Ann resolved to speak her mind to Father in an effort to obtain a Writ of Releasement that might allow her to pursue the object of her true desire.

———

I ALSO learned in those first months in the colony how to live with the fear of war, although this surely is a boast on my part, for I don't think one ever really learns to *live* with such a fear but simply to accommodate its terrifying grip on the mind and the soul while summoning up the courage to carry on as best as one can.

Even before I left the city, the talk among the Saints there—which I had heard in every quarter, from the pulpit to the dry-goods store—had been of the coming confrontation with the United States and the need to prepare for the imminent war with the troops of Johnston's army, who had been marching toward our colony since the early months of summer, dispatched by President Buchanan to quell what were perceived in Washington as "irregularities" within our territory—meaning the United States did not wish us to practice our Divine Principle, nor did they want us to build up our Sacred Kingdom in the West, free of secular rule and interference. Only an early winter, and disorganization in the federal army, had spared us an attack in the fall and left the troops stranded, quartered at Fort Bridger for the winter, where they were awaiting better weather in order to march forward against us.

We knew it was only a matter of time before they arrived.

And we were much afraid. The thought of war filled our minds, and the preparations for it—the drilling of the militia, the laying up of crops, the securing of hiding places deep within the fastness of the mountains—took up much of our energy that winter.

The Prophet, who, like so many other Saints, had endured the earlier persecutions, had vowed to stand and fight to the last man rather than let our people be driven from their homes again. I had heard his sermon in the tabernacle before leaving the city. *Before I will bear this unhallowed persecution any longer, before I will be dragged away again among my enemies for trial, I will spill the last drop of blood in my veins and will see all my enemies in hell,* he had proclaimed. *I will fight with gun, sword, cannon, whirlwind, thunder, until they are all used up in the pocket of the Lord.*

And that is what we shall do with those soldiers if they come here, Father would say, as he urged us on with our preparations. We'll dispatch them to their maker. They'll find themselves used up in the pocket of the Lord. Used up and destroyed forever. For God is on our side, ready to help us prepare for the Final Battle and the Second Coming of Our Lord Jesus, and in this, we cannot fail.

———

FATHER HAD so many different sides to him.

I came to see this as time went by.

Yet the more I came to know about the wives, with whom I spent such long hours every day, the less I felt I knew about Father, who was often absent from the fort, engaged with military preparations and busying himself in the fields, or gathering timber in the canyons, and putting the finishing touches on his mansion.

———

MANY TIMES in those first months following my arrival in Harmony, I paused to ask myself this question: *Whom had I married?* Our courtship had been so brief, our marriage so swift. And yet, if I imagined I would remain in such a state of ignorance for long, I was greatly mistaken in my understanding of the workings of the female community, for in time I went from knowing almost nothing about the man I had married to learning a great deal about him, thanks to the gossip that passed so freely among the wives and the other women in the tiny settlement that I now called home.

Aggatha, Father's first wife—the wife of my youth, as he was wont to call her—was the source of much of this gossip. She seemed to take delight in reminding me that she had known Father much longer than anyone else and traveled with him through many hard times. I believe it gave her a feeling of superiority to be able to recount the tales of their struggles together, and while the conspicuously heroic light in which she often cast her own actions often oppressed me with its self-serving tone, I listened quietly to her stories. I always listened. What else could I do, trapped as I often was in her company? The clamorous tide of her memory, once loosed from its distant horizon, rolled on and on, like the endless waves of an incoming sea, delivering detail after detail concerning her years with Father. And I admit to having curiosity—especially when her tales veered from her own trials and tribulations and triumphs of spirit and came to rest on the more prosaic facts concerning Father's own history.

In any event, in what seemed like a rather short time, I found that I had accumulated enough details concerning Father's past to form quite a complete picture of his life.

And this is what I learned.

THREE

H E WAS BORN in Kaskia, Illinois, in 1812. His father was an alcoholic and disappeared when he was young. His mother died when he was three. Shortly thereafter he was sent to live with his grandfather, a trader who spoke an Indian dialect as well as English and French. There he was placed in the care of a colored nurse who spoke only French to him.

When his grandfather died, Father was only seven. He was taken in by an aunt who often abused him and forced him to speak a new language. By the age of fifteen he was making his own way in the world, carrying mail on horseback through the sparsely settled region of Illinois. He worked on a riverboat on the Mississippi and drifted through mining camps, until he met the Woolsey family in a town called Vandalia, Illinois, and fell in love with the oldest daughter, Aggatha. They were married in 1833.

Their first child, William Oliver, died before he was two. Their second child, Elizabeth Adaline, also died young. Around this time, a neighbor named Levi Stewart, who had recently been converted to a new religion, gave him a copy of the Book of Mormon and he read the book, finishing it on the night he sat up with the corpse of his second child.

From that moment on, his life was changed.

Utterly changed, as Aggatha put it.

Longing to know more about this new religion, Father and Aggatha made their way west across the Mississippi River in 1838 in the company of Levi Stewart and other families, finally arriving in central

Missouri where the Saints had gathered in a place called Far West. There Father met the Prophet Joseph Smith in person, and was baptized by him, along with Aggatha.

They took up land on the Missouri prairie and Father soon earned a reputation for his industry and trustworthiness. But life was not easy. The Saints among whom he settled had already been driven from Ohio by angry mobs and now the Missourians turned against them as well. They burned their farms, torched their houses, and tarred and feathered the Saints. Father, being strong and full of vitality, joined the defense of his people. He became a leader in the Host of Israel, the private militia formed by the Prophet, who was now also known as General Joseph Smith. In the skirmishes that followed, Father showed a fearlessness for which he would later become known. After the massacre at Haun's Mill, where so many Saints were killed, the Prophet chose to surrender, and the church leaders were taken to prison. Forced to give up their land, their homes, and all their property except their teams and wagons, the Saints once again prepared to move. Thus, six months after they were baptized, Father and Aggatha were on the way back to the safety of Vandalia, with their new baby girl, Sarah Jane.

Yet persecution only strengthened his commitment to their newfound religion, Aggatha said. It sharpened his sword and gave him the gift of a silver tongue.

For the next five years he traveled as a missionary for the Gospel, working chiefly among the well-to-do class. He developed a way with words and, when it suited him, he mixed his knowledge of French and Indian dialects into his sermons, often to great effect. He was a powerful orator and told wonderful stories. He possessed a natural charisma, and he could charm both women and men, and in no time, he had baptized over a hundred people, working tirelessly for his faith and even traveling to Tennessee to proselytize among strangers. Later he and Aggatha decided to join the Saints who had gathered in Nauvoo, the City of the Beautiful, built by faithful on the banks of the Mississippi River. There he set about helping to erect the Great Temple.

In Nauvoo, Father took his first plural wives, with Aggatha's consent, as she was quick to inform me.

In February of 1844 he married Nancy Bean.

Three months later, he married Louisa Free and Sarah Caroline Williams. He also married Aggatha's younger sister, Rachel, as well as their widowed mother, Abbagail. All four women became his wives on the same day.

When Aggatha told me this, I felt such surprise I could not help but ask, He married your sister and your *mother*? as if I might have heard her wrong.

He married her for her soul's sake, Aggatha said coldly, eyeing me with some disdain, as if to suggest my question contained an aspect of the unseemly.

My mother was nearly sixty when they were wed. His only interest was her spiritual welfare, she added, and then continued on with her story.

In 1845 he took four more wives: he married Polly Workman, Martha Berry, Delethia Morris, and Nancy Vance.

A year later, he married Emoline Woolsey, Aggatha's youngest sister.

By quick calculation, I realized this meant he had by then married four Woolsey women—the widowed mother and her three daughters— and I could not help but wonder at this, though I knew better than to interrupt Aggatha again. Perhaps, I thought to myself, these Woolsey women *needed* marrying. Perhaps there was no one else to care for them and Father had been doing them a kindness. In any case, Father had by then accumulated eleven wives, not all of whom, Aggatha freely admitted, could he publicly acknowledge.

The Holy Doctrine of Plurality of Wives, introduced by the Prophet in 1841, was still largely practiced in secret. Only an inner circle of elders was permitted to engage in what was known as the Principle and Father was part of that inner circle. The Principle held that it was the natural order of things in God's Kingdom for a man to have many wives. And Father was not a man, Aggatha said, to refuse what God had ordained.

In 1844 the Prophet decided to run for the office of the president of the United States, a move that angered his enemies, and within months he was murdered by a mob at the Carthage jail. Father, who was away on a mission at the time, returned to Nauvoo to be with his wives during this time of turmoil. By then the Saints had chosen Brigham Young as their new prophet and leader and Father was appointed as his secretary. But new troubles soon arose. Threatened by their hostile neighbors once again, the Saints prepared to abandon Nauvoo, the City of the Beautiful they had worked so hard to build. To avoid further bloodshed, the leaders agreed that the Saints would leave the state of Illinois as soon as the grass grew and the water ran.

In the middle of the winter, Father crossed the icy Missouri into Iowa and established a camp with his wives, including his youngest wife and her six-week-old baby. Soon afterward the Prophet Brigham and his wives joined them, and other Saints followed. Fighting bitter cold and winter storms, the exiles camped there on the prairie, slowly inching westward as the weather permitted.

Oh, it was cold, Aggatha said to me. Bitter, bitter cold, such as you likely have never known.

I did not bother reminding her that I had been with the Willy Handcart Company and survived the blizzards on the Wyoming plains that took the lives of seventy-eight of my companions. Instead I simply listened.

I listened very carefully.

In late August, Aggatha said, they arrived at a place in Iowa they called Winter Quarters, where they set up tents and prepared to wait out the long winter.

Now all the talk was of moving on to the mountains in the West when spring arrived and weather permitted travel. But first there was the winter to survive. It was Father who was sent on several missions of vital importance. In 1846 he was given the entire sum of money accumulated by the Saints and directed to go to Missouri to buy wagon covers and material in preparation for the great migration. Then the war with Mexico broke out and the Saints raised a battalion of five hundred men to fight for the States. A few months later Father was sent across the continent to Santa Fe, New Mexico, to collect the wages of the battalion in order to buy food for the starving colony. Riding horseback, with a minimum of rest, he traversed unknown lands and braved attacks from the natives and carried out his mission.

He became a hero to us then, Aggatha said, and he also proved there wasn't a country he couldn't navigate, or a mission he couldn't see through. You must imagine this, that with just his horse and his dog and a few chosen men for company, he made a ride into the unknown and returned with enough money to keep us from starving.

After that trip, which lasted three months, he outfitted two wagons and set off for Missouri to bring back food and supplies. Traveling weeks through bitter weather, he returned in February of 1847 and distributed the dried fruit and honey and tallow and twelve hundred pounds of pork to the needy families at Winter Quarters.

He also brought back potatoes, Aggatha said. It was the potatoes that saved us—that effected the cure from the scurvy-like affliction that had begun to decimate our ranks.

Yes, it was the potatoes that saved us, she said, the raw potatoes.

By then he had married three more women, Nancy Armstrong and the two sisters, Polly and Lavina Young, all girls whom he had converted while serving as a missionary.

Yet I gathered from what Aggatha said that the exact composition of his family was in a state of flux since several of his wives were in the process of leaving him, or had already left.

Why did they leave? I put the question to Aggatha as delicately as I could.

The strains and privations of frontier life, she said, after gazing away for a moment and giving my question some thought. His long absences on trips for the church, she added. And, as to be expected, the natural jealousy common to women resulted in considerable disharmony in the household.

She said this in an even, quiet voice, as if attempting to bring a detached analysis to a situation in which she herself had had little involvement. But then her voice grew more agitated.

One wife, Delethia Morris, left him to marry a trader. She departed suddenly, riding off one night and leaving her child behind for us to care for. I could have told him he never should have taken her to his bed. She was too young. Too selfish and too young to live the Principle.

What of the others? I asked.

She admitted that her youngest sister, Emoline, had become insubordinate, giving aid to one of Father's enemies, and so she was separated from the family. Polly Workman, who was also prone to stir up strife, was sent to live with her brother. Nancy Armstrong fell victim to the plague and died at Winter Quarters. Nancy Bean and Louisa Free, each of whom had borne a child by him, grew tired of living the Principle and left him to return to their parents. And Sarah Caroline chose to live with her aunt rather than stay with her husband, although later she would rejoin the family.

So many defections, in such a short period of time. I couldn't help but wonder, what did this mean? I also found her choice of words telling . . . the "jealousy common to women." The "considerable disharmony" in his household. The "insubordination" of one wife and the suggestion another was "prone to stir up strife." It sounded to me as if the wives were fighting, and who could blame them? Eleven women, all attempting to share a household that had been reduced to a cluster of tents on a cold and inhospitable prairie.

But it was what Aggatha said next that most interested me.

There really was no truth to the rumors that began circulating at the time that our neighbors began locking up their daughters to keep them safe from him, she said, shaking her head. It was quite the other way around: they all came willingly to him, as kittens to milk. And as for the incident in Winter Quarters, when he was tried by a tribunal of his peers on charges of rape and adultery, there was no truth to that. Jealous forces were at work there, jealous and *evil* forces, and we only paid the fine in order to put the whole affair behind us and move on.

But it was then that the tide began to turn against him, she said. It was then our enemies began to show their faces.

There were those who spoke out against him now, and yet he continued to enjoy the trust of the Prophet Brigham Young who, as if to announce his loyalty to his old friend, adopted Father as his spiritual son and named him to the Council of Fifty, the secret governing body of the church, often referred to as the Council of Ytfif in an attempt to confound our enemies.

He was disappointed not to be chosen to accompany the Prophet on the first exploratory expedition to the West, Aggatha said, but Brigham ordered Father to stay behind to oversee the cultivation of crops that would be needed by later companies of emigrants. He proved himself to be a good farmer and raised thousands of bushels of corn to help feed his people during their planned exodus into the wilderness.

The following year, in 1848, they prepared to move west. Father was chosen to lead a company of Saints on the great migration to the Rocky Mountains where, the previous fall, the Prophet had established the New Kingdom in the Valley of the Great Salt Lake. There were those who did not want him as their leader but the Prophet intervened on his behalf, once again silencing his enemies, and Father took his place as head of a company of fifty wagons.

He set out to cross the plains in the spring, with his seven remaining wives and eighteen children.

We had four wagons, Aggatha said, and seven span of oxen, fifteen horses, six chickens, three cows, two dogs, and all our worldly possessions. Many companies departed at the same time. The line of wagons stretched from horizon to horizon, a great exodus of humans and beasts yoked together in one divine purpose.

The three-and-a-half-month journey was plagued by many difficulties. Overloaded wagons were pulled by underfed teams and, one by one, his animals began to die. There were those in his company who did not believe it was right to lay hands on beasts and pray for their recovery, but Father put the matter to prayer, Aggatha said, and received a revelation from God in which the Lord told him He did not object to the elders anointing the beasts. And so, when his oxen fell down in the yoke, suffering from exhaustion, he doused the animals with gunpowder and sweet milk mixed with salt pork and then laid hands upon the beasts and prayed for their recovery. Time and again the animals did recover, and he soon became known for his healing touch, for the way he could lay hands on animals and humans alike and dispel the sickness and fatigue.

His dreams had always guided him, but now his night visions increased, and in them he often saw the future foretold. He gained a reputation as a mystic and dreamer, a man who could communicate with the heavens above and thereby help direct the affairs of men on earth.

In many other ways, he became indispensable to the company.

He was a superb hunter and woodsman. When supplies ran low, he killed rabbits and prairie dogs and roasted them over the fire. He shot antelope, and deer, and kept many hungry families supplied with fresh meat with his sharp hunting skills.

He could be depended on for his leadership and steady nerves and for his quick judgment in any emergency.

Once, at a crossing of the Platte, the wagons had to wait an entire day while a herd of buffalo crossed the river in front of them, plunging in an endless and undulating flow of ragged hair and horn into the swift blue waters, creating a living, writhing bridge of beasts that stretched from horizon to horizon. The herd was as wide as the world, and the beasts emerged from the water blacker and sleeker, carrying the river with them in the weight of their woolly, sodden coats.

It was like nothing we had ever seen before, Aggatha said, the way the buffalo filled the entire world. It was like nothing we had ever felt, the way the earth shook beneath our feet as they passed. That day we came to understand that in the New World, in the kingdom that awaited us in the West, the beasts would rule our lives. Beasts with outsized heads and scaly horns and eyes that looked out from the sides of their heads. Wolves that howled in the night and stole from the herds. Eagles that plucked the eyes from newborn calves, and lions and bears who held humans in their dark power.

There was much sickness and death on the trail. Children were born, and other children died. Aggatha's mother, Abbagail, fell victim to malaria. She gave up the ghost near Pacific Springs after several days of fever. Father made a rough coffin out of wagon boards and buried her above a spring that lay like a huge mirror in a boggy meadow. The next day his best ox died from drinking alkali water. He put a sick ox in the yoke and rolled on to Soda Springs, but just before they got there the weakened ox dropped dead in the traces. So he yoked a cow by the side of the remaining ox and pushed on until that cow died too.

Many days were like this, Aggatha said. The animals grew spent and died, and the trail was soon lined with the stench of their bodies.

By the time their company reached the Sweetwater, divisions had appeared in the ranks. Arguments broke out among the men, some of whom began accusing each other of petty crimes—the theft of an ax, a reluctance to stand watch, or even unwanted attentions cast upon a daughter or wife. Still, Father prevailed as their leader, stepping in to settle disputes, and the company pushed on, making its way farther and farther into the wilderness, trudging into the ever dropping arc of the westerly sun.

It was late September by the time they reached the Valley of the Great Salt Lake where the Saints had established their little colony the year before. They had no time to build cabins, Aggatha said, before the weather changed and the first snows came, snows that were heavier and deeper than any they had ever known before. The first blizzard whitened the sky and lasted all day and night and when it cleared they found themselves snowbound in their tents and wagon boxes.

The remaining animals suffered badly that first winter.

Not only did the weather take its toll but the lions and wolves and foxes raided the herds in the darkness and filled the black nights with their cries.

Father had chosen a spot for his family some distance from the main settlement. They camped on the benchland, high above the valley, near the place where the Big Cottonwood Creek flowed out of the mountains. The granite peaks rose steeply behind them, tall cliffs cut by deep canyons where the trees and wood were plentiful. He was kept busy that first winter, riding out to check on his herds, fighting deep snow to ferry wood and supplies to his family, now numbering nineteen children and seven wives. Many mornings, Aggatha said, he went out into the frozen dawn only to find fresh kills among his herds. How, they wondered, would they ever survive the winter with the wasters and destroyers decimating their stock?

It was not long before a decision was made. Before the New Year arrived, a council was held and the elders declared war—the War on the Wasters and Destroyers.

It was decided to turn it into a contest, Aggatha said, in an effort to spur the best hunters to action. All the men in the settlement were divided into two teams. Father was chosen to head the first team, Elder John Pack captained the second. The rules for the contest were laid out. Whichever team registered the most kills would be treated to a feast by the losing team. Proof of kill would have to be offered and the game would be counted as follows:

The right wing of each raven would count as one point.

The wing of a hawk, owl, or magpie, two.

The wing of an eagle, five.

The skin of a polecat or mink, also five.

A wolf, fox, or wildcat, ten.

The skin of a bear or panther, fifty.

The contest began on December 24th, that first winter in the valley. It was decided that the wings of the birds and the skins of the animals would be produced by each hunter at the recorder's office on the first day of February, when the contest would end and the winning team named.

The slaying, however, was so successful that the contest was extended for a month. Each day the hunters went out into the snow-drifted world and came home at night with the dead animals and birds hanging from their saddles. The wings and skins piled up around the tents and wagon boxes. As the weeks wore on, the mounds of pelts grew steadily higher around the dwellings, sheltering them from the bitter winds that came down from the north. Snow fell upon the pelts, obscuring the colors, then new skins were added, and more snow fell, the darkness and whiteness building up there in alternating layers.

Fortunately, God was on our side, Aggatha said, and soon the cries of predators in the night began to be silenced as the hunters went tirelessly about their work.

When the first of March arrived, the contest was declared over, and a tally was taken.

It was discovered that 15,786 wasters and destroyers had been killed.

Father's team was named the winners, by a margin of five hundred points.

Later his enemies would say that he had cheated. They would accuse him of counting kills that weren't really his but rather pelts and wings provided by the Indians with whom he had become friendly during those harsh winter months.

Still, our victory was sweet, Aggatha said. The celebration lasted far into the early hours of the morning, with dancing and feasting. In the meeting hall where the Saints gathered for worship, the sound of their singing carried far out into the night, where a new silence had fallen over the land. Now little stirred in the darkness, except the cattle and oxen and horses, the beasts that would now have dominion in Zion.

There never was a more perfect slaughter, Aggatha said.

Nothing to match our War on the Wasters and Destroyers.

Almost sixteen thousand kills, in a mere three months.

And I can tell you this, she said, her eyes glittering. There never was a finer hunter than Father. Or a better match for this raw, wild country.

———

THIS WAS the point at which Aggatha's account of her life with Father always ended. With the story of the victory in the War on the Wasters and Destroyers.

After that, she would say, we came south. The Prophet ordered us to leave the valley in 1850 in order to lead an expedition to settle these terrible southern regions.

And here we have been ever since, laboring in the heat and the cold and the wind and the dust, with these poor godless heathens, among whom we are fated to live.

FOUR

F IVE DAYS HAVE passed now, and my sons have still not returned. I am much worried for their welfare. I tell myself they
have undertaken much more dangerous missions in the past, and they
have always come through. Surely they will do so again.

Billy is so much the little man at the age of seventeen, and Ike, at
fourteen, feels that it is his duty to demonstrate that he, too, is made
of strong stuff. They are responsible and trustworthy boys, as capable
as men twice their age, for their father made them so. He turned them
into able horsemen and woodsmen when they were yet young and
instilled in them the skills and the good judgment needed to survive in
this harsh and dangerous world.

Still, I am beset by fear and worried for their safety. They should
be home by now, and they are not. And I can do nothing but busy my
mind until they come.

———

I AM WELL aware that, to the uninitiated, to those who live outside
the realm of our kingdom, our lives must appear unfathomable, or like
a labyrinth, especially with regard to our marriage customs. When my
own mother and father learned I had been wed to a man with seven
wives, they despaired for me. I received a letter from Uckfield begging
me to come home. "You have fallen into the clutches of white Mus-
lims," they wrote, "shameless fanatics who have even writ their own
Bible and who keep harems for their pleasures. We cannot send you
money for we have none, but surely if you were able to get to that god-

forsaken land, you'll be able to make your way back to England. Return to us now, dear daughter, while you can, before it is too late to make another life, this we beg of you."

I did not return to them, needless to say. Instead I wrote to them and informed them in no uncertain terms that I loved my new home and I loved my husband as well. I sang the praises of the New World. I said I preferred to be one wife among many, the eighth wife of a great man, with a Lord for a master, than to be one lonely wife yoked to an inferior.

Of course, I did not mention that I was actually not Father's eighth wife, but his seventeenth, for this I was afraid would have sounded the death knell to our relations, for I could just hear my father saying, The seventeenth, is it? The seventeenth wife? Let me get this right, girl: there were seventeen, and now there are only eight? And what would have happened to the others, lass? I pray ask you?

――――――

I SUPPOSE that anyone with their full faculties about them might well have wondered how I received the news of Father's history, including the account of the number of women who had married and left him over the years.

But I can truthfully say it disturbed me not in the slightest to learn of Father's past.

Not one jot or tittle.

For I believed in our Principle, in its Divine Origin, and I pitied those who had not the courage to live by it—the Delethia Morrises, the Emoline Woolseys, the Polly Workmans, Nancy Beans, and Louisa Frees of this world. I felt certain that it was not Father's fault these wives had failed to live up to their vows and honor their covenants with him. It was surely their failure, and their loss, not his.

――――――

SOMETIMES IN the evening, when the day's work was done and the dishes from supper had been cleared and washed, Father would call us together, all his wives and children, and speak to us on matters pertaining to our spiritual well-being.

Often he spoke on the Divine Principle, expounding on the subject of why polygamy should be the privilege of every virtuous female who has the requisite capacity and qualifications for matrimony. He said women should demand of either individuals or governments the privilege of becoming an honored and legal wife and mother, even if it were necessary for her to be married to a man who already had several wives, or, as Jesus said in the parable, to take the one talent from the place where it remains neglected or unimproved and give it to him who has ten talents.

That is as it should be with women. Every woman, Father said, had the right to a husband. Even if it meant, as the Prophet himself had declared, marrying one's own sister in order to grant her the crown of motherhood.

For all persons who attain to resurrection, Father said, and to salvation and to the joys of eternal union must first have that union with the opposite sex here on earth or they will remain in a single state in their saved conditions, for all eternity, without the joys of eternal union with the other sex, and consequently without a crown, without a kingdom, without the power to increase. For one must be married to become a god or goddess in the next life, Father said. And that is what we are striving for.

To become gods.

The rulers of our own planets.

Often Father took the opportunity to remind us, his wives, that the blessings of the Gospel come to women only through men. It is through men, and the Holy Priesthood they hold, that women have access to God.

In temple marriage, Father said, you will remember that each man and his wife are given a new celestial name. On the day of resurrection, the men who have been righteous and paid their tithes will be called from the dead by the Angel Moroni by their new names, and then, in turn, the men will call out the celestial names of their women and thereby raise them.

If a wife does not obey her husband, Father said, the husband can threaten not to raise her from the dead.

Did we understand this?

I did understand it. I understood it very well. And I did not want this fate to befall me.

I very much wanted to be raised from the dead on the Holy Day of Reckoning. To take my place beside Father as his Queen and Consort, the Mother of a New World. And so I took care to obey him.

When he asked me to toil at a task, I toiled beside him with all my might.

When he required me to make an arduous journey with him to a neighboring settlement to trade goods or stock, I went willingly, no matter what the weather and without regard for the strains or dangers of the expedition.

When he wished to celebrate an occasion and called on me to prepare a meal to feed the entire family—or, on more than one occasion, to entertain all the brethren and sisters from the colony—I cooked and baked and served up every specialty I knew would please his heart and also garner the compliments he so loved to receive.

And when he came to lay with me, I took him happily to my bed.

Because I always wanted him.

I wanted him in ways I had never wanted any other. Not the boys of my youth for whom I felt the passions that rise so fast and pass so easily, and not the men who later tried to lay claim to my affections, such as Brother Kippen in whose house I first lodged in the city, working as a servant in order to pay off my debt to the Perpetual Emigrating Fund. Poor Brother Kippen. With his stern-faced wife who abused me from the beginning and then came to despise me, as she feared nothing so much as the possibility of a younger woman finding a place in her husband's affections. She was right to harbor such fears, for not once but many times during my year of service did Brother Kippen suggest that he would do me the favor of making me his plural wife whenever I wanted. But I did not want Brother Kippen. He repulsed me, and I left his household to take up my position at Brother Stoddard's.

I wanted only Father, and I wanted him in ways that, in the light of day, might cause me to blush.

I wanted him because he could stir me and because I believed he was a man of God and because I wanted the possession he offered me.

I wanted forever to be possessed by him. For him to *occupy* me as he had that first night we lay together, and that I could not lay with him every night, that I was not permitted to allow him to occupy me night upon night and leave his seed in me that we might have the child I so desired, was, in the beginning, one of my greatest trials.

And yet he never failed to reassure me of my place in his affections.

Even on those nights when he lay with Aggatha. The wife of his youth.

Or her sister Rachel.

Or Polly.

Or her sister Lavina.

Or Leah.

Or Sarah Caroline.

Or even when he came to Mary Ann and took her to the next room, and lay fondling her and cooing in an attempt to win her favors, as I listened through the wall.

Throughout it all, he always let me know that his desire burned for me. That I was his English bride, the only English girl he had ever married, and that he was much pleased with me and that I stirred in him the deepest longings.

Give me my little tummies, he would say in the morning, coming into my room, and, with great joy, I would comply.

———

THE INDIANS in the region were of great interest to me. They were of a very poor nature to begin with and had become exceedingly destitute and turned upon the white settlers to beg for their subsistence. Driven from their water sources, they had grown increasingly desperate, and they hung about the fort day after day, often begging from kitchens, oppressing the settlers for food. Sometimes the more advanced and warlike Utes paid us visits: they arrived from the north and brought us children they had stolen from the weaker tribes, offering them for sale to the settlers. Father had bought a number of children from the Indian traders and, although some had died, being in such poor condition and so badly treated by the slavers, four had managed to survive and had been adopted into the family.

Of these children, Lemuel, at twelve, was the oldest. He worked the fields with Father, rarely spoke, and in general presented an altogether pitiable picture of degraded youth, with his ragged clothes and thatch of bushy black hair. Father had given a side of beef and a rifle for him when he was but five years old. Rachel had also acquired a little girl named Mahala who worked in her household. The other Indian children were named Sarah, a five-year-old girl being raised by Aggatha, and Sally, a three-year-old whom Father had purchased for Leah.

By the time I arrived in the settlement Father had been appointed Indian Agent, in charge of all affairs relating to the natives in the southern regions. His chief work was as Farmer to the Indians, ordered by the Prophet to instruct the natives in the arts of agriculture so that they might cease their wild, nomadic ways and take up more stable Christian lives. This meant we often had occasion to interact with the Indians, both in the settlements and as we traveled throughout the region. In the morning, before I was up, the house was often crowded with Indians desiring to confer with Father about one matter or another. They had a name for him, and by this name they always greeted him. They called him "Yawgatts," which in their language signifies a tenderhearted man, one who would weep at the sufferings of any person in distress.

Among the Indians who came one morning was Moquetus, the chief of Kishere, whom Father had baptized a few years earlier. Father was away in Cedar City on business and so many of the Indians left, saying they would return later, but Moquetus waited all day, biding his time just outside the gates of the fort where he had tethered two small children to the ground with rawhide ropes. Finally Father returned and, after having a talk and smoke with Moquetus, he bought the two little girls, one about six years of age which he called Alnora, and one about four which he called Alice. They were of the Sebee'tes tribe. For the two girls he gave a rifle and ammunition and a young horse and Moquetus went away happy with his goods.

After Moquetus had gone, Father called us together and, after some deliberation, he gave Alnora to Polly and Lavina, and then he brought Alice to me and asked if I wished to have her.

I looked at the small, naked child cowering before me. She appeared ill and much abused. Her thick hair was matted and her nose caked with effluent, her eyes dull and lifeless, like a creature only half alive. The flesh on her ankles and wrists had been rubbed raw from the constant irritation of her restraints. Her skin was so covered with filth she appeared even darker than she naturally was. I did not know how to tell Father that it was my own child I wanted, not a little naked, half-starved Indian girl. But I remembered what Father had told me, how the Prophet had advised the Saints to buy up as many of these children as possible and instruct them in the Gospel so that not many generations should pass before they became a white and delightsome people. I know the Indians will dwindle away, Brigham had said, but let a remnant of their seed be saved. Now the time had come, Father said, for the gates to be opened and the seed of Manasseh brought back to the fold. The millennium was nigh, and before Christ could come again, the Lamanites—this remnant of the ancient tribe described in our Holy Book—must be gathered up and baptized into the One True Church.

And so I took Alice. As my duty. As my calling.

In order, as the missionaries had said, to play my part.

Alnora would die before the week was out, but Alice, my little

Alice, lived. I washed her and dressed her, as I had the dolls of my youth, and I applied a carrot poultice to her chest to cure her cough. I tended to her flesh wounds and nursed her for weeks until the life came back to her eyes. And then I set about learning a few words of her language in order to communicate with her.

I learned to say "pesherrany" when I wished to speak with her.

And "eetish," meaning a long time ago, as in your people and my people were friends a long time ago, in the Book of Mormon times.

And "cot tam posujaway"—I do not understand—a phrase I often had occasion to use as I attempted to comprehend her needs and wants.

And I learned the word for fear—"sherreah"—because I saw so much of it in her eyes. No sherreah, I would murmur and pat her little woolly head as she cringed at my touch. No sherreah, my little dear. Toojee ticaboo toinab, I would say. I am your friend.

She, however, seemed to know only one word, which she used over and over again in those first weeks. "Shutcup, shutcup," she would whimper. Food, food.

Give me food.

———

FOOD, IN TRUTH, was always in short supply in the colony and often the source of much contention. Many times I was forced to gather wild duck and pheasant eggs or concoct pot pies made of squirrel. Little Alice and I wandered the valley and hills looking for *yant*, a species of the wild rose that the natives had taught me to bake into cakes that tasted like chestnuts, and still many evenings we went to bed hungry. The irrigation canal that brought water from the mountains to the settlement was not entirely adequate and could sustain only a certain number of fields. Crops often failed for lack of water, and upon such crops we were dependent for our survival, for there was no *yant* to be gathered in winter and game animals were often scarce. Increasingly quarrels broke out among the brethren as to how to allocate the water, this precious resource. Father, as President of the Branch, as well as Farmer to the Indians, had his hands full trying to settle disputes between whites and Indians alike in a fair and amiable manner.

And still there were those who spoke against him. There seemed to be an undercurrent of sentiment working against him, for reasons I could not understand, and a general mood of whisperings and innuendo relating to the Indian Depredation and Father's increase of wealth in its aftermath.

The vehemence of his enemies often shocked me.

I remember a certain brother, whose name need not be recorded here, who took such a bitter dislike to Father that he went out of his way to slander him. He accused him of using broken, rotten adobes to repair a section of the fort wall, for which he was being paid a very meager sum, and then simply dismissing the building committee and appointing another when the situation was discovered. He took umbrage at Father's relating his dreams and visions in his sermons, claiming that his position as leader did not entitle him to claim such visions were divinely inspired and came from his close association with the heavens but could very well be nothing more than the night wanderings of a mortal mind. In fact, he questioned whether most of Father's important revelations did not come from eavesdropping and claimed that Father had a habit of sneaking about and listening to other people's conversations. He said he knew for a fact that Father had listened behind a fence to Brothers Peter Shirts and William Young, who were talking of what they called Father's "immeasurable selfishness," and then claimed that Father repeated what he'd heard at the next meeting, purporting to have read it from a sheet let down from the heavens in a dream. He said this caused much ill feeling among the brethren, for Father had been seen listening by a third party. And there were many more complaints. The list went on and on and included the accusation that Father had said he himself would not hesitate to steal from Gentiles who had so often robbed the Saints, and would not find this in the least immoral.

Father, however, said he "cared not a shit" for those who spoke out against him, and so ready was I to join in his defense, I did not even mind his profanity.

In the end I will prevail, he would mutter, and then add, Every dog will have its day, every bitch two afternoons.

But he has not prevailed. He has been bitterly betrayed by those he loved most.

———

I WANT TO put this right.

Father disdained the brute strength of a world of fists. He was a knight heroic. A man beyond ordinary men, one who carried himself with a great reverence for this world—a world which I often found perilous *and* blessed, yet transitory.

I want also to say this: he always wore his endowment robes. He stayed true to the church, even after his excommunication—even after the Prophet, to whom he had been so faithful, abandoned him, casting him to the wolves.

No. He never lost his faith.

He was changeable, it's true, and he liked the exercise of authority, but it was always in the service of his faith. At times he became a strict imposing figure, like a Hebraic patriarch of old who takes his orders directly from Jehovah and stands upon his own Mount Sinai.

But what can one expect of a man of God?

Still, even when I thought I knew him well, I was often surprised by his actions.

Later, when we were forced to hide, exiled to one place more remote than the last, there was so much I could not understand about this man, my husband, our husband, and the life we led because of him. My thoughts, my inquiries, were often blocked by my feelings for him, by the sense I was joined to him by destiny, and by the sheer power of his personality, which relentlessly leveled everything, until it seemed we had no personalities of our own but existed as one great female brood—a gaggle of geese following our gander wherever he led us.

His authority was absolute, and yet in truth, over time I came to see how little control he had over his wives. Just as he couldn't control the winds that reduced his cornfields to tatters or the rains that washed out his dams. We, too, were our own force of nature, and we required careful tending in order not to overleap our banks.

———

I SEE THAT I have begun to speak of him here in the past tense, as if he were already gone. And yet this may not be true.

There may still be hope.

For I believe in miracles, and in the Lord who says, *I am God, and mine arm is not shortened; and I will show miracles, signs, and wonders, unto all those who believe on my name.*

I do believe. I believe all things, I hope all things, I have endured many things and . . . yes, I hope to endure all things.

———

THAT FIRST year in Fort Harmony there was little rain. The crops failed and hunger stalked our settlement. The wind was our ever present enemy. It blew night and day for days on end, drying out the soil, sometimes filling in the ditches with sand so the water couldn't run. In the winter it blew from the north, drifting the snow into banks so high the cattle could walk over the fences. In the summer, it brought dust and sand. The sand blew through the cracks around windows and doors, it crept through the chinking and filled every crevice. It lodged in our food and our beds, and when we stepped outside, it filled our eyes and our noses.

Conjunctivitis was a great problem. The eye trouble that sorely afflicted the southern colonists. Many days I bathed my eyes to relieve the redness and sore feeling, and still the wind blew and the sand filtered in everywhere and my eyes grew red again. When forced to work outside, I took to wearing pieces of cloth tied about my head, like blinders on a horse, to spare my vision a little.

More children were born to our family that year.

In February, Rachel gave birth to a boy and named him Ralph.

In April, Leah gave birth to a large girl she named Lucy.

And in May, Sarah Caroline brought another little girl into the world and named her after Rachel.

Each time I stood by, using my midwifery skills and helping my sisters during their layings-in and, once they were delivered, I washed and swaddled the new babes after treating their navels with scorched flour, and then held them to my breast where the desire for my own child burned so fiercely.

In time, Father would say, as he lay next to me, stroking my face while the purple light began to leak through the curtained windows. I promise you, dear Emma, my English bride. In time you shall have your own child.

———

BY SUMMER the threat of war had passed. Word reached us that Johnson's army had marched into the city only to find it deserted, the Saints having fled on Brigham's orders. A nonviolent resolution to the impasse was reached when the Prophet agreed that a new governor, appointed by Washington, D.C., could take up his post in the territory, although everyone knew that Brigham would still rule, for the Saints would listen to no other. In the south, we breathed a great sigh of relief, and Father, taking advantage of the new climate of peace, began to expand his holdings, buying farms in the settlements of Toquerville and Washington, some twenty-five miles away. He established a tannery and a molasses mill and expanded his herds, and he also began experimenting with silkworms. On a city lot in Washington he began to erect another mansion where Polly and Lavina were to live. The sisters, whom Mary Ann and I privately referred to as Miss Muss and Miss Fuss on account of their peculiar ways, would be ensconced finally in an atmosphere more befitting their fragile natures. Even before the mansion was completed, I could already imagine them sleeping in their fine new quarters, the two pale sisters breathing in unison night after night, their hearts beating to the same rhythm, as the common blood of their ancestors coursed through their veins.

I, however, stayed where I was, in the little cabin within the fort that I shared with Mary Ann and little Alice.

With the increased prosperity, I felt our familial bonds loosening, however, as first Aggatha and Rachel and their families moved away to live in their mansion in New Harmony, and then Polly and Lavina left to occupy theirs in Washington. Leah also moved, settling her family across the valley on a farm in the village of Kanarra, and Sarah Caroline chose to go with her. We were all within a long day's journey of one another, but it meant that Father was now often absent for days at a time as he made his rounds of properties and wives, and more and more I came to rely on Mary Ann for the intimate companionship I so longed for until at last she, too, made her move. Just after the new year, she finally mustered the courage to speak to Father about John Alma, and I think his response surprised us all.

She began by telling him that she was not pleased with their marriage arrangement and that for some time she had been unhappy. He told her that if he could not make her happy that she should have her liberty, and if there was any other man that she could be happier with to say so and he would use his endeavors to have her sealed to that man. She replied that she could love him and respect him as a father but not as a husband and that she wanted his oldest son, John Alma, for her companion, that she loved him more than any other man she ever saw. Upon reflection, he answered that her request should be granted.

And so, on January 18, 1859, almost one year to the day after I arrived in the colony, Father—acting with permission from the Prophet, who had agreed to grant him a divorce—married Mary Ann and John Alma in a ceremony in the great hall on the second floor of the mansion in Harmony, and afterward he gave them a sumptuous social party and supper, which I myself prepared, and to which he invited all the inhabitants of the settlement.

And with that, everything, I am afraid, soon changed. Mary Ann set up housekeeping with John Alma in a small dwelling he erected for just the two of them outside the fort, and now I was left alone in the cabin, with only my little Alice for company. Father was often away, and many times my heart ached for him. I might have let the spirit of discouragement descend upon me had I not had the comfort of knowing that the thing I had longed for had at last come true.

I was with child, at last.

And not even the arrival of Terressa Chamberlain, nor the haunting visit of my old friend Elizabeth Summers, could dampen the great sense of excitement and happiness I felt, though each event, in its own way, troubled my heart for a very long time.

It was, perhaps, the last time when I understood anything clearly at all.

FIVE

I REMEMBER ONCE, a short while after I had arrived in the household, Aggatha took me aside to give me advice. She said she wished to help me avoid the sorts of difficulties that had arisen in the past when certain women, whose names would remain unspoken, had entered the family and begun to stir up strife. The rules of Father's household were really very simple, she said, and she felt it her duty, as the eldest wife, to lay them out for me.

In a polygamist family, she began, the key is to conform to the established rules of the house and be careful how you set up your own idea of government, for it was the collective, not the individual, that most counted.

The main rule, she proposed, was Perfect Obedience.

Perfect Obedience, she repeated. Did I understand? She did not have to say whom it was I should obey. Of course we all knew that Father's word was law.

Also, she suggested, a respect for order was absolutely necessary. I was to keep my quarters neat, respect others' property, retire early, and rise before the sun was up. Early to bed, early to rise, she said cheerfully, that is the motto that guides us. At 9 P.M. the dwellings were to fall dark; at 5 A.M. the candles could be lit again.

Speak no words when angry, she advised. In a plural home, this is the rule, for otherwise much hurt can result, and this kind of damage is very difficult to undo.

Keep your lovemaking for your husband until you are alone. Show no signs of affection when others are present: you do not wish to create an atmosphere of jealousy.

As DIFFICULT as this advice was for me to accept—especially the idea that I could not show Father any feeling in a spontaneous manner—I managed to take Aggatha's words to heart and put them into practice. We all knew we were creating a new order of living and that it was a higher order, requiring a higher standard of behavior in all matters. And truly, I felt much harmony among us. The children, especially, were a delight to me and I relished my role as "auntie." Among the wives, there were those who engendered fond feelings in me, and those for whom I held no special affection. But none did I actively dislike.

That is until Terressa Chamberlain arrived.

I knew something of her even before Father decided to take her for a wife, since she had already been living in the settlement at the time I arrived. The Chamberlain family had come south in Father's company of nineteen wagons as part of the first wave of emigrants to expand the kingdom into the southern reaches of the territory. They arrived at Parowan in 1851 and, a year later, Solomon Chamberlain had helped Father establish the fort at Harmony. All this time Terressa had been married to Solomon, who was thirty-two years older than she and whose disposition, like hers, had not improved with the years. And yet, if Solomon appeared ill disposed and dour, Terressa struck me as cruel. She was the sort of woman given to making harsh remarks and judgments, usually singling out the weak for her abuse. In meeting I had heard her bear insufferably long testimonies and observed how she liked to claim a high moral ground for herself so that she might look down upon others from a very great height and deliver her little sermons. More than once I had taken a quick detour when returning from the bowery, the open-air, thatch-roofed structure where many of our meetings were held, in order to avoid meeting her face-to-face. I might add that hers was not a face that pleased: some anger had permanently etched itself upon her countenance, and advancing age had robbed her of whatever physical charms she may have once possessed, hollowing her out into a brittle, dry hull of a woman.

So why did Father marry her?

What induced him to bring such a hard-hearted, arrogant woman into our midst?

Many years later I asked Rachel this question. Dear honest Rachel who, out of all Father's wives, seemed to harbor the least suspicion and jealousy.

Why it was a favor he did her, Rachel said in response to my question. Terressa weren't happy with Solomon yet she couldn't very well go husbandless. Who would care for her? No, it was a kindness Father did her, taking her as wife. Also, I reckon he figured he could use the extra hands.

They were married in March of my second year, much to my dismay.

I did not prepare this wedding feast.

Nor did I take the news happily that Terressa would be living with me, sharing the rooms that had been so recently vacated by Mary Ann.

I had resolved not to be jealous of anyone. My concern was to keep a place in my husband's heart that would be all my own by putting his welfare before everything else, by serving meals that he could be proud of, and by maintaining a haven to which he could come whenever he was weary or discouraged or in need of affection. But within a week of Terressa's arrival, my haven was beset by the most terrible strife.

It began with a few offhand remarks.

What a poor little stock of goods, she would say, glancing through my pantry. And, You have only two spoons? And you eat from wooden bowls? Why, even Solomon managed to provide me with real china. But perhaps John is waiting to see just what sort of wife you will make before he invests too heavily in your welfare?

It bedeviled me, too, that she addressed him as John when the rest of us had accustomed ourselves to calling him Father and, wearying of this, I confronted her one day. But you see I've known him so *long,* Terressa said, climbing to her invisible pulpit from which she could look down on the world. Much longer than you, my dear.

Soon she began moving my things.

She took my blankets out of the wooden chest and stowed them on an open shelf so she could have use of the space, and when I objected, she said my blankets were only *cotton* quilts whereas hers were pure wool and thus needed the protection of the chest.

She set the two wooden chairs Father had made for me out on the porch so she could make room for her own furniture which she likewise claimed to be of a higher quality. When I complained of this, protesting my chairs would soon disintegrate in the open air, exposed to the elements as they were, she laughed and said, Dust to dust, my dear. Or in this case, willow to dust—it's all nature, anyway. I found her chairs and tables to be too large for the tiny space which left Alice and I nowhere to place our games of skittles.

And yet she pretended to affect a generous spirit.

By all means, dear, she would say to me in that haughty voice she reserved for inferiors, feel free to use my blankets, or my chairs, and you're welcome to eat at my table. Just don't let the little savage touch anything or sit on the furniture. She's so wretched and filthy I don't know how you keep her.

In other ways, she began to abuse Alice. One day I came back from the fields to find she had tied the child to the porch. Alice was weeping, distraught at being so confined. Later, when I confronted her, Terressa said, I didn't want her making trouble about the place.

There was no point in trying to talk to Father about Terressa. I knew it would only bring on accusations of troublemaking and discontent, especially so soon after their marriage, and in any case, I saw him much less frequently now. He spent much of his time overseeing the farms and the labors of his other wives, all of whom were assigned to toil either in the fields or in his factories. Caroline and Leah were raising vegetables and silkworms. Polly and Lavina worked in the molasses factory. And Aggatha and Rachel were taking in paying guests, teamsters from the East who'd begun passing through the territory en route to California. Father had put up a large sign of the eagle over their door and many nights now the mansion was full of lodgers, for whom I was often required to cook. To me he had delegated the task of getting in the dock root for the tannery and managing the poultry flocks. He had instructed Terressa to help me, but she was a poor worker. She complained continuously and often refused to go into the mountains to hunt the root, saying she didn't feel well enough for such tiring labor. And when she did come, she criticized my methods, constantly questioning my every decision, from where to find the root to when we had a sufficient load to haul to the tannery. She seemed to find nothing pleasing about my person and she criticized everything—from the way I wore my hair to my housekeeping and the affectionate play I indulged in with Alice, until at last I lost my temper.

It happened on a day when we'd spent the afternoon together in the canyon. In her usual fashion, she was finding something to criticize. This time it was for failing to pick a spot where the trees would shade us as we worked, even though in the place I had chosen, the dock root was plentiful. She complained loudly that it was a wonder Father could eke out a living when he had to depend on the likes of me to sustain his endeavors. As the day wore on, she grew more cruel in her accusations. She said I would be lucky to keep my child, for the firstborn are often weak and fare badly in the southern clime, and in any case, I did not look in the best of health. And then she hit Alice, whipping her on the bare legs with a willow for simply having wandered out of our sight for a few moments.

On the ride home I said nothing to her. I drove the team in silence. Alice sat between us, hugging close to my side to avoid any contact with Terressa.

When the team had been put away and we had entered our cabin, I turned to her and let my anger fly. I said that if she ever came with me again to dig root I should be boss over the work for she was worthless at the task and she might be careful how she twisted and flung words at me for without more humility than I saw in her I could bear but little more. I said she had abused me shamefully that day, and Alice too. I informed her that she had said things she ought not to have said and talked very saucy to me and I told her there was the door, pointing to it, and she could walk through it and never return unless she could carry a better tongue in her head.

That evening we spent in silence, and the next day Father returned.

Of course she told him everything and he made it plain he was most displeased with me.

For three nights in a row, he lay with her, in the room next to mine. I know she told him many falsehoods and tried to turn him against me. In the days that followed Father said many hard things to me. And then, quietly, slowly, it passed.

Terressa finally moved out. She moved into the quarters only recently vacated by Leah and Sarah Caroline.

And so once again, it was just Alice and me. Dark, silent little Alice who nevertheless had begun to trust me more each day.

In time, all was forgiven. And once again he came to me.

In the morning.

With the first light, when the horizon reddened and the new day leaked slowly in.

SIX

The RIVER IS running high this morning.

I went down early, just as the sun was striking the tops of the cliffs, to see if I might not glimpse the boys coming down the road. I could not see them, but I am sure they will be home soon. They must have grown tired on their long journey and stopped to rest a while. I feel sure they will come today.

Frank French came by while I was walking back to the cabin. He is the bachelor miner who works a claim up the Paria.

No word yet, Emma? he said.

No word, Frank.

I brought you a loaf, he said, and handed me a handsome round he had just baked. I could still feel its warmth and smell the warm sweet odor of the bread.

Most thoughtful of you, Frank, I said. He inclined his head and touched his brow and then hurried up the trail, a shy mouse but nonetheless a good-hearted one.

———

THIS RIVER has claimed my soul, I think. If ever I should leave it, I believe it would always run in my dreams.

No one thought that we could survive so far from the settlements, nor keep the ferry running without assistance from the outside. But God was with us. God has always been with us. Even when men have abandoned us to the cruel whims of fate.

And even here at Lonely Dell.

We were never without those who showed us kindness.

Major Powell once gave me 150 pounds of flour. That was when the Great Geological Expedition to the Grand Canyon stopped here and left behind their ailing photographer, Mr. Fennemore, for me to nurse back to health.

That flour saved our lives. God works in mysterious ways, I thought at the time. Even through a one-armed, river-obsessed major.

Fennemore was a great trial to me. Perhaps it was the fever that made him so incautious. Once he was well, he tried to tempt me into leaving with him. You deserve better than a murderer for a husband, he said.

I turned him out shortly after that. If you are well enough to insult me, I said, you are surely well enough to get on that mule and find your way back to the city.

One day, perhaps, someone will ask me this question:

When did you know?

And I will have my answer.

When Elizabeth came to visit.

———

I HAD NOT seen my old friend for some time when she arrived in Harmony one afternoon, not long after Terressa had moved out of my cabin. She made the journey from her home in Cedar City in the company of her husband, Isaac, who immediately upon their arrival had sought out Father and found him at work in his fields, and her visit took me entirely by surprise. I simply heard a knock on my door late one afternoon and opened it to find Elizabeth standing there.

I was shocked to see my old friend. She seemed to have aged in the few months since our last visit and, even more, she appeared uncommonly troubled. Her naturally bright nature had become weighted to such a degree that to lay eyes on her was to feel how oppressed her spirit had become.

She arrived at the end of a trying week. A number of the settlers had decided to move away, and Father had been very busy, trading for goods, buying up land from the departing colonists, and attempting to calm tempers that seem to flare for reasons I could not understand. Earlier in the week, I had assisted him in planting potatoes and building a stone wall and I had also spent several days alone in the mountains, engaged in the difficult task of washing raw wool in a cold stream. I felt I had earned an afternoon of rest, and so I had retired early one day, retreating to my cabin within the fort, in an attempt to replenish my tired body, and also to remove myself from the grumbling and whisperings of the discontented settlers who were preparing to leave.

I do not think it would be unfair to say, though it may perhaps sound a trifle boastful, that there wasn't a cleaner or neater dwelling in the settlement than my own modest little cottage. With the help of young Alice, I kept my floors swept, my furniture dusted, and my windows clean, and my kitchen and pantry were as well organized as any and, considering our shortage of food, stocked with many precious spices and condiments essential to my trade as cook. It was a humble dwelling, it's true, but it gave me pleasure, and on the afternoon of Elizabeth's visit I was indulging that pleasure, sitting by the hearth with Alice and singing a hymn. Alice loved hymns: with the exception of a few English words, she had shunned speaking or learning the language, but in singing she eagerly raised her voice with mine, happy to substitute a humming sound for the words she didn't know.

It was in this state that Elizabeth found us. Alice and I. Sitting by the fire singing hymns, and I must say that our peace and contentment stood in stark contrast to Elizabeth's distraught demeanor as she passed through my doorway.

At first, I could make no sense of what she was saying but simply caught a few disjointed words—*soldiers, must go into hiding.* I sat her down by the fire and made her a cup of tea while Alice entertained her with more singing, and then I finally joined her at the hearth and listened to the news she had brought me.

She began by talking about the Indian Depredation. She said she had recently learned the truth of the affair and that the story was not what we had been told. White men had been involved in the slaughter of the wagon train of Arkansas emigrants, she said, and not just white men but *Saints*. She whispered this last word, giving it a hiss that reminded me of nothing so much as a snake.

For much of the year I had spent at the settlement, I had heard such stories but I did not believe them. Who could believe such a thing? That our men, our brethren, would willfully murder innocent men, women, and children? It was unthinkable to me. They may have been there that day—even witnessed the events—but taken a part in it? No. This I did not believe.

Dear Elizabeth, I said. These are just stories. I myself have heard them repeated often enough. But where is the proof?

Emma, she said, there is no such proof, at least not yet, but perhaps it soon will come and then what shall we do? Both our lives will be ruined.

How can our lives be ruined? I asked. Whom have you been listening to?

Everyone, she said, and her eyes grew wide with fear. Everyone. The Saints returning from San Bernardino. The settlers who are leaving the area. And the teamsters from the East. They all tell the same tale. Word has gotten out. And now they are coming. *They are coming.*

With this she began weeping and I had to calm her in order to persuade her to go on with her story and enlighten me, if possible, as to how our lives were now in such peril.

Who is coming?

A group of officers and soldiers are coming, she said. They are coming to investigate the massacre.

It was the first time, I believe, that I heard that term used.

They have a list of names of the brethren who were present at the meadow that day. Isaac's name is on that list, and so is your husband's. There are others, too, but they're seeking the leaders. Elders Dame and Higbee and Klingensmith, and Isaac and John. That's who the soldiers will be looking for. And if they find them, they'll be arrested.

She put her face into her hands and began weeping. In the silence that ensued, Alice started singing again. She began singing "Nearer My God to Thee," substituting Pah-Ute words here and there for English ones, and I had to take her chin in my hand and press my finger gently to her lips to silence her so I could think.

What are you saying, Elizabeth?

She lifted her face and looked at me and I saw the desperation and fear in her eyes.

I am saying, my dear friend, that our husbands had a hand in the killings. And if they are captured they stand to die for it. And then where will we be, Emma? What will happen to us then?

I tried to keep calm.

What is this you are saying about soldiers coming?

It's true. That's why we've come here today. Isaac felt he must warn John.

Where did this news come from? How do you know the soldiers are coming?

A dispatch arrived from the city, from our friends in the north. It came last night. The soldiers are already on their way.

And Isaac? What does he say? Does he admit he had a part in this affair?

Elizabeth looked down at her hands folded in her lap. He admits nothing, she said. Only that an oath was taken by all the men. The affair cannot now be spoken of without breaking the oath, which is to court the wrath of the Destroying Angels. She paused and then looked up at me.

But I have learned this, she said. There were many men there that day. Many of *our* men. Some were part of the killing and some were not. Some killed the women and children, and some killed the wounded and the able men. And others killed no one. They laid down their arms in horror. But when it was over, more than a hundred people were dead. Do you hear me, Emma? Over a hundred! Including many little children. And those few children who survived? They did so not because they were rescued by our men, as we were told, but because our Doctrine of Innocent Blood forbids the killing of children under the age of eight.

I shook my head. No, I said, I cannot accept this.

Understand, I do not know what John did. Nor do I know my husband's part in it. Just that these events took place.

But we have no proof, I cried. No proof at all!

Mark my words, Elizabeth said quietly, the proof will come. I'm sure of it. And then where will we be? We did not bargain for this, Emma. Where in the sermons and in all those lofty words of the missionaries to whom we listened does it say anyone has the right to take another's life? I ask you that!

Perhaps you should ask your husband, not me, I said.

I did. And do you know what he said? He said, Elizabeth, if the Lord requires blood atonement to accomplish his purposes here on earth, then His agents shall be ready at hand. If called, we answer; it is our duty to the priesthood. Now, what do you say to that, Emma? What do you think of this Doctrine of Blood Atonement? Is that what we left our families for, to join a pack of holy murderers?

I felt she was very near losing control of herself, and that nothing I could say might possibly relieve her extreme condition, and so I fell silent while she continued to stare at me.

Elizabeth left a short while later. We clasped each other in an embrace before she departed and promised to see each other again soon, but our gesture of solidarity lacked heart, and I think we both knew it.

———

THE NEXT morning Father went into hiding. He left for the mountains with the first light, taking his finest riding horse and a mule packed with supplies. The night before he left he called us together—those of us still living in Harmony. Aggatha and Rachel were there, and their children, and Mary Ann and John Alma, as well as Terressa and myself and little Alice, and Sarah Caroline and Leah, who had driven from Kanarra in the pony trap. He said he wished to speak to us, and he started by asking us to kneel in prayer.

After the prayer was over he said he was forced to leave us for a time. He would be going up into the mountains, to a place not far away where he would be able to watch us through his field glass. He did not know how long he would be gone but he expected us to carry on with our labors in his absence. To John Alma and his older sons he gave instructions concerning the disposition of some animals. He asked that Mary Ann and I continue with the planting. He told us which crops were to be seeded in which fields and he warned us against letting the fields go dry. Remember that our food for the coming winter depends on the success of your planting, he said.

After he had given out all his instructions concerning temporal affairs he began preaching to us on the vileness and treachery of our enemies and especially did he rail against those who had murdered our Prophet Joseph and had boasted of it, and others who had recently murdered our Apostle Parley P. Pratt and done the same—the cutthroat heathens from Arkansas. (Only as he said this word, *Arkansas,* did I begin to make the association that the wagon train of emigrants had hailed from the same region as the men who had so recently murdered Pratt, and this gave me pause . . .). He went on to say that if a man is walking a path of sin and does not veer from his course, then it is incumbent upon a believer to stay his decline into hell by relieving him of the burden of his life and that in spite of anything we might have heard about the unfortunate affair at the meadow we should remember this: To be relieved of a sin-ridden life was better than to go on living in such a degraded manner. To pay for sins with one's blood was a way of gaining Heaven for the unrighteous.

When he had finished speaking he told us we could all retire and he said he would send an emissary to notify us of his hiding place and that one by one, or in the case of his wives, two by two, we could soon come and visit him and spend the night but that our movements should be made with extreme caution and in no instance were we to be so careless as to allow anyone to follow us.

———

LATER THAT evening, he came to me. When I heard him enter the cabin I lifted Alice from her place next to me in bed and carried her to the narrow cot by the fire to make room for him. I had not been expecting him and my hair was twisted in little pieces of rags to give it curl and these rags I removed quickly and shook the hair loose so that it fell about my shoulders. He undressed slowly. I watched him from the bed, not speaking but rather observing his every movement. He seemed weary and I imagined him to be deeply troubled but when he turned and faced me I saw that he was smiling. He climbed into the bed beside me and he placed his hands on the swell of my stomach, within which my child—our child—was growing. I reckoned that in two months, or perhaps a little less, I would be ready to deliver.

Do you think it is a boy, Emma? Or a girl?

I don't know. It could be either, couldn't it?

He laughed at what I'd said and I realized how silly it sounded. Of course it could be either. What else could it be?

Which would your heart prefer?

A boy, I said.

Then I prophesize here and now that you shall have a boy, Emma. He kissed me on my forehead and drew me to him, but he must have sensed my reluctance.

He drew back and looked at me and I saw the bemused look on his face.

You look frightened. Are you frightened, Emma?

A little.

And what are you frightened of, dear Emma, my English bride?

The moonlight was bright upon his face. I could make out the creases around his eyes and the fine lines radiating from the corners of his mouth. Unlike the other elders, he did not wear whiskers, and his skin appeared youthful in the moonlight. Looking at him, I felt his strength and goodness and it caused me to feel that I had nothing to fear. I could see he was sure of himself in ways that I was not. I wanted to trust him and rely upon him forever because I felt there was nothing he could not set right.

What frightens you? he asked again as he began undoing the buttons on my nightdress.

The soldiers are coming, I mumbled.

Do you know what we shall do with those soldiers if they trouble us too much?

I shook my head.

We'll see that they're used up, he said. Used up in the pocket of the Lord. My enemies have good reason to be afraid. But not you, my dear Emma.

He began to take me and I asked if it was wise to engage in the deed with the child so far advanced inside me and he assured me that the baby could not be injured by our congress and in fact, he said, the feelings that result are known to energize both mother and babe in the most healthful ways—didn't I know that? As a healer and a midwife, surely I must know this.

I felt that he was teasing me then and I stiffened and tried to pull away but he murmured, Emma, Emma, be with me tonight for tomorrow I am gone, and at this thought I gave in to him and I let him lead me, and once more he occupied me and I felt him take me up to that place of shimmering light.

———

I WATCHED him ride away the next morning. Later I learned that Bishop Klingensmith was already in hiding, as well as Elizabeth's husband, Isaac, and others would soon take to the mountains. Once Father was gone, there were those who felt free to speak of him in any fashion they wished. I heard an elder say that Brother Lee had gotten us into this mess, and it was up to Brother Lee to get us out of it. I heard a sister say he was the very devil, a son of perdition, and another called him a curse on our house. Another accused him also of being a devil, but of the worst kind, namely, a *saintly* devil, a monster cloaked in righteous attire. But of all that was said, it was Solomon Chamberlain, the old man Terressa had left in order to marry Father, who most frightened me.

He accompanied me to the fields one day, in order to turn the water onto the crops, and as we worked beside each other he began speaking of the unfortunate affair at the meadow. He said he himself had not been there that day, but sometime later he had occasion to pass by the scene, and he described what he had found there.

The scene, even at this late date, was horrible to look upon, he said, stopping to lean upon his hoe and shaking his head. Women's hair in detached locks and masses clinging to the sagebrush and strewn over the ground. Parts of little children's dresses and female costume dangled from the shrubbery, or lay littered about, and among these, here and there on every hand, for at least a mile in the direction of the road, there gleamed the skulls and bleached white bones that had been scattered by the wolves.

The wolves dug them up, you see, he said. Dug them up and feasted on their bodies.

I am not saying that they did not deserve their fate, he added, taking up his hoe once again. Anyone who blasphemes our Prophet shall not be allowed to pass from this land alive, and anyone who kills our apostles shall suffer the same end, even if they be guilty only by association. To murder a Gentile may sometimes be expedient or even to a certain degree wrong, but it is seldom a crime or an unpardonable sin. My objection is with the method that was used. It was your husband who led the Indians to attack the train first. And it was also he who rode into the camp, a few days later, carrying the white flag of truce and promising the emigrants deliverance from the natives if they would lay down their arms and march out single file. He told them to send the women and children out first and then ordered each man to march out so one of the brethren could walk by his side and lead him to safety. Only that is not what happened, is it? Instead they shot those people and clubbed them to death. All was arranged, you see. All of it arranged with the natives. I have no quarrel with this. If it had to be done, so be it. But how could they have departed the scene without conducting proper burials, leaving the bodies for the wolves to feast upon, and for the next train of emigrants to discover? Now the troops have come, and who knows what is to follow?

I felt my face flush. The sun was blazing in the sky and seemed suddenly to swing back and forth on an invisible axis. I looked at the old man, Solomon Chamberlain, whose hands trembled upon the hoe and whose long white beard lay flat upon his chest like a woolly scarf, but he seemed unperturbed by my lowering gaze. He is jealous, I thought. Jealous of Father for having taken his wife from him.

Why have you told me this? I cried. These are lies, terrible lies. I believe you will roast in hell for saying such things. I turned and fled, running across the broken earth with little Alice stumbling along behind me.

When we reached the road, I stopped to catch my breath. I thought about what Solomon had said, and I thought about all that I had seen and heard. Alice took my hand and turned her black and questioning eyes upon me and I glanced away so that she could not see the tears welling up in my eyes. I remembered the rows of shoes I had seen in the bishop's storehouse not long after I arrived—and the dresses stained with dark marks, the children's clothes, and the stacks of bedding for sale, and I saw the face of little Charley Fancher, trapped in his muteness, and none of this could I bear to think about for long.

Come Alice, I said, lifting my head and blinking the tears away.

Come. Let us pray. And there in the road I dropped to my knees and buried my face in Alice's dress, for she did not kneel with me but stood quietly before me, her mouth drawn down in fear. I clasped her shoulders and bowed my head and I prayed. I prayed for my husband, and I prayed for all those whose lives were in peril, and I prayed for strength, that my fears should not overcome me. It was as if life had decided I didn't need any favors, but right then and there I prayed for God's favors, that He might remove the threat from our midst and restore peace to our family. I felt the strength of my faith inside me. My faith was like a fire shut up in my bones. I burned with belief in the One True Church, and in the goodness of my husband and the rightness of his course. I could see fields of light and intelligence all around me, and I knew it was the truth, and that this truth would make me free. Jesus said, In the world ye shall have tribulation, but be of good cheer; I have overcome the world. I, too, prayed that I might overcome the world, and I heard a voice then, and it said, Let not your heart be troubled, neither let it be afraid.

And I knew this to be the answer to my prayer.

What I could not yet understand, I must take on faith.

Above all, I must not be afraid.

———

IT WAS TRUE what Father said. He had not gone far away. His hiding place was across the valley in the bluffs east of the farm where, with his field glass, he could watch the family go about their duties.

Each evening two of his wives would go to him with food, and visit with him, and tell him the news, then one would remain overnight while the other returned home.

What is it like there? I asked Sarah Caroline the first time she came back from a visit.

He is not suffering, she said dryly, for he sees to it that he has all he needs. Even his physical wants do not go unmet, as long as we are there. And with that she smiled at me in a way that left my heart a little sore.

I wanted very badly to visit him. But he had sent word that I was too far advanced in my pregnancy to risk riding out to visit him. I told myself that a letter might even be better than a visit because Father could read it over and over and keep it with him forever.

And I was right. Later I discovered that Father had gone to the trouble of copying my letter into his journal, where I later found it. The entry read:

Emma, my English girl, sent me a letter the better to express her feelings, as she was unable to come, expecting to be confined soon. The few words are as follows:

My dear companion—It affords me joy that I cannot express to know that you are alive and have been safely delivered from the hands of your enemies thus far, who have been hunting you like a roe on the mountain for the Kingdom of Heaven's sake. Yet I cannot but feel melancholy at times when I think of the sufferings and hardships that you must necessarily undergo in the mountains; saying nothing about the society of your family whom you love as dear as life. My prayers for your deliverance and safe return to the bosom of your family who loves you dear, have been unceasing. And although I cannot be with you in person to share your sorrows yet the Lord knows that I am in spirit, and I also bear testimony that your spirit visits us. May God speedily permit you to return home, for I feel as though I could not stay from you much longer. I am sometimes tempted to try to climb the mountains in search of you but then I think of our child. God bless you, my dear, to live long on the earth to bless and enjoy the society of those who love you dearest, among whom I humbly count myself. Your devoted wife, Emma

Two months later, he was back home with us and the soldiers were gone, having given up on their quarry.

The rest I cannot tell in my own words, for it still causes me such pain, so I will report only what Father committed to his journal:

On Thursday morning, the thirtieth of June, at one o'clock, Emma, my seventeenth wife, was delivered of a stillborn son. The child was large and proper but the mother was hurt in a fall some days before its birth which was supposed to be the cause of its death. By its mother's request I gave it the name of John Henry, after her father and myself. At ten a.m. this morning its remains were neatly interred in the Harmony graveyard.

So it was.

I sometimes still see myself falling.

I see the horses bolting at the sound of the thunder and I feel my hands on the reins as I pull with all my might, I hear my voice calling out the horses' names—Babe! Blacky! Whoa there! Whoa Babe! Blacky! But they do not stop, they do not listen, and when the wheel catches on the rock and the wagon begins to tip I realize that there is nothing, nothing to stop my fall, and then there is only blackness, the great dark void that opens and begins to swallow me up.

SEVEN

A NEW FIERCENESS came into me with the death of my child, John Henry.

I cannot explain it except to say that a terrible willfulness that had been present in me since my youth now took commanding possession of my soul. When I was young and often ran wild, my mother, in exasperation at the failure of all efforts to control me, would grab hold of my arm and shake me and say, What I wish for you is that one day you will have a child with an incorrigible spirit such as the one you possess so that you might know firsthand the difficulties you have caused me. But I have had no such child. The twins are as sweet as a summer morn, the boys filled with a goodness beyond reproach, and my babe is yet too young to know whether she, in the end, will fulfill my mother's curse.

I only know that the passing years have made me strong as any man, determined that no one shall take from me what is mine. Even now, as that cunning old fox Brigham, the Prophet I once revered, plots to wrest this ferry from me, I feel my old fierceness rising up. To him I say, you shall have this ferry over my dead body.

I know I have earned the reputation of being the most difficult of all the wives of my husband, and I am happy to assume this title with pride, for it is for him I have fought the battles I have—for him, and for my own place in this world. To live as I have, on the brute edge of civilization, as the companion of a fugitive, has often required the strength of ten women. Let those who wish to call me unladylike go ahead and do so. Better this than to be known as a coward.

All throughout the summer following the loss of my baby, I toiled endlessly in the fields, hoping the hard labor would take my mind from my sorrows. I was never afraid of hard work, and it's a good thing as it was a strong part of the religion that had won my heart. In Uckfield, from the earliest days of my youth, I had worked as a kitchen servant in the manor owned by Lord and Lady Hook. I was no stranger to the kind of work that stretches from dawn to dusk. But I had never toiled at so many different kinds of tasks, nor felt the physical burdens more heavily than I did during those first years in Harmony.

It seemed there was no end to our laboring. Father not only set his entire family to work, including our Lamanite children, but he also took on a number of hired hands that season, men who were kept busy at harvesting, plowing, ditching, building, and repairing, for he was constructing for himself a little empire of prosperity.

The soldiers were gone, it was true, but the fear of arrests still remained, and even more destructive to the fabric of our society was the sense of shame that increasingly crept into our lives. More and more Saints began to flee the southern settlements, creating increasing opportunities for Father to trade animals they desired for their journeys, or to acquire goods and lands they wished to leave behind. Inevitably, this also caused much jealousy, for the prosperous man always engenders envy, and it was no different with Father. The more wealth he acquired, the more he was whispered against. And yet he seemed untroubled by this.

Every dog will have its day, he would repeat, every bitch two afternoons.

In early August of 1859—the year my baby John Henry died— Father decided to take a four-horse team and visit some friends in Pocketville and he asked me to accompany him. He also invited Mary Ann and John Alma to come along for the ride. On the way we were to gather dock root for the tannery.

The melons were ripe and plentiful that year and we took several with us to eat along the way. There were many patches of wild berries for the picking. At Pocketville, we supped at Brother Pollock's and returned home about sunset, bringing with us twelve bushels of dock root and several shaunts of berries. On the ride home, Father made an agreement with John Alma, who had taken up the distasteful habit of smoking. If John Alma would give up the use of tobacco, Father promised to give him the best mare and colt that he owned. Of course, John Alma eagerly agreed to the bargain, although Mary Ann and I teased him, saying he was a boy of little will and should he fail to keep his bargain, not only should he not get his mare and colt but he should be the one to have to give Father a present. This put him in a fine state of mock outrage and caused us all to laugh, and the teasing went on, back and forth, resulting in much merriment until at last we reached home.

I mention this only to cite an example of the good feelings that prevailed in those days, especially at those times when Father and I were alone or in the company of the family members I particularly enjoyed, such as John Alma and Mary Ann. Perhaps it was the loss of our child that caused Father to draw so near to me, but we experienced a change in our relations that summer. I felt myself become his favorite, and I basked in his unceasing attention. Instead of coming to me in the morning, as was his custom, many nights in a row he would now lay with me, from dark until dawn. It was as if he understood how very much I needed him, especially at night, when the sorrows descended most forcefully. The burn from the oil lamp threw an ocher glow across our tiny room as he arrived each evening and took me on his lap and fondled me and whispered to me and we talked our way slowly into the lovemaking, with the space of black hanging outside the window gradually growing lighter as the dawn came on. Every night he was mine. And every night I was his.

Very often we set off on journeys together. Risking the ire of his other wives, he would nevertheless choose me to accompany him on a trip to one of the neighboring settlements. And very often I proved my value to him on the road, for I was eager and industrious and ready to assist him in improving our lot in any way that I could.

You are a strong one, aren't you, Emma? he'd say, watching me at some task.

Strong as an aleman, I'd reply, and you can bet your last farthing on that.

One day we started for the settlement of Washington with a heavy load of lumber and provisions. The going was very difficult and the teams were much taxed by the weight of the wood. At the distance of eight miles from town, we encamped for the night and lay under the stars together. The next morning we resumed our travel but the roads being rough and our load heavy, we broke four spokes in one of the wheels, which forced us to leave the lumber by the road. It was hard work, unloading the wood—a man's job. But I didn't mind the labor, and I saw how my willingness to toil at such an arduous task brought out Father's tender side.

Are you certain you can manage? he asked as I hefted the end of a large timber. I don't want you hurting yourself.

But I could manage. I did manage. I was young and strong and I wanted him to see the strength in me. I wanted him to see that I wasn't like Aggatha, the wife of his youth who had grown feeble with age. Nor was I like Rachel, small and thin and constantly deferring to her older sister. And neither was I like Polly or Lavina, the pampered sisters, nor Leah who had grown even fatter and more useless with her swooning and talking in tongues. Nor was I a bitter, weak crone like Terressa, the most useless of them all. I was myself. His English bride. Strong and sure and there to assist him in all his labors.

When we had finished unloading the lumber, he insisted we take a rest before journeying on. He led me into the woods to lie down. But we did not rest. He seemed much heated by desire, and there before the crows and the magpies, beneath the cottonwoods that shaded us from the blistering sun, we lay down upon a bed of leaves. I remember the sound of the birds in my head. I remember the heat rising from the stony land and the smell of dust, dry and acrid. And I remember afterward thinking, I have conceived again. I have conceived another child, here in the open, beneath this wide blue sky.

Later we traveled on a distance of six miles before the hind axle broke and rendered the wagon immobile. It was then I offered to take one of the horses and ride to Toquerville, a distance of some eight miles, in order to bring back some augers. I set off riding bareback, without fear, taking joy in the landscape surrounding me. I descended the steep rim of the basin and caught sight of great mountains ablaze with color. The view was perpetually changing. Rocks on rocks confusedly hurled into great red loafs, the remnants of an earlier world. Everything grew red. The rock strata of sandstone and the peaks beyond the valleys that opened one upon another. The sunshine was so brilliant that the glare was almost unbearable, and the rocks appeared emblazoned by the sun, as if lit from within. There was no homelike scenery here, no green fields of England, no rolling hills. Here a scene painter's nightmare would be tame compared to nature's productions, with the blood-red land, the cliffs and the soil, all red, all red. It had become my land, my home, my Zion, and I realized that day I preferred it to all others. Harsh, dry, and windy though it was, inhospitable in all manner of ways, it was mine, and I felt at that moment it had claimed my soul forever, and I rejoiced in the splendors of this New World. All this way hath the Lord they God led thee, I thought, and to give thee peace in thy latter end.

When I returned with the augers, many hours later, Father spliced the axle and we rolled on, but not before retiring to the woods once more to satisfy our love.

He was always a man of great appetite but, in those days, I preferred to believe that none could stir him as I did.

———

ALL COURAGE is a form of constancy, of holding steady in the face of changing fortunes. In that rufescent world, so vast and violent and filled with an ever increasing number of enemies, my new fierceness took the form of an aggressive defiance, as if I had discovered, at the center of my being, an undisclosed molten core.

In part, I have to admit, it was the land itself that hardened me.

The heat and the cold, the endless toiling beneath the sun, scratching at the brick-baked earth while the ever present wind leached the moisture from everything and darkened my complexion until I resembled little more than an Indian.

The wind blew all day. It picked up the red dust in great round balls and it sucked it into funnels that danced across the land. Often, when working in the fields, I dared not rest in the shelter of the cottonwoods for fear that one of the large old branches might blow down upon me.

From all quarters of this world I felt the hidden dangers in nature, and in the hearts of the wicked, who wished us nothing but ill.

———

I REMEMBER one day that season in particular, for the lingering distress introduced into my soul. It was the 4th of July and I was to journey to Kanarra with Mary Ann and John Alma to take part in the Independence Day festivities that had been planned there. Father and the others had left earlier, and I looked forward to the ride with just the two of them. The day was hot, but not unbearable. I had dressed in my finest clothes. Early in our marriage, Father had made me a present of a beautiful blue dress, a dress unlike any I had ever owned. Made of an excellent French silk, it was trimmed in velvet and lace, and although I knew it had come to me secondhand and bore evidence of lingering stains, the dress was nonetheless a thing of beauty and it had engendered great consternation among the other wives who were jealous of such a gift.

We arrived in Kanarra before noon and joined with the crowd gathered at the bowery. There were many people there, Saints from all the southern settlements who'd come for the festivities, including many newcomers to the colonies. The Prophet had recently ordered a large group of Swiss emigrants, expert at the art of wine-making, to establish a new settlement on the Santa Clara River, and another group had been called to plant cotton in the valley of the Rio Virgin. The first of these new emigrants had just begun arriving and still relied on the older settlements for certain necessities, and they had turned out in numbers to celebrate Independence Day with us.

The atmosphere was one of merriment. Father had contributed fifty gallons of his finest home brew and the men were making free with it. Not long after I arrived at the celebration, an argument broke out but it was quickly settled and the rowdy youths were admonished to cease their intake unless they could behave with more decorum. The brass band soon began playing. Father gave a short speech to a great round of applause, and then an old Indian named Big Finger arrived with his ragtag band of followers and, with whoops and cries, they circled our party on their horses before dismounting and settling down at the edge of the grass to partake of the festivities.

The food was laid out on a long table and we commenced to fill our plates and take up places on the grass, picnic-style, when the incident that caused me such distress occurred. A child I had never seen before, who had arrived earlier with Jacob Hamblin and his wives, came and stood before me.

She stared at me for a few moments and then began to cry.

Her cries grew to such a volume that the entire crowd assembled there beneath the bowery fell silent, just as the girl pointed at me and cried, That's my mother's dress you are wearing! Where is my mother?

I felt the blood rise to my face.

There is some mistake, I said. Surely you are confused. I reached out for the child but she shrank away and continued in her agitation.

Where is my mother? she screamed.

I looked about me: all eyes were directed toward me, and in those eyes I saw such accusation.

A mistake, I said again. Surely the child is mistaken.

It's no mistake, a woman sitting near me said. I had never seen this woman before and I assumed she was part of the new wave of settlers. The child is an orphan of the massacre, and you dare to wear the spoils of the slaughter, replete with the stains of blood. But the child knows the truth and she speaks to your shame. Butcher's wife—

I was on my feet in a flash and at the woman's throat. I felt hands grabbing at me, pulling me away, and still it took three men to subdue me, so great was my wrath. I felt blinded by my anger and shame. The child was quickly led away, and the woman whom I'd attacked lay prostrate on the ground, gasping for air. Soon other sisters surrounded her and began to minister to her, all the while casting sidelong and reproachful glances at me. Father held me tight, with my arms pinned to my sides, and still I struggled against him.

Let me go, I cried. Let me go!

Not until you can hold your temper, he said, and tightened his grip on me. A few of the brethren began to laugh.

Hang on, John, one called out. You've got a wildcat there!

My tears began to flow. It was then I looked up to see Terressa, my archenemy, smiling down at me. She wore a look of haughty contempt.

Some women will do anything for a new dress, she proclaimed, loud enough for all to hear. But what can you expect from a lowborn foreign termagant?

This drew more laughter from the crowd.

I felt the fight go out of me then and my only wish was to escape, to flee the mockery of that crowd and run far away and hide myself in a place where I could stop my ears against the sound of their jeering.

Father felt me go slack in his arms and, taking me by the hand, he led me away. I felt the rough tug of his clasp as he dragged me to where the horses had been tethered by the stream. Out of the corner of my eye, I saw that Alice had followed us. She stood beside a wagon, peering fearfully out from beneath her thatch of black hair. I sunk to my knees and wept into my hands.

You are the most high-strung woman in this land, he said, and you'll cause us all a time in hell before you're through.

You didn't tell me, I said.

What didn't I tell you? he thundered.

You never told me where this dress came from. That it was taken from the dead at the meadow.

I pulled at the dress, shaking the skirt at him, wishing to tear it from my body, but it was well made and did not give but only produced a rustling noise, like dry leaves stirring in a breeze, as silk rubbed against silk.

I heard no complaints from you at the time you accepted it, he said. And what matters its provenance? All that we have has come from God, and no other. You will remember that. Now get up, and comport yourself with dignity. I'll not have a wife of mine fighting like a common shrew.

Shrew or not, I said, I've had my fill of this crowd. I'm going home.

Do as you wish, he said. But you'll not be taking a horse or wagon of mine to get there. You can walk home if you like. Perhaps by the time you get there your temper will have cooled.

And thus I set off with Alice, in the heat of the day, with no bonnet for protection. It was a very long walk from Kanarra to Harmony, but I did not begrudge one step of my journey as each one took me farther from the scene of my humiliation. My shoes pinched my feet and the heavy fabric of that dreadful dress trapped the heat of my body until I felt I might faint. Alice walked beside me silently, sad-faced and uncomplaining. The crows circled overhead, their black wings creating scimitar shapes against the burning yellow sun. I kept seeing the face of that child, contorted in such grief, as she cried, *Where is my mother?* I kept hearing those hissed words, directed at me, *the butcher's wife* . . .

And worst of all I kept seeing the face of Terressa.

The day grew extremely hot. I trudged on, thinking of the time not long after my marriage when Father had taken me down to the cellar of the bishop's storehouse in Cedar City and shown me the rows of shoes lined up on the shelves. Men's shoes, women's shoes, children's shoes of all sizes, some stained, other with holes in them, and all worn into the shapes of their previous owners' feet.

Choose a pair for yourself, he'd said.

There was a smell in the cellar that came from the shoes and from the mounds of unwashed clothes, a cold metallic odor tinged with a whiff of disease.

I thought of what Rachel had once told me, how the morning after the slaughter she had driven out to the meadow with a few other women from the settlement to strip the dead of their clothes. The women had undressed the dead women and children while the brethren attended to the men. The clothes were stacked in mounds just as a light rain began to fall. Jewelry had been removed from the corpses. And then one by one the naked bodies were dragged to shallow pits and covered with a thin layer of soil.

WHAT WAS I to think of those deeds in which I took no part and yet which had begun to haunt my life and create scenes such as the one that had occurred today?

Will you love your brothers and sisters, Brigham had said. Will you love them likewise when they have committed a sin that cannot be atoned for without the shedding of their blood? Will you love that man or woman well enough to shed their blood?

Life was composed of hardships and insults. But the flame of the true religion was burning and God was with his people.

What was a world without vengeance anyway?

Who would right the wrongs if not the righteous?

I thought of such things as I trudged through that tenantless world, feeling both spectral and ponderous. A storm blew up. Spits of rain carried on the wind and it began to grow dark. I left the road, not wishing to meet any wagons returning from the celebration, and wandered through the rucked fields, beside the dross and wrack of a red stream. Thin wires of lightning erupted to the north. The sky darkened overhead and the air smelled of the devil himself.

My little Alice grew tired, and I knelt down so she could climb onto my back. I felt her small brown hands around my neck as I stood up and, leaning forward to balance my load, trudged on with the creosote and buckthorn catching at my skirt and with Alice breathing heavily in my ear. A bronze moon rose and cast an imitation of itself in the silty ditch water. In the darkness, I trod through the fecal mire of cattle. My skirt grew heavy with the weight of moisture from the rain-soaked plants. In the phosphorous dark, I could make out the shapes of candelilla rising like torches amidst the tules and pokeweed.

Shutcup, Alice whispered. Shutcup.

Soon, I said. Soon we shall have some food.

There is nothing for it, I thought, except to grow stronger. To grow stronger and fight fire with fire.

I was poor as a snake and yet in good health and never so nimble since I was a child.

It is not enough for us to be adapters, Father once said. We must be controllers. It is God's will for us to be so. We are the finishers of nature.

Everything, I thought, is possible for the sake of love. And it was for love, love for those sinners, and for our slain leaders, that those lives had been taken.

I pondered the nature of God and spirit and will and the meaning of grace in men's lives. In the moonlight I could see the red alluvial fans spilling out of the clefted canyons and the little skirted hills sang to me, calling out, *carry on, carry on.* I would prosper in this old red world. Let them call my husband a butcher and me the butcher's wife. What had been done had been done for the betterment of the Kingdom of God and in the end we would win out.

Every dog would have its day, every bitch two afternoons.

Just as Father said.

———

IT WAS LONG past midnight when I finally reached Harmony. The houses were all dark. I heated water and bathed Alice's little feet and doctored the scratches on her legs before putting her to bed.

The next morning, in the gray and malignant dawn, Father came to me.

All is forgiven, he said.

If I desire forgiveness, I'll ask for it, I replied.

You are a fighter, aren't you, Emma?

A fighter I am, I said. And you'd do well to remember it.

After he had gone, I washed my dress out and hung it outside to dry where it could be seen by all who cared to view it.

The Lord giveth and the Lord taketh away, I thought. But I would keep what was mine, and from that day forth, I would wear that dress with pride.

I knew Zion was within me and would grow until it covered the earth. Christ was coming. Christ was coming very soon. Then we would have one hundred years of peace. There was no stopping place in our religion. It was a warfare and finally would overthrow all opposition. Man was the head of woman. And the only way to be saved was to be adopted into the great family of polygamists and strictly follow their examples. And to strike down one's enemies with a vengeance.

For vengeance is mine, sayeth the Lord.

And we had taken some for Him.

EIGHT

I WAS NOT the only one in the family to give birth that year.

In January of 1860, I accompanied Rachel to Washington for her laying-in and delivered her of a boy, named John.

In March, I attended the birth of Leah's son, also named John. And in November—just a few weeks before my own confinement—I helped Sarah Caroline bring her baby Sarah into this world. My skills as a midwife were increasing and much valued by my sister-wives. However, when Aggatha delivered twins prematurely, just before Thanksgiving, no amount of skill or training could have saved the babies. Both were deformed, and both born dead. Father and Aggatha suffered unduly when Leah, out of dumb carelessness, threw the fetuses into the fire before their sex could even be determined. I wished for them not to see the little monsters, was her explanation later, which did nothing to calm the parents' nerves.

When my own time came, Father sent for Priddy Meeks and he delivered me of a boy whom I named William James. My little Billy was a proper child, nine and a half pounds' weight. A proper handsome child. My joy was now complete.

———

WHEN THE snow melted that spring I left my small cabin for larger quarters within the settlement. At Father's request, I set up a boarding-house for the ten hired men who came to work for us that season.

If I had imagined when I left the green isle of my childhood that I was forever bidding adieu to my fellow countrymen, it was only out of ignorance and a lack of understanding concerning how many of my compatriots would follow me to America, for that summer it seemed to me that representatives of the British Isles, as well as all the countries of Europe, were flocking to Zion, having been converted to the Gospel. The Swedes and the Danes, the Swiss and the Germans, the Irish and Welsh, as well as Canadians and Australians—all had heard the call and were engaged in the great gathering in preparation for the Second Coming.

My boarders were representative of such diversity. Among them were three young men from England, one of whom hailed from Tunbridge Wells, a town near Uckfield. I had always enjoyed the company of men and in my new role as matron of the boardinghouse I took much delight in being surrounded by such a robust and diverse group. Many evenings my kitchen was filled with laughter and singing and more than one bawdy tale. Alice soon became their little darling, and she seemed to grow in confidence as the hired hands showered attention upon her. Soon she was joining their songs and ferrying plates from the stove to the table, like a proper little helper.

In time Father saw to it that I had my own cow and chickens and pigs, and I became skilled at animal husbandry, increasing my flocks manyfold. Each animal was precious to me. Each contributed to my wealth, and I tended them all with care.

When my cow went into labor and the calf was too long in coming, I pulled it myself, and when it was slow to breathe, I lifted it to my face and placed my lips over its nostrils and blew the tenderest puff of air into its lungs, then massaged its chest and blew again, until with a shake and a shudder, it opened its eyes and breathed on its own.

When my sow gave birth to nine healthy piglets and one deformed one, I put the latter out of his misery. This is how I helped him die. He was a tiny piglet, no larger than my hand, born with a gaping hole in his skull. I lifted him from his mother's side and held him a moment against the warmth of my beating heart. I stroked his underbelly, as smooth and soft as a baby's bottom, and hummed a quiet melody to still his fear. Then I placed him gently on the ground and smashed his fragile little skull with a hammer.

There were those things that needed my assistance to live, and those that required my help in dying, and to both I gave my fullest measure.

I learned to make a living fence of black willow and cottonwoods, to cut the branches from larger trees to lengths of six feet or so and then set these starts in the earth a foot apart and water and nurse them until they took hold. I soon had a living fence to protect my dwelling from the wind, which when carefully pruned, also produced wood for fuel.

I taught Alice to hiss at the geese and send them away when they threatened to chase her, and when it came time to kill them, I did the job myself. I learned to throw a ewe after birthing and check her bag and milk the wax plug out of each tit so the lamb could suckle.

When I was forced to sleep outdoors on the hottest summer nights, I learned to lay down a rope around my bedding, for a rattler will not cross a rope in the night.

I learned to know when the mare had waxed and was ready for foaling by watching for the signs of dripping milk that clung to the hind legs and muddied up her white stockings.

I learned to snub up a balky cow for milking, and to castrate my own piglets, and bring the boar to the sow for breeding.

I even learned to listen to the other women's woes without sharing my own. I cultivated an indifference to gossip and petty squabbles. I came to understand that silence is power.

The winters were more difficult to bear than the summers. Sometimes, when Father was gone for weeks at a time, visiting Aggatha and Rachel at the mansion, or Polly and Lavina in Washington, or Caroline and Terressa in Kanarra, or Leah in Toquerville, I felt so lonesome I sometimes walked into the snowy hills and yelled a while, just to hear the sound of my own voice. The hired men left in the winter and I missed their easy company. When they returned in the spring, I was happy to see them again.

Make us some of your biscuits, Emma, was their first request to me, and I was always happy to comply, for a woman values nothing as much as a man's appreciation of her skills.

———

FATHER CONTINUED his work with the Indians and when chores permitted I often accompanied him on his visits to their camps. For the most part, they lived no better than animals. At night they slept curled up together in the sand, like pigs. Their food was comprised of snakes, roots, locusts, and reptiles of every kind—in short, everything and anything hogs will eat and some things that hogs will not eat, such as cats and dogs. Once we had one of our cats killed and we gave it to them and they ate it insides and all.

And yet they were not without moments of grace. One night Father took me with him to witness the Ta-vo-Kok-I, or circle dance. Under the December full moon the natives circled in the moonlight around a cedar tree from which all branches had been removed except a small tuft at the top. The leader, or poet, stood in the center and recited words for the next song. All then joined hands and circling around in a sort of shuffle sang the words proposed. They wore their rabbit fur dresses and woven mat sandals for the ceremony, and watching them, there beneath a great round moon, I felt I was seeing a spectacle as old as the earth itself.

Most of the time, however, I sensed only their abjectness, and they roused me to pity.

They did not smile. I never saw a smiling Indian. Father said they found our smiles foolish and did not understand them.

In the spring they gathered in various places along the streams to plant their meager crops of corn and squash and melon. They erected their wickiups, using forked sticks to create rounded frames onto which they piled brush, and in these crude shelters they passed their days in idleness.

Generally speaking, the women fared better than the men. The older women developed heavy haunches but the maidens were lithe and lean, with upturned breasts and graceful limbs. I came to know two young sisters, Won-si-vu and Ku-ra-tu. They often arrived at dawn and hung about my kitchen door, wearing their conical basket hats and sad dark looks. They were young, plump girls with breasts like ripe tubers, elongated like yams. In time I convinced them to cover themselves with blouses I made myself, though I noticed they never bothered to wear them except when they came to beg at my door.

There was always some new excitement with the Indians. Enos, an Indian raised in Fillmore by some Saints there and known to be a notorious thief, was captured and kept in chains but he escaped. George Chrisman reported he had seen Enos ride off with his horse right before his very eyes. A hunting party was got up by Father. After two days of searching, they returned with Chrisman's horse, but I never saw Enos again.

Roving bands of natives began making their way north from the Kaibab Plateau and often harassed the settlements. These natives were different from our Pah-Utes. The men had beards and shaggy hair and wore loincloths and very strange hats made of buckskin that looked like scarves tied so that the tails stuck up like rabbit ears, leaving a top-knot of coarse, filthy hair. One evening, when I was alone, an old native arrived at my door. He was barefoot, his skin caked with dirt and white dust. His testicles drooped from his skimpy loincloth. He presented altogether the most frightful appearance, and yet he approached me with an attitude of peace. He had a lump and scars on his abdomen. The lump looked like a huge boil, and through means of sign language he made it known that he wished me to lance the boil and dress it for him, and this I did. He later returned, bringing me a basket of roasted locusts for my payment. I did not have the heart to refuse his gift, though neither could I eat them for I had not yet sunk so low as to consume the insects of the earth. Instead, in a wicked flash of inspiration, I made a cake for Terressa, adding the ground locusts to the flour, and left it at her door with a note that said, "Something special for you."

The natives were under a curse, the curse of the dark skin, and yet we knew them to be a people of destiny, descended from the same fathers as we were. Treat them kindly, the Prophet admonished us, but treat them as Indians, not as your equals. In return for settling on their lands, Brigham offered to help the Indians learn to grow better crops and teach them to read and enlighten them concerning their history as revealed in the Book of Mormon.

This of course was Father's job, as Farmer to the Indians. He had been called to teach them the skills of agriculture, and to baptize as many natives as possible in order to bring them into the Kingdom of God, and in this he was very successful. Once, in just one afternoon, he baptized over a hundred natives, taking them down into the waters of the Rio Virgin.

They trusted him. They trusted us. They knew the Mormons were their friends and that the Americans were not their friends because we told them this was so. Mormony good, they would say, Mericats bad. They did not harass us in the way they did other whites. I have heard it told that travelers through this territory, when accosted by natives, are often required to strip off their shirts so that the Indians might ascertain whether they wear our holy garments, and if they do, all is well, they are treated as friends. If not, their fate is considerably less certain.

The natives know they have no greater friend than Father, whom they persist in calling Yawgatts, or The Man Who Cries Easily. When he speaks with them, they listen. They do his bidding willingly, and he is generous with them to a fault. They think his medicine is powerful: they have seen him lay hands on the sick and cure them. They have heard him prophesize the future and witnessed that future arrive.

And yet I often despair for their souls, for they are such a backward people, content to dwell in their brute realm, and yet we have made matters worse, I fear, by taking the best land and water for ourselves. Brigham preaches that Alice and others like her will become a white and delightsome people one day. But what if it should work the other way around? What if it is our own whiteness that gets erased over time, darkened by this treacherous land, by the wind and the sun that beats down so relentlessly, turning our own skin red and coarsening our natures until we become no better than them? I believe the Prophet is right and the Indians will perish one day, for I see them dropping even now. Yet what is to keep us from perishing with them? Who can say the land will be any kinder to us? Or that someone else will not come along and eventually displace us from our water sources and take our lands, leaving us to beg for mercy?

I sometimes think that time will erase all color difference upon this earth, and that in the new dispensation, when Christ again comes to rule, he will find only one people of a single muted shade of brown.

Brigham has counseled the men in the settlements and told them they are free to take the native women and girls as wives. But if a brother wishes to do so, he should first gain her affections and take the proper pains to instruct her and baptize her, and then have her sealed to him by the proper authority—the same precisely as a white woman.

Yet few of the brethren have done so.

I once asked Father whether he had ever considered marrying a native girl, and he answered no. When I inquired as to why this was, his response surprised me. He said that until one of the General Authorities took a native girl as wife, he could not think of doing so for it would seem an inferior choice.

What if you fell in love with her? I asked.

Love, he said, was not as important as standing. There was his standing to consider, his place among men.

I would not have once believed that the religion that had claimed my soul could reflect such a worm-ridden preoccupation with position, but those early years in Harmony taught me that even among the Saints—perhaps especially among the Saints—there were betters and lessers, the rich and the poor, the highborn and the lowborn. A constant struggle for betterment went on. Yet many of Europe's poor arrived in our colonies so bereft of goods and skills they were relegated to the meanest existence and looked down upon by the brethren and sisters who had climbed to the upper reaches of our society. Generally speaking, the elite lived in the north and the further south one traveled, the more one encountered poverty, and with it, ill-treatment. Even in the smallest settlements, where there was little in the way of wealth, there were always those ready to lord it over others. I learned that snobbery exists everywhere, even on this raw frontier, and even among Christians who are taught we are all the same in the eyes of God. At no time was this more evident to me than on the occasions of the Prophet's visits, during his annual tour of the southern settlements.

The first time he arrived, we had little notice of his coming, and when a rider from Parowan arrived one day to inform Father that Brigham and his entourage would be coming to Harmony the following day and expect to lodge in our mansion, it sent Father into a flurry of activity in an attempt to prepare for this important visit. A wagon was dispatched to Toquerville to retrieve the china and linens from that household, a pig and beef were slaughtered, and produce was hastily gathered from the fields and trees stripped of their fruit. I was put in charge of all meals and in the early morning hours, I began organizing the other wives and children into teams and assigned them tasks, from shucking corn to stuffing sausage.

By the end of the day, when the Prophet and his entourage arrived, we were ready to greet them. The entire town turned out to welcome our leader, who rode in a specially made carriage at the head of a procession of twenty-three wagons. Numerous other riders on horseback accompanied him, including his chosen counselor, Apostle George A. Smith, whom the Indians called The Man Who Takes Himself Apart at Night because of the way he removed his false teeth and wig and spectacles before retiring, and indeed, these appurtenances gave him a strangely contrived appearance. Nor was the Prophet himself without his oddities. In the years since I had last seen him, on that day when he had sealed me to Father, Brigham had grown in size. He had gained so much weight that, in truth, it required several men to help him descend from his carriage. Two of his wives accompanied him, including his reputed current favorite, Emmeline Free, whose sister, Louisa, had once been married to Father. Father once told me that he had hoped to marry Emmeline, too, but the Prophet had fallen in love with her and talked Father into giving her up to him.

The women in particular seemed relieved to have finally reached their destination, following a long and dusty trip. After washing up at our well, the entire party settled themselves in our social hall and proceeded to take part of the feast we had prepared for them.

I couldn't help noticing the extraordinary quantity of meat and biscuits, puddings and cakes that the Prophet managed to put away, nor did I fail to observe the frontier quality of his manners. He burped purposefully and loudly when the urge overtook him. He let grease hang upon his chin, untended by a napkin. His hands were large and his fingers looked like bloated sausages, with the skin parched and cracked across his knuckles. His stomach swelled against the table, making it necessary to haul each forkful of food a good distance to his mouth in order to consume it, and not always did it make this trip without leaving something on his waistcoat. All in all, he seemed less a prophet and more the untutored, rough ruler of an ancient fiefdom. And yet no one could mistake his power, or the force of his personality.

When he had eaten his fill, the Prophet excused himself from the table and took up a spot before the fire. Others quickly followed suit and in no time Brigham was surrounded by listeners, the faithful of his flock, eager to hear what words he had to say.

He began by pronouncing that God was about to redeem the world from sin and establish the millennium, and as proof of this he cited the destruction of the Union through the Civil War which was raging in the South, a war which the slain Prophet Joseph Smith had predicted long ago, even to the very place where the first battle would be fought—Fort Sumter, South Carolina. Brigham reminded us that

Joseph had predicted this war would destroy the Union, after which time the Saints would step forth to rule the land. Jesus himself would appear in this century, and the Prophet had even predicted the exact year: 1890.

Brigham said the leaders in Washington wished to see our people destroyed, and they had fixed on the issue of polygamy as the means to hasten our end. In the Senate a cry had gone up against the "twin relics of barbarism," meaning slavery and polygamy. The war that was now being fought in the South was an attempt to end the former, and it would be only a matter of time, the Prophet said, before the government of the United States turned its attention toward the Latter-day Saints in an effort to break us apart and destroy our plural families.

But in this they would not be successful, he said, for the Lord was on our side. God was about to redeem the world from sin and establish the millennium and if bloodshed was required to usher in the new dispensation, then blood would flow where it must, but in the end, the Saints would triumph. The Civil War would destroy the United States, and when that happened, the Prophet said, he would be ready to become king over the ruins.

After discoursing awhile on such large matters, Brigham turned his attention to more commonplace topics. He said that in all the settlements he had passed through on his journey south he had observed a lack of order and piety among the colonists. He spoke of the necessity for cleanliness and removing filth from our habitats. He cautioned against letting refuse accumulate near our dwellings, and laid out instructions for erecting privies for each household.

Then he turned his attention to the topic of women and their dress. He spoke on the impropriety and folly of women following the fashions and customs of the Gentiles in their dressing. He said that the authors of those fashions were of the lewdest character; they emanated from whorehouses and brothels, and yet the women wish to cleave to them as close as life. But are such fashions any advantage to them? No, they are an injury. Women who dress in such fashion lace themselves up and carry such a load of petticoats across their hips that it destroys their kidneys and the strength of their loins and causes them to degenerate, and thereby destroys their very existence and purpose, which is to bear children, for without children they soon would cease. Such folly and extravagance must be done away with and women must fashion themselves after the order and council of Heaven.

All the while, as he spoke thus on the subject of women's dress, I could not help but notice how his eyes rested upon me, as I sat there in my fine silk dress with the layers of petticoats arranged artfully around me. However, I met his gaze evenly. I met his gaze with a determination never again to be intimidated over my choice of attire.

He finished his little sermon by admonishing all the women present to adopt the Mother Hubbard as the style of dress most conducive to the requirements of modesty—as suitable for work in the fields, he said, as it was for worship. And he exhorted us with these words: Arise and thrash, O Daughters of Zion; for I will make thy horn iron and thy hoofs brass; and thou shalt beat in pieces many people; and I will consecrate their gain unto the Lord.

And then abruptly, as if he had exhausted his reserves of energy, he announced he was ready to retire and after offering up an evening prayer, he made his way to bed in the company of his wife Emmeline.

As they left the room, I couldn't help noticing what a fine dress Emmeline wore and how she had been laced into it. Her voluminous petticoats rustled as she followed him downstairs to the room that had been prepared for them. No Mother Hubbard for her, I thought. Not for the chosen wife, who wore such a load of jewels she could have been mistaken for a sultan's consort. What was good for the goose was obviously not sufficient for the gander. But I would be no one's goose. I would dress as I pleased, in silk if I wished, and with as many petticoats as I could manage.

In the morning, after a sumptuous breakfast at which the Prophet once again ate enough for several men, the horses and carriages were made ready and the party prepared to depart. After a moment of struggle, the Prophet managed to hoist his bulk onto the carriage seat, and his wives set about making him comfortable, wrapping his legs in a blanket and adjusting the fox cape that draped his shoulders.

The last thing he did before setting off was to face the elders assembled before him and raise his arm to the square, which I knew to be one of the secret signs of the brotherhood.

Let no man betray our cause, he said, lest he find himself used up in the pocket of the Lord.

With that, he departed, as regal as a potentate, with the air of a princely ruler, in command of his multitudes and forces.

Later, as I tidied up the room in which the Prophet had slept, I came across the chamber pot in which he had left his night soil, and I took it to the privy to empty it. I was curious, as unbecoming as it was, for I imagined that somehow the offal of the holiest of men would somehow differ from that of an ordinary mortal. But it did not. I emptied the pot and held my nose, for the shit of a prophet, I discovered, smells like any other.

———

THE WINTER of 1861 came on with a vengeance. Father traveled through early storms to preach in the outlying settlements of Pinto and Grafton and Pocketville, warning the people against filth and iniquity, informing the Saints concerning the state of the Union and the Civil War as heralding the Last Days and the Triumph of Israel. He visited the Indian settlements, too, and counseled his red-skinned friends. Everywhere he went he was called upon to lay hands on the sick and infirm, for it was known that the Power worked through him and he could make the sick well. His fame as a healer had spread, and he was much in demand that season.

On Christmas Eve a fierce storm set in, and Harmony, being situated higher and on a northeast location, received the brunt of the weather.

The storm continued for several days. On Sunday, the 29th, the prospect appeared dark and gloomy. The snow had turned to cold rain and the earth seemed a sea. The weather became even more violent on New Year's Eve, as 1861 came to a wet close. Then it changed overnight, and the rain once again turned to snow.

By January 4th, the snow was a foot deep. Fort Harmony, being constructed chiefly of unbaked adobe brick, began rapidly to decompose in the rains and snow and constant wetness. Many of the settlers in the fort were hastily evacuated to the township.

Yet there was really no place for them to go, for even the houses in the newer settlement were melting down. Nor were we in Father's family any safer. Terressa's adobe house was the first to collapse, then my own dwelling decomposed and returned to its native element. Wagons were arranged one next to the other in the shelter of trees and in these we attempted to take refuge. And still the rain and snow continued. Some of the family took shelter in the rock mansion until it was flooded to a depth of three feet and they were compelled to abandon that dwelling and attempt to weather out the storm in shanties made of planks.

It was bitter cold. Temperatures continued to drop and there was little dry wood to keep a fire burning. Soon many in our family fell ill with ague and the cough. The children suffered terribly, and I feared for my little Billy who, in spite of his strength, had gotten the chills. During the entire storm, which had by then raged for nine days, the wind was from the south, but now it shifted and the weather became even more severe. Temperatures dropped further, and still we thought it better to suffer in our crude shanties and wagon boxes than to risk being buried alive in our melting adobe abodes.

On Tuesday, January 7th, it snowed heavily throughout the day.

By Thursday, January 9th, the snow was two feet deep.

On Sunday, January 13th, the storm still raged, spreading a mantle of gloom over Harmony. Father summoned another portion of his family to the mansion, and there, against one rock wall, we all huddled together, wet and cold, with many now ill.

The next morning the storm continued to rage. Our feeble fires guttered out in the wind that blew through our insubstantial shelters. The children cried. There was nothing dry to be had, no way to dry our clothes or bedding, and many of the family were now seriously sick and suffering terribly in these brutal conditions.

That afternoon the barn fell. The side had been washed out several days before and only the timbers had supported it, but these, too, finally gave way. Several horses, calves, and hogs were inside when it fell but nothing was lost.

We spent that night huddled against the west wall of the one remaining building and in the gloom and darkness heard parts of the walls falling in. This was a time of watching as well as praying, for there was every prospect of being buried in the remaining ruins of the dwelling in which we sought shelter from the bitter winds. About midnight part of the south wall collapsed with an awful crash, killing two chickens and injuring Aggatha's son.

At length daylight came. And the storm still raged.

For the next eight nights running we had very little sleep and even less to eat. Father went without undressing or putting on dry clothes. With the help of William Pace and George Sevy, he outfitted three wagons and eight yoke of oxen to each wagon and removed all the remaining families from the fort, with the exception of Sarah Caroline and her children, who refused to leave. She considered her house the only place of refuge, and felt sure it could stand up to the storm.

Reports reached us that the Rio Virgin and the Santa Clara River were overflowing the country and doing much damage. Orchards and vineyards had been desolated. The towns of Adventure, Rockville, Grafton, and Pocketville were all destroyed. Homes and furniture, sawmills and cane mills were all downed in the floods. We heard that Bishop Tenney had lost all his houses and part of his family, and rumors of more deaths began to reach us.

On Monday, January 27th, more than a month after the storms had begun, six more inches of snow fell.

The next morning, it began to rain, but that afternoon it turned again to snow.

Was there no end to this siege of bad weather? I began to feel that perhaps the end was nearer than we thought, and that, as with Noah, the earth was on the verge of a deluge. The fever raged through our shanties. Terressa and Aggatha both were seriously ill, and many of the children were suffering. But my strength held, and so did my little Billy's. Alice was another matter: she became so chilled one night that I was sure her cold had turned into pneumonia and, fearing for her life, I held her next to my breast and wrapped our bodies together in my coat, hoping the warmth of my body would transfer to hers. Not since I had been trapped on the plains of Wyoming had I experienced such misery and fear. Our homes, one by one, were being destroyed. Everywhere there was sickness. Little dry wood could still be found, and without warmth, our prospects were growing grimmer by the moment.

As with Noah, our deluge lasted forty days and forty nights, yet we had no ark to carry us across the rising waters. Neither had we dry wood, or medicine, or enough food.

We had only one another.

Yet I had made a promise to my Lord God, back on the plains of Wyoming, that if I should be spared and survive those storms I would never again complain of the weather. Throughout the long deluge I kept my promise. When others despaired, I maintained a calm cheerfulness. I saw to meals when my sister-wives were too weak or ill to feed their own children. I administered to the sick. I fed furniture to the fire and kept the water boiling, in which I cooked the dead chickens that washed up in the barnyard. At one time there were thirty-four of us in one shanty, huddled like hogs in the mud, and into each of those thirty-four mouths I poured hot broth and sustenance.

And then the tragedy occurred.

Sarah Caroline and her children had insisted on staying in their house within the fort, believing it still to be sound, even after the south wall collapsed and the roof had been removed by wind and snow. Finally Father insisted they leave. The dwelling posed too great a peril, he said, and it was not agreeable to him that they should remain there any longer. He planned to remove them the next morning. During the night, however, the walls in one room collapsed, killing Sarah Caroline's two youngest children, George and Margaret Ann.

Sarah Caroline was inconsolable. I had just turned my back, she said. I had just left the room. She could not stop blaming herself for their demise. The family was left demoralized by the deaths, as well as by the prolonged suffering and exposure, the crowding and deprivation, and the illness that had taken its toll. Even Father seemed to degenerate into despair as he surveyed the ruins of our lives.

The storm finally did end and spring came. But our family had lost much, and in some sense it was never to be the same. The mansion still stood, but all our other homes had been destroyed. The flour mill was gone, as well as the tannery and the molasses mill. The yard, the fishpond and outhouses, the orchards and stores of crops, all had been swept away, and many animals had been lost as well as the most of our tools and farming implements, which was perhaps the greatest loss of all, for without them the task of rebuilding could hardly begin.

Also arriving that spring was the disturbing sense that the tide had turned against Father. A decided chill came over all relations between him and the General Authorities. It was as if they wanted nothing to do with us anymore, as if they had decided that Father was a liability. They seemed to subscribe to a growing feeling that he could be blamed for the lamentable affair at the meadow, and that by shunning him, they could take away the blame from others and spare the leaders any implication of having sanctioned the destruction of the emigrants.

And so, whether by coincidence or design, the decline in our material wealth was accompanied by a growing enmity toward our family. The elders began shunning Father. He was removed as President of the Branch. Our children were subjected to taunts, and we wives were whispered against. When the Prophet came south the following spring, he declined our hospitality, preferring now to lodge with the Apostle Erastus Snow who had erected his own fine mansion in the thriving new settlement of St. George.

So began our descent, our rapid decline into disgrace and ignominy.

By then, every man who had been at the meadow on that terrible day had left the area. Some had gone to Arizona; others were living in Nevada at Panaca or Pioche, working in the mines there; still others scratched out a subsistence on the Big Muddy or established lonely homesteads in the regions beyond Kanab. Even my dear friend Elizabeth and her husband, Isaac, had fled and were rumored to be living in isolation at Las Vegas Springs, where Elizabeth, childless and barren, was said to be most unhappy. Only Father had chosen to stay in the area and carry on his business as before, and this seemed to irritate the Authorities who wished that we, too, might just disappear.

But we did not disappear.

Instead, we built new dwellings. We pretended not to notice the new iciness in the air. Father finished a small house for me on the upper site where I had long ago, on that day with John Alma and Mary Ann, imagined myself living, and once again I slowly began to accumulate pigs, chickens, cows, and arranged to board a few workingmen.

No, we did not disappear.

Instead, we increased.

In November of 1863 I gave birth to another boy, a husky healthy lad whom we named Isaac, or Ike. How wonderful now to have two boys, my three-year-old Billy, and my baby Ike.

Sarah Caroline and Rachel and Leah all gave birth again that year as well. We were rich in children and our babies all thrived. We tended to one another's children as if each were our own, and to all those who would denounce our Holy Principle I would say this:

A child thrives under the care of multiple mothers.

And a mother thrives, too, when aided by her sisters.

For the next three years I continued to live in my little house high above all the other houses and to board the hired men. I came down to the mansion when important company arrived to help with the cooking, though fewer and fewer visitors stopped now to see us. Still I was happy, even in the midst of such shunning. I had my boys and Alice. I had my little house and my herds. I enjoyed the company of the hired men, all of whom like to sing and dance in the evening and tease me with their tall tales. I had my husband, whom I continued to view as a prince among men. And perhaps best of all, I had my independence, for even though I was the seventeenth wife, I was the mistress of my own domain, and my wealth, as meager as it might seem, was my own.

I considered myself a happy woman. The yard resounded with the noise of animals, seeking calm and rest as they settled into the night, and the cold sharp air was filled with the powerful smell of urine, droppings, and fermented manure, the smell of wealth to me. Songs flowed from my kitchen, and the laughter and gurgling of children filled the air. My husband came to me often: I felt myself adored by the hired men, who often said they considered Father a lucky man. Yes, I was happy, and my happiness might have gone on and on, stretching unhindered into the future, had it not been for the arrival of Ann.

NINE

I CAN RECALL very clearly the first time I saw her.

She lived on a farm near the settlement of Beaver with her mother and stepfather and her younger brother, David. Her stepfather had bought a ewe from Father and we stopped there to deliver it one day. Just as we were preparing to leave, I turned to see someone standing silhouetted against the light in the doorway of the barn, a tall figure, cast in shadow—so tall that I at first mistook her for her mother.

Once she stepped outside, however, I saw her for what she was: just a girl. Very tall and large-boned but, nonetheless, just a girl.

Here's Brother Lee, her stepfather said to her. You remember him, don't you, Ann?

Yes, she said, not smiling, not showing any eagerness at all. She had long black hair that fell loose about her shoulders. She had large blue eyes. She had brown tanned feet and her limbs were long and well formed. An attitude of directness, and of surety, permeated her being, in spite of her youth. She stood tall and straight, looking at Father in the most calm and engaging fashion.

The last time you came you promised to bring me something, she said. Did you bring me something?

Well, now, Father said. I believe I do have something for a certain girl. Let's just have a look here in this wagon.

We all walked over to the wagon together, the girl, her stepfather, Father, myself, and Rachel, who had accompanied us on our journey. The girl wore no shoes and her feet were the same color as the earth. Her dress had been mended in many places and seemed too small for her, yet even in this poor outfit, she had a natural grace that her sad attire couldn't diminish. Her skin was honey-colored and smoothed by her youth. Her full lips were tinged with pink, as if painted. All in all, she was an unusually comely girl, and I felt a blackness arise in my breast as I looked at her. I knew it by its name of jealousy.

Father walked beside her and took her hand. I knew very well then what was happening, what had been happening, perhaps, for some time. Just as I knew how powerless I was to stop it.

From the wagon Father produced a coil of satin ribbon that we had just purchased that morning in Parowan. I had hoped to use the ribbon to trim a dress I was making for Alice.

I believe this might look very pretty in a certain young girl's hair, he said, and placed the ribbon in her hands.

She thanked him and pressed the ribbon to her breast. And then she looked up at him and in that look, so full of knowing, I saw the dissolution of my future.

———

RIDING HOME I felt as if the sun and sand were sticking to my eyelids. Everything was red. The sun came down so hard it pulled the hairs from my head and then it climbed inside my skull and I felt the points like needles going down through my tongue all the way into my heart, and sticking there in dots of shooting pain.

Her name was Ann Gordge, soon to be Ann Gordge Lee, for not more than a month later he took her to the city where he was sealed to her in the Holy Covenant.

There was no point in showing my distress or attempting to discuss the affair with Father. If you believed in the Principle, as I did, there was nothing for it except to embrace your husband's choice, for man was the head of woman, this is what we were taught. And if at times I chafed against such a notion, I had only to remind myself that it was Father, not I, who held the priesthood and with it the Keys to the Holy Kingdom. Besides, there was this to consider: I loved him. He continued to win my affection as no other ever had. I knew he was a man of God, an exceptional man, a man any woman would want in the home. In all our years together he had never once abused me. Nor had I ever seen him mistreat any of his other wives or children. He loved his family with an uncommon intensity. He put our needs before his. He flattered us and wooed us with kind words and gifts. He ruled from strength, in other words, and used his considerable animal magnetism to keep us willingly on the bit. Just as he used that same power to lure young Ann to his marriage bed.

She made me feel so old.

So suddenly aged.

Yet I was only twenty-eight when he took her for a wife.

He was fifty-six.

And she? She was in full possession of all of her thirteen years.

———

LATER I came to wonder why she ever agreed to marry him in the first place, given how everything turned out. She once said she married him for her parents' sake because he had promised her stepfather five fat ewes and a blooded horse. Another time she said it was because she feared for her mother's safety because her mother had spoken out against the Saints and there were those who wanted her out of the way and Ann believed that Father would protect her mother through his influence in the settlements. But I believe none of this was true. She was simply ripe for the picking, and he arrived in time for the harvest.

I know that when we returned that day from the visit to her parents' farm my heart was as sore as it had ever been. The black beast of jealousy had lodged in my breast, creating the most frightful wrath. I understood what Aggatha must have felt when Father first brought me home. When I thought of the ribbon Father had given Ann, I remembered the pretty shawl he had bought for me. I could see the worm turning again, dangling on its silvery thread, and there was nothing to be done about it.

What cannot be cured must be endured. I had learned this as a first principle of medicine. It would now be my lot to apply it to my marriage.

I asked only that God might grant me the patience to possess my soul. And to hold my tongue, which was growing sharper every day.

———

AFTER THE marriage she came to live with me, in my house high on the hill. Father said she was to be my sister-wife, and in this I had no say. She brought with her a small wooden box that contained all her worldly possessions. These amounted to one worn dress, a tattered petticoat, a rag doll, a set of wooden animals her stepfather had carved for her, a brass Masonic pin that had belonged to her real father who had drowned when she was only two in their native Australia, and a set of four postcards she had acquired in San Francisco after her mother had emigrated to that city with her two children.

And, of course, the length of satin ribbon.

It turned out that she had never owned a pair of proper shoes, a situation Father remedied by trading George Chisom for some leather and making her a pair himself. Still she preferred going barefoot, and neither did she mind wearing her old dress, even after Father had acquired a new one for her.

I knew better than to abuse her in Father's presence, but when alone I concocted a myriad of tasks for her to perform at my bidding and in doing so firmly established who was to be in control in our household. She seemed not to mind the hard work. In truth she had a sweet and rather dreamy nature, and appeared to often sleepwalk through her daily chores.

In the evening, after the dishes were done, she sat outside on the porch and bantered with the hired men, who all seemed smitten by her beauty. She liked to sing. She had a very pretty voice. She knew some ribald songs, including one that went

> *My wife and I lived all alone*
> *In a little log hut we called our own*

She loved gin and I loved rum
I tell you what we had some fun

When she sang this song the hired men always joined in on the chorus, singing *ha ha ha, you and me, little brown jug don't I love thee,* and sometimes she rose from her chair and hoisted her dress and danced in bare feet to the clapping of their hands while I watched from my place at the window. The men still favored my cooking, but in all other ways she now commanded their attention.

Father, too, soon made her his favorite, and he made no attempt to hide his preference. Often he arrived after dark, coming directly from his chores and carrying a small jug of whiskey, and together they would set off up the trail and disappear into the woods and the summer night. Later, when they returned to the house, I could smell the liquor on her breath as well as his, and I wondered if he offered her the whiskey as a means of smoothing the way to their lovemaking. The thought of him coupling with her in the woods like common forest animals filled me with disgust, but then I remembered all the times we had done the same, including the afternoon when, to the sounds of crows, we had conceived our son Billy.

That summer I conceived again, on one of the rare mornings when he came to me after a night with Ann. I took great joy in my condition, for I had come to understand there was much power in being able to produce children. Aside from the happiness each child brought me, every birth also pleased Father greatly and increased my standing within the family. For we were taught that the size of a man's family and the number of wives and descendants he had would profoundly affect the degrees of glory earned in the next life.

Still, even with the new life growing inside me, I often felt such misery, sharing my house with Ann, the beautiful child-bride. Most of the time I pretended to pay her little mind. But the truth was nothing she did escaped my attention. I was always watching her.

One day she did something that so angered me I flew into one of my rages. I had ordered her to gather oose—the root of the yucca plant which we used for making soap—and instead she had gone down the hill to Terressa's house and the two of them had whiled away the afternoon eating plums and playing cards. When Terressa drove Ann back to the house at sunset, arriving in the little pony trap, I was waiting for her, and when I saw that she had no oose and could offer no excuse for having gathered none, I tore into her, calling her all manner of names. In a moment of high passion, I slapped her face.

I suppose it was the slap that did it. Suddenly the sweet-natured girl who had taken all manner of verbal abuse from me in the past and never uttered a complaint jumped upon my back and began clawing me and tearing at my hair. I screamed for help and threw her off, but she managed to grab me again and pushed me to the ground. She began hitting me with her fists while sitting astraddle of me, and I was astonished by her fierceness, and more than a little frightened. My little Ike started howling while Billy ran off to find Father as Ann continued to pummel me. More than once I managed to push her off but she always overpowered me again, for she was younger and quicker and much stronger. During all of this Terressa simply looked on and made no attempt to separate us or cool our tempers. Finally Father arrived and the scene put him in a fine rage. It was difficult to say who he was most angry with—Ann and me for fighting, or Terressa for doing nothing to settle the dispute.

You are like children, he thundered, once he had pulled us apart. She had bloodied my nose. I, for my part, had left deep scratches on her face and arms.

And you, he said, pointing a finger at Terressa, are perhaps most to blame for doing nothing to stop this affair from reaching the point of violence. You should have used your influence, as the elder wife, toward a quiet settlement of the differences between these two girls. What *were* the differences, anyway? he demanded.

Neither of us said anything for a moment. And then, in a funny little high voice, Ann said, Oose. The word sounded so silly, and the tone of her voice so funny, that I burst out laughing. Oose, she said again in her squeaky made-up voice, and then she began to giggle. We both dissolved into helpless laughter then, a mirth that only we shared, for both Father and Terressa were frowning at us in deepest disapproval.

Finally Father prepared to quit the scene.

Clean yourselves up, he said, and I warn both of you, I won't be so tolerant of this kind of behavior in the future.

———

THAT NIGHT he did not come to lay with either Ann or me, but sometime after the midnight hour, I heard her cross the room and felt her slip into my bed.

She found my hand beneath the covers and held it.

Her breath was shallow. I could not see her face in the darkness. I waited. And finally she spoke.

We shouldn't fight, she said, and I'll tell you why. I am just like you.

The moment she said this I knew that it was true. I think I had known this from the beginning, that I was more joined by nature to her than any of the others. She had a rebellious streak, just as I did. And as she had proven that day, she was not above a good fight. There was mischief in her, and there was mischief in me. Moreover, as the seventeenth and the nineteenth wives (number eighteen, Terressa, hardly counted for anything) we were fated to bring up the rear together. The older wives would always have more say than we did. I saw at that moment how we might need each other, how an alliance between us could make us each stronger. And truly she was a sweet child, although I had come to see how her youth disguised a very old soul. In many ways she possessed a wisdom and a calm far beyond her years. After all, it was she who had come to my bed that night, seeking a reconciliation, as if she was the more generous and mature.

We lay in bed holding each other's hands and talked in whispers for a very long time that night.

She really is the ugliest old crone, isn't she? Ann said, and I did not have to ask whom she meant.

I think he married her for her soul's sake, I said.

It certainly wasn't for her beauty. She could scare the feathers off a chicken. Do you think he sleeps with her?

I don't believe she likes the deed anymore.

Do you?

Do I what?

Do you . . . like the deed?

I felt myself blush a little, for I had never spoken of such things with anyone before.

Yes, I suppose I do well enough.

Does he wiggle his finger against you, too?

Ann! Really—

Don't worry. No one can hear us. Did you ever know such a thing could feel so good?

I believe if it had not been so dark in the room I could never have continued this conversation. But somehow the darkness made it possible. I felt cloaked by the darkness, enfolded in a stillness that permitted me to tell the truth without fear of consequence.

No. I had never known such a feeling before.

He was not my first, she said.

But you are so young. How is that possible?

A neighbor boy took me in the fields last year. But it wasn't the same. His willy was so little. Father's is very big, don't you think?

I laughed and said, I have nothing to compare it to, lass.

This boy, he later had a mishap with his sister while they were herding sheep together one summer and she had a baby and her brother was the father. When the baby was born the father of the brother and sister attempted to say the child was not theirs, but everyone knew the truth. That girl went a little mad. They took the baby from her and gave it to a relative. I suppose the boy could have given me a baby, too, just as he did his sister. If I don't want a baby with Father, what should I do?

Why wouldn't you want a baby?

I don't much care for them. They cry so much and you always have to tend to them. I wouldn't like that.

You are a peculiar girl.

She ran her hand down my shoulder and let it rest lightly on my breast.

I like you very much, she said. I liked you right from the beginning, even when you talked cross to me.

You must not, I said, and took her hand from my breast.

And why not? We can do as we please. There is no one here to say we can't. We can even make our own pleasures, now that we have been instructed how to do so.

But it isn't right, I'm sure.

Why would it be wrong?

I don't know—

Then perhaps it is not. She slipped her hand beneath my gown again. This time she let it rest near that most secret of places. My breath caught in my throat. But I did not stop her.

If you do not wish to conceive a child with Father, I said, this is what you must do. After you lay with him, you should take a little vinegar and mix it in a cup of water. Then go to the creek and wash yourself thoroughly with it. If you can, hoist your bottom up on a rock so your loins are tilted up and pour the vinegar water over you—

Over me, or into me?

Into you, of course. It's his seed you want to kill.

A girl I know in Beaver who is older than me gave me fits for marrying such an old man and one with so many wives. But I told her not to be alarmed, that I would make dollars to cents of him before I got through. And I will. I intend to have many adventures in life, and this is only the first.

You really are a peculiar one, I said again.

I don't mind being peculiar. I've never wanted to be like everyone else.

But do you love him?

I don't know. I don't think so. I like him well enough, though.

You could have married a boy nearer your own age. Did you not think of that?

I could have, it's true. But it wouldn't have been so interesting. I liked the way he looked at me. He said he would give me presents. He said he would build me a house of my own one day. My stepfather told me he was a rich man. But it wasn't only the gifts. Or the money. I don't know how to express it except to say he excited me. When he came to visit and took me on his lap, I felt how hard his willy got. I could feel it through the cloth of his trousers. That excited me.

I know no one who talks as you do. It's scandalous.

No, Emma. The truth is never scandalous. It's just the truth. And it can't ever be wrong to tell it, can it?

It was perhaps such talk that led to our excess that night, an excess which was never to be repeated. Later I was to think of this as the means by which we pledged our bond to each other, after the fashion of natives, who are reputed to mix blood from self-inflicted wounds in order to seal themselves as brothers. We did not mix blood, but a substance even more powerful and forbidden. We became sisters that night, not just sister-wives but true sisters, through the act in which Father had initiated us and which we would never again feel the need to replay.

———

HER BEAUTY and her youth made her the belle of the ball for a while. Ann was a commanding presence at all that season's dances. For the Saints, dance has always been not only a means of recreation, a way to cast off the worries and labors of the day, but a form of worship as well. However, religious love is the very neighbor of sexual love and they often got mixed up in the intimacies of social excitements. At the dances, it seemed all the men were perpetually in the market. At such gatherings, which were often held at our mansion in the upstairs social hall—it being able to accommodate the greatest number of people— the men and boys all vied for the chance to partner Ann. I do not say that she flirted with them, or intentionally cast her charms about in a free and wanton manner in an effort to attract the males. Rather it seemed a natural consequence of her presence. Men flocked to her. And even though Father had claimed her as a wife, he could hardly lay claim to or contain her spirit, which had an element of freedom to it beyond any I had ever encountered in the female sex.

In truth I came to believe over time that she thought more like a man than a woman, and in such a way she also moved through the world. She maintained a cool attitude toward the other wives, as if they came from a different species whose concerns and habits she did not share. She never joined in the idle gossip that occupied the other women in the settlement. And yet she was not without firm opinions, nor was she afraid to speak her mind, as I had learned that first night she came to my bed. There was a forthrightness about her. She could deflect the unwanted attentions of men effortlessly, without leaving any offense, though in truth she seemed to enjoy the company of men much more than women. Raucousness didn't offend her; she enjoyed a good laugh, and she was never far from a song.

She was good to Father. She sat on his lap and stroked his hair, rubbing his shoulders after a long day's work. Or, sometimes in the manner of an amateur theatrical performer, she rose to her feet and danced for him while singing one of her pretty little songs. Our house high up on the hill soon became his favorite stopping place at the end of a long day. I provided the delicious meals, as I always had, and she provided the entertainment, while the hired men afforded the manly company Father had always relished. And at the end of the night, it did not much matter to either of us whether he went to her bed, or mine, or, as eventually happened, whether he coaxed us both to lay with him and take our turns.

———

I ONCE heard him brag to a group of men that in his earlier days he had been quite the rooster among the pullets. He did not know that I was listening when he spoke these words. This was when he was jailed for the second time, as he waited for his second trial to begin. His listeners were all reporters who had assembled from various parts of the country to interview the now famous man. I did not think it was a wise thing to say for it confirmed the then prevalent view of him, that he was a rapacious man, capable of all manner of excess.

No, I did not think it was a wise thing to say.

Even if it was true.

———

As my pregnancy advanced, Ann became more and more of a help to me and our bond of friendship deepened. I found her to be the most amusing company. We could be very wicked together. She sometimes liked to dress the part of a man, and because she was so large-boned and flat-chested, she could do this to great effect. We worked up a little skit together that we performed one night for the whole family in the social hall. It was called "The Gent Comes Calling," and detailed the trials of a hapless suitor trying to win the affection of his beloved. Ann of course took the part of the suitor, dressed as a man, while I got myself up as the much painted object of desire. As I was then very far advanced in my pregnancy—and much larger than I had been with either Ike or Billy—the effect was quite comic. Or so we thought. But of the adults present, only Father and Mary Ann and John Alma seemed to enjoy our performance. Of course, all the children laughed. But the other wives who were present—including Aggatha and Rachel, Leah, Sarah Caroline and Terresa—all sat stony-faced throughout the play, and afterward I heard Aggatha cluck to her sister and, shaking her head, remark that there was something a touch too unnatural about it all, and that we had blasphemed the holy state of motherhood.

In time, of course, we invented names for them all by which we referred to them in secret code.

Aggatha was The Bucket because of her steely manner and graying hair.

Rachel became The Mouse for all the attributes she shared with that creature.

Leah we called The Big Swooner, or simply B.S., in reference not only to her considerable size but to her fits and the nonsense that poured forth from her mouth when she babbled in tongues.

Polly and Lavina, whom we rarely saw unless we happened to journey to Washington with Father on some errand or another, retained the names Mary Ann and I had first given them—Miss Muss and Miss Fuss, or simply "M" and "F," as in mother and father, or male and female. For in such a way—as immutable and fixed partners—did the sisters so often appear to us.

Sarah Caroline we were only slightly kinder to, in deference to her loss: I still pitied her the deaths of her children in the terrible storm, an event from which she had not fully recovered. To us she became The Weeper because of the tears that always seem to flow so freely now.

And Terressa? That aged amalgam of ire and ill humor? That self-righteous, prim, horse-faced dispenser of gaseous advice and perpetual venom? She was simply The Viper, to be avoided as rigorously as any snake.

―――

IT WAS AT about this time, just a few months before my laying-in, that an incident occurred that soured relations between Father and myself for some time. During one of the family evenings at the mansion, Rachel made some passing remark about having produced three daughters and no sons while I had given birth to three sons, though my first had died. She said how very much she would like to have a son, and in jest, I said to her, Well, Rachel, if it is a boy I am carrying, I'll give it to you; since I am so good at producing boys, I can easily have another!

To my complete surprise, this comment put Father in a terrible rage. I had only made my remark in a spirit of bravado, egged on, I might add, by Ann, who loved to see this side of me emerge. But Father took me seriously, and he rebuked me in front of everyone for having made such a wicked statement. And then, as was his wont, he held forth with a prophecy.

You are carrying not only a baby girl, but twin girls, he said. The name of the first shall be Rachel Emma, for you two sitting here, and the second born shall be called Ann Eliza, for your companion wife and your friend Elizabeth Summers, with whom you traveled the first part of your trip to Zion. I cannot promise that you will be able to keep both these little girls because of your rebellious spirit and caustic tongue. You yourself will be most responsible for the outcome.

He frightened me when he said this. It seemed true that I might be carrying twins, so great was my size, and I did not want to lose them to my wickedness. Later, on the walk up the hill with Ann I began feeling rebuked and remorseful and I wept many tears until Ann began chiding me for taking Father's words to heart.

Don't you see, she said, how for his part he simply wishes to keep us in line by instilling fear in us? He wants to control not only our actions but our tongues as well. Pay no mind to his words. A soothsayer he is not.

But he himself believes he is most capable of foretelling the future.

It's another method for gathering power unto himself and attempting to wield it over others. This is what men do, she said most matter-of-factly.

All men? I inquired.

All I've chanced to meet. But then I am still young. Perhaps one will surprise me yet.

———

A FEW WEEKS later Aggatha died. Her demise was not sudden. She had been ill for many months, suffering from a variety of maladies related to age, and although Father had laid hands upon her many times and prayed fervently for her recovery, it was not to be.

She suffered terribly at the end. It was the only time in all my years of offering assistance to the sick and dying that I had ever witnessed a body become so generally necrotic before the actual death took place. The flesh of her breasts and shoulders turned dark and putrefied long before she had taken her last breath. I attempted to ease her suffering as best I could but, truth to tell, there was little any of us could do. The stench at the end was awful, and her agony was great. Before she died she gathered her children around her and blessed them. She asked her sister, Rachel, to be their mother now. People came to bid her goodbye, and to bring messages for their own dead which they hoped she would carry to the other side. To each wife she said a few kind last words. When my turn came to bid adieu to the dying woman, Aggatha drew me close and whispered, May God bless you to keep both of your little daughters, for she knew of Father's prediction.

———

ONE MONTH after Aggatha's death, I brought forth a pair of twin girls, just as Father had said I would, and they were assigned the names he had already chosen—Rachel Emma, or Emmie, and Ann Eliza, or Annie. They were born on Sunday, July 22nd, 1866, the first about 4 P.M., the second perhaps thirty minutes later. Never had I had a harder labor, for the girls were very large. One of them weighed eight and a half pounds, the other eight and three quarters, making the babies seventeen and a quarter pounds at birth. Several witnesses present bore testimony of the promised girls and confirmed the fulfillment of Father's prophecy.

But all I could think was, I have two boys, and now I have two girls, and I have not lost any of them to my wickedness.

———

ALMOST NINE months later to the day, having failed to avoid the fate she did not wish, Ann bore her first child, a boy named Samuel James. I cannot say she made the most natural of mothers. Her milk was slow to come, and finally, to protect the health of the child, I took him to my own breast. Long after I had weaned the twins, I still suckled little

Sam, and soon formed a bond with the child stronger than that with his own mother.

Ann much preferred to be outdoors rather than assume the burden of household work. She was happy to toil at hard tasks more suited to men as long as it took her from the home. She had a particular love of horses, and since Father owned some of the finest-blooded stock in the territory, she had her pick of the best mounts to chose from when she set out for a ride. She had a natural rapport with all animals, and in time she convinced Father to let her accompany the herds into the high pastures during the summers. With her yellow dog, Nero, she lived for weeks at a time on Kolob Mountain, leaving me to care for Sam, and having but little contact with the other hired men, some of whom were also employed as herders. Soon, however, the men began bringing me stories of Ann. How she shot a mountain lion in midleap. How she pulled a breached foal herself, thereby saving the life of Father's favorite black mare. How she had been bitten on the face by a bobcat she'd trapped and tried to tame. And how she had fashioned for herself a pair of riding breeches out of an old canvas wagon cover and made a matching coat, trimmed in the fur of the bobcat she'd shot for having bitten her. This outfit I saw for myself when she returned to the settlement after a month on the mountain. She rode in astride a fine gray horse, wearing a sombrero she'd gotten off an old Indian named Jim. When I first spied her, I felt for all the world I could have been looking at one of the Mexican traders that came through periodically, so sunburnt was her skin, and so thoroughly disguised was she by her manly outfit. Her appearance astride the horse in this getup caused almost as much consternation amongst the brethren as Jane Meeks had when she'd been caught cutting the Spanish Rusty with one of the soldiers from the fort. (To cut the Spanish Rusty meant to ride astride a horse in front of a man rather than behind as was considered proper, and this was deemed immoral: for Jane's offense she had been disfellowshipped for a time.) But although Ann received her share of stares and quite a few clucked tongues when she rode in wearing her homemade pantaloons and her wide-brimmed hat, she provoked no punishment. Times had changed, and as for straddling a horse, we had become a practical-minded people who could ill afford to stand on ceremony where the demands of our daily labors dictated otherwise, and no one could argue the fact that Ann's outfit made sense for a herder, whether that herder be a woman or not.

————

IN MANY WAYS it was an uneventful time, that summer that Ann spent on the mountain, filled with small occurrences and petty squabbles. Peter Shirts was reprimanded and made confession of whipping Mary Morse, and Mary Morse made confession of abusive language toward Peter Shirts, and both were forgiven by the bishop after some explanations were given. Amasa Lee and Samuel Groves confessed their faults in playing and cutting up in the way they did one evening, running about in the corral in a state of nudity, and they, too, were forgiven their sins after a public hearing.

Old man Chamberlain attempted to win Terressa back by offering to give Father another of his wives and her two children, but Father said he did not believe in trading wives as if they were mere livestock and declined Solomon's offer, much to my bitter disappointment.

Dudley Leavitt bought two more Indian girls but both died within the first week of naming. A number of wives asked for a Writ of Releasement, finding themselves unable to live by the Principle, and they soon left the settlement in the company of soldiers with whom they'd taken up. The bishop felt compelled to lecture us all from the pulpit on our increasing iniquity, especially the public displays of drunkenness he'd frequently observed in those brethren who traded freely with the Swiss colonists for the product of their vines. A few children caught the measles and were quarantined. Others fell ill from the same disease, but all recovered in time.

The one exception to these prosaic events was the incident that occurred in the middle of September, when Sarah Dalton, Father's oldest daughter, shot her husband in the heart while he slept in his bed. She then placed his head carefully upon the pillow and put the gun in his hand and claimed it was a suicide. No charges were brought against her, even though it was generally known that he'd abused her for years and on more than one occasion she'd threatened to shoot him.

In the fall we hauled in the squash and pumpkins. We harvested a good crop of corn and potatoes. On October 14th the snow fell about two inches deep, and Father said that, according to the Old Dutch Proverb, it being the first tracking snow, there would be only six more tracking snows this winter, as the moon was six days old when the first snow fell.

We sold a number of ewes and calves. We traveled to Dog Valley to gather cress, and made a trip to Parowan for shingles, cotton yarn, spades and shovels, factory needles, pins, shoe patterns, thread, buttons, calico, stamps and envelopes, salt, pepper, coffee, tea, writing paper, painkiller, and shoe leather—all of which were sorely needed.

We butchered hogs to trade for these goods and we came out on top and even had enough left over to purchase twenty-five gallons of the best-grade whiskey.

In January, Father accidentally had his testicles hurt by the jumping of his horse and they commenced to swelling to an alarming extent. I used spirits of turpentine, coal oil, saltpeter, wild sage, and vinegar to treat him, and last of all I applied a poultice of charcoal and raw grated carrots, and after a week of lay-up, he was able to resume working again. At the same time I was tending to Father's injury, Ann was nursing a foal. Father had bought a heavy claybank mare and colt but his ox hooked the belly of the colt and Ann, instructed by me, sewed up the wound herself and was most pleased that the colt survived.

The first telegraph message was sent and received at Cedar City and this caused quite an excitement among the people, who all said it was a great thing, but neither Ann nor I could fathom its import and found their enthusiasms to be excessive and silly.

That year Sarah Caroline conceived, and so did Rachel and Leah, and by spring both Ann and I were pregnant again, much to my joy and her disappointment.

In the fall of 1867 Father announced that his sons Joseph Hyrum and John Willard, Aggatha's oldest boys, had been called to go on missions. The boys were eager to see the world and readily accepted the call. Joseph was twenty-two, and Willard, or Will, only eighteen, but they were good, hardworking youths. To support them while they were in the mission field would put a strain on our family resources, but Father was determined they should go, just as he had gone forth and preached the Gospel in his youth. He decided to drive a herd to Salt Lake City to sell in order to raise the money for their expenses. Best of all, he chose me to accompany him. I would take the twin girls but leave the boys—including Ann's little Sam, whom I had only recently weaned—for Ann to care for in our absence. I was elated by the prospect of this journey, for it had been ten long years since I had left the city to take up life with Father.

On April 25th, 1868, the herd started north, driven by the boys, Joseph and Will, and Father and I soon followed in a wagon outfitted for the long journey. It would take us ten days to reach the city. We had heard that the Prophet was also traveling north with an entourage and at Chicken Creek we came upon his party. In a hasty conference, Father indicated to Brigham that he thought his boys should be sent to England, where he was certain they would have much success in making converts. But Brigham had other ideas. The Sandwich Islands, he said, were in need of missionaries, and he intended for Joseph and Will to spend their time there, working among the natives of the South Seas.

Before parting, Father tried to gauge the mood of the Prophet in terms of the ill will that had long been building up against us in the southern colonies. He told him about the shunning we had increasingly suffered as a result of the unfortunate affair at the meadow—sore treatment that others, even more responsible for these events, had somehow managed to escape. Father said he wanted the Prophet's assurance that he still held him in highest regard and that he could be counted on to stand by us in the future, and the Prophet gave him such assurance. He went so far as to sign a paper that said, "Brother John D. Lee is a staunch, firm Latter-day Saint who seeks to build up the Kingdom of God and live by its Principles and is in full Fellowship and Good Standing." This paper was to prove important, especially when we reached the city, as it helped guarantee Father a market for his cattle and insured he received a warm welcome wherever he went to trade.

We arrived in the city on Monday, May 13th, and I was most amazed to see how it had grown in my absence. What a thriving, busy place it had become! Immediately we sold our beef cattle to a Brother Feramorz Little who treated us to beer and a sumptuous dinner. I later learned he had the reputation of having the best table of any in the city, and if our meal was any measure, this was certainly true. That night we lodged with Sarah Jane, Father's daughter with whom I had had my picture made long ago, and the next day I witnessed an event that greatly impressed me.

Brigham and his party were returning from their trip south, and all the city turned out to welcome him. Like an ancient Roman ruler, he entered the city to great trumpet and fanfare. He rode in a grand carriage at the head of a procession of horses and wagons, dressed all in black and clasping a gold-topped cane, the very same cane, it was said, that had once belonged to the Prophet Joseph. Twenty-five thousand people lined the main street of the city, including many youths who had been organized into cadres by their school teachers. The military was there in uniform, as well as a brass and martial band, drawn by prancing matched horses that accompanied the procession down the parade route. It was a sight I knew I'd never forget—the Prophet, appearing larger than life, his white-bearded jaw set firmly and his chin raised, waving to his people as if they were minions of his kingdom. Several of his wives, in expensive satin frocks with jewels dangling from their ears, rode in separate carriages and his eldest sons, only slightly less massive than their father, sat astride prancing horses, followed by a retinue of counselors and advisers, all hailed by a populace filled with adoration and enthusiasm for their leader. The people looked so much more affluent and worldly than I was accustomed to seeing in our poor southern settlements. For the first time, I felt the true prosperity of the Saints, as well as our solidarity. And when, as the Prophet approached Temple Square, the great banner was hoisted which read, WELCOME HOME BRIGHAM, FRIEND TO ALL MANKIND, I knew that truly the Saints were fortunate to have such a wise and cunning leader, a leader who had steered us so often across the shoals of opposition and strife, and I felt that perhaps Father was most fortunate of all, for long ago the Prophet had adopted him as his spiritual son. As long as Brigham was in our camp, I felt we had nothing to fear from our detractors, and this allowed me to view the future with more hope and confidence than I had for some time.

The next day, a Sunday, we attended sacrament meeting in the tabernacle and heard Elder George Q. Cannon speak on the subject of communitarianism. With great eloquence, he laid out the concepts behind The New Economic Order by which the Saints were now expected to live. He denounced the "aristocracy of wealth on the one hand, and the class that lived in degradation and poverty, on the other." This disparity, he said, was due to an incorrect organization of society and the power to address this evil required the Office of the Holy Priesthood. Under its authority, all were now to be equal, with equal claims on communal property—every man according to his wants and needs, inasmuch as his wants were just. This would be accomplished by turning over all private property and increase from flocks and fields to the Lord's storehouse to be supervised by local bishops and to become the common property of the church, and from this every man might draw his share according to his talents and his needs.

At this point in Brother Cannon's sermon I found myself thinking, But will not the careless and indolent take advantage of this system by requiring that the industrious share unfairly in the fruits of their labors? But Brother Cannon soon answered the point. The man who was energetic and faithful would receive his reward in the Day of the Lord Jesus, or in Heaven, in other words. The cooperative system was meant to apply to all, not just Saints but ultimately to all society, and this would introduce the millennium, spreading a communitarian gospel over the earth and bringing to the world a system free of class and injustice. That would be the consummation of our mission as Saints, to bring a new order of justice and peace to the world, and to accomplish this, we were to all consecrate our wealth and labor to the church, who would distribute it according to need.

It sounded wonderful to me. Having spent the first part of my life as a servant in England, and the second living among the poorest of the Saints, I knew injustice and discrimination firsthand and I had often thought how unfair it was that some enjoyed such luxury while others struggled for their crust of bread.

But later Father remarked to me that he could not see the sense of this system, for he believed it was private ownership that spurred a man to his best labors, and he had no wish to support the lazy and weak through his own hard labor.

It is doomed, this communitarianism, he pronounced as we left the tabernacle that day. As it turned out, he was right, for men are essentially selfish and wish to lay up their own rewards, both on earth and in Heaven, even good men filled with the spirit of God.

A few days later, Joseph and Willard received their anointings and were set apart for their missions. Father made arrangements for them to travel with a family who was taking a wagon to San Francisco, and from there they would board the ship that would carry them to their faraway destination of the Sandwich Islands. The Sandwich Islands! The very name frightened me. I could not begin to imagine what might await them there. Were there cannibals afoot in those lands? Did the natives wear bones in their hair and sharpen their teeth, all the better for tearing human flesh? Did the women run about in a state of nakedness? And eat all manner of strange things? Most importantly, would we ever see Joseph and Will again? I could tell that the boys, too, were beset by anxieties and fears, and many tears were shed at our parting, especially by Will, who begged his father's forgiveness for his past rebellious spirit.

Before leaving the city, we attended the theater and witnessed a production of Shakespeare's *Hamlet*. The opera house was so grand, and the audience decked out in such finery, that I felt myself quite out of place in my much worn silk dress, and yet nothing could diminish the sense of wonder and happiness I felt that night, sitting there in that ornately decorated hall with Father beside me. He looked most handsome in a new black coat and white collar, with his hair freshly cut and his face clean-shaven. He squired me that night as if we were new lovers in the first bloom of romance, and I felt what it might be like to have a husband all to myself, one whose attentions were focused utterly and solely on me, and I wished then that we could stay forever in the city, with its excitements and lavish entertainments, and never return to the poor feudal settlements in the south, where only enmity awaited us, not to mention eight other wives.

But return we did.

The trip home was uneventful with the exception of one disturbing occurrence. While encamped on Chicken Creek, near the farm of Thomas and Mary Woolsey, Aggatha's brother and sister-in-law, Jane Woolsey, Father's niece, came into our camp one night and tempted Father. That is the way he later reported it to me, in any case, after I discovered them in a most compromising situation: I returned suddenly from a walk that evening and found Jane sitting astraddle of Father's lap, laying kisses upon his brow. From the expression on his face, he was much enjoying this experience—until, that is, he looked up and saw me standing there.

What is this? I demanded.

Jane, who was a child no older than Ann, abruptly rose and scurried away, and Father set about offering an explanation.

The girl climbed on my lap, only a few moments ago, overcome by delight to see her favorite uncle—

I loosed my tongue at him then and let him have my mind. I

demanded he tell me the truth. I said I wanted to know whether this, in fact, was to be the beginning of another courtship, and if so, I had a right to know his intentions. What I had witnessed was not the innocent behavior of an uncle and niece. My eyes did not lie to me. What were his *true* feelings regarding Jane Woolsey? Did he actually intend to make this girl his twentieth wife? A child who seemed even younger than Ann?

He said he could not answer my question with any surety at the present, as things were not yet settled. He claimed that Jane had come to him, shortly after she had seen me set off for my walk, and announced that she wished to become a member of his family. She said she wished to be his wife. She brought the matter up, not he. Father claimed he had tried to discourage her.

I said, Jane, you are a young girl in the bloom of youth. You can marry both young and middle age. Why me? I am an old man now. You certainly would be better satisfied with a young man.

And she? What did she say to this?

She replied, Uncle, I have known you since I was a child. I love you more than any other man on earth. I always loved you. A home is what I want, and a kind friend to protect me. You are the man that I want.

Do you expect me to believe this tale?

But it's true!

And what did you tell her then?

I said, Jane, if the Lord wills it, I expect to return to the city in the fall, and if you conduct yourself as a prudent girl and remain in the same mind, I will take you as wife. We shall go to the city and be sealed in the Covenant. But I will not place you under obligation to wait for me. If you get a good chance to marry, do so. It was then she climbed onto my lap and said, Uncle, I hope the Lord will kill me if I do not prove true to you and laid a few kisses on me. That is when I looked up and saw you standing there.

An extraordinary account, I said bitterly.

Ah, but true, Emma, true.

Your prospects for wives seem to be getting younger and younger as you get older and older.

It is not my doing—

Soon I think you may have to begin adopting babes and raising them up yourself to a ripe matrimonial age of seven or eight—

Watch your tongue, Emma.

And if you marry Jane, will you stop at twenty wives? Or do you propose to give the Prophet a run for his money and aim for thirty, or thirty-five?

You are treading dangerous waters. I warn you to keep a civil tongue in your head or pay the consequences.

I'll hold my tongue, for now anyway. But not before telling you this. You give your enemies ammunition by chasing after girls so young. And this one, I warn you, is a fox. Put her in your henhouse, and I guarantee a row.

———

WITH THAT we dropped the matter and broke camp and traveled on to Dog Creek in the coolness of the night. The next day, about day-break, we met a Dutchman on foot without any money and without food for two days. We gave him a loaf of bread, and traveled on, but a wheel was broken in crossing a ditch over Wild Cat Canyon, necessitating a stop for repairs. While Father fixed the wheel, I entertained myself by watching the antics of a whole village of prairie dogs. My thoughts, however, were very far away.

For the first time in a long while, I began thinking of England and of the home and the parents I had left behind. I could see the neat and orderly redbrick houses of Uckfield, the many-chimneyed establishments lining the High Street, and the stone houses and barns of the countryside where there were no surprises left to either the land-scape or the people. I remembered the old church in the center of the village with its vaulted apse and the balconies on either side of the pulpit and the embroidered cushions for kneeling in every pew. I remembered the strange fashion in which the parson parted his hair. I could see the green and folded landscape, Ashdown Forest stretching toward Tunbridge Wells, and the sheep dotting the emerald fields like clean white boulders. In the spring the rhododendrons and lilacs and azaleas bloomed along the roads to Groombridge and Boarshead and Lewes and the grapes hung from bowers like jewels. Duddleswell and Nutlety, Rotherfield, Eridge, Temple Grove, and Crowborough. The names of the villages ran through my mind like the names of old friends. And what of my parents and my sister and brother, I wondered. Were they well? Did they miss me ever? Or had I become a lost memory to them, the daughter swallowed up by a land so distant and a religion so foreign I might as well have disappeared into Arabia.

I grew sad thinking that most likely I would never see my parents again or behold the rolling hills of Sussex, the fields of mustard and blue flowers growing among the hedges, and the trees of Ashdown Forest whose bark was greened by moss. No more green and gentle world for me. Instead, I realized I was destined to live out my days in this dry, red land, and the finality of this thought, this sense of a past closed off forever to me, left me feeling hollowed out, as if some core of my being had been removed.

That evening we camped near a migrating band of sheep, and their incessant bleating filled the air. The herders, as it turned out, were from California and had heard of the incident at the meadow. When Father gave his name, one of them said, So you are the butcher they speak of? This prompted him to stay up until the late hours, giving them a correct account of the affair, while treating them liberally to our stores of whiskey. By morning, it seemed he had won them over, for he parted from them like old friends.

The next day we drove to Beaver, where Father preached in the new large brick meetinghouse, laying out the case for rebaptism to cleanse the soul of accumulated evils, and many in the congregation were melted down to tears. Later he was called on to administer to the sick in the village. He laid hands on Brother Jeter's son. Then Sister Mary Riddle, who had been lying at the point of death, hearing that he was in town and being advised of his great powers, dispatched a message asking him to come to her. He went and prayed and laid his hands on her and through the power of faith she felt instant relief. No sooner had Sister Riddle amended than one of her children, a little girl, was suddenly attacked with a raging fever and began calling for the man who had prayed for her mother. So we returned to the house, and Father anointed the child with holy oil and rebuked The Destroyer and that child, too, was made well.

And then, having loaded our wagon with presents and provisions bestowed upon us by the grateful families of the sick, we departed for Harmony, where we found that in our absence the atmosphere had deteriorated considerably.

The Saints, it seemed, had become even further debauched in their habits. There was much indulgence in Gilbert's, a drinking whiskey, and the evening we arrived we found several of the brethren making public displays of drunkenness. Some were sitting near the bowery, smoking and chewing tobacco, and when they saw Father drive up, they made lewd signs. We learned that a number of the men, including some of the boys in our own family, had taken to swearing and carousing about town. Furthermore, it was rumored that Ann had taken up with a certain young soldier named Matt Carney and made free with her favors in Father's absence. She denied having done so, but Father remained unconvinced by her protestations of innocence. Over the next few days, several loud rows between them ensued, during which Ann more than held her own. Before it was over, a set of crockery had been smashed, and the entire town felt compelled to take sides, though many chose to denounce them both as aberrants and adulterers.

Added to this was the news of Leah's defection. She had removed herself and all her belongings to Toquerville, where she had lodged a complaint with the bishop there, charging Father with neglect and asking for a Writ of Releasement. This was to be the end of their marriage. It turned out, as we later discovered, that The Swooner had been dallying with one Joseph Pruitt in Father's absence, a man to whom she would soon be wed.

Now it was not only Father's worldly goods that were being pilfered, stolen out from under his nose, but also his wives. I sensed a wild spirit in the settlement, a breakdown of the reigning social order, so different from the coherence and refinement of society I had observed in the city, and the exact opposite of the new social order I heard preached by Brother Cannon. Here, in this harsh outpost, among the rude fellowship of these ruffian saints, it was every man for himself. The moral code had broken down, and not even the priesthood could save it. I came to believe that the horrible events at the meadow, even though they had occurred over ten years earlier, were most responsible for this general demoralization among the people. Slowly, over the years, an erosion had occurred. The massacre of the Arkansas emigrants not only had branded the hearts and minds of those men and boys who had been involved but had also shamed those Saints who had not even been there that day and instilled a searing sense of guilt in everyone. It was as if those events had even poisoned the land itself. The very atmosphere of this brute red world seemed impregnated with sorrow and evil, colored by all the innocent blood shed that day, and this had brought forth a scavenging coarse nature in those otherwise not inclined to brutishness.

In response to the disarray Father found in his households he held a general meeting of his remaining wives at which he forced each of us to stand and confess our sins, beginning with whom we might have had unlawful congress over the past few months. To my surprise, The Mouse had been very naughty indeed, and confessed to a dalliance with Matt Carney—the very same man with whom Ann had been accused of consorting. The Weeper shrank from confessing anything worse than failing to attend church meetings, and shed a few tears. Miss Muss and Miss Fuss hotly denied wrongdoing of any sort, and considering their icy primness, it wasn't hard to believe. When he came to me I said no opportunity had presented itself for me to betray him or indulge in sin and, since I was not given to sitting astraddle of my uncles' laps, I had nothing to say—a comment that caused him to visibly fume. But so eager was he to get to Ann, he overlooked my sauciness and pressed on. And you, he said, facing my young sister-wife, who seemed to have matured in some indefinable way in my absence, are you finally ready to tell the truth?

As a matter of fact, she said, standing up and yawning, I'm really ready for bed. I find it so tiring being so good.

With that she sauntered out of the room, and I had to cover my mouth to hide my smile.

———

AND SO WE resumed our lives, in that ever shifting, ever changing landscape, where the winds never ceased to blow, for the ill or the good. Many a time I thought we were foolish to stay there. I felt it would be prudent to follow the example of others, like Isaac and Elizabeth, and the Klingensmiths and Samuel Knight, all of whom had fled long ago. It seemed to me only a matter of time before the authorities would come again, sending their troops like bloodhounds, and who would they find when they arrived? Only Father, for all others who took a part in the affair were now long gone. All except Father, whose name increasingly was attached to the incident as chief instigator. I had come to accept that he had played a part in the massacre, though I believed his account of the affair—that he had ridden into the emigrant camp with every hope of saving the party and leading them to safety, that he had pleaded with the Indians to cease their siege and even wept in an effort to dissuade all parties from the butchery, thereby earning him the name of Yawgatts, and that when the slaughter had finally commenced, he had been so absorbed with caring for the littlest children that he had taken no part in the actual killings.

I believed this because I wished to believe it. Whether it is true or not, I still do not know. And in many ways, it doesn't matter. Men are moved by their faith to commit acts only God understands, and oaths are taken to seal those acts in a brotherhood of silence. What I do know is that Father continued to carry on his affairs as if a more innocent man didn't exist. He acted like a man without a worry in the world, an attitude that many mistook for arrogance. And given the increasing attacks on our property, the looting of our goods, the insubordination of certain wives, and the growing ruffianism in the settlement, I felt it would be only a matter of time before our fragile peace would be destroyed, and in this suspicion, I would be proven right.

TEN

THE NAVAJOS HAVE a way of keeping time by tying knots in a buckskin string. If you say to them, I will meet you in seven days, they will tie a knot in the string for each day that passes and at the end of seven days, when they have tied seven knots, they will appear at the appointed place.

So it is with my days now. I feel them slipping through my hands, like a string of knots without end. They now pass with no appointments to keep, and with no prospect of another earthly meeting with the man who has been most dear to me.

The boys returned last night. They brought me the news that he is gone. He has been laid to rest in the cemetery in Panguitch. There was no graveside service, Billy said, but John Alma spoke a few words, and Frank offered a prayer before the grave was filled.

———

A WHILE ago I walked up the canyon, wishing to be alone. As usual, an immense silence greeted me—silence, rocks, emptiness—the currency of this land. The sky was mourner's gray above the vermilion cliffs. I heard no sound. No bird, or voice, or falling rock. This, I thought, was the way the world would be when all mankind had gone, when the cleansing wind of prophecy had swept all sins and virtues from the earth and the wilderness was strewn with fallen and abandoned faiths.

My own faith is lost to me. I have no more belief in the Gospel than I have in the tiny winged creatures moving noiselessly on the air.

As for the Prophet I once revered, I wish to send him cross lots to hell. I pray that his tongue turns black, as black as his darkest mortal sin, so that he might choke on his betrayal and die a quick and unmourned death.

The boys brought with them several items when they returned last night. The first was Father's handkerchief, which still carried the scent of him and into which I wept as I received their news. The second was a photograph of Father, sitting on his coffin, taken by Mr. Fennemore—the same Mr. Fennemore whom I once nursed back to health when he stopped here with Major Powell's expedition. With the picture came a note:

"It was your husband's last request that I send you this likeness of him, taken in his final hour. It comes with my deepest sympathy. I shall always remember your kindness to me. Sincerely, James Fennemore."

The boys informed me that he sent the same photograph to both Rachel and Sarah Caroline as well. A copy for each of the remaining wives.

There are only three of us now. Only three wives left.

And we are no longer wives, but widows.

————

SEVEN YEARS have passed since I first came here to this river. When I followed Father into hiding, I knew not what was in store for me, how this land would grasp me by the short hairs and require that I do its bidding. No one bargains with this land. This much I have learned.

I remember we arrived in the night after a difficult journey down the Paria. I could see nothing in the darkness. There was a musky smell of arrowweeds and willows and the clayey odor of mud clinging to the damp night air. I could hear the sound of the river, a great roaring in the darkness. As dawn came on I left the wagon and climbed a ridge in order to stretch my hips and back for I was pregnant again and the child pressed hard against my bones. I also wished to take stock of my new surroundings. And what I saw emptied out my heart. From my place there above the canyon, I saw a world blasted into rock, hard and unforgiving. I saw how ancient trees had been turned to bits of whitened stone at my feet. I saw scree and slag and scarp, fallen debris, seams of purple rock laid down next to blue, and orange against red—and canyons as deep as the sky. I saw a river—the mighty Colorado, running red with the burden of the desert soil. It roiled away into a chasm so deep it seemed to lead straight to hell. And below me, between the cliffs that fell like folded curtains, I saw our wagons and our animals and the shanty, a cluster of life, huddled there on a narrow delta below the remnant of the glinting globe of moon. This then was my future, I thought. We are banished to the end of the earth, with no human society but our own.

Then I heard footsteps and turned to see Father climbing toward me. He had a strange expression on his face, as if filled with a kind of pride. When he reached the place where I stood, he looked down upon the rude homestead, set just a short distance from the river, and asked, What do you think, Emma?

Oh what a lonely dell, I murmured.

He told me that would be its name from then on. Lonely Dell. Only we won't be lonely here, he said. We shall follow the instructions of Isaiah, who said, Prepare straight to the wilderness a highway for our God.

———

THE BOYS also brought me a letter from Rachel last night. I believed myself beyond jealousy now, and still I find myself anguished to think it was The Mouse and The Weeper who dressed him for burial, and not myself. Her letter was brief, informing me that she considers me her bosom friend. The phrase rankles me. We were never of like mind. Why must she presume that things have changed?

I wish to finish my account before I have not the will left to do it. The story of our final exodus is one still painful to me. Yet we had four good years together here at the river before Father was forced to flee to Moenabba with Rachel, and then a short while later made the mistake of returning to the upper settlements for supplies. There, at Sarah Caroline's house, in Panguitch, he was apprehended by a certain Marshal Stokes while attempting to hide in the corncrib. The rest is a sad tale of treachery and betrayal, of rigged juries and bitter lies, and hearts broken by separation.

———

IT STARTED with a letter.

One day, shortly after we had returned from our journey to the city to see Joseph and Will off on their missions, I found a letter addressed to Father, waiting for him at the post office. As he was away at the time, I took the liberty of opening it and reading it myself. It was a warning, in the form of a threat. The author, a purported "Major Burt," gave Father ten days to leave the territory forever or face being arrested for crimes he had committed at Mountain Meadows.

The moment I read the letter I knew it to be a forgery. I felt certain it was the work of George Hicks and John Lawson, two of Father's most vociferous critics, and I took matters into my own hands. I confronted Hicks on the street the next day and accused him of fabricating the letter in an effort to frighten us and drive us from the settlement so that he might lay claim to Father's fields—land that he had coveted for some time. I let him have the full force of my tongue and temper. I told him he was a poor sneaking pusillanimous pup, always meddling in other men's matters, and that he had better sing low and stay out of my path or I would put a load of salt into his backside.

Hicks, enraged that a woman would dare to give him such a public tongue-lashing, immediately went to Bishop Pace and preferred a charge against me for unchristian behavior, and we both were told to appear for a hearing, at which we were each held to blame and ordered to undergo rebaptism—me for loosing a train of abuse, and he for provoking it by attacking my husband in such a sneaky way. When the sentence was pronounced, I asked for the privilege of naming the man to rebaptize me, and the bishop, not suspecting my intent, granted it.

I am much obliged, I said. I demand baptism at your hands, Bishop, seeing that you are so inconsiderate as to require a woman to be immersed when the stream is full of ice and snow, just for defending her husband. You should pay a little of the penalty for making such a decision, and perhaps if your backside gets wet in ice water you will be more careful how you decide things in the future.

Many people had turned out for the hearing, and the majority of those in the packed room laughed upon hearing my remarks, and one even went so far as to cry, Stick it to him, Emma! But the bishop was not amused. And in the end, he made an excuse of having to go to Kanarra to get out of it, and instead Brother John Larson took me to the creek and forced me to undergo immersion in the icy water, and then did the same to George Hicks.

The months that followed were very troubled times, and my only solace was Ann, in whose friendship I took increasing refuge. The fact that Terressa now lived in our house helped to draw us nearer, for we knew Father had placed her there as a spy. She was to keep an eye on us and report to Father any irregularities she observed, especially with regard to Ann's behavior with other men. As far as I could see, Ann had no desire to betray Father with anyone else, especially given her condition, though increasingly she took to making little remarks against him. It wasn't easy for her. She was heavy with child, and once again she had no wish to bring forth a babe. Her condition seemed to depress her, while my own less advanced pregnancy only fueled my energy and hopes for the future. She would stand at the stove in the morning, boiling black coffee, her swollen abdomen pressing against her thin shift, and tap her bare foot against the floor nervously, her mouth drawn into a frown—not speaking, but just jiggling her foot against the wooden floor and staring at the black liquid as if some dark feeling were trying to work itself out in the bubbling she observed there. Ann, I would say, it can't be that bad, and she would turn and look at me over her shoulder, fixing her sad blue eyes on me for a moment, and then smile thinly and say, Well, if it can't, how come it is?

She delivered a little girl that winter and we named her Merabe Emma, after Ann's mother and myself. The name Belle was soon attached to her, for she was a most beautiful child. Now Ann had Sam and Belle, and I had Billy and Ike and Lizzie and Annie, and in the spring I gave birth to another boy, little James, or Jimmie Gribble, as we took to calling him, after a boy in a fairy tale. We had seven children now between us. So deep was my love for all these children that I made little distinction between Ann's and my own. And I once again nursed her littlest babe, Belle, freeing her that summer to take to the outdoors again, where she felt so much more at home.

I lost my Alice that summer. She succumbed to diphtheria in June. I had not known what ailed her, only that she fell suddenly ill and grew rapidly worse. I had tried every remedy I could think of, to no effect. One night an old woman appeared in the settlement. It was said she was a healer, just passing through with her husband, and I called for her and asked her to look in on Alice. It turned out the old woman was blind. She entered the room where Alice lay, and stood very still, sniffing the air. And then she said, Diphtheria. I can smell it. And it's already far advanced.

She had never been a strong child, Alice. Not since that day when Father had bought her from Moquetus as a half-starved, half-dead baby, caked in filth and her own excrement. Nor had she ever overcome her inclination toward silence. And yet between us the tenderest love and trust had grown up, and I wept profusely at her passing. As I washed her body in preparation for burial, Terressa happened to come into the room.

Better the little wretch is gone, she said. Such a defective little savage can have no purpose here on earth, save to illustrate the extent of human ignorance and misery.

I turned and, without uttering a word, flung the basin of water in her face.

Speak to me again of such things, I said, and it won't be water you'll receive but something with a bit more lead. She began to protest but I pushed her up against the wall, twisting her arm behind her, and told her I wanted to hear not another word from her, and then I hissed, Get out of my sight, and let her go.

It was but one example of my growing anger and unrest. I grew defiant in those days in direct proportion to the degree of threat I felt, whether it was George Hicks fabricating a letter or Terressa abusing the memory of my dead child. What was becoming clear to me was how much more frequently I lost my temper, and how my ferocity was taking an increasingly violent form.

I believe I might have done some permanent violence to Terressa that afternoon when she interrupted my washing of Alice's body had a gun or an ax been at hand. I had come to loathe her so deeply. After this incident, I think Father understood he had to separate us, for safety's sake, and he decided to build a larger house for Ann and myself and our children, leaving Terressa to occupy the little house on the hill. In October, he commenced laying the adobes for our dwelling. The house was to be located on the outskirts of Harmony, along the prettiest little stretch of the creek where the trees were thick and plentiful.

Two weeks after it was finished, however, John Lawson and George Dodds came onto our property one morning and proceeded to chop down the trees along the creek. We sent word to Father, who hastened from the fields to try and stop them. He ordered them off our property and they threatened one another with guns, but eventually Lawson went right on chopping, until Father forcibly took his ax away from him and set off to get a writ from the justice of the peace, prohibiting Lawson from trespassing on our land.

But Lawson came again early the next morning when Ann and I were alone. Hearing the cutting going on, we determined we had to stop it. We set pans of water to boiling on the stove, and when the first was ready, I took it to the yard and attempted to throw it at Lawson but he ducked away at the last moment, and only laughed at me, calling out, Pour it on, Emma! Go ahead, pour it on! Ann soon came out with another dose, and this time he was hit full force with the scalding water and while he was thus distracted, I jumped him from behind, grabbing the arm that held the ax, and tripped him onto his back.

In a flash I was on him, striking him with my fists, and Ann soon pitched in. By the time Father and several others reached the scene of action, we had bloodied his face. Ann had him by the hair and was still pounding his face as I continued to deliver doses of hot water. When finally we were pulled off of him, Lawson looked a bloody gore and, enraged and still in this condition, he made his way to Kanarra where he took out a writ against us for assault and battery with an attempt to kill.

We had to appear before Justice Pollack on December 4th. Witnesses were examined by Bishop Roundy. In the end, Lawson was fined for trespassing and Ann and I were exonerated by Pollock, who said we had simply been defending our property.

Nevertheless, we had now earned the reputation of being the two most incorrigible women in the settlement. Women did not brawl, even in defense of their property. We felt the incident only illustrated the dangerous level of disregard for our rights and property that had infiltrated the thinking of our neighbors, an attitude that was to grow worse in the future.

And yet, little did we care what others thought of us. Ann and I and our children formed a little society unto ourselves. The more Father was disrespected (and we with him), and the more he was held in contempt and abused by his peers for his presumed role in the massacre, the more we closed ranks and turned toward each other for comfort.

And then, in August of 1870, everything changed.

The Prophet sent word he wanted Father to join him and his party on an exploring expedition up through the mountains to the headwaters of the Sevier River and over onto the Colorado Plateau. They were to descend the Paria to its confluence with the Colorado River and explore the possibilities of establishing a ferry there. For twelve days Father was gone. When he returned he called the families together and told us the news.

I shall not go into any detail about my recent trip, he said, except to tell you that we must sell everything—all our holdings and property here in Harmony, as well as in Kanarra and Washington and Toquerville—and move out to the Colorado River. There we will set up a ferry, for it is Brigham's wish that I should remove myself from society for a time to ensure my own safety and to further the expansion of the kingdom. Brigham has put out the call for the Saints to settle in northern Arizona, and without a workable ferry to take the families across the Colorado River, his plan cannot be accomplished. We are to help him with this undertaking, and take up a new mission.

I knew that what he was telling us was that he had been ordered to go into hiding. As the figure whose name was now most often linked to the massacre, his continued presence in the settlements threatened to keep suspicions aroused and focus attention on the Saints, rather than on the Indians, as the main perpetrators of the horrible deed. Brigham wanted Father out of the way in order to quiet the growing clamor for justice for the crimes committed against the emigrants. And because the Prophet was a shrewd and cunning man, he saw how he could both banish him to the harshest of outposts *and* put him to work building a ferry, thereby furthering his own ends.

What I didn't know—what none of us knew, including Father— was that even then plans were afoot to cut him off from the church. The news of his official excommunication was received by letter in October of 1870. He was much upset, and claimed evil forces were at work. When the wives heard this news, they were most frightened and anxious, for everyone understood what it meant. To be excommunicated was to become a pariah, an outcast, in this world, and to join the realm of the damned in the next. No longer could we expect any kind of support or protection from what Father liked to call his "friends in the north," meaning Brigham and other high officials in the church. Furthermore, our goods and property were now wholly subject to plunder. As his wives, we were encouraged to disassociate ourselves from him, and were told that we would be granted immediate divorces and deeds to our property if we did so.

When word of his excommunication reached us in Harmony, he was away. He returned a few days later to find his wives—with the exception of Ann and myself—all lodged in the mansion and in full rebellion. The Weeper and The Viper had locked their doors against him. The Mouse did the same, although she later relented. Miss Muss and Miss Fuss had already applied for an official divorce and refused to see him, shouting from behind a closed door that he should go away. Bewailing his treatment, he spent the night in his wagon, drawn up on the street in front of his mansion, as if he wished first thing in the morning for everyone in the village to see for themselves the full scale of his rejection and humiliation.

The next afternoon he came to see us. He told Ann and me that he had managed to forestall the sale of our house and that we might remain there for a time while he journeyed to the river to explore the conditions there. However, he hoped that when he returned we would be of one mind to join him in his new undertaking. He wanted very much for the two of us and our children to come and live with him at the river.

Ann, to my surprise, informed him that she was pregnant again and that she had no wish to move just then. Father expressed great happiness on learning she was with child. But Ann showed no such joy. She stood up and went to the window and looked out for a long time, and then she turned and faced him, looking more miserable than I had ever seen her. She said she was not yet twenty and already she had two children and another on the way and that people made fun of her and said it was folly for her to have married someone so old and with such bad feeling attached to his name. Now he had been excommunicated and whatever power he had once had would be forever diminished. She said she was afraid. She said she was tired. She knew she was still young yet she felt so old. She looked thin and white standing there in her patched dress, sweating in the heat with her dark hair sticking to her pale neck.

I don't got a bit of sense in me I don't think, she said. I don't know how I got in this. She began weeping and Father went to her and attempted to hold her but she shoved him away and said, Leave off it, John.

I had never heard her call him John before and the word sounded so funny.

Leave off it, John.

I've done the best I can here, Father said. I gave you everything—

No you didn't. The mare you give me you even took back—

Well I needed her, he said.

I just don't know how I got in this, she said again. She flung an arm up in front of her face and the bones looked so big and thick and the skin as sallow as last week's butter, and beneath the arm shielding her eyes I could see her mouth working wider and wider over her teeth as it opened in grief.

Well I don't know, he said, I just don't know what you think a man ought to do.

He looked wounded. He looked like he was hurt to the core but I could see how in truth she hadn't made a dent in him. He was rising to a moment of oration; that was all.

Talking about such things like you knew something about this whole affair and I don't know how the hell a man can ever get one up in the world with his wives helping his enemies and accursing him and accusing him of all manner of things when all he has done is keep their welfare in mind from the very first day. It's only a trick of the devil. The hand of the Lord must still be acknowledged in all things and in his lot being cast here among us even in our misfortune, even when we can't see the good to the thing. Why the people back north say I have done what no other man has done for this mission. When the mob came against us in Missouri we thought it an awful thing that a mob should be suffered to rob and pillage our goods without being brought to justice in a land of equal rights and boasted liberty, but the Prophet said that this was only a drop in the bucket to what it would be, and now I see the red tide coming among my very own people, I see this mob right in our own settlement aturnin on me and I think finally the end of the wicked is near and the redemption of Zion is at hand and I weep with joy mingled with grief even in the midst of my misfortune—

Stop it! she cried suddenly. Stop talking like you knew something when nobody believes you anymore. You have robbed me of my youth is what you done.

I don't remember forcibly taking anything from you. It seemed quite freely given.

You said if I was big enough I was old enough but I wasn't neither.

You were big enough to climb up on my lap and delight in what you found waiting on you there.

I don't want this child, she said and placed her hand upon her abdomen. The look she gave him was full of wild anguish.

You are a most unnatural woman, do you know that?

And you are a wicked man.

I hold no woman against her wishes. If you dislike me so, go ask the bishop for a Writ of Releasment and see how much you like making your own way in this world.

I'm not afraid of the world. It's humans I mistrust.

The house seemed suddenly stuffed with wet yellow light. The kitchen had a half door and the top was always open to help the smoke escape. Through this square came the bright heavy sunlight that flooded in as a cloud passed from the sun. I could see the poplars blowing in the wind and I could see the sty just down the hill where a boar and a sow were locked together. There was one small window that didn't open opposite the door and this is where Ann stood. An oil lamp hung by the window. Between the door and the window, we had a wooden table and several chairs carved from pine with straw seats. On one of these sat Father. We had a wooden rack next to the stove for drying damp clothes. In the room behind the fireplace were two bedsteads. One was mine. One was Ann's. This was all our furniture. Our children slept on the floor, on mattresses filled with straw. This is all we had in the world, besides the clothes upon our backs.

I'm not afraid of the world, she said again.

He turned away from her, feigning a weariness.

And you? he said, looking at me. What about you?

I found there were no words in my mouth. I felt pressed unnaturally between them, standing at the stove halfway from him and halfway from her with them both staring at me and waiting. He mistook my silence for some kind of complicity, I think, and stood up abruptly.

I leave for the river in the morning with Rachel and her children. The older boys will drive the cattle and extra wagons. Terressa has elected to go north for a while. Polly and Lavina, as you know, are seeking a divorce. What shall you do?

He looked first at me, and then Ann.

I won't go, Ann said sullenly. Not until this baby comes anyway. She stared at the floor and pointed her toe and rubbed it back and forth across the rough boards.

I'll stay to help Ann, I said, at least until you come back.

In six months I'll send the boys for you. That should give you both time to make up your minds.

I want my mare back, she said to him just before he left. He stared hard at her for a moment. And then he promised to bring her the horse in the morning.

———

WE WORKED together through the fall, harvesting our vegetables from the fields, picking the fruit, and drying and canning the produce. We slaughtered two pigs and hung the meat to cure. We killed a number of chickens. We had more pork and eggs than we needed and these we traded to Aunt Kisiah Redd for some sewing. In this way we managed to get new dresses for ourselves and our girls. We found we liked living alone. We didn't mind the shunning anymore. We were glad the others were gone. We stopped going to Meeting.

We made our own Christmas that year. I baked. Ann carved and painted the wooden toys for the children. We took all the children into the woods to cut a Christmas tree, harnessing the black mare to the old sled, and returned with a fine yellow pine. On Christmas Eve we sang carols and feasted on goose and plum pudding. We danced with the children, Ann dressed as Santa Claus in a white beard and red cap. She gave me a brooch she'd bought in Cedar City with money earned from breaking horses that fall. I gave her a pair of riding boots for which I had given Charley Redd a year's worth of egg money.

In February I delivered her child, a large well-formed boy we named Albert. She took no joy in him. As I was without milk, she had to nurse him herself. Her nipples soon cracked and festered. Many an evening I sat across the room from her, watching her face as the babe suckled. I saw the way she winced and fought back tears. He was a difficult child and cried often, as if he imbibed her own unhappiness in her milk.

———

By SPRING I was missing Father very much. I knew I should make up my mind soon whether to join him or not. Busy tongues were wagging now. Wherever I went I heard the gossip. People said Ann and I had abandoned him to his misfortune. They said it was only a matter of time before he had no wives left. They said he was already cast into deepest hell. They said no woman in her right mind would want to saddle her fortunes to his.

———

I DREAMED one night that I saw him. He was standing near a willow shanty and he looked so poor and sad. The earth was black around him, as if burned by a terrible fire. Shortly after I had this dream, word came to me that Aggatha's boys were leaving from Harmony soon, taking him a load of flour and some tools he'd left behind, and I could go with them if I wished to visit Father. Taking my leave of Ann, I made the trip in five days. He had not known I was coming. When he saw me drive up in the wagon, he rushed to meet me with open arms.

He already had a cabin up and next to that, a willow shanty.

It looked just like the shanty in my dream.

———

Two weeks later I returned to Harmony in the company of the older boys, in order to pack my household goods and gather up my children. I told Ann I was joining Father at the river, and I pleaded with her to do the same.

He wants you to come, I said. He told me to tell you he's waiting for you. We'll all go to the river together, and start a new life there.

She stood in bare feet looking at me, one foot on the floor, one tucked behind her ankle, the thin blue veins wrapping themselves around her ankle bone and running like little rivulets along her feet. She had lost weight in the time I'd been gone. Her big bones pushed against skin everywhere, making her dress hang like a tent from her sharp, hard shoulders.

I got to think about it, she said.

The next day, she said she would come. She said for me to take the children in the wagon and she would follow later with Aggatha's boys. She said to take Sam and Belle in my wagon and she even tried to give me little Albert, but I convinced her she must keep him with her as he was not yet weaned. As I prepared to set off, she embraced me and said she would see me soon. She slipped a small object into my hand, and I realized it was her father's Masonic pin, which I knew to be one of her most treasured belongings. When I objected to such a gift, she insisted she wanted me to have it. I should have known then what it meant.

———

Later I learned from the boys what happened.

Just before they were to set off the next day Ann, in some way, fell through a hole in the top of the potato cellar. As she went down, her legs went up and her arms were pinned next to her sides so she could get neither up nor down. When she called for help, the boys came and, seeing her predicament, they began to laugh and refused to help her at first. They only meant to tease her, they said. They had only wanted to have some fun. However, Ann was not only angry but embarrassed, to be so caught, with her dress hiked up that way, and the boys laughing at her, and her so helpless. By the time they got her out, she was pale and shaking. She said she would not go with them. She said she did not ever want to see them again.

She went into the house, where Albert was crying, and shut the door.

The boys waited for a while. They were feeling contrite by then. They could hear the baby crying for a long time. It seemed he would never stop. Once they peered through the window. They said she was sitting at the table. Just sitting at the kitchen table, staring at the wall, with the baby on the floor, cushioned by a pillow, crying for all he was worth, his fists furiously waving in the air. They said it seemed she did not even know the baby was there. It was like she couldn't even hear it.

At sunset one of the boys knocked on the door and said he was sorry. He apologized for all of them and he said they were waiting for her and they were sorry for laughing so and for not helping her quicker.

She did not open the door. From the other side, she called out that they should go on without her. She said she would not come with them. Not that night. Not the next day. Not ever. She repeated that she did not ever want to see them again.

The next morning they left. They left her in the house with its bolted door and with the sound of the baby crying once more.

And that is the last anybody has ever seen of her.

———

LATER, FATHER said she made a shipwreck of her faith and of their marriage. He accused her of planning to stay behind so she could cash in on his misfortune. He accused her of squandering away hundreds

of dollars' worth of property and making his goods fair game to anyone who could get to them. He said she had even burned the house
down in spite. Furthermore, he said he believed she had a younger
man waiting on her somewhere, and that is why she defected that day.
But I say any woman with a nursing child is not prone to be seeking
other men.

I say she did not leave him for that reason.

Rather, she left him for the world. *I intend to have many adventures,* she had said to me that night when she came into my bed, *and
this is only the first of them.*

––––––

WHAT WE do know is that she left Harmony with her baby a few
weeks later. She had disposed of everything by then, except the black
mare and a few personal belongings. She took her baby, Albert, and
made her way by horseback to Beaver where her brother David lived.
On the way she spent the night in Paragoonah with one of Father's old
friends. He said she looked poor. He said the baby cried a lot. He said
Ann spoke very little and that she left in the morning early, without so
much as a goodbye. When she got to Beaver she left the baby with her
brother. She asked him for provisions and these she packed in saddlebags before she lit out on the black mare, heading north. Her brother
agreed to keep the boy for a while. When he asked her where she was
going, she said she didn't know.

I kept Belle and Sam, and Sam is with me yet. It breaks my heart
that I let The Mouse take Belle from me last year, but it was done at
Father's insistence. He claimed Rachel needed the girl to help her with
her chores, as her own daughters had married and moved away.

In the beginning, when Sam and Belle asked me where their
mother was, I said, Your mama couldn't come with us to the river and
we are sorry about that but we'll all love you here and take care of you
the best we can. In time they ceased thinking of their mother. At least
they didn't ask about her anymore.

Occasionally we have had word of her but we don't always know what to believe. We heard she had traveled down to Mexico with a band of Indians, dressed as a man, and that she lived a winter with them in the mountains of Sonora. Some say these Indians were Geronimo and his band. She also was reported to have lived awhile in a convent in the Mexican state of Chihuahua. Supposedly she became a Catholic there. Others say they later saw her in the mining towns of Montana and Idaho, where she was plying a fallen trade.

What I do know is that Father was angered by her defection. He claimed to be most deeply hurt. And perhaps to compensate for the loss of their mother, he made Belle and Sam his favorites for a long time. He explained it once in this way.

I was orphaned young, he said. I grew up an unwanted child in a home not my own. And I know what that is like. It does something to you. To your basic character. I have only the vaguest memory of my mother, lying pale and sick on a couch. I loved the Negro mammy whom my grandfather hired to take care of me. She loved me, too. She had an interest in me. But when Grandpa Doyle died and I was sent to my mother's sister, I realized she already had more children than she wanted. I always felt in the way. I wasn't loved there. I just didn't belong. Never a good word. Never a word of praise, no matter what I did.

Never a bit of affection.

I tell you, I don't want these children to have it that way. If I pay especial attention to Sam and little Belle, you will know the reason why. I'm trying to make up for their mother.

I'll appreciate it if you'll remember this.

Be kind to them.

————

ONCE WE heard she was in Missoula, running a laundry there. Then supposedly she moved to Red Lodge and took up with an itinerant horse trader. Other places have been named in connection with her. The Bitterroot Mountains. The Camas Prairie. The northern railroad town of Corrine.

I don't believe she ever went back for her boy, Albert. Sam seems like my own child now, and Belle did, too, before she was taken away. I don't think they will ever see their mother again.

And I don't think I will either.

———

I DO KNOW I loved her for a while as I have loved no other woman. She was the best friend I ever had. When I think of her I think of the fun we had. I think of that Christmas when she made the toys and I made the cakes and pies. I see her dressed up as the suitor, playing the part of the gent. I see her dancing in bare feet before a row of clapping men. I remember laughing so hard with her at times. I remember feeling wicked and free. I did not think there was anything that could ever keep us apart. Except Father. I believe I always knew he was the only thing that could come between us.

And in the end, he did.

PART THREE

Ann

S HE RODE HUNCHED up against the wind, letting her feet dangle loose from the stirrups, her eyes half shut against the billowing dust. Her knees had cramped from the long hours in the saddle and the weight of her legs swinging free eased the pain in her joints. The sun had already crested and begun to drop in the western sky and now each bush and plant and tree cast a little dark imitation of itself in the form of long shadows lying quivering upon the broken ground. Her own shadow moved slantwise behind her like the steadily tagging darkness of some other.

The wind cooled the horse out and dried the sweat on its neck so that the hair felt hard and stiff beneath her hand as she patted the red mare and urged her on. Just a little farther, she said, and the horse cocked an ear to the sound of her voice.

It was a stern country she traveled. The land climbed and fell and rose again in great sweeps. Earlier she had crossed the prairie, following the creek, keeping to the south side, and the going had been relatively flat and easy until she struck the lava beds to the south, the jagged rocks formed by an ancient fire, a place no horse could cross. The great black flow required a long detour, with the heat rising up from the sun-warmed rocks offering a comfort against the chill of the day. All along the creek the air was cool and the birds greeted her approach—the ducks and geese hidden in the willows and the swallows thick before the pocked cliffs. Swallows like bits of dark ash blown hither and yon against the blue sky. No pattern to their flying except one of their own mad devising.

Meadowlarks called out in their high tweeing fashion and once in a while a killdeer flushed up ahead of the horse, dragging a wing and crying out sharply in an attempt to divert her from its nest. At one point, when she had already left the creek and was traveling across the broad and grassy flatland, she looked up to see a sight that startled her. What she first took to be two humans with a dog, visible there in the distance, turned out to be a pair of tall sandhill cranes and a coyote. She had not been able to understand what the cranes had been doing, standing there so close to the coyote. The cranes crying out and lifting their wings and dancing about upon their long skinny legs while the coyote kept its muzzle to the ground, oblivious to their commotion. For a long while she had puzzled over this as she rode along until she'd come up with an explanation that satisfied her. She figured the sandhills were a mating pair, an adult male and female, who had been hatching out a nest when the coyote had come along and commenced to eat the eggs and, instead of flying off, the sandhills had elected to stay near the nest on the chance there might be something left. But there would be nothing left, except perhaps the sticky bits of broken shell. What did they feel, those cranes, as they watched their unborn get taken that way? Most people didn't think animals had much feeling but she knew differently. She knew that animals could feel many things, including such things as humans often felt and perhaps things they knew nothing of.

Now as she rode up through the loose scree, she thought again about the cranes and the way their great heavy wings had spread as they took to the air and the sound they made as they flew low overhead. She thought how she might describe that sound if ever called upon to do so and she came up with this: it was like the croak of a frog mixed with the coo of a dove except it was much louder than either of these sounds and once heard it could never be forgotten.

She had long since lost the trail of the men she was tracking and had been moving by instinct alone. For a while the tracks had been clear and easy to follow. The spavined mule leaving outward-turning prints, small and neat. The smaller, perfect tracks of the unshod mare pressed deep into the earth so as to suggest she was carrying a weight.

More than likely Waddell was riding her gray mare. The boy walked. His boots left sharp-toed prints intermixed with those of the dog that followed closely on his heels. The man and the boy—they had not headed north as they had said they intended to. They had not traveled toward the Princess Mine but turned south, following the creek and crossing the prairie. She had been grateful for the rain that left the earth soft and easy to read. She figured she was at least three, maybe four hours behind them and she had kept the red mare moving at a jog trot all morning until she came to the lava flow, and then she'd lost the track and begun guessing, moving at a slower pace.

———

THE MAN and the boy had arrived at her cabin the evening before, leading the spavined mule, and asked to put up in her barn for the night. The man's name was Waddell, and his son, Boone. She had not cared for the look of the fellow, nor the rough way he treated his boy or his animals, but she had not turned them away. She learned they had come up-country from Kanarra by way of Beaver, where her own kin lived. Perhaps she let them stay because of this, or because Beezer had been away so long and she pined for human company, no matter how rough. In any case, she had given them permission to spend the night, and later, tempted by the whiskey Waddell had offered her, she stayed up drinking with him. In the course of the evening, Waddell had given her the news about Lee, that he had been executed two days earlier. Was it this news that had made her so incautious? In the end, she had drunk far more than she should have. Later, she had taken Waddell into her confidence, bragging on the value of the horses she and Beezer owned. In the morning Waddell and the boy were gone, and with them, the gray mare—the finest-blooded horse she had ever owned, and due to foal soon. She might have known he was a thief from the look of him. She had made a costly mistake. Let her guard down, unbalanced by the news of Lee and more than one too many whiskies, and it had ended up costing her more than she was willing to pay.

SHE CRESTED the ridge and drew up her horse, then dismounted stiffly and stretched her legs, looking out across the wide valley below. A dark patch of trees stood out against the far hills. The timber was no more than a spot of runty pines growing at the head of the valley where the melting snows fed into the stream running out of the cleft of the brown hills. If a man and boy were to rest, that's where they would be. But they were not there, or not that she could see, nor was there any evidence of a living thing stirring as far as the eye could travel.

For some time she stood fixed to the spot, the reins loose in her hand, while the red mare cropped at the short grass and rested from its climb. She sent her eyes from one point to the next, letting her gaze veer off to the snow-covered ridges and the bare brown scarps and broken rock outcroppings, over the slanting shoulders of bare hills, taking notice of the world a piece at a time as if it were a land worth studying. She looked for anything that didn't belong, a movement or change of light, a flash of white or color. She looked for a boy and a man and a mule and a dog, and especially she looked for the gray shape of a horse, but all she saw was a bowl of a valley covered in browse and the slopes of particolored stone upthrust in ragged shelves and the lone blackened stump of a lightning-struck pine.

And looking at all that emptiness, the ordinary heart-squeezing emptiness of the wide and lonesome world, she wondered if she was still moving in the right direction or if she hadn't set herself on entirely the wrong course hours ago.

The sound of the mare's teeth tearing at the grass and the wind and sun and the quiet of the day reminded her of something, some common moment from the past, but she could not think of when she had stood in such a place as this and listened to that sound of a horse grazing and why it would make any difference if she had.

How could she know which direction they had taken?

She knew there was no knowing these things, there was only the instinct behind the imagining of something, and she tried to still her mind, thinking of Beezer as she did so, remembering all he had told her in the past, about how a man could read the world with his heart if he had the strength and stillness of mind, just as a horse could read a man by instinct alone whether that man wanted to be read or not.

He had gone to Montana to sell some yearlings. Providing all went well, she expected he'd return today or, latest, tomorrow. She had left him a note explaining what had happened and she had written it the only way she knew how, in the script of the Deseret Alphabet. She did not know how to write in English. She had never been taught though she had promised herself one day she would learn, because what was the use of writing if you could only write in Deseret, the useless script of the past, forced upon her as a child? They had not taught children how to write in English when she was growing up in the southern colonies: the Prophet had decreed the Saints should have their own alphabet as a means of confounding their enemies. For many years it had not occurred to her that there was anything strange about this or that everyone didn't devise a secret code by which to communicate just among themselves.

In order for Beezer to understand her note she had left him her primer which showed all thirty-six characters of the Deseret Alphabet and their roman counterparts. When finished, the note had looked like this:

With the help of the primer he would be able to translate the note, character by character, as he had once done in the past when she had written to him for help, and he would discover what it said: "Dear Beezer, two strangers came last night and stole Vittick when they left this morning. I am setting out to track them down and bring her back. The man's name is Strophius Waddell, his son, Boone. He come up from Kanarra. I couldn't wait lest I lost their track. They headed south. I'll be back soon as I can. Ann."

She knew he would worry when he read the note and there was nothing she could do about that and still she wondered if she had done the right thing in setting off alone. There were half a dozen ways Waddell could have skirted the lava flow but something told her he had picked the same route she had and that he was just ahead of her, there somewhere in a valley beyond this one or in the one beyond that.

Late in the day she crossed the stony bottom of a dry creek where broken shards of Indian pottery lay strewn among the pebbles. The red mare she rode had not drunk since morning and she hoped to find water, a welled-up isolated pool lying still against the cutbanks, but the bed was hard and dry and she rode on down its course until she struck a deer trail and cut crosswise up a ridge.

At sunset she found herself atop a gaunt rill, looking down across a green valley at a sod-roofed cabin and the few sheds that surrounded it. She could make out two figures in the field behind the cabin and the stock milling about in the large enclosure to the south. There was no telling if it was Waddell and the boy she could see. The figures appeared blurred and indistinct from such a distance and after studying the scene for a time she decided there was nothing to do but descend the ridge and ride on toward the homestead.

No one was about when she rode up to the cabin and she sat her horse quietly and gazed around and then called out before dismounting. She crossed to the porch and climbed the steps. A weathered woman appeared at the door, holding a babe in her arms, and regarded her with a look that was both timid and fearful.

Evening, ma'am, she said.

The woman shifted the child in her arms and looked toward the barn and called out a name and a tall man appeared from within the dark confines and began walking toward her across the barnyard. He carried a full pail that slopped its contents onto the earth. With each step he took, the white milk dribbled onto the tops of his boots, and a trail of cats followed closely on his heels. Several children emerged from within the cabin and stood watching her silently from the porch.

She knew from the look of the children and the way the woman was dressed and the man's full beard that more than likely they were Saints, perhaps part of the wave of Danish emigrants the Prophet had sent north to colonize the area south of the Snake.

When the man reached the place where she stood, he handed the pail to his wife and then turned to her and said, in a thick accent, "What can I do for you?"

She took her chances and introduced herself as Brother Gordge and said she had come down from the prairie and had been riding all day and she would appreciate it if she could water her animal before continuing on her way.

The man clasped her hand and shook it firmly and said his name was George Gustafson and that a brother was always welcome on his place and then he ordered one of the children, the largest boy, to show her to the trough and said that if she cared to, she could join them for supper and stay the night.

I'll most likely move on tonight, she answered, but I thank you for the offer.

It's a dark night to be riding, he said.

It was true: it was set to be a cloudy night and, she said, she did not know the country well, but her purpose was such she feared losing time and thought she could not afford to stop the night with them.

He asked her what purpose could contain such urgency.

She explained to him she was tracking someone who'd stolen a horse from her, and described Waddell and the boy and the animals they traveled with and asked if he might have noticed such a party passing his way.

They have a dog with them, she added, a strange-looking dog. Half its face is black, the other half white—

Sure I seen 'em, he said. They stopped here a few hours ago and left behind nothing but bad feeling in their wake. We got no use for Gentiles here, especially the sort that don't mind using foul language in front of children and take more than their share from your table with no thanks for your trouble.

Do you know where they were headed?

That I cannot say. I know they were pushing their animals hard.

Did they have a gray mare with them?

They did. A nice-looking mare but she came in ridden hard and dropped down soon as they had stopped. A while later she had a hard foaling—a stillborn colt.

The gray mare? She dropped her foal here . . . ?

Out in that pasture yonder. And not an hour later the biggest feller mounted her up again and pushed off down the trail at a good hard pace and left the boy to follow with the mule.

She set her jaw and looked away.

Would that be the horse you are looking for?

She nodded.

I reckon if you find her you'll be lucky if she's in one piece. She looked in pretty poor shape when they set out.

Could you show me to the trough so I can water and be on my way?

Take him along to the water, boy, the man said to his son, and she followed the youth to the back of the cabin where the stream ran and let the red mare drink her fill.

There was a narrow chine of yellow rock running down the ridge behind the stream and she focused her eyes on this and let her anger settle as she listened to the mare sucking in long drinks from the stream. She felt the boy watching her and turned to look at him and found herself gazing at a gangly big-eared youth who nonetheless wore an expression of wisdom and calm on his face.

Sorry about your horse, he said. I give her a pail of oats after she . . . after the foal died.

What'd you do with it?

With what?

The foal.

I left it out in the field yonder. I figured the coyotes would have it.

Show it to me.

It was black. Perfect, and black, with the finely shaped head of its mother. In the fading light she stood looking down at the foal. It had a white star between its eyes, and two white stockings on the forelegs, otherwise it was solid black. It would have turned eventually, dappling out as a yearling, taking on the gray color of the mare. Its hooves were like tiny crescents of obsidian, shiny and hard. Gently, she lifted one hind leg to check its sex and saw that it was a filly. Not a colt. And not stillborn either, as Gustafson had said, but live-born. It had sucked air and moved its legs. Its mouth was still open and she could see where the earth had been freshly stirred around its hooves. She knelt down and placed her hand on its delicate neck and bowed her head.

You want to bury it? the boy said.

She nodded, grateful he'd thought of offering this.

I'll get the shovel.

When the boy had gone she wept briefly and then dried her eyes on her sleeve and when he returned with the shovel she dug the hole as he watched and together they lifted the still-pliant body of the foal and laid it the hole and covered it over with the dark earth.

I heard them say something as they were leaving, the boy said, as they walked toward the barn.

What was that?

I heard the boy say he didn't want to go back to Canary—

Kanarra, you mean?

I guess. It weren't no place I ever heard of. I just overheard them talking when they were saddling up, getting ready to leave—I was up in the loft and they didn't know I was listening.

What else did you hear?

I heard the boy complaining.

What exactly did he say? Think on it. It's important.

He said he didn't understand why his pap had changed his mind about going to the mines and I heard his father hit him and tell him to shut up.

What else?

His pap told him he had his reasons and it wasn't for him to question what they were. He said they were going to Canary whether the boy liked it or not, and then he rode off on the mare, and after a few minutes the boy followed with the mule.

I appreciate you telling me that.

I hope you get your horse back. She's weak. And he was pushing her hard when he left.

She reached down and picked up one of the kittens that had been milling about her feet and held it to her face and looked into its clouded eyes.

They just opened their eyes yesterday, he said. Two already died. But there's still three left. You like cats?

She nodded.

You could have one of these if you wanted.

I couldn't take it now.

Maybe you'll come back this way.

Maybe I will.

I'll keep one for you.

She smiled at the boy and thanked him and said if she did come back this way she'd like to take a kitten and she thought the little calico she held in her hands would be the one she'd want to have.

She stopped at the cabin to bid Gustafson and his wife goodbye and found the family gathered before the fire, readying for their evening prayers. Gustafson asked if she would care to join them and she could not see how to refuse without giving offense, and so she knelt with them, dropping down upon the hard wooden floor and joining hands with the little children who knelt on either side of her.

Their hands were so tiny and cool and smooth-fleshed they felt like tender little flowers. Gustafson prayed first. He asked God to remember those who in their ignorance did not understand His merciful ways and he thanked Him for His bounty and he prayed for a pure heart and a forgiving soul and said he was thankful in the name of Jesus Christ amen. Then several of his children joined in, offering up their own short and simple beseechments. Finally the big-eared youth who'd helped her bury the foal spoke a simple prayer in which he asked God to speed the way of their visitor and give him strength for his journey and bless him in his quest.

His words moved her. She had long ago lost the innocence and faith that allowed her to believe in prayer but she understood that the youth still possessed such things in a purity of form and if there was any possibility of evoking a power of guidance and protection, he had done so on her behalf and she could not help but be grateful, for a prayer was a prayer, and if it came from a believer, from the true of heart, it was not to be refused.

When they had risen from their knees, Gustafson's wife gave her some cold biscuits and dried meat to take with her, and she took her leave of the family, thanking them for their kindness, and especially she thanked the boy for helping her bury the foal.

The way was dark. She moved through a shoreless void, a night so black she could not see the landscape around her but only sensed it through the pores of her skin and by registering the noises her ears picked up, by the subtle changes of sound resulting from the steps she took and the feel of the earth beneath her boots.

She walked. She walked slowly, leading the red mare, sparing the animal her weight after so long a day of traveling. It felt good to stretch her legs and feel her body grow warm from the effort of walking. She needed to have her feet upon the ground, to keep a close contact with the earth in order to sense her way in the featureless night. Gustafson had promised that if she managed to stay to the trail she should have no trouble and she could reach the northern edge of the lake by the next evening. That was the key. Staying to the trail. Feeling always the hard-trodden earth beneath her feet and being able to sense if it changed to unpacked earth which meant that she was straying from her course.

For hours, she kept moving, feeling her way through the night. When she came to a stream she mounted the mare and crossed it and then dismounted and continued on her way. She heard owls calling in the dark and felt the bats skim by overhead on their leathery wings. All the creatures of the darkness were moving in the night and after a while she became one with them and the world grew less uncertain.

When the crimson dawn appeared she stopped beside a stream and drank and allowed the mare to graze while she rested sitting up against a tree and setting her mind free to travel at will.

She thought about a dog she once had, a yellow hound named Nero, and how he had saved her once from drowning when the wagon on which she'd been riding with Lee overturned during the crossing of a river.

Bright and June. Those were the names of the oxen. Bright and June. They had been lost in the crossing, trapped in their yoke as the swift current carried the wagon downstream, turning and tumbling it in the water like so much weightless flotsam and finally lodging it against a logjam. Lee had hauled the oxen from the river with a team of horses and butchered them on the spot to salvage the meat but later she had not been able to partake of it because she had felt such a fondness for those animals.

At the thought of Lee some deep sadness turned in her. It felt like regret. And something like shame, and this she knew had to do with the children.

The morning came on with a glowing radiance, the orange light flaring in the east as the desert doves began to stir and coo in their fashion. A weariness overtook her and yet she was afraid of sleep, afraid of the hours it would steal from her. The red mare had ceased grazing and laid down in the nearby meadow. She thought about horses and their patterns and how they could sleep in three different positions—standing on their feet, or lying down with their head still raised, or else by spreading themselves flat out against the ground, inert and immobile as if they'd been felled by death. It seemed to her that in each position they purchased a different degree of rest but only in the latter did she believe they really dreamed.

Once Lee had said to her, I'll hamstring any horse you try to ride out on. Don't you ever even think of leaving me. But he never could have cut a horse. A man, maybe. But not a horse. He had too much regard for them.

A light rain began to fall, precautionary and lifeless, coming down in a tediously fine spray, and she moved farther beneath the bower of limbs and drew her coat up around her ears.

She thought, How often have I lain unprotected in a roofless world and thought of home? All those days of traveling in the years following that moment when she had decided to leave Lee. In the beginning always moving, living for a time among the Apaches, high in the Jacarillos, and then later she'd begun the long journey south to Mexico, traveling with the Indians who had come to accept her. She had dressed as a man and passed her way in the world as such until she arrived at the convent in Monterrey and resumed the wearing of skirts for a while because the nuns would not take her in otherwise.

She listened to the sound of the rain and thought of Beezer. Would he have returned from Montana by now, bringing with him the money from the colts?

They had never bothered to marry and she did not think they ever would.

For one thing, she had never been properly divorced from Lee, and even now, when his death released her from her old covenant with him, she saw no point in entering another marriage. She did not believe her union with Beezer needed sanctioning by either church or state.

It troubled her slightly, though, to think that she had been sealed to Lee in the Holy Covenant and by the laws of such sealing was promised to him for Time and All Eternity. Even if she no longer believed in such things, it still cast a small dark shadow across her mind, because what if they were right and she was wrong? What if their version of Heaven, in which a man would have all his wives with him forever—all the wives who had been sealed to him on earth—were proven to be true? She would find herself joined to him in an immutably fixed contract, unable to be altered by any mortal change of heart, and all those promises and vows she had made that day in the Endowment House would yoke her to him forever, even in death, and this idea she could not bear.

She remembered the day they had arrived in the city and gone to the temple to be sealed to each other.

Everything was white. Never had she seen so much whiteness. For the ceremony she had changed into all white clothes, lent to her by Aggatha, Lee's oldest wife. They smelled of mothballs and age and had fit her poorly.

After she had dressed in these clothes she was taken to join Lee in a large room painted to look like the Garden of Eden. There were other couples there, waiting to be sealed to each other, including many older men with young girls. The room was the most beautiful she had ever seen. Painted on the walls and ceiling were all kinds of animals, birds and serpents, and trees. A man and a woman dressed as Adam and Eve stood at the front of the room and enacted a drama. They pretended to eat of the fruit of the Tree of Knowledge and then an elderly man dressed as God appeared and banished them from the garden and gave them green satin aprons in the shape of fig leaves, supposedly to hide their "nakedness." She had been given her own fig-leaf apron, which she tied around her waist.

Then everyone moved to a different room and certain passwords, signs, and grips were shown to her and she was given a secret name and instructed as to the meaning of the marks on the holy undergarments that she would wear from that day on.

There were four marks, one over each breast, one over the navel, and one at the hem above the knee.

The mark across the stomach, she was told, meant that you would suffer yourself to be disemboweled rather than reveal any sign, grip, or password or repeat anything you saw or heard in the Endowment ceremony.

The mark on the left side over the heart meant you agreed to avenge the blood of the Prophet or have your heart taken out.

The mark on the right side of the breast indicated that you had to work for your living and be industrious and faithful in paying your tithes.

The mark on the hem above the knee was meant to suggest constant prayerfulness.

Later, she had been ushered into another room upstairs with a curtain drawn across the middle and the marks of the garments were repeated on this curtain. The men were led to one side of the curtain, the women to the other. She was told to touch the person on the other side of the curtain—to press her knee against his. She had no way of knowing if it was Lee she touched but whoever was there, hidden from her sight, reached through a hole in the curtain and gave her the sacred grip. The actual marriage was performed in another room before an altar shaped like a coffin and upholstered with red velvet. When her turn came she knelt down beside Lee and the elder who was officiating asked Lee if he took her to be his wife, and he answered, Yea, and in turn, she was asked if she promised to obey Lee for the rest of her life, and, after a moment of hesitation, she said she would.

Her hesitation did not go unnoticed. Later she heard the official say to Lee, I hope you do not rue the day you brought this girl to this altar, and Lee answered, She is young, but in the course of time she'll learn and make a good and faithful member of my household.

Aggatha and Rachel were waiting for them when they emerged from the temple. She had ridden in the back of the wagon during the long journey home while Lee sat up front with his older wives and from that day on she never doubted that they regarded her as little more than a servant, required to perform any duties they might choose to assign her. She had done the hard work. She had milked the cows and worked the fields and then later, when her herding skills became apparent, Lee had entrusted her with the horses and she had taken the animals high up on the Kolob to graze. This she loved because it allowed her to escape to the outdoors where she had always been happiest. By then she had moved in with Emma. And he had made her his favorite, bedding her more than he did the others. She had not only allowed this but encouraged it, because in time she came to crave his attention, as a child craves the love of a parent, and also because it gave her a feeling of power over the others.

She knew his first trial had ended in a hung jury, and she believed then that he would go free. She'd heard he had gone back to the ferry and was living with Emma, and later she got word from her brother that he'd returned to Moenabbe, in the Arizona Territory, to be with Rachel and her family. After that she'd heard no more. Least of all that he'd been arrested and tried again, then found guilty and executed. Waddell had told her it was an all-Mormon jury that had convicted him the second time, and that it was generally agreed it was done so on Brigham's orders.

When she first told Beezer about her marriage to Lee he asked her, Were you in love with him?

I don't know, she had answered. Sometimes when he was not around for a while I thought perhaps I was. I knew that it gave a kind of new excitement to the days when he arrived and stayed a few nights with me. I remember the first time I caught him looking at me. Even then I knew what that look meant.

What do you mean you knew what that look meant?

I knew it meant that he wanted me in a way he didn't want the others. That he liked me more than them.

If what Waddell said was true, Lee was gone now. Dead. Taken to the meadow and shot, twenty years after the thing happened for which he was being killed. And this was hard to believe. Not that so much time had passed, but that he was finally dead, and that they had chosen to punish only him, out of all the others just as guilty.

———

SHE HEARD a grunting and looked over to see the red mare struggling to her feet, straightening her forelegs and bracing her front hooves against the earth as she heaved herself up and scrambled to gain a purchase against the dew-slick grass. Slowly she, too, raised herself from the ground, her body stiff and chilled from the dampness that had seeped into her bones. After she had eaten a little cold biscuit and meat, she caught up the mare and saddled her, then let her drink her from the stream and, filling her own canteen, mounted up and set off down the trail.

It was noon before she stopped again.

She passed through a settlement and halted just long enough to inquire at the bishop's storehouse, asking whether anyone had sighted Waddell and the boy, but the brother who tended the store could give her no information and so she pushed on again, riding down the dusty street between the bowering trees and the rows of stone houses in the windows of which she could see the pinched faces of the women who followed her with their eyes.

Leaving the settlement, she took a trail through an open field where a herd of slat-ribbed cows had bedded down to wait out the heat of the day. They sat chewing their cuds, then scrambled to their feet as she passed by and stood looking at her with their legs splayed, gazing out with fearful eyes. The naked skulls of cows and whitened bones—scapulae and laddered ribs and knobbed leg bones—littered the landscape and she wondered if this was a place of butchering or if some less intended misfortune had befallen a previous herd, a hard die-off from the previous winter or a ravaging band of wolves.

The farther south she rode, the warmer the day grew and the more the landscape changed, becoming less green and forested. The earth turned sandy and dry and as she crested a ridge she caught her first glimpse of the lake shimmering in the faraway distance. She came down out of the hills and struck a course due south and crossed a broad gravel riverbed, dry and white in the sun. Now cacti and agave and clumps of feathery mesquite dotted the ground and there were beds of saleratus and wide stretches of bleached alkaline soil. The brightness of the sun burning down on such a pale world caused her eyes to ache and she took to closing them for short periods during which she sat the horse and rocked sightless through the world.

She camped that night near a little stream the name of which she knew not. She slept fitfully and woke to the sound of ducks gabbling near the blackened water with it not yet light. Dawn found her sitting up against the trunk of a dead cottonwood watching the shape of the desert form itself out of the dingy light. She rode all that morning without rest, passing through two more settlements before beginning a long climb up through a narrow gap in the sage-covered hills, and now she had to force herself to stay awake as a great and deep weariness began to overtake her. In such a state of aggrieved exhaustion, her mind weakened and she began to doubt herself, not believing then that she would ever find Waddell or see her gray mare Vittick again. She let her head drop. She tied the reins in a knot and draped them over the saddle horn and then closed her eyes and gave herself up to her tiredness and in a state of half-consciousness she allowed the rhythm of the mare's rolling gait to rock her to a light sleep.

She awoke sometime later with the feeling that something was wrong, as if some great disturbance had just occurred of which she had been perilously unaware, but it was in fact the lack of movement that had awakened her.

The mare had stopped and stood quietly now with her ears pressed forward and nostrils flared and she could feel the animal's muscles tense and bunch beneath her as the horse fixed its gaze on some distant point ahead.

She looked out across the rolling scrubland and the barren dark hills and the mountains and the flat brush country that surrounded her, wavering there in the crenulated heat that rose from the pale land, and saw nothing for a while, her eyes still heavy with sleep, and then gradually her senses sharpened and she smelled the fire and she saw them, two figures camped by a stone outcropping with a wisp of smoke rising from their midst like a pale string drawn toward the heavens.

There was no possibility of covering her approach, no trees or rock rills or mounded hills to break her visibility, and she thought perhaps they had already sighted her anyway and there was nothing now to do but to ride on toward them, and so she urged the mare forward, keeping her eyes fixed on the camp where she could see the spotted dog moving around, its white and black pattern showing up starkly against the dun-colored land.

She had no plan, and as she slowly closed the distance between herself and Waddell and the boy, she tried to still her mind and fix upon it some scenario that might have the desired outcome. She carried no weapon except the knife tucked into her boot, and she knew she could not overpower Waddell and the boy in any case. She realized that she had intended to elude them, that she had envisioned no moment of specific confrontation. Rather she had seen herself sneaking down upon their camp under the darkness of night and slipping away with the mare and that during all of this she had assumed she would somehow make herself invisible.

Instead, here she was, riding toward them in the light of day and in full view of their wondering eyes.

She felt her heart tapping high in her chest, the wind wheezing in and out of her nostrils with each breath and she tried to make everything run still in her mind, as if waiting for a sign or some bright flash of inspiration that would tell her what to do, but instead she felt only the fear running in her veins, turning her mouth dry and her flesh cold with the dread of it all, all that she did not know, those events she could not yet begin to fathom.

SHE AWOKE THINKING she was someplace else altogether, in another land far removed from the spot where she lay on the cold uneven ground with the stones pressing into the small of her back.

She had been dreaming an old dream. She was back in Mexico, in the town of Juárez, walking down a dusty flyblown street, and the pigs that always ran loose through the town were swarming about her feet. A woman suddenly appeared and studied her with dark and craven eyes. In the dream the roosters were crowing and a low rumbling that she took for thunder came down out of the hills like the approach of a distant herd. And then she was back in the convent with the sisters gathered around her and she could see the small gray birds perched in the branches of the olive trees outside.

She lay quietly for a while with her eyes open, slowly blinking and thinking on the dream and then she tried to sit up but her hands were tied behind her and she could find no purchase against the earth to lever her body forward. Her ankles, too, had been bound, tied up so tightly she had lost the feeling in her feet.

She rolled over and faced the fire and felt its warmth against her chilled and aching body. The boy sat across from her on the other side of the fire. By inching forward a little she could bring his face into full view.

He held something in his hands and he was turning it over, passing it from one hand to the other and keeping his eyes cast down, unaware of the fact she had awakened and was now watching him.

The dream lay over her like a second world not yet fully closed off, a world only half as close or real as the one enclosed by the night folding in around her, but the pigs and the woman and the familiar feeling of Juárez were nevertheless still there in some penumbral form. She remembered another part of the dream now, how one of the nuns had bent over her and whispered something in her ear and then slipped a tiny silver cross into her hands.

She did not know how long she had been asleep. The night had a complete and gauzy darkness to it, as if the midnight hour had long since passed. She could see the dog lying just beyond the circle of light cast by the fire. Its half-white, half-black face visible there in the shadows like a strip of particolored cloth. Her tongue felt thick in her mouth and her thirst was a hollow rasping dryness that seemed to grow worse with every breath she drew.

Boone, she said quietly and the boy jumped a little and looked her way. She had startled him and she could tell that he had not liked it by the way he looked at her.

What you want? he said and looked down again at the thing he held in his hands.

A drink of water.

Pap said not to give you nothin. He said to stay clear of you till he gits back.

Where's he gone to?

It ain't nothin to you.

She heard a coyote howl and thought it came from very nearby. The dog lifted its head and looked in the direction of the sound and then stood up and wandered over to the fire and circled twice before settling down again upon the ground. Its teats lay like flattened pink pouches splayed out from its speckled belly.

What happened to her pups? she said after a while.

It don't matter.

It don't matter to who?

It don't matter period.

Maybe it matters to her.

The boy spat. I don't reckon it does.

You don't think she cares what happened to her pups? That she doesn't miss them?

That's right, he said. I don't think she cares a damn about any of it.

Well what *did* happen to them?

Quit botherin me. He stood up and poked at the fire, sending a shower of sparks racing up into the darkness.

Did you kill them?

I didn't kill em.

He killed them then, didn't he?

You jes got to know don't ya? Okay, he kilt em. Yeah he sure did. All seven of em. One by one. Wrung their necks and throwed em to an old boar who ate em right up fast. The boy grinned at her and said, Ain't you sorry now you asked?

She held her gaze steady and said, Why'd he do it?

Why'd he do it? The boy looked at her and swiped his greasy sleeve across his nose then blew a wad of snot into his fingers and wiped it off on his boot.

Can't you figger nothin fer yerself? Why you think he done it?

I don't know. I wouldn't have asked you if I knew.

Cause we were settin out for the mines, that's why. And he weren't gonna let me bring her lest we got rid of the pups. Only now we ain't even goin to the mines cause he's got a whole other idea in his head.

He threw whatever he was holding in his hands into the fire and settled into a dejected look.

What was that?

What was what?

What you threw there into the fire.

Weren't nothin.

You won't tell me?

No, I won't tell you and I wish you'd quit talkin.

She let some time go by before she spoke again.

I want you to think on this, Boone. I need your help. If you help me I can help you.

How kin you help me?

That depends on what you want.

Ain't nothin I want.

I don't believe that.

How kin you help me then?

That depends on what you want but whatever that thing is I think I can help you get it. She paused only a moment and then went on.

Maybe you'd like to leave your pa. Maybe you're tired of him smacking you around like he does. I saw the way he treats you and you're old enough you don't have to take that anymore. Maybe you want to get free of him and set out on your own.

The boy spat again and looked at her and then gazed down and studied his empty hands as if he was surprised to find they now held nothing.

Or if you were to tell me you'd like a horse—a good horse of your own—I could see to it that you got one. And it wouldn't be one you'd stolen either.

How you gonna do that given the fix yer in?

Well, that's the thing. You'd have to help me get out of this fix before I could get you the horse. But you'd have my word on it. A horse and some money for a new start.

You think I'd trust you?

You'd have my word on it, she said again.

What do I need you to git me a horse for when I already done got two of em. A nice gray one and a nice red one.

Those horses aren't yours and you know it.

Well they sure ain't yers anymore. Not as long as yer the one tied up there and Pap's callin the shots.

Let me have a drink, she said wearily.

I tole you Pap said not to give you nothin.

Yeah. I know. But who gave you the corn bread and chicken when he said not to? Who saved some supper for you the other night when you lost your appetite cause he was drunk and hittin on you?

He stared at her and then he looked away, gazing back into the fire.

Just a drink of water, Boone. That's all I'm asking.

He didn't move for a long while and when he did it was to fetch the canteen from the place where it lay next to the panniers. He picked it up and took it over to her and dropped it by her side then started to walk away.

Boone . . . you got to help me sit up. You got to untie my hands, else I can't drink. You know that.

Jesus, he muttered. Pap finds out I done this and I'm done fer.

He leaned over her. He bent over and grabbed her by the front of her coat and hauled her up roughly until she looked steady enough, centered there on her haunches, and then he let go of her and stepped back quickly as if he couldn't bear the nearness of her.

I cain't untie yer hands.

Yes you can, Boone. You have my word on it that I won't try anything. Just let me have a drink and get some circulation going and then you can tie me up again.

I cain't do that.

She started to say something but a feeling of light-headedness suddenly overtook her and she felt herself falling, tipping sideways on her buttocks with no means to right herself or break her fall. She hit the ground hard and felt a hot stinging pain above her ear where her head had struck a stone.

She lay there breathing quietly and let the pain course through her and cast her mind somewhere above her body as if she were not the bundled strictured mass lying there on the ground but free to wander far beyond the pain. The collar of her shirt pressed hard against her throat and caused her to feel suddenly sick. The bile rose up in dry spasms and wracked her body yet there was nothing there in her stomach to issue forth. A rusty taste of dried blood came to her as she licked her swollen lips and swallowed against the heaves that shook her body. Gradually the sickness subsided and in the new quietness she found a welcome peace. The boy mumbled something but she could make no sense of his words.

I said you okay?

She did not speak for a long time and when she finally did it wasn't to answer him.

You're a fool, boy, she said quietly and felt the way the words purled out from between her swollen lips like thick smooth objects. He's only gonna keep abusing you, long as you stick around and let him do it. I don't say this for me but for you. Get free of him while you still can. If you stay with him and get caught stealing horses—

Shut up, will you? Will you jes shut it up now?

She rolled over onto her back and looked up at the night sky enclosed there by the circle of trees. The fire threw an upward dying light that faded against the branches and dissolved into the spored darkness of the night sky. A round vaulted sky struck with stars swinging through their orbits. No moon. Just a great black night spattered with gauzy clusters and sharp points of light. She could make out the Great Bear and the Pleiades and other constellations whose names Beezer had taught her but which for some reason she could not remember now and it didn't seem to matter for it wasn't the name of the thing that she wanted but rather the forgetting of it, the absence of any word or thought that might interfere with the pure sensory rush she felt in seeing the endless celestial display, at once turning and twinkling and falling into the depths of the immeasurable void. In the brimstone land of Christian reckoning, each one of those stars was another world where a Saint had met his reward and now ruled over all that imploding light as a god, but to her they were just stars, the perfect renderings of beauty on the vastest possible scale.

She felt him tugging at her again, pulling her upward by the front of her coat, and she didn't resist but neither did she help him. She remained limp, her body suffused with a carelessness and a complacency that made her feel drunken and light.

Yer bleedin, he said. You done cut yer head now.

She turned her face to him and looked directly into his eyes. Let me have some water, boy. Untie my hands.

The commanding tone she'd adopted seemed to work and she felt him loosening the rawhide straps and then her hands were free and she reached for the canteen and took a long drink.

When she finished she pulled herself across the ground until she could rest her back against the stump of a tree and propping herself up, she faced the fire and began rubbing her wrists until the painful tingling had passed and the feeling returned to her hands.

I got to tie you up agin now.

No you don't, she said wearily. You don't got to do nothing of the sort. What do you think? That I'm gonna run off on you with my feet still tied?

It's Pap I'm thinkin on. He comes back and finds you loose and it's me that gits the beatin.

He isn't going to show up without any warning. We'll hear him coming.

The boy looked over at her and wiped his nose again on his sleeve and then looked away. A swatch of oily dark hair was plastered across his forehead as if it had been painted there and his face looked gaunt and sunken in the quivering light.

I dunno. He ain't always predictable.

Where'd he go?

He said not to say.

He rode in to Corinne, didn't he?

What if he did.

Did he take the gray mare?

The boy didn't answer.

I said, did he take Vittick, my mare?

Naw, he rode out on the sorrel.

Where's the gray?

With the mule. Down by the creek.

What kind of shape is she in?

The boy shrugged.

Come on, Boone. Tell me.

She's down and breathin hard. Somethin happened durin the foalin. Pap went to town to see if he cain't git some saltpeter and gunpowder to douse her and try and save her.

She let her weight settle against the stump and slumped back and looked at him. She looked long and hard at him and in that look she invested all the contempt and anger rising up in her, yet in the end she felt her face go slack with the deep sadness that overtook her at the thought of Vittick suffering.

It weren't like we done nothin to her. She had a hard foalin. Like as not it would have happened anyway. I mean whether Pap took her or not.

That's what you'd like to think, isn't it.

She reached out and pushed a stick farther into the fire, using it as a poker to stir the coals, and then threw another branch onto the flames. The dried leaves ignited in a dozen little blazes that flared with a suddenness and crackled sharply in the night.

Go check on her, Boone. You got to go see how she's doing.

I ain't leavin you here alone if that's what yer thinkin. I ain't that stupid.

Nobody's saying you're stupid. But if that mare dies you won't have anything left for your trouble.

Ain't nothin I kin do fer her anyway. She's either gonna make it or she's not.

Listen to me, Boone. I got a feeling about you and I don't think I'm wrong. I think you can help her. If you won't untie me and let me go to her, just go yourself. Talk to her. Put your hands on her and talk quietly to her. Let her know you're with her, that she isn't fighting it all alone. You got nothin to lose and she's got everything to gain. If you think she's not scared, you're wrong. And if you think it won't help her to know she's got someone pulling with her, you're wrong again. I think you know that much.

She could see the boy thinking over her words, how they had not gone entirely unheard by him, although he seemed to sit there for such a long time she thought perhaps she was wrong about him and he was beyond being moved to feeling for any animal or human. But then he stood up and said, I'll take a look at her but I got to tie yer hands else I cain't do it.

It was a bargain she could live with and she told him so. As he set about tying her up again, she asked him once more to put his hands on the mare and stroke her and speak calmly to her in a tone she might find soothing. She added that she'd known many horses in her time but none had ever been more intelligent or strong-hearted than this mare and she felt sure that the animal would understand his touch and feel encouraged by it, especially if he was able to offer it in a true-ness of feeling. She said also for him to look into the mare's eyes, if there was light enough to do so, and try to contact the horse in order to read her condition so as to learn as much as possible about what might be done to save her. And lastly she said he might try this, to reach into the birth canal and see if anything might still obstruct the passage and if so to remove this as best he could to stop any contract-ing or bleeding that still might be occurring.

When the boy had gone, she stared into the fire and felt a calm come over her in the wake of the sudden rush of words. She could not be sure how much he'd understood of what she was trying to tell him but the mere telling of it had made her feel better, as if somehow she had purchased a small sense of relief by sending forth a surrogate. The dog had remained behind, choosing to stay near the fire instead of fol-lowing the boy, though it now stood quietly staring off into the night. She found this strange. Not the dog's staring—the mesmerized fixa-tion upon that place where the boy had disappeared from sight—but that she had chosen not to follow her master. Which said to her that the boy was not her master at all, that in truth she probably had no real master. Because every dog she'd ever known to have sided with a human would never have chosen to let its companion head off into the night alone. Whatever the dog's relations with the boy, they were not of that variety.

She clucked to the dog, using the same sound she employed to urge a horse on, and the dog turned and looked at her.

It was a sentient thing, filled with a troubled spirit. Its confusion was palpable to her. Lacking the litter to mother, it had been left with all the mistaken instincts—the baggage of milk and swollen teats and the ripe caring urge—and there was nowhere to put it now, not any of it, and it seemed to her that the animal had turned inward on itself in a flood of urgent confusion, drawn down by the sorrows of its losses and the longings for the absent young. Some fear bound it now, she could see that. It was fear that kept the dog pinned there by the fire. She realized now that this was why she had not followed the boy. She held to camp for good reason. Perhaps she even imagined the possibility of the pups appearing again, restored to her as suddenly and inexplicably as they had been taken away, and she would be waiting for them, waiting there near the packs and the food, all that was familiar to her and held scent of home.

She heard a sound from the woods and stilled her own mind as if this would enable her to hear better. The dog, too, picked up the noise and together they listened, drawn into a perfect complicity.

But the noise, whatever it was, did not occur again. It could have been a coyote or the burred call of an owl, or a fox moving through the darkened woods—any one of a number of creatures that hunted by night. Or it could have been Boone, returning from the creek, or even Waddell himself approaching. And yet it had sounded like none of those things to her.

It had sounded like nothing so much as the muffled whinny of a horse.

With her mind already cast there in the darkness, she imagined the boy bending over the mare. She sent her thoughts to them. She put herself beside the boy and joined him as he stroked the horse's neck, running his hands from her ears to her withers all along the sleek and muscled flesh. She sent the horse her own touch and she felt it go out from her strongly and she also felt the mare receive it. She pictured herself looking into the mare's eyes and holding a steady gaze while studying the big dark pupils flecked with gold and she saw a terrible pain there, a pain and a fear much worse than what she had seen in the dog's eyes. It filled her with such a sudden worry that she felt herself lose her place there beside the mare and she knew that the moment had passed and she would not be able to go back there. She could not send the horse anything now except her own worry and it had no need of that.

———

THE NIGHT was still. Without wind. Without a sound except the crackle of the fire.

She remembered once she had spent a winter in a place called Ross's Hole near the west fork of the Bitterroot River. The placer mining had been good in that place but often the men could not work on account of the Indians who harassed them and kept them fearful. Still, wherever there were miners, there was money to be made. A girl could make a small fortune. She had left that place in the spring with Beezer, bringing to an end a way of life she had never meant to enter in the first place. Together they had crossed over the main fork of the Bitterroot River and made their way south. Later she learned that if they had taken the Indian trail they need not have crossed the river at all, but they were traveling with a wagon and so took the road and thereby had to cross the river eleven times. Eleven times, fording those waters, and each time worse than the last. They made little progress by day as the Indians were bad and the effort of keeping constant guard during their movements made the going slow.

But after three days of hard travel they had come to a place called Squaw Man's Ranch, owned by a man named Doolittle. He was harvesting when they got there and he had been very kind to them. He gave them a cabin to live in and treated them kindly in exchange for a season's work. Beezer had toiled all summer in the fields. Doolittle had given her cows to milk and before she left he gave her a very fine horse because she had proven her worth to him in a very unexpected way.

There had been some disease among his horses and many of them had died over that summer. Doolittle had not known what to do for them. When his favorite horse had fallen sick he said to her, If you can save that horse, I will give you this other one. And she had saved the horse, though at the time she did not know how she had done it. She had simply given the horse grated potatoes, remembering a story Emma once told her about how raw potatoes could effect a cure for many things. Grated raw potatoes, mixed with a little oat mash. This had cured not only Doolittle's favorite horse but several others as well. Later Doolittle tried it on two stallions but he had let them run too long before he tried the remedy and they had died.

She and Beezer stayed there until he'd gotten the harvest in, after which they started down the Bitterroot to a place called Gund Creek. They stayed there all winter with a man named Joe Pardee. She had milked cows and in return gotten half the butter and sold it for the money. She worked through the harvest and thrashing, toiling alongside Beezer, for which they had each received forty dollars a month. But before they got through thrashing there came up a very severe storm and two men and eight horses froze to death. The storm lasted up to the first of December. Then it cleared off and there came the Chinook wind which melted all the snow off the ground and they had no more winter that year in Montana. Everybody went to plowing and putting in their crops in February and it had been the queerest of winters, brutal at the start and then uncommonly mild. Later they traveled north to Missoula and bought a stove and rented a house and started a laundry there. They took in washing at twenty-five cents apiece for handkerchiefs, twenty cents a pair for socks, and fifty cents for shirts and all other articles except dresses and white shirts, which were a dollar apiece. They had stayed in Missoula from March until the middle of June when the water got very low and then they moved on to Pioneer. In this place, flour had been very scarce but while in

Missoula they had taken on a considerable quantity of flour for seventy-five cents per hundred. At Pioneer she and Beezer sold the flour at a good profit and with this money they moved on to Deer Lodge and opened up another laundry which they ran for about a year until some miscreant without the fear of God before his eyes had set fire to the place and burned it down. The stables next to the house had burned at the same time together with some of the finest horses that ever came to Montana. And after that, after they had gotten burned out, they decided they'd had enough of Montana and, wandering from place to place, they bought their first mares and finally moved down to Idaho and homesteaded on the wide flat grasslands beneath the peaks of Horse Heaven.

In all that long recollecting she could think only of the potatoes that had cured Doolittle's horse and she wondered if there might not be some way of trying such a thing with Vittick. Or if there was some other cure she might think of that could have an effect.

She clucked again to the dog. She bid it come to her for comfort's sake and it did. It came and settled at her feet and studied her with sunken eyes. She spoke to the dog for a long while. She talked to it softly and she knew it listened to her and she felt it understood her.

She wondered if she might have done anything differently. Because it seemed to her that it was her own folly that had brought her to this sorry state.

———

SHE HAD ridden directly into their camp because she had seen no other course and it hadn't taken Waddell long to show his colors. When she had demanded her horse back he dragged her down off the sorrel and shoved her up against a tree and held her there and that was when he had felt her chest and said, What's this? And then he tore the front of her shirt open and began to laugh in his coarse cracked fashion. I knew something weren't right with you, he'd said, but goddamned if I didn't figger you fer a man. As she stood there with her shirt ripped open, she caught the boy looking at her in a way that made her think he had never seen a woman before and she watched him turn away in shame.

His blows had come as a surprise. She had not been expecting that Waddell would hit her the way he did and the sharp swift punch he'd delivered to her stomach sent her doubling over in pain. You wanna act like a man I'll treat you like one, he said. And then he'd caught her on the chin with his knee and brought his fist down on the back of her head and she'd fallen to the ground thinking, This is the place and time where my life is going to end.

But it had not ended there after all.

He had forced her to her feet and marched her into the woods, telling the boy to stay where he was. It was late afternoon and the raking light slanted through the stands of pale aspens. Slubs of grainy snow still lay on the ground in hardened patches on the north sides of the trees and the scent of rotting leaves kicked up from the earth. Maybe it ain't such a bad idea to treat you as a woman after all, he'd said, and she'd known then what was coming. But it hadn't happened the way it seemed it would. Not because Waddell hadn't tried but because he was not able to accomplish the deed and after a while he'd given up.

When he brought her back from the woods the boy had been sitting silently before the fire and he glanced up with a knowing look and then turned his back and began breaking branches into short lengths by snapping them against his foot. As if to cover his failure, Waddell began laughing and bragged to the boy, saying he'd had better, but then he'd also had worse. The boy blushed as Waddell commenced to tie her hands and it was then she had pleaded with him to let her turn her shirt and he had done so before binding her wrists.

Later he had taken his gun and headed off toward the low brown hills that sloped down behind the stand of aspens. She had seen him moving up a draw and then he had disappeared from sight. He was gone a long time and in that time she did not speak and neither did the boy. Darkness fell about them. The boy fed the fire and she quietly studied his movements, watching him as one watches the clumsy and deliberate efforts of someone who knows he's being observed and doesn't like it. The light flared up against the gaunt sockets of his eyes, which he never once turned on her.

When Waddell had returned he was carrying a badger he'd shot and he set about skinning it before the fire. He made a deep incision along the belly and pulled out the pearly innards and threw them to the dog, who set upon them with a singular ferocity. Waddell roasted the badger whole over the fire and then divided the carcass with the boy, carving it into sections with his knife. He hadn't offered her any of the food and she had asked for none although the smell of the roasted meat had deepened her sense of misery. Huddled there by the fire, tearing at the meat with his bared teeth, enveloped in a brutish silence, Waddell had resembled a starving animal set on devouring its kill though she could think of no animal so foul and ungainly in its movements.

After he had finished eating he ordered the boy to bring him the sack of dried apples from the panniers and when he'd had his fill he lay down upon the saddle blanket spread out over the ground and fell into a deep sleep. Not once since he'd brought her back from the woods had he looked at her or uttered a word except to issue orders to the boy. It was as though she had already ceased to exist. As if she were nothing now but a bundled inert mass lying just outside the light of the fire, like the discarded remnants of a hunt. Though she struggled to stay awake, her own weariness overcame her and she had fallen asleep herself, only to wake and find him gone.

———

THE DOG blinked slowly and gazed into the darkness, its ears cocked forward. No sound came from the woods. By doubling her fists as the boy had bound her hands she had managed to secure for herself a certain latitude and by flexing her fingers now and straining against the leather ties she began to work them loose. After a while she freed one hand, and then the other. The knife in her boot had not been discovered and she used it now to cut the straps that bound her feet. She crawled to the panniers, not yet trusting her legs to stand, and emptied the contents until she found what she was looking for.

The dog followed her into the woods. She could feel it tagging her as she moved between the pale aspens, stepping carefully and stopping now and then to listen for any sound. She circled above the camp and crossed the creek, climbing up out of the trees and moving along the sloping bank of the hill until she could see the shape of the horse before her, outlined faintly against the darkness. The mare was lying on the ground with her head raised. She could not see the boy and had no way of knowing where he was. She crept to the mare's side and knelt down next to her and spoke to her softly. She stroked her neck as she spoke. She tried to coax the mare to her feet but the horse would not stand. When she heard the snapping of twigs, she flattened her body against the ground, keeping her hand on the mare's nose, and listened. But no sound came again. She stood up slowly and, after whispering a few last words to the mare, she made her way back to the stream and crossed through the shallow water. After a while she began moving up the slope, crouching low and feeling her way across the loose scree until she struck a boulder slide and began climbing up over the broken stones. On the far side of the slide she discovered a draw and followed it to the top. She could no longer feel the dog tagging her and she was glad of this, for its spotted pattern showed up starkly in the night. The draw narrowed and she was forced to take a steep route along a broken shale shelf that led to a large rock outcropping. There, in a cave formed by overhanging boulders, she sat down, exhausted by the climb.

The dawn found her crouched there in her den amid the animal droppings and the bits of fur and twigs and the schistose layers of mica glittering in the pale morning light like a sacerdotal offering placed there long ago by some wandering priest. Far below her, to the south, she could see the edge of the lake and the smooth gray water. The rising sun reflected in the water appeared as a funnel of fire spreading out over the lake and turning the surface molten. She left the cave and crept along a rock wall until she could look down upon the camp. The sorrel horse had already been saddled and stood picketed between two trees. Waddell knelt by the creek, filling the canteen. When he had finished, he called to the boy and the boy led the mule and the horse to the place where he stood. Words were exchanged though she could not make out what was said, only the harsh tone of Waddell's voice and the boy's muted response.

Not far away from Waddell she could see the gray mare stretched out flat against the ground. Unmoving. Just a pale mounded shape lying motionless against the tawny grass, whether dead or alive, she could not tell. Suddenly Waddell crossed to the mare and nudged her with his boot. The horse lifted her head in one sudden jerk. He fitted a halter over her nose and tied it at her cheek and called out Hup now, and the horse struggled to her feet and took a few steps forward and then stopped and shook, sending a small gray cloud of dust into the air.

In the yellow morning light the man and the boy readied the animals for travel, strapping the panniers to the mule and snubbing up the gray mare. Her joy at knowing the mare was alive and on her feet overcame her, and she pressed her knuckles to her lips. From her hidden place there among the boulders she studied the preparations for departure and wondered what had become of the dog, for it was nowhere in sight. She watched as the boy returned to the camp and kicked dirt onto the remains of the fire. He lifted his eyes and studied the hills as the smoke billowed thickly and rose around him and she knew what he was looking for. It did not escape her, the knowledge that she had betrayed him and broken her word by freeing herself when she had promised him she would not. Undoubtedly he had paid for it and it seemed to her that at some future place and time she would have to set it right with him. Because surely there would be another time with its own set of reckonings still to come.

———

THE SUN crested the ridge behind her and cast the land in a drowning whiteness by the time Waddell and the boy set off from the camp. Waddell riding in her saddle astride the red mare and leading the gray. The boy tugging at the rope attached to the spavined mule and following his father at a distance, walking slowly as if drawn down by the forces of his own dark reluctance. She kept her eyes fixed on them as they moved across the hard and knotted land until they reached the far end of the narrow valley and disappeared from sight and then she began working her way down through the scrub and the loose scree until she came to the cave where she had spent the night, and there on the dead leaves and sloping shale sat the dog, looking up at her.

She held out the back of her hand and the dog came to her and she felt the warm tongue upon her flesh and was moved by it and by the way its tail began to rotate in slow and then ever widening circles.

Okay, she said. She knelt down in front of the dog and stroked its head and looked into its eyes to settle the matter and, when she was certain it had understood her, she rose and the dog followed her as she headed down the draw, moving quickly now through the brush.

THREE

ALL MORNING SHE walked. She walked across the broad and broken plain following the same well-trod path that Waddell and the boy had taken and when she ascended a low hill and crested its ridge she half expected to see them in the valley below her but they were not there. She sat on a flattened rock and rested her legs and studied the land spreading out before her and the dog rested, too, sitting beside her feet and gazing out over the broad dry valley. To the east the tall peaks of the Wasatch Mountains rose up purple against the pale sky and appeared washed-out and flat at such a distance. Across the valley she could see the edge of the lake and to the west there was nothing but water. Water the color of fresh bruises lying dark and reddish against the runcinated shore.

Where do you figure they got themselves to? she asked the dog and it turned and looked at her, lifting its nose and sniffing the air as if to test the odor of her words. She stroked the thick white ruff at the back of its neck and the dog leaned into her touch and they stayed that way for a while, the dog pressing against her shins while her fingers gently kneaded its fur. She wished she had something to eat. She thought of dried apples and roast hare. Her hunger caused her to feel drained and tired and she had to force herself to quit thinking of food and take to the trail again. Halfway across the valley she came to a sluggish stream clogged with a brackish foam which she skimmed from the surface in order to drink and the water refreshed her and took the edge off her hunger.

The country began to grow more familiar. She crossed over another ridge and dropped down into a fertile valley watered by a wide river lined with fernbush and blackbrush. Clusters of serviceberry grew here and there and the odor of their small white blossoms filled the air. She knew this to be the Bear River or believed it was so and if this was true she thought she might follow its course and make Corinne by nightfall.

The going was slow. Her body ached from the blows she'd received and the hard days of travel and she was forced to stop often and rest. During one of the stops she discovered a stand of golden current growing beside the river and knowing the flowers to be edible, she picked them, slowly foraging among the branches like a feral animal, but the blossoms did not sit well on her stomach and later she gorged them up and afterward felt the weaker for it.

By nightfall she was exhausted and knew she would not make it to Corinne. She began thinking of where she might pass the night. As she came up out of a brushy ravine she saw the smoke rising beyond the draw in a south-facing valley. The blue haze collected over the roof of a cabin where a yellow light shone in the windows. The dog lifted its muzzle and sniffed at the air and for a long while they stood together and studied the scene. For a great distance beyond the cabin there rose the humped shapes of something she could not at first make out and then she realized they were wickiups. Wickiups clustered together and stretching into the distance, silhouetted and presenting no evidence of life. There were more wickiups than she had ever seen in one place and she could not imagine why they were there, why they had been constructed in the first place, and why they now appeared to stand deserted and empty. The humped stick dwellings stretched across the valley like the crude wattled nests of some oversized animals, gathered into a colony. There was nothing about the scene that she liked, except the familiarity of a lighted cabin, which held out the possibility of a meal and a bed for the night. The fields to the south of the cabin had been recently plowed and a small herd of white-faced cows stood out against the falling light.

She clucked to the dog and told it to stay close and it kept to her side as she crossed the plowed fields and approached the cabin. Long before she reached the yard the dogs came out and commenced to bark. Large dark hounds with spittle slinging from their muzzles. A door opened and a man stood silhouetted against the light. He called to the dogs and told them to shut up and they ran back to where he stood and fell to circling his feet.

Evening, she said.

The man said nothing. He was old and white-haired and he wore a shirt full of holes and through the holes she could see the gray of his undergarments.

She removed her hat and ran her fingers through her short hair and looked down at the dog and then back to the man and waited.

I thought you was somebody else, the man said. I reckoned you for George. But you ain't George.

No, she said. She told him her name, giving it as Andy Gordge, and said she had traveled a long distance that day, hoping to reach Corinne, and she had eaten nothing for two days and wondered if he had food to spare and if she might bed down somewhere for the night. Without answering the man turned and stepped through the door and the hounds commenced barking again and came toward her until he told them to be off and they fell silent and slunk away into the night, and then he beckoned to her and she followed him into the cabin.

There was only one room, full of a smell of unwashed bodies and the odor of cooking. The floor was made of packed dirt and like the walls it was badly out of true. At the far end of the room a fire burned, and at a long table made of rough-cut wood sat two women—one old, one young, both Indian.

He spoke to the older woman and she rose and retrieved a plate from the cupboard and went to the stove and ladled something from a pot and then set the plate down on the table and motioned for her to sit across from the old man, who had taken up his seat again before his half-eaten meal.

She sat. All eyes upon her, as if she were a curiosity imported from afar. She spooned the first taste of the food into her mouth. Some concoction of meat and onions spiced with red peppers and some bitter-tasting herb. A taste like nothing she had eaten before. She gazed at the young woman. She appeared to be recovering from the pox. The sores on her face and hands had not yet healed and her skin had a waxen and unhealthy pallor. Through a small window she could see the lilac sky darkening and a bronze disk of a full moon rising over a ridge. Occasionally a cow bawled, the sound drifting up from the corral. The old woman never took her eyes off her. This unsettled her, because she had never known an Indian to stare in such a bold fashion.

The man asked her what purpose there was to her travels and why she had no horse and she explained her horse had been stolen and she was looking for the man who'd taken it. She described Waddell and the boy and the animals and the old man looked at her blankly and said he knew nothing of such persons or beasts. The old woman studied her with eyes set back between the folded lids. She could not be certain what if anything the Indian woman understood of the conversation but she appeared to listen to all that was said with a consuming interest.

When they had finished their meal the old man asked if she had any tobacco with her and she said that she did and produced the pouch from the pocket of her coat. Together they stepped outside and sat on the steps of the cabin and rolled their cigarettes and lit them with a twig brought from the fire. She stared up at the sky. The light was almost gone.

She asked about the wickiups and the old man told her the story.

He said his brother had been a missionary to the Lamanites. Did she understand the word Lamanite?

She said that she did: she had heard it before.

All the Indians hereabout are called that, he said. The Pah-Utes and Utes and Shoshonis and Bannocks and Goshutes. The whole bunch of em.

He said that he and others like him, including his brother George, believed the Indians to be the children of Jacob from the tribe of Manasseh, known as the Lamanite people in the Book of Mormon, the religion to which he had long ago been converted but now had left. The Mormons believed according to their prophecy that a spiritual awakening among these Lamanites was a sure sign that the millennium was nigh and because of this belief he and his brother had responded to the call and had begun preaching to the natives.

You might have heard of my brother? George Washington Hill?

She said that she had not.

The old man drew on his cigarette and looked out toward the mountains.

Brigham says that one day all the Indians will become a white and delightsome people. That through righteous living and baptism their skins can be changed from red to lily white. Do you believe that?

No, I don't, she said. I wouldn't think that possible.

Nor would I. But that's what he believes.

People can believe all kinds of things for all different reasons. That doesn't make them true.

He said his brother was a big man who loved to talk, a man full of a good-natured bravado and unlike himself he possessed a gift for speaking in the native tongues and the Indians had all liked him and he had great success in converting them to the faith. He had baptized over a thousand Shoshonis in less than three years and then he had returned to this place near the Bear River and encouraged the Indians to follow him. And they had come. Hundreds came, thousands. They came for food and for instruction in the arts of agriculture but mostly they came to be near his brother George, whom they believed could help save their people with his prophecies and visions.

Over two thousand natives gathered here, the old man said, raising his arm and making a sweeping gesture in the direction of the wickiups.

Two thousand Indians, all in this place.

She nodded in appreciation of such a large number and the old man went on.

For two years they kept coming. Not just the Shoshoni but the Bannock and Nez Perce and Piedes. My brother told them that they were the Lord's Battle Axes and that if they joined the faith and embraced God no harm could come to them. He told them that only when they and others like them had been converted would Jesus come again and the game would be plentiful once more and the whites would give them back their lands. He said this valley belonged to them and that if anyone tried to drive them off their guns would have no effect because bullets couldn't penetrate their holy garments. The garments he had given them. The same garments the Saints wore.

The old man fell silent and she pondered what he'd said. In the darkness she heard a flock of geese pass low overhead, their wings making a rhythmic sound, sodden and squeaky on the night air.

The Indians believed him. The old man looked at her and shook his head. They believed in the magic marks on the garments. The mystic markings signifying that they had been cleansed of the blood of their generation and were prepared to receive the bridegroom. My brother told them Jesus was the bridegroom and he was going to save them but that he could only come in the fullness of time and when they, the Lamanites, had made the way ready. They placed great store in this mysticism. This form of medicine, and especially they valued my brother's assurance that the garments would protect them from any harm.

The old man spat and then hacked up something and spat some more.

But they weren't protected. They weren't protected at all. He drew the last smoke from the cigarette and flipped it into the darkness where it arced through the air like a newborn cinder tracing a dying path, darkening to nothingness before it hit the earth.

People around here got scared. They became alarmed at the idea of two thousand Indians gathered not five miles from town. All those red savages right at their back door. Corinne is a Gentile town and always has been, as you probably know. People here have no use for Saints who stir the natives up. The townspeople started arming themselves, thinking they were about to become victims. Victims of the Indians and the Saints. They got to thinking, By God the Mormons are going to do us just like they did those emigrants at Mountain Meadows. Pretty soon soldiers arrived from Fort Douglas, dispatched to protect the town. One morning the captain rode out here and told my brother he had to move his Indian camp. It wouldn't be tolerated anymore. He gave him two weeks to clear the natives out.

Well, that was pretty much the end of it. The Indians left, and so did George. He went off to Nevada to live with Chief Walker and his band. Took his followers with him and left me here. All that time he said, Come to Utah and be washed. You are the chosen people. It's time to redeem the remnant of Jacob before Christ. All it done was cause the natives to raise up their own prophets and seers. It caused them to make up their own garments and believe they could dance the evil away. They think they can get help from their own gods now but they cannot and do you know why?

No, I don't reckon I do.

Because their gods are no match for ours, that's why.

She said nothing to this.

The Saints believe that Jesus Christ will come again in 1890. That's thirteen years from now. Do you believe that?

No, I don't.

You should. Everyone should live as if the end is nigh. As if the door could darken any time. Even if the rest of it don't make any sense. I don't believe all of it anymore. In fact, I believe very little of it. But I do believe the part about being ready for the end. That I do believe.

The old man rose slowly to his feet and looked out into the night for a very long while as if he could see something there that ordinary mortals could not see. Then he turned and climbed the stairs, saying he would get a blanket and told her she could bed down wherever she chose. She could sleep in the corner of the cabin or in the shelter of the porch. She said that she preferred to sleep outside. He asked if she would like to have the Indian girl for the night and she said no.

She looks worse than she is, he said. The pox has passed and I don't believe she can infect you anymore. You might have her if you want her.

She shook her head and said, No, she preferred to sleep alone.

When the old man had gone to fetch the blanket she sat still in the darkness and thought how to be taken for a man was to have access to a world otherwise closed and unfathomable and how it caused her to feel of neither world, as if the glimpse of men's souls and their own forms of weakness held no more attraction than the jealousies and bickerings of certain women she had endured. She wondered if it wasn't the case that only in the pure fit of true partnership could one escape the weaknesses of either sex. In such a union a wholeness might be achieved through a mixing of sensibilities. Maybe then and only then could one's nature be known, in opposition to another, and by melding in some fashion. She wondered if this might also be accomplished in the joining of human souls to animals, thereby freeing nature to run its course.

The night passed quickly. She chose to sleep in the fields. She took the blanket he gave her and wandered among the abandoned wickiups until she found one whose brush walls still offered good protection from the wind and she curled up there in the bowered hut where she could see the stars twinkling through the webbing of branches like flecks of light caught in a dark skein. Only once in the night did she awaken and it was to the sound of the dog crunching something in the darkness, eating the cast-off bones of some animal long ago consumed by the misbegotten inhabitants of these rude dwellings. It took her a long time to fall back to sleep. She thought of what the old man had told her and how she, too, had once believed that the holy garments could protect her and how she had one day stopped believing in this and in all else they had taught her. When she removed her garments for the last time she had not known what to do with them and so she had buried them in a hole, as if interring a dead and useless part of herself.

In the morning the Indian woman gave her a bowl of porridge to eat, sweetened with goat's milk, and she ate half of it and then took the rest outside for the dog, turning the mush out on a flat stone for the animal to lick up. When the old man saw this he chastened her and said it was for men to feed men and for dogs to feed themselves and he had not intended for his food to be wasted that way.

She apologized but said she did not mind sharing with the dog because it was hungry, too, and, for better or worse, she was responsible for it now.

The man shook his head and said, Shit if you ain't.

She returned the blanket to him and prepared to leave. She thanked the old woman and pressed into her hand the remainder of her tobacco and the woman smiled for the first time. As she began to walk away, the old man called to her and offered to sell her a horse but she said she had no money and he said that without money he couldn't give her one. She nodded and thanked him anyway.

One more thing, he said. He looked at the old woman and chuckled. She says—and here he stopped and pointed to the old woman— she says you ain't a man but a woman. Is that true?

She smiled slowly and said, Could be, could be, and then she turned and walked away, leaving the three of them standing against the doorway of the cabin staring after her. When she looked back later she saw that they were still there, a trio of dark figures, standing motionless in the soiled morning light.

———

IT WAS PAST noon and the sun had already crested by the time she reached the edge of town and looked out over the lake where a steamship was moving slowly toward the shore, its covered side wheel turning in the water. On its side were painted the words "Kate Connor" and on the top deck passengers had lined up at the curved railing to glimpse a view of the landing.

She made her way into town, walking past a gristmill and a row of adobe houses looking pale and forlorn against the bleached land. Farther on she came to the saloons and canvas shanties and the merchant shops and gambling places fronting the railroad tracks. She passed a large new two-story building with "Montana Trading Company" painted on the front in bold letters. There were no trees or shrubbery of any kind, giving the town a bare appearance, and white alkali dust blew down the street. A few wagons drawn by fat ox teams or high-mettle horses passed by, loaded with goods. She kept the dog close to her now. At one point a pack of yellow curs came out from behind a wattle fence and they circled and gnashed with their teeth until she let loose with a hail of rocks and the dogs slunk back and retreated to the place from whence they'd come. At every blacksmith shop and livery stable she stopped and looked over the animals milling about the pens.

At every corral or fenced enclosure she did the same.

No one spoke to her. Nor did she speak to anyone.

She walked the entire length of the town, searching out any possible place where someone might hide a horse if they were of a mind to hide one but she found no trace of Vittick or the red mare. Nor did she see Waddell and the boy and their mule. Although she did not believe it would do much good, she searched out the sheriff and found him at home, preparing to take his midday meal, and she told him what had happened, beginning with the theft of the mare and ending with the beating she'd endured. The sheriff, a young man with a long serious face, listened quietly to her tale and promised to keep an eye out for Waddell and confiscate the horses should he happen to see them. He suggested she might notify the livery stable of the theft and named its owner. She recognized the name and wondered if it could be the same man she had once known, long ago, and asked where she might find him, and then, thanking him, she bid the sheriff goodbye.

At the far edge of town where the railroad cars stood shunted on a siding she came to the blacksmith shop and stood in the doorway peering into the darkened interior where in one corner the bright incandescence of a forge illuminated the shape of a large man bent over an anvil. The man took no notice of her and she stood for a while watching him until her eyes had adjusted to the scene. Cats of every color were lying about in the shadows and when they saw the dog they seemed to swell within their own skins and grow bigger and their gazes became keener as they watched the dog for any sign of sudden movement. But the dog did not move. It stood quietly at her side.

She shifted against the light and the blacksmith looked up and then set down his tools and crossed to where she stood and studied her then broke into a broad smile. He wiped his hands against his apron and said, I'll be damned.

Hello Farley, she said.

It is you, isn't it?

Yeah, it's me.

Ain't you a sight.

I reckon I am.

He leaned down and kissed her lightly on the mouth.

I couldn't ever figure why a woman as good-lookin as you has to go about dressed like a man. Unless you just had your fill of us and don't want nothin to do with us no more.

She smiled and took off her hat and swept her hand across her cropped hair and said, I never got sick of men. I just got sick of the work it takes to get myself up like a woman. You got a drink of water around here?

He led her to a place behind the shop where a crude ramada had been constructed out of pine posts and roofed with willow boughs. She sat in the shade while the dog circled and sniffed at the posts. The water barrels were weighted with heavy stones to keep the lids from blowing off and he removed the stones and then lifted the lid and took down a battered tin dipper from its hook on the wall. He ladled a cup full of water and brought it to her. The cup was old and where the handle met the tin a leak had sprung and as she drank the water dribbled down her chin and the dog tried to catch the drops that fell.

Dog's thirsty, too, she said. The blacksmith called the dog over to the barrel and ladled some water into the bottom half of a broken crock lying on the ground and the dog drank greedily.

Where's your horse?

She told him the story of Waddell and the boy and the horses they'd stolen from her, and said that for all she knew Waddell could be right there in town, or he could be miles away by now, but either way she figured she wasn't yet ready to give up on the possibility of finding him.

I figure he's headed south. His boy said he was going back to Kanarra.

And you plan on following him all that way?

She nodded. If I have to. Thing is, I need a horse.

I reckoned that was comin.

What have you got here?

Not much. My best animals are all out. I got two—a gelding and a mare. The mare's too old for hard travel, and the other's just green broke. You can take a look at him.

She followed him through a gate and past a row of run-down coops where speckled hens were pecking at the dirt to where a round corral had been fashioned out of unpeeled cedar posts. Two horses stood back to front, swishing their tails to keep the flies off each other's faces. The blacksmith took up a halter hanging on the post and undid the gate and stepped into the corral and the horses lifted their heads and grew still.

Whoa now, he said, as he approached a tall yellow horse, holding out his arm to keep the horse from bolting past him. The horse rolled its eyes and lifted its head and turned to the side and pressed itself against the fence as the blacksmith circled its neck with the rope and then fitted the halter over its head and led it out of the corral.

She stood looking at the horse. Not saying anything.

I know what you're thinking. He's not much to look at.

She smiled and said, I won't be riding his looks.

The horse's mane had at some time in the recent past been roached and had now half grown out and stood up in a ridge along its neck. It was a poor-looking animal, slack-rumped and bow-necked with a Roman nose, but its eyes were keen and she sensed an intelligence in them. She placed her hand on the horse's shoulder and felt the way the skin ran and quivered under her touch. She had never liked yellow horses. It was nothing she ever would have said aloud because only a fool would judge a horse on its color. Still, it was true.

He'll do, she said.

She asked the blacksmith if he had a saddle he could spare and he said he'd just gotten one off a Mexican in trade and she could take that if she wanted. They led the yellow horse past the chickens and tied him up near the ramada at the back of the shop. He asked her if she was hungry and she said, Weren't I always? And he said, Yes, that's the way he remembered it. He told her to stay where she was and rest while he got up some food and he disappeared through the door of a shanty attached to the shop. In a little while he emerged with a plate of boiled eggs arranged on a platter. He'd opened a can of sardines and stacked some crackers on the plate as well. While they ate the old mare in the corral began to whinny and the yellow gelding answered with a high shuddering sound.

The old gal's gonna be pretty upset to lose her boyfriend.

Funny thing about mares. They always get more anxious over being left, don't they?

What ever happened to that feller anyway?

What feller?

The one you took up with in Montana?

Still with him, she said.

I wouldn't have figured that.

Some things you can't figure.

I expect you heard about Lee?

She nodded.

She turned away and looked out toward the lake. The sun falling through the loose willows stirring overhead cast a pattern of swinging and shimmering light. An old tarpaulin draped over the fence luffed in the breeze, filling with air and deflating like a living breathing thing. It did not quite seem possible he was dead.

The blacksmith rose and went into the shanty attached to the shop and when he returned he carried a newspaper in his hand. He laid it out on the table before her and she looked at it.

Read it to me, she said.

The article described the scene at the execution and it also described the prisoner's last weeks in jail. There was a long passage about his wives and their last visits to him. When he came to a part about Emma, she asked him to read it again.

Lee's concubine, Emma, the belligerently inclined plural wife, made matters lively for the guards when she arrived to bid her husband goodbye. She stopped her buggy in front of the Beaver jail, and as she approached, she heard one guard say to the other, Who is that handsome woman? Oh, she's just one of John D. Lee's whores, was the answer that came back. Quick as lightning Emma delivered a blow across the guard's face with her buggy whip, and when he made to come at her, she put up her fists and pleaded with him to step forward as she would take great pleasure in turning his face to gore.

Another wife, Terressa, was heard to complain that she had not been to see Lee because there was his English wife, Emma, a firebrand in the way. She claimed this dark-eyed English hussy had been bestowed upon Lee for his heroic service at Mountain Meadows but that from the time she arrived she had introduced discord into the household and it had been a hell upon earth ever since. This old lady was shriveled but decently clad, showing some breeding in her deportment, and she talked with good sense. She now calls herself Mrs. Terressa Phelps and still considers herself a legal wife of John D. Lee, though she has left his home and is now living with an unmarried son. She still speaks in the highest terms of her uxorious lord and feels the deepest affliction at his present disgrace and position of jeopardy. The old lady says, John D. Lee has been made a dog of by his church and he hasn't the wit to see the lifelong tool they've made of him. But he's kind to his family. He always treated me well—I'll say that for him— and he treats his other wives well, and all his boys and girls are well brought up. She claims her husband is being sacrificed in a most cowardly and dastardly manner and lays the blame on Brigham Young. Poor John, he went for wool and came back shorn, she said. He has made a foolish bargain and will come out at the small end of the horn.

The jailor attending to the prisoner said that before his execution Lee was shown a copy of his likeness that appeared in one of the nation's papers and he declared himself displeased with it. This picture he considers a libel on his personal beauty, and makes bold to say so. He remarked, I'm better-looking than that. If I am not, how is it so many women have fallen in love with me?

It's a question, at the moment, beyond answer.

That's enough, she said, I don't need to hear any more. He closed the newspaper and folded it over and placed it on the table, weighting it with a stone so it wouldn't blow away. She stood up slowly and said it was time for her to leave. The blacksmith made no move. He looked up at her and said, Remember that time in Missoula?

Yes, I do, she said.

The horses continued to call to each other and she could hear the sound of the wagons moving down the street out front. The heavy slow-going freight wagons coupled together and drawn by oxen and mules. She'd never liked Corinne. It was a freighting town, a railroad town, but most of all it was a Gentile town and therefore a place where a man could get anything he wanted, flesh or foul, rum or gin. She had worked here a short while but in the end she had left. She found she preferred miners over drovers or railroad men.

Maybe you could get me that saddle now, she said.

The saddle was an old square-skirted Mexican outfit with half-rigging and heavy *tapaderos* covering the stirrups. It had a big flat horn, as wide as her hand, and the leather had been tooled into ornate, flowery patterns. Silver conchos were affixed to the skirting where the leather thongs emerged and there was more silver rimming the cantle and the horn. She had seen such saddles in Juárez, a saddle fit for a *jefe* or *hacendado* but not a real cowboy.

The blacksmith saddled the horse for her while she made her way to his outhouse and when she came back he had finished and the horse stood ready. He had tied a blanket behind the saddle, rolled in an India-rubber poncho, and hung a canteen over the horn. She waited in the celadon light filtering through the ramada while he returned to his shanty and came back out with a small sack and tied it to the saddle. Just a couple of tins of meat, he said, and some cornmeal and dried peaches. He then reached into his pocket and pressed a leather pouch into her hand and she could feel the coins inside.

She looked away from him and thanked him, overcome by his kindness. She said she didn't know what else to say and he said, Ain't nothing you have to say, we go back a long ways, don't we, Ann? She said it was true, they did. He held the horse's head while she fitted her boot into the stirrup and mounted and settled her weight in the saddle and the young horse danced to one side and laid his ears back and kicked out with its hind legs and the blacksmith yanked him up and the horse froze, its nose in the air and its eyes rolled back to reveal the whites. The gelding began pulling away from him, backing up suddenly and trying to wheel.

Sumbuck, the blacksmith said, holding tight to the reins and yanking on the bit until the horse reared up and pulled away from him.

You can always take the old horse if you want to—I'm afraid this idjit here'll end up hurting you—

I reckon this one'll be fine once we get to know each other.

Well, who knows. Could be this here colt might even bring you luck.

Why's that?

It's a known fact that yellow horses are lucky. Ain't you ever heard that?

No, I never heard that one before, she said.

Well, now you have. That's how he got his name. Lucky.

She laughed and said, Well, okay now, guess me and Lucky'll be off.

You be careful now.

He released the horse's head and stepped back and the colt jumped forward nervously as she pressed her heels against him, and then she turned the animal and waved goodbye and headed down the street between the rows of shanties and the board saloons and canvas tents where the *nymphs du pavé* and the soiled doves plied their trade. Farther on she passed the booths and dugouts where men sat at the faro tables or played three-card monte in the muted gray light leaking through the canvas walls. She kept the horse on a tight rein, riding slowly along the street, looking carefully for any sign of Waddell and the boy, but she saw none.

The wind had risen and the dust from the wagons filled the air. She passed the Metropolitan Hotel and Uintah House and Montana Street, where the drinking saloons fronted the tracks. She rode behind the saloons to check the corrals once more. A train was pulling out, releasing great clouds of steam into the air, and the yellow horse shied and pranced sideways and threw its head. She rode on down a back street, past stagnant pools of water lying in the low areas, sloughs of green water filled with rotten, putrified, stinking matter that she could only barely identify as the maggoty carcasses of dead animals. The dog trotted behind her, keeping its head low.

She rode on out of town to where the tules began at the lakeshore and the salt crust broke beneath the horse's feet. She rode with no destination in mind and with no sense of purpose other than a wish to know the horse and to let it sense her ways. When she turned and looked back the town appeared as nothing more than a few squat buildings on the horizon and beyond that rose the steep mountains that looked much closer than they really were. She kept the horse moving forward and every once in a while she circled a stand of pig- weed or saltbush, forcing the animal to respond to her touch and command, and then let it travel on again forward at its own pace. She tried to form a picture in her mind of what she wanted the horse to do before she asked him to do it, and in this way she hoped to trans- mit her desires quietly and without fear and to join her spirit to the animal's. Yet it was a fractious thing, high-strung and nervous, and already it had worked up a sweat. She passed an old cemetery, a dreary, neglected place, low mounds sunken and ragged and the headstones listing and tilting in the dry white sand amidst the leavings of cattle and sheep that had at some time in the past broken through the warped fence of spectrally white boards propped in the sand. She rode down to where the river emptied into the lake and sat the horse awhile and looked to the south and to the west where the water stretched to the horizon. The horse was restless and stood uneasy.

She talked aloud to the horse, telling him she never figured they would actually kill him and she still couldn't quite believe it, and at the sound of her words the horse cocked his ears and grew quieter.

It was the most remarkable sight anyone ever saw. The old man never flinched, and it made death seem easy the way he went off. None of his family was present. His body was sent to his sons and his wife Rachel who took it to Panguitch for burial . . .

She rode on, out across the alkali flats, heading directly into the dropping sun. At one point she felt the shadows darken about her and she looked up to see a flock of white pelicans soaring overhead, and the world seemed both blessed and fraught at that moment, resplen- dent with beauty and yet fragile and transitory. She pointed the colt toward a stand of dark trees rising up in the distance and let it break into a gallop, keeping a tight hold on its head. They came upon some white bones littering the sand and the horse suddenly shied and reeled to a stop. He stood with his legs stiffened and his head lowered and blew through his nose as he backed away from the bones, dropping his head ever further. She stroked his neck and spoke to him and urged him forward, attempting to bring him to the bones so that he might judge for himself their harmlessness, and slowly, by circling them and urging the colt on patiently, she got him to approach the fearful objects and drop his nose and sniff them and she felt his fear abate and saw the way he suddenly lost all interest in them.

She rode on, crossing the alkaline plain where the corrugated sand had hardened into ripples and the wrack of branches and twigs left behind by the receding water lay in little scalloped ridges. The setting sun cast a funnel of gold across the wavery surface of the lake. When she came to a stand of willows she dismounted and stood gazing out over the flat rufescent water. The day was ending. She thought of Lee and she could see his face very clearly. She could see it one way, and then another. With different expressions writ upon his countenance. She saw him as he was when he was filled with desire. She saw his cunning and his humor.

In the beginning he had fed her bits of food from his fingers and kissed and fondled her and stroked her hair and told her all manner of things about her beauty and the life they would have together. Later on he'd lost much of the tenderness and took her as he pleased, with no thought to her own pleasure.

The yellow horse cropped the stunted grass as the cold blue dusk settled over the lake.

One time, after he'd taken his sons to the city, he returned full of suspicions and accused her of taking up with a fellow by the name of Matt Carney when it was really Rachel who'd been about to elope with him. Still it caused a devil of a row in the family. Lee called a meeting where everyone was taken to account and ordered to confess. He asked them one by one to get up and ask forgiveness for what they'd done and he demanded they pray for one another. He went through this with all the wives and each confessed whether they had at any time had intercourse with a Gentile and who that Gentile was. It was this kind of confession that almost cost Matt Carney his life. When he finally came to her she told him she had nothing to confess and left the room. When she came out into the yard she met Harvey Pace, who had been listening at the window. Harvey said, How long before they're through in there? And she said she didn't know. It was then she overheard Lee tell Rachel to kill some chickens and get dinner ready and Rachel had said, Why don't you ask Ann? She has hams and everything else to get up a first class-dinner for you. That was when she heard Lee say he would not speak to that woman, meaning her, for three months. And he had kept his word. He had not spoken to her for three long months.

She had never betrayed him with anyone and he was wrong to think that she had. Others did. Rachel. Sarah Caroline. Even Terressa, toward the end. She wondered if Emma still had both children with her. She hoped she did.

The dog had wandered out of sight and now it returned carrying in its mouth the dark limp form of some rodent that it now prepared to devour. Settling down on the packed sand, the dog took the animal between her paws and nuzzled its soft belly and then tore at it and pulled forth a long string of shiny blue guts.

She waited. She waited until the dog had finished eating, standing quietly beside the horse and stroking it and speaking in low tones about such matters as then seemed important to her although she understood these were things of consequence only to her and could never matter to anyone else, which is why she confided them to the horse and not a human. She felt a sense of fear and she tried to understand it as she spoke to the horse. She knew it had to do with Lee's dying, and dying in the way he had. The newspaper said he had met his death bravely. Minutes before the shots were fired he had described himself as feeling calm as a summer's morn.

Calm as a summer's morn.

She wondered how it was possible for anyone to face death with such serenity. Perhaps he really did feel that. Or perhaps he didn't. But she admired him nonetheless for saying it and for going to his end that way. It couldn't have been easy. She told the horse it was the same with men as with horses and dogs: nothing wants to die.

She looked to the south as if she expected to see in the bronze moon rising there all the events that had transpired in that faraway meadow where a man who was judged and condemned was taken forth and shot but all she saw was the same tainted disk with its dark unfathomable shadows.

She mounted the horse and followed the trail back to town, riding through the darkness and sawing the horse down when it tried to bolt, keeping the reins short to prevent the colt from getting the best of her. The streets were quiet now and the canvas tents glowed like sulfurous boxes. She stopped before one such tent and through the doorway she could see a few men eating at a long wooden table. She dismounted and tied the horse to a post and told the dog to stay.

She ate well on baked squash and bean soup, sitting at the common wooden table with three other men. The men did not look at her and did not speak to her and neither did they appear to know one another. All ate in silence. Men who worked for the railroad perhaps. Or drovers from Montana headed south with herds. They had cleaned themselves up for the night and in their newly scrubbed appearance all traces of their day's work had disappeared and all they had in common now was sunburned flesh and a line of demarcation across their foreheads above which the white, hat-protected flesh gleamed with a necrotic pallor.

She ate. She ate the soup and the squash and the corn bread and when she'd finished she asked the woman who had served her if she might have a cup of coffee. She sat savoring the taste of the coffee and the heat of it. The walls of the tent billowed in the wind, sucking in and out as if the shanty itself were breathing. Through the open doorway she could see the dog and the horse and their eyes looked incandescent in the dark.

Some mornings Emma would get up first and make coffee before the children awoke and bring it back to bed and the three of them would linger there together, Emma in her proper nightgown, always pink or white, with the fabulous bows down the front, and Lee and her in nothing at all. Her with her legs folded so he joked she looked like some wading bird, with those long hinged legs, and them all laughing. The thing was hard to explain. It was really beyond explaining, but they had been happy in those days.

She thought of Beezer. She could see the cabin sitting up against the mountains and the prairie stretching away, tilting like the land had been turned a little sideways. She could imagine him fixing his evening meal. What men wanted had always been something she found easy to give. All she expected was appreciation, some kind words, no rough behavior. She had gotten much more than this from Beezer. Much, much more.

One by one the men at the table rose and left and she was alone with the waitress, a big heavy woman with hair dyed the color of boiled beets.

She thought about how she could head north, or she could head south. She sipped her coffee and thought about the various possibilities and likelihoods. She wished she knew the condition of the mare. And whether or not she had survived the day of traveling, wherever it had taken her, and whether even now she might be somewhere nearby, closer and more available to her discovery than she could imagine. She thought of Kanarra and the difficulty of making such a long journey. And then she thought of Vittick and of Waddell and it angered her to think of him presuming he could get away with stealing such a horse. A horse that would stand out no matter where he took it. It seemed to her she had no choice but to go on.

She picked up her hat from the table and put it on and rose and paid her bill and walked back out into the night and stood looking first in one direction, and then the other. Laughter came from a saloon across the way and a woman emerged, pulling a man in tow, and they crossed the alley and lifted the flap on a little tent and went inside and she heard the creak of the springs as they fell upon a bed.

She untied the horse and walked it down the street and then she stopped and tightened the cinch and mounted and the horse crow-hopped and reeled and seemed set on heading back to the blacksmith's shop where the old mare waited and she was a long time in changing the colt's mind but in the end she did. She did it without once putting the spurs to him or whipping him. Instead she talked him down and waited him out and urged him on until she had convinced him he had but one course left open to him and that was to travel forward into the darkness.

She slept that night on the alkali ground at the northern edge of the lake, near a small acrid pool. The wind blew all night and filled her blanket with salty sand. She rose while it was still dark and drank some water from the canteen and rolled up her blanket and attempted to tie it behind the saddle but the horse sidestepped away from her, nervously pivoting on the long rope staked in the ground, until finally she gave the rope a sharp jerk and told the horse to give it up and he did. He stood still in the cool morning and she finished tying on the blanket and tightened the cinch and mounted and set to traveling at a trot out over the dried cracked earth where platelets of whitened mud lay curled up like the broken shards of teacups. A desiccated land that smelled of sulfur and brine. She skirted the town, taking a southerly course, and the dog trotted behind her as the dawn broke in a widening band of laminate crimson and pink.

An hour later she drew up the horse and sat looking back in the direction from which she had just come. She sat that way for many minutes. And then she said, Oh, just go on, and turned the horse and rode south as the dark clouds scudded up against the mountains and a light rain began to fall.

FOUR

S HE RODE ALL that day without cease, staying to the wagon road that took her through the greening country with the light rain falling on and off. Every now and then she stopped to let the horse rest and it blew hard and stood with its sides heaving against her legs while she stretched in the stirrups and studied the land. The mountains to the east shut in the long valley and rose up in crags and snow-laden peaks and to the west the lake stretched forth unending under a gray umbrageous sky.

At noon she came to a stand of trees and dismounted and shared a meal of biscuits and jerky with the dog and when she'd satisfied her hunger she mounted and rode on, passing through the settlement of Ogden, on the outskirts of which she found men toiling in the fields. Once she had spent a few months in this place but that was long ago. She had worked for a season in an establishment run by a woman named Buelah Pritchett—Puke-up Pig-shit is what the hired men had called her, for her meanness and the way she often abused them and for the slovenly state of her being. She had left there poorer than when she'd arrived and was glad to be quit of that life. It did not seem to her that anything had changed in the years since she'd left, except a new and larger meetinghouse had been constructed in the center of town. She stopped at a mercantile and bought a tin cup and a metal plate and tobacco and then she rode on, happy to leave that place and all its weary memories behind.

She camped that night near an old burn and the sky cleared and the gray trees shone silver in the moonlight. The air turned cold. Stars came out. She sat for a long while with her blanket around her shoulders, smoking, with the dead and broken trees fallen at every possible angle and leaning against one another in precarious repose. The moon shone upon the horse cropping the sparse tussocks of grass and the fire sawed in the wind as she stared into the flames. The dog lay before the fire with its head resting upon its paws and every once in a while it lifted its head and studied her, as if to ascertain her thoughts. After a while she stood up and checked on the horse and spoke to it in the dark and then she returned to the fire and took off her clothes, stripping down to her underwear. She built up the fire and hung her damp clothing on a log near the flames and then she laid the poncho on the ground and wrapped herself in the blanket and, with the dog nestled near her for warmth, she fell asleep.

Once again she dreamed of Mexico. She dreamed she was riding through the plateau colonies of Colonia Juárez on the blue-roan tobiano paint that Lee had once given her and in all the towns she passed through, in Dublan and Diaz and the mountain villages of Pacheco and Garcia and Cuichupa, she searched for the gray mare but she found nothing, only the abandoned remnants of old dugouts carved from the banks of the Piedras Verdes River, the crude shelters of natives who had squatted there long ago.

In the morning the world was born again out of the darkness and she lay shivering in her blanket until the sun had crested the peaks and then she rose and dressed and rolled the blanket inside the poncho and tied it with rope. The sun's yolk rolled above the ridges as she walked out through the dew-laden grass to where the horse stood tethered to the ground and she unstaked the horse and led it back to where she had left the saddle. All along the horse's back she could see the marks of old wounds, the crescents of lighter hair, evidence of old bites and abrasions. The horse was so thin the points of its shoulders and hips stood out under its skin and she noticed how the hair had begun to rub from its withers, worn away by the heavy Mexican saddle. To keep from raising a sore, she doubled the blanket over the withers before throwing on the saddle. Her breath misted and hung on the morning air as she tightened the cinch and the horse laid back its ears and turned to looked at her, its single visible eye rolled back to reveal the white. He would not stand still for her to mount and once she was up on his back he set to lunging and bucking before she could find her seat and she took the horn hard in the stomach before she managed to pull his head up and saw him down. He stood still then with his legs splayed and his breath coming hard, as if preparing for some new form of nastiness. It seemed a tiresome start to the day and she told the horse so. She said they still had a long ways to go and if he kept that up it wasn't going to be much fun for either one of them.

She clucked to the horse and laid her leg against him and in response the horse spun and tried to unseat her again and she let him have the spurs and he reared up and stood on his hind legs and for a moment they both hung there in the balance, horse and rider improbably located in space, until she threw herself forward, stretching her body long against his neck and he came down on stiff legs and proceeded to buck across the broken earth. It was all she could do to stay with him. The dog, growing excited, circled around behind the horse and nipped at its heels and barked until she called it off. Once again the horse grew quiet, though she could feel the way the muscles quivered over his shoulders, the flesh running in spasms, and she stroked him there and talked to him for a long while and soon his ears came forward and he moved off, prancing and traveling sideways for a while until he finally settled into a steady gait.

It was a day's ride to Salt Lake City and she knew the route well. There was little movement on the road. A Sunday. The Lord's day and all the Saints in church, forbidden to work on this day of rest. She was glad for the quiet. Happy to have the road to herself. She kept the horse moving at a good pace all morning. The rain had ripened the country all around. God's country, Lee had called it. The Ark of Refuge and Asylum of God's Chosen. Now his name had become a hiss and a byword and he was gone from this world forever. How could such a furious brutality ever be forgiven? Or atoned for by the death of one man?

She crossed an arroyo where the road wound past a flood barricade of boulders, the big stones tumbled in a dry wash, and followed a stand of cottonwoods along the empty river course. When she came to a pothole she stopped to let the horse drink but he could not see to the bottom and he blew nervously at the surface of the water and backed away in fear. All right, have it your way, she said, and rode on, choosing a course that took her past the city. She did not stop again until the sun had gone down and a canescent pall descended. By then she had reached Willow Creek where she camped for the night. There she found good grass and water. In the morning she pushed on, making the hard climb over the hills that separated the valley of the Great Salt Lake from that of the Utah Lake and dropped down in the basin just after noon. There was no water until she came to the American Fork and here she stopped and rested in the shade, looking out over the shallow swales where the land dipped into shady dells. She opened a can of tinned meat and turned half out for the dog and the rest she ate herself. She finished her meal with a handful of dried peaches and drank her fill of water. Then she refilled her canteen and mounted up again and traveled on, with the doves and quail flushing from the deep grass around her. She left the main road and followed a trail that wound through the low stands of kinnikinnick carpeting the ground, skirting several small settlements. She passed a child driving a herd of goats and later came upon a cluster of Indians squatting around a low fire and then she didn't see anyone for a long time. She rocked in the saddle and let her thoughts drift.

Some people said he was as good a man as ever lived. That he had a tireless energy and courage. A more than average intelligence. Walter Winsor had once told her he thought Lee was the best man he ever knew. Never a more tenderhearted man, he said. Never one more generous, a friend to everyone. He was a good hand with a horse, that much was true. A good builder and provider. You could put John D.

Lee on a desert island, Winsor had said, and in no time at all he'd have raised a fortune, so clever was he at making money.

But she had seen the other side, too. The way he bullied people to get them to do his bidding. How he was not quite honest in all his business dealings. He had a habit of spying and eavesdropping and claiming that his visions set him apart from other men. He once told her that this world was controlled by the other world of invisible spirits, although some had bodies of flesh while others were disembodied. When the Lord desired to accomplish a work among the wicked for their destruction He generally employed disembodied spirits. But the killing at the meadow had been done by ordinary men. Men prepared to wield the sword of destruction for the greater good of the kingdom.

Levi Stewart once told her a story about Lee. When he had lived in Illinois, Stewart said, Lee began taking more and more wives until he had so many he couldn't keep them all. Still, there were two young sisters, Louisa and Emmeline Free, both great beauties, on whom Lee had set his sights. He was determined to make these sisters his wives. Charmed by his good looks and courtly manner, the sisters had been prepared to marry him, until Brigham intervened. The Prophet fell in love with one of the sisters on first sight and pleaded with Lee to let him have her. Of course Lee agreed, being ready to defer to Brigham in all things. And yet he was so upset by this turn of events that, according to Stewart, he had gone out and frigged several women to whom he was not married and then returned home and frigged all his wives, all on the same night, and afterward he had gone boasting about it. About how he had frigged twelve women in one day. Why are you telling me this? she remembered asking Stewart, who by then had turned against Lee. Just so you'll know what kind of man he is, he replied.

In the beginning, during those first few years with him, there were times when she counted herself lucky to be his wife, and they had all prospered, but that was before the tide had turned. In those days she and Emma had their own house and their own pigs and chickens and cows to do with as they wished, and they had husbanded their animals well and turned a good profit each season. They even made money on cats. Once she acquired a mother cat who gave birth to four kittens and shortly afterward a man they called Frankie, a Gentile cook for an outfit passing through the territory, had stopped in the village and seeing the kittens pleaded with her to sell him one. She told him that there were but few cats in the country and that she wished to keep them for herself. He said that in Nevada where he came from they had none at all and he was bound to have a cat to take back with him and he would not take no for an answer. In the end he gave her twenty dollars for one of the kittens. A very good season for cats.

The next spring they made extensive preparations to put in the largest crop they ever raised, and they got it in all right and everything looked favorable for a bountiful harvest until the grasshoppers came along and cleaned up everything, destroying all they had planted except the potato crop and the peas, which for some reason the insects would not eat. This had been the beginning of their decline.

That season the first Mrs. Lee died and he had taken her death very hard. Still, he had hoped to replace her with another wife and he set his sights on a young girl in Santa Clara. But his attempt to win another wife met with failure, though he bought the girl dresses and other presents and got her to lay with him and fondle on him, but in the end she did not become his wife, but gave him the slip and, wearing the clothes he had given her, eloped with another man.

During that time, everything appeared to flow backward. The cattle and horses died off, and the storms came one upon another, proving disastrous to the fields so that everything had a depressing appearance and for the second year they lost their crops and had little to eat. It seemed like everything was changing. The Gentiles were becoming too numerous for comfort and threatened their way of life. Rumors about the massacre grew into accusations and always Lee was named as one of the chief instigators. Winter came on and they had nothing to sell. There appeared to be a dark and impenetrable cloud hanging over their lives and they were not themselves anymore.

All this seemed to have happened long ago, and yet these events remained so fresh in her mind they could have transpired just yesterday.

———

SHE CAMPED that night away from the settlements. Before darkness fell she gathered wood and built a fire. The night was cold and a wind blew unceasingly and the ground was luminous beneath a full moon. In the morning she awoke to find the horse gone. It had pulled up its stake and wandered off. For several hours she searched the country, tramping through the brush and the thickets of elderberry and snakeweed, until she finally spotted the yellow gelding grazing quietly upriver from a grove of willows. The horse moved off as she approached. She squatted on her haunches and waited. When she moved again the horse also moved, trailing the long rope through the grass. In this way she passed the better part of the morning, following the horse, with every attempt to approach him thwarted. She recalled how once she and Lee had lost their horses high up on the Kolob, and it had taken them three days to finally catch them, and remembering the trick Lee had used, she set about gathering the tops of wild oats in her hat. Then she turned her shoulder to the horse and, feigning indifference, she waited, shaking the hat once in a while. Curious, the horse began to move toward her. She set the hat on the ground and circled behind the horse, driving him slowly before her. When the horse came to the hat he stopped and dropped his nose, and while he was thus distracted she managed to grasp the end of the rope. By then the afternoon was almost gone and she felt hungry and tired. It was several miles back to camp and she walked the distance, leading the yellow horse as the wild hares scattered before her.

The next day she came to Peeteneet Creek, a small stream of pure clear water, and crossed a divide that brought her to another valley and she spent the night camped on Chicken Creek. Here she had once laid over with Lee during a fearful storm. They spent three days in this place on account of the storms. A man they did not know had been killed in the storm by lightning while sheltering beneath a tree. This happened on their wedding trip, as they returned from the city, and it seemed to her a bad omen. The first Mrs. Lee had been traveling with them, along with her sister, Rachel. After the storm abated and everything looked clear, they traveled on to a place called Mill Creek, where one of the horses took sick and died. This delayed them two more days. Lee had called on a man in the horse business to buy another horse and the man had tried to sell him an animal with Lee's own brand on it. When Lee asked the man where he had gotten the horse, the man said he bought it from a trader earlier that week and Lee then knew it had been stolen in his absence. He said the horse was his and took it, refusing to give the man any money, and the trader had cursed him and called him all manner of names.

From there they had traveled on to Beaver, stopping at her mother's house. There a row ensued when she tried to give her mother her share of the wool they had bought in the city. The older wives claimed the wool was not hers to give, even though Lee had already promised her a share, and she and Rachel had fought bitterly. That raised the devil. From that point on the sisters had turned against her, and for the next six years they had done all they could to make her life a hell, unless they happened to want a favor from her and then they were good as spit.

It seemed the land itself was impregnated with all these memories. In almost every settlement she passed she had been a visitor with Lee. In every little colony he had been known, and he was either loved or despised. He was the sort of man for whom no middle feeling existed. People either thought him generous and friendly and kindhearted, or shifty and power-hungry and dishonest. Still, in every meetinghouse up and down the line, from Santa Clara to Salt Lake City, she had heard him preach from each pulpit and seen the way he could melt people down to tears with his words.

It had always seemed to her that he was a man with a great need to be liked—not just liked but *loved*—and this caused him to change his

shape and sentiments to fit the circumstances in which he found himself. When preaching, he was holy and God-fearing and full of fire.
But when drinking with the hired men or playing cards with drovers,
he was coarse and full of good-natured bravado and swore like one of
them. With Brigham he was the fawning acolyte. With his wives, the
firm yet seductive—and often cheerful—master. He tried to be all
things to all people. And now he was nothing, or rather he'd been
made the goat, which was pretty much the same thing.

It caused her to feel dispirited, remembering these useless things
from the past, and she turned her mind from Lee, focusing on the
landscape around her and the distance she still had to go. A rackety
wind blew down from a canyon. She followed the dirty slip of a narrow stream that slapped along beside her. The valley was broad and
long. She could see a great distance, to both the south and the west,
and she felt the space around her as a kind of freedom and blessing. A
person could acquire an exaggerated notion of mastery over destiny
from the simple act of riding horseback way far across such spaces, she
thought. Perhaps this is what this land had done to them all—given
them a bloated sense of power—and why such willful violence, in all
its forms, had marked their lives.

———

IN THE NIGHT the wind rose and a light snow began to fall. She
awoke to find a world turned white beneath a layer of rime hardened
by the cold. In the gray oppressive dawn she built a low fire and made
coffee and cooked a pot of cornmeal mush and then she saddled the
horse and set off, keeping to the wagon road. Even so, the going was
hard. The road was slick as butter. With every step, the horse skidded
on its hocks in the thick red mud as it struggled to descend the steep
hills and ascend the next. She traveled all day, fording a swollen river,
passing scattered homesteads and the crumbling walls of abandoned
adobe dwellings. She came to a settlement where she had once seen an
Indian named Baptiste dance naked in church. This had happened

on a Sunday when Lee was visiting the village to preach. Baptiste and his band arrived just as the service was beginning. The Indian strode into the meetinghall and, after a few moments, he stripped and began dancing naked in front of the congregation. One of the brethren sitting near a window thought to look out and, seeing the other Indians surrounding the church, whispered a warning to Lee. But Lee had remained calm and pretended to take no notice of Baptiste and continued the service, only preaching a little louder. After a bit, Baptiste stopped his dancing and stood there naked, listening to Lee's words, and then he stole out and took his band away.

Why did Baptiste do that? she had later asked Lee.

It was done to banter us, he said, and insult us. He thought if he could enrage us through his indecent behavior and therefore provoke a confrontation it would give him and his band an excuse to conduct a raid.

Whatever the reason, the settlement had taken it as a warning and for days the colonists had been on the alert. What she remembered about the incident now was how strong and defiant Baptiste had looked, standing there naked in the raking light streaming through the windows, surrounded by the solemn bearded men and the women in their big sheltering bonnets. How he had looked like the Original Man, perfect in his creation.

———

FOR THREE days she rode south across a land that fell and rose in great swales, through different colors of nascent green with the snow sometimes falling in tiny hard grains and then clearing or turning to a weak rain. When the sun came out it melted the thin layer of snow to a pellucid wetness and warmed her hands and face and the light fell upon the white peaks causing such a glare it made her eyes ache. She rode with her hat pulled low. She passed what looked like a mountain of salt and came upon a bloated ox abandoned beside the road and the stench of death stuck in her nostrils for a time. The wild hares were so numerous they ran in every direction and it seemed the earth itself was alive and writhing with their motion. She flushed a sage hen with five chicks and the birds ran before her, the pale downy feathers of the chicks loosed and hanging on the air as they flapped their untried wings. Dismounting, she stalked the birds into the sage and managed to fell the large slow hen with a stone, and this she cooked over a midday fire and gave a portion of the meager meal to the dog.

On the evening of the eighth day she climbed up from the plain covered with a stubby growth of wormwood and passed into the cedar-struck hills. At the summit she found herself in a thick stand of cedars—trees so ragged and dwarfed, so evidently small for their age, that they looked as if a forest had been set out and buried to its neck in drifting sand. The road was rough and bordered by black volcanic stone. Rocks full of bubbles and holes and cast about the land, rocks upon rocks, like the confusedly hurled remnants of an earlier world. A great ragged range of mountains rose to the east, glowing roseate in the distance, and more mountains rose beyond that, and even more beyond those. It was a country with no end to it—no beginning and no end. Farther along the trail a stream rushed out from the hillside, leaping down several feet between banks fringed with ice, and then swilled into the sand and disappeared, and here the horse bogged down in quicksand and only by struggling did he manage to pull first one foot loose, and then another, and another, gradually finding solid ground to free himself of the mire.

By the time she reached Indian Creek the next morning the horse had thrown a shoe and pulled up lame. Now she walked, leading the yellow gelding. The road followed the course of the creek, and her boots grew heavy with mud. The creek was strewn with the bones of horses and cattle and here and there beaver had backed up the water into ponds where trout dimpled the surface. The water was impregnated with saleratus and acrid to the taste. Geese and ducks were plentiful here and she sat on the banks of the stream, listening to the gabbling while she ate cold meat from the can, food that tasted of metal and left her feeling sour. The dog set about digging for gophers and, meeting with success, proceeded to devour its kill. In eight days, ever since she had left Corinne, she had spoken to no one except the dog and the horse, to whom she occasionally confided her thoughts. As she unsaddled the horse that night, she spoke to it again. She felt overcome by a deep weariness after a long day of walking and she spoke of her tiredness and how she wished there'd been no need to force him on such a long journey. The horse was badly drawn down, unused to such hard days of traveling. You're a good old boy, she said, a good old yellow horse. She stroked the bony cheek and the horse pressed into her touch and dropped its nose. Tired as she was, she rubbed the gelding down, massaging its legs, and checked its feet for stones before staking it out and building a fire.

In the night she lay awake and listened to the coyotes. The sharp cries carried through the darkness. The world seemed vast and lonesome and she sensed no good in the hearts of men. She felt the hope drain from her. It seemed to her she had undertaken a misbegotten quest and a deep despair settled over her. In the morning she awoke feeling fearful and far from home. She wished she were back on the prairie. With Beezer. Lying next to him in the little cabin, with the sound of the water running outside. She could not calm her fears, nor could she name them. She felt lost, as if she had wandered beyond the pale, when in truth she had come home. She thought perhaps it was this that made her so fearful.

As the sun rose she walked, heading toward town, and leading the lame horse. When she reached a rise she stopped and looked down on a scene she knew only too well. Her brother's farm lay nestled in the green valley below her, a cluster of log buildings with one lone tree rising up in the barnyard. This was the place where she had lived out her childhood, where her mother and stepfather had struggled to make a living until cholera had killed them both and her brother had taken over the farm. For a long while she stood on the ridge and studied the scene. After a time her brother emerged from the cabin and proceeded to draw a bucket of water from the well. A boy came out and followed him across the barnyard and stood in the weak morning light filtering through the heavy flat-bottomed clouds. Her son. Albert. Whom she had not seen since the day she had ridden in and left him there. The boy had thick brown hair, like his father's. He had grown tall and straight.

Sam. Belle. Albert.

She remembered how once, when Sam was about four, he had asked her if he should get up on the chicken coop and jump off and break his neck. This because Emma was always warning the children they were going to break their necks if they weren't careful and he had thought this was something to try. The next day he wanted to know if she wanted him to go outdoors and let the wind blow him away. A funny child, Sam, always with the odd thing to say, always bright and curious and full of a questioning nature.

Lee had carved horses for the boys out of soft pine and amused them for long hours by pointing out to them the good points, telling them that these were blooded horses and suggesting which would be worth the most if it were only made of flesh and blood instead of wood.

We remember the fish, which we did eat in Egypt freely, the cucumbers and the melons and the leeks and the onions, all the bounty of the land and our joyous long days upon this land . . .

Other children came out of the cabin. Her brother's sons and his daughter. The children chased one another, brandishing sticks, and their cries and laughter drifted up to where she stood on the break of the hill with the cold wind blowing against her.

For a long while she considered the possibility of walking down the hill and surprising them all. She imagined sitting down at the table with her brother and his wife and the children and sharing a midday meal. Taking Albert on her lap. Sitting in those rooms where she had so often sat with her mother and her stepfather and her brother. She imagined all the things they would say to one another. How she would tell them about Beezer and about their herd and the way they summered up in the high valleys of the Big Smokies and how the prairie turned purple each spring under a carpet of camas flowers. Her brother would be happy to know that she now shared her life with a good man and that her days of wandering had ceased. They would reminisce about the past. She could conjure up all sorts of scenes that might unfold, each one lovelier than the last. What she could not imagine was the moment of parting. She could not see how she might take leave of the boy again, or what she would say to her brother if he asked why she did not take her son with her now.

This she could not see at all.

————

WHEN THE afternoon light began to fall she rose and led the horse back the way she had come. The lameness seemed to have eased and so she mounted up when she struck the road and turned south and rode slowly through the deepening dusk, taking care to keep the horse at an easy walk. The stars were beginning to come out and swing in their orbits overhead. An hour later she reached the town of Beaver. She could make out its shape from a distance, the pinpoints of light standing out in the dark discolored vastness of a bowled valley. The street was deserted as she entered the town. Two soldiers emerged from a saloon and watched her pass in the soiled evening light. She rode directly to the blacksmith shop and was pleased to see the forge still lighted and a man at work. She asked him to replace the shoe the gelding had lost and told him she would return for the horse in an hour. She also asked if he had chanced to see a man and a boy traveling with a mule and a red horse and gray mare but the farrier shook his head and said no such party had caught his attention and she thanked him anyway and left.

She ate by oil light sitting at a small pine table in the downstairs room of a boardinghouse called Mrs. Quinn's. Across the street was the saloon where they had tried Lee. Upstairs, in a room big enough to hold all the onlookers. She knew this from what Farley had read to her from the newspaper—this and many other details she had not been able to put from her mind and which she thought about again as she ate. Two little girls sat at another table and watched her eat. The proprietor's daughters. They had bows in their hair. Identical blue bows that matched the color of their eyes. She thought of Albert while she studied the girls, and she thought of Emma and Sam and Belle and then she tried not to think of them anymore and kept her eyes lowered to her meal.

When she finished eating she ordered a whiskey and she held the glass to the light, as if toasting the flame, turning the amber liquid until it warmed, and then she downed the liquor in one gulp and stood up and put on her hat and strode to the door, her spurs making a tinkling sound against the wood. The little girls waved to her as she left and she waved back.

Outside a wind had come up and the night was filled with the sound of rustling leaves. She sat on a bench beneath a pole-and-brush bowery. The dog lay at her feet. Several Indians rode by on slack-rumped ponies, slumped forward with their blankets pulled around their shoulders. She remembered how Lee had always kept a suit of buckskins and when it suited his purpose, he darkened his face and dressed as an Indian. Much mischief was gotten up this way. Later it could always be said that the Indians did it. That's what they always claimed.

The Indians did it.

Nearly all the deviltry committed by the Saints was laid to the red man and often no one was ever the wiser. It was said that at the meadow many of the brethren had gotten themselves up as Indians. Later, the children who had survived told stories of seeing the white men wash the paint from their faces.

There were things she had seen that she had never spoken about to anyone. Things that often still haunted her dreams. Things that could never be forgotten.

She had seen the carnage at the meadow with her own eyes. When she was eight, her mother and stepfather had left California intending to join the Saints in Utah. After crossing a desert for many days on the Old Spanish Trail, they entered Utah Territory and came upon a meadow. It was winter then, but the brown pastures had not yet disappeared beneath the snows. The weary families had planned to camp near this spot and let their animals recruit but what they saw there changed their minds. The broad fields were littered with scattered bones and scraps of clothing, and in several places locks of long hair clung to the bushes. The wagons all drew to a stop and the men climbed down and walked among the bones. So it is true, her mother said when her father returned to the wagon. Everything we heard is true, isn't it? We're pushing on, was all he had said in reply and they had rolled on silently through the landscape of bones as a light snow began to fall.

It was a rude world and no one knew this better than she. The apostle had been right when he told Lee on the day of their marriage that he did not believe she would ever make a good Saint. She did not have the fire shut up in her bones. And she had seen too many things.

There had been a phrase they used when someone was put out of the way. They said he was *pushed over the rim of the basin.*

She remembered a young man named Anderson. Rufus Anderson, who fell in love with one of the girls in town named Lucinda Crandall. This had interfered with the desires of the bishop, however, who had hoped to take the girl for his wife, even though he already had many wives living with him at the time. Anderson, however, loved the girl with all his heart and would not give her up, and she fully reciprocated his feelings. They were secretly married and the girl became pregnant. When the bishop saw her condition, he was so enraged he called a meeting to dispose of the matter. Anderson was called to account and charged with adultery, even though he tried to explain how he had secretly married the girl. Lucinda was then called before the council and ordered to renounce Anderson, which she would not do. So they sent her home. Anderson wished to accompany her but they would not let him go. After she had gone, the elders bound Anderson's hands and feet and blindfolded him. And then they took down his pants and castrated him.

This was done on a Saturday.

They hung his privates on a nail near the bowery, and the following day, they remained there for all to see. It was meant to be a warning to be careful and not cross the designs of the authorities, and to indicate what would happen to adulterers.

She had been only a child when she had seen the privates hanging on the nail at the bowery and she had not known what to think of them, knowing that they were part of a man, but what part? The bloody and unrecognizable remnants, posted there for all to see. When her mother caught her staring at them she let out a little cry and hurried her away. That was the point at which her mother's faith was lost. She turned against the church, denouncing its violence. She took to speaking out against the Saints to all who would listen. This proved a dangerous course to take, for the people in the settlements were preparing for war with the States and no dissent was tolerated and especially were apostates reviled. Her mother could very well have been sent over the rim of the basin, had it not been for Lee's intercession on her behalf. The price, of course, had been her daughter. And although she had been young at the time, she understood all of this well enough, and that is why she married him. Later she would admit the greater truth of the matter, which was this: she would have married him anyway because she had desired him.

If they're big enough, they're old enough. That's what Lee had said.

And she had been a big girl. A big strong girl.

Poor Anderson. In spite of his maiming, he had survived and, with all his misfortunes, the girl never forsook him. They fled from Beaver and the last she heard they were still living together as man and wife in Nevada.

———

SHE ROSE from the bench, her body chilled from the dampness of the evening, and started down the street, heading toward the blacksmith's shop, with the dog trailing behind. Suddenly she saw something that caused her to stop and stand very still. There, before a saloon, she could see several horses tied to a hitching rail, standing in semidarkness. The horse closest to her appeared to be her red mare, though she could not be sure of this. She approached the horses quietly, glancing about her, but no one was in sight. When she reached the place where the horses were tied the sorrel turned its head and she saw the white blaze running down its face and the white stockings on its forelegs and she recognized her saddle, the one Beezer had made for her. Next to the mare stood the mule. And next to the mule, Vittick was tied to the rail.

She worked rapidly. The night was dark and the street empty and yet she could hear the loud voices of men issuing from within the saloon. A window facing the street was open to the night air and through the window she could see Waddell and Boone. The boy stood at the bar talking to a young girl in a red dress. Waddell was hunched over a glass, sitting at a table with several other men. All he had to do was turn his head and look out the window. And he could see her. She had difficulty untying the rope. It seemed at any moment the door might swing open allowing the light to spill out and with it, the man she least desired to meet.

She freed Vittick first. The gray mare neighed softly. She ran her hand down the horse's nose and spoke to her and the mare nuzzled her hand and blew softly against her flesh. She led her around behind the mule and untied the red mare and clucking to them softly, she set off down the street. She led the horses past another saloon where the door was open to the night and inside she could see the men gathered at tables and the women standing at the bar in their gaily colored dresses. The mule began to bray, calling to the horses, and the red mare answered with a long shrill whinny, and turning, she caught a glimpse of two figures emerging from the saloon. She turned quickly down an alley between two squat buildings and made her way along the fenced pens where the low grunts of pigs mingled with other noises, like the sounds that come from the throats of certain birds.

The yellow horse stood tied to a railing outside the blacksmith's shop. She hastily paid the farrier and mounted the red mare, snubbing up the gray and the yellow horses, and then turned and without looking behind her set off at a trot, riding out of town between the rows of darkened houses with the trees rustling in the wind. She rode through the night at a steady pace, leaving the road where it crossed a creek and riding on across the broken fields without stopping. She rode until her arm grew numb from the effort of leading the horses and then she stopped and rested and in a short time moved on again. Dawn found her on a summit, sitting against the trunk of a dead cottonwood near a stream covered by a thick layer of ice. She waited, passing an hour and fighting off sleep while the horses grazed on the spring grass, and then she set off again.

For three days she pushed hard, always watching her back. She rode through rainstorms and unseasonable cold and she camped far from the wagon road. She rode through breaks in the weather when the sun emerged and steam rose up from the land and her clothes half-dried on her body before the night fell again and the dampness closed in around her.

On the fifth day the fever came on and she could go no farther. She chanced upon an abandoned herder's cabin set among the broken wrack of an old cornfield and she left the horses in a fenced enclosure. She gathered as many cornstalks as she could carry and threw them to the horses, expending what little remaining energy she still possessed, and then she laid down upon the bare boards in the cabin and from this place she stared up at the roof and its missing portions and through these gaps she gazed at a sky that grew dark and light and then dark again. Her body shook with the chills and she could not stop the shivering nor could she rouse herself to build a fire and in any case the chills alternated with spells of fever when her body burned so fiercely she could not stand the blanket. It seemed to her the life was passing out of her and she tried to fight the passing but she felt no strength for the struggle. The fever grew worse and she became delirious, calling out the names of those from the past. She lost all sense of time and she no longer knew where she was. At one point it seemed to her that she was back in Harmony, in the house she shared with Emma. She heard her voice, the lilting English accent calling out her name. And she heard other voices, too. The voices of children. But it was Emma's voice that came most clearly to her, telling her it was time to eat, and then she was supping on roast beef and Yorkshire pudding and Emma's plum cake. The men were there, too, clapping for her and singing in a chorus. The hired men. Jacob and Soffit and Marley and Thomas and all the others. All singing and clapping and calling to her and she was dancing and spinning, spinning and dancing, only it was the house and the faces of the men that spun about her while she stood fixed and gazing at the whirling world and then she lost a sense of that world and all others and slipped into deepest blackness.

When she awoke it was dark. A darkness unrelieved. She longed for a lamp to cast light upon her surroundings. From the corner of the room came a steady scratching noise. The sound of mice or rats. The dog lay next to her, its face touching her shoulder. She spoke its name. The name she had given it that morning near the cave. And she felt its feathered tail stir across the floor. The dog rose to its feet and licked her face and the warmth of its tongue felt good against her cold flesh. She managed to roll to one side and crawl to the door and look out. The night was clear, the stars were strung across the sky, broken and scattered flecks of light running across the heavens. She could see the horses standing in the corral, blanketed in the light of the moon. By pulling herself across the floor she managed to reach the saddlebags and the canteen and she drank some water, taking short gulps and swallowing with pain, and then she put her head down on the saddlebags and slept.

In the morning she felt able to stand and she made her way outside in the weak gray light and turned the horses out of the corral and drove them into the field bordered by a fence made of stones and left them to graze. She built a fire on the ground and heated water in her tin cup and gathered leaves from an ephedra bush growing nearby and made herself a weak cup of Mormon tea which she sipped while warming herself at the fire. Then she ate. She ate the last of the jerked meat and cornmeal boiled together and gave a portion to the dog. Throughout the afternoon she slept while her clothes warmed in the sun. In the evening she felt strong enough to gather more wood for a fire. Before dark she caught up the horses and penned them in the corral. The red mare and the yellow gelding looked rested, but Vittick was restless and appeared thin. Her hooves had broken up and she seemed listless and poor. She passed her hands over the mare and spoke to her and then she walked out into the fields and gathered more corn, making several trips to the corral. She left the horses penned for the night. In the morning, still weak, and with a pain coursing through her head, she saddled the red mare, and leading Vittick and the yellow horse, she set off once more.

In the settlement of Scipio she spent the last of the money that Farley had given her on supplies, buying hard bread and jerked meat and a small bottle of whiskey. Two days later she dropped over the rim of the Utah Valley and three days after that she rode down the main street of Corinne and drew up before the squat low building in the fading evening light. Farley came out and stood looking at her. When he saw her condition he helped her down off the horse.

She leaned on the railing while he pulled off the saddles, first from the red horse and then the yellow, and these he left on the ground while he led all three horses to the wattled corral and turned them loose. He returned to find her sunk to the ground, her arms around the dog and her face buried in its fur. He helped her to her feet and led her inside a small dark cabin and eased her onto a bed. Kneeling down he removed her boots and then he swung her legs up on the mattress and covered her with a quilt.

She wept. He sat by her side holding her hand and she wept openly and freely. Every once in a while he took the edge of the quilt and dried her eyes and nose but he did not try to speak to her, nor could he see her face clearly in the darkness.

After a while he stood and crossed the room and lit an oil lamp. A cat slid past him and leapt upon the table where the lamp sat and he said, Get down from there and pushed the cat to the floor. He drew up a chair and sat beside her, staring at her face. Her eyes were open but fixed on the ceiling and she seemed not to know he was there. The dog whined at the door and for a while this was the only sound, mournful whimperings issuing now and then from beyond the closed door.

She spoke something to him, words he didn't catch, and he leaned closer and said, What?

Let the dog in, she mumbled.

The dog came to the bed and leapt up and settled by her side, holding its head aloft, its half-white, half-black face turned to hers and motionless, its gaze fixed upon her.

That's the damnedest-looking dog, he said.

Nero.

Nero?

That's her name. She lifted her hand and stroked the dog's head and then let it drop heavily to her side.

Nero? Ain't that a man's name? What's the point of naming a bitch Nero?

What's the point of any of it? she replied.

You've had a rough go of it, haven't you?

He used to say every dog'll have its day and every bitch two afternoons. But he never got his two afternoons, did he?

I don't reckon I know what you're talking about.

I don't expect you do.

I'm going to get you something to eat and then you're going to sleep.

I saw my boy, you know.

I never knew you to have a boy.

Two. Two boys and a girl. Albert and Sam and Belle.

He did not know what to say to this and so he said nothing.

He don't look a thing like me. He looks just like his father.

He put his hand on her forehead and the dog let out a low and menacing growl.

Shut up, he said to the dog. I ain't gonna hurt her. First damned dog I ever let up on my bed anyway.

How long have you been running this fever?

She shook her head.

Think on it. How long since you took sick?

There was a storm. It snowed. I got wet and took the chill.

I'm going for the doctor. Will you be all right til I get back?

Do you think this will be the end of it?

You ain't that sick I don't believe.

I mean the end to . . .

To what?

All of it that started at the meadow . . .

I don't see that it makes much difference now, does it?

I'm afraid of meeting him again.

Meeting who?

Lee. I mean on the other side.

I figure you got enough to think about without worrying about that.

I do worry about it though. I think about it. How we were sealed to each other to be raised up in the fullness of time, all his wives together with him, as rulers of our own planet.

Jesus Christ, he muttered. I heard it all now. Would you just quit thinking and try to rest while I fetch the doctor?

She passed the week in grave illness. Sometimes she was lucid and calm and other times she spoke nonsense and thrashed about the bed, throwing off the covers and calling for someone named Emma. He had a hard time getting the dog to leave her side. It seemed to trust no one but her, and not until the need to relieve itself sent it outdoors was he finally able to shut the dog out and even then she woke full of worry and asked that he let it back in.

At the beginning of the second week she had improved enough to sit up in bed and eat by herself. The color returned to her cheeks and the doctor no longer stopped to look in on her each evening. He washed her clothes and dried them in the sun and laid them over the end of the bed and one morning she got up and dressed and sat outside in the shade of the ramada where she could see the horses in the corral. Where she could watch them scratching each other's backs and dozing on their feet. Sometimes she made her way slowly to the rail and studied the mare and felt relieved to see that she looked better.

One afternoon a man came to see her, an editor from the East who was staying at the Hotel Criterion and who had heard about the wife of John D. Lee. He said he wished to interview her for his paper. When she discovered his purpose she asked him to go away but the man was persistent and after a while she found herself answering his questions, sitting outside in the shade of the ramada with a shawl wrapped around her shoulders. In the beginning it was easy.

He asked where she was born and she said, Australia. I was born the thirtieth of May, 1849, in Adelaide.

That makes you twenty-seven years of age now?

I reckon it does.

Where was your mother born?

In England.

And your father?

He was born in England, too, but I know little of his history. He died when I was two years old in a drowning accident. My mother was pregnant at the time with my younger brother, David.

What brought your mother to America?

I never asked her that. I know that she settled in the gold fields of California and there she met and married my stepfather, John Phillips. Eventually they joined the Mormons and moved to Utah and settled in Beaver.

And that is where you meet John D. Lee?

Yes.

How old were you when you married him?

I was thirteen.

I was told that you were his nineteenth wife. Is that true?

He only had eight wives when I married him. The others had left.

At the time you married Lee, did you know about the massacre at
the meadow?

Everyone knew. Everyone who lived thereabouts.

And still you agreed to be his wife?

I did not know his part in it.

Did he ever talk about the massacre with you?

He talked of it all the time, especially later when he could see that
they intended to make him the goat. He always said that if Brigham
tried to lay the blame on him he would see to it that the saddle got put
on the right horse.

Meaning?

Meaning, I suppose, that he would tell who had really ordered the
deed.

Why do you think he went to his death rather than "put the saddle
on the right horse," as you say?

Because he loved him. Because he always loved him more than any
other man, even after he sold him down the river.

Loved . . . who?

Brigham, who else?

Did you love him?

No, I never loved Brigham. I thought him pompous and conniv-
ing and full of a loathsome self-interest.

That's not what I meant. Were you in love with John D. Lee?

She looked away, toward the corral, where Vittick and the red mare
were stretched out flat in the sun. The yellow horse stood beneath the
overhanging roof of a shed, its eyes closed.

Yes, I reckon I did love him. Once. Long ago. He wasn't a hard
man to love. That's what people ought to know.

The editor laughed. With all those wives I don't find that difficult to believe.

She shot him a cold look. He died a man, don't forget that. You ought to ask yourself if you could do the same.

He also killed people. Innocent women and children. Helpless wounded men. People he'd tricked into trusting him.

I don't believe anybody knows for sure who did the killing that day.

It's said that just before he was executed he confessed to killing five people.

He wasn't the first and he won't be the last to kill for righteousness sake, to slaughter innocents out of some misbegotten notion of obedience or revenge.

Then you believe he and the others were ordered to do what they did by some higher authority, like Brigham himself?

She smiled at him, a thin, tight smile meant to convey her bitter feelings. I believe the whole kit and caboodle were in on it, she said. I believe that wagon train was doomed long before it reached the meadow. But things didn't go as planned. Maybe they had meant for the Indians to do the deed for them, but when that failed, something had to be done.

Something had to be done? But why?

You're asking me questions I can't answer, she said tiredly. And I think I've said more than I ever wanted to about any of this.

You know your husband has become one of the most famous men in the land. His name is known in all parts of the country. How does it feel to be the widow of such a notorious criminal?

It don't feel like anything.

When was the last time you saw your husband?

I don't believe it matters. But it was some time ago.

In all the newspaper accounts, it's said that only three wives remained loyal to him to the end—Emma, Rachel, and Sarah Caroline. Does this mean you decided long ago to abandon him to his misfortune?

Things just took their course. I can't say more than that.

Do you blame Brigham for his death?

I don't reckon there's much point in it.

But do you blame him?

Yes, I do. I believe it was on his orders that the jury voted to convict. After all, they were all Mormons, weren't they?

Of course many would agree with you. It's generally believed that Brigham ordered people to testify against your husband at his second trial in order to assure a conviction, and that the jury, composed as it was entirely of members of the priesthood, was told to find him guilty. Why do you think this was done?

She stared at her hands for a moment and then she looked up at the clean-shaven editor in his pressed black suit and said, Because I think Brigham thought it better to sacrifice one man rather than let a whole people dwindle in contempt and disbelief. Even if that man was his adopted son, one who done his bidding his whole life.

If you met Brigham now and he wanted to shake your hand, what would you say to him?

I'd say, let a dog shake its own paw.

What will you do now?

I believe I'll go to bed, she said. I'm feeling awful tired.

The editor thanked her for speaking to him and she said, That's all right, and then she rose and turned her back on him and made her way slowly to the cabin and once inside she crawled into bed, calling the dog to her, and rolled on her side and looked out the window, out to where the sun settled on the lake, breaking apart there in blisters of light, carried upon ripple after ripple toward the barren waiting shore.

————

TWO DAYS later she walked out to the corral and said goodbye to the yellow horse. She stood for a long while, stroking his neck and scratching his cheek. She told him he had earned his name, that he was as lucky as they come, or at least he'd been so for her. She took from her pocket a lump of sugar and laid it in her palm and flattened it, offering it to the horse who took it up with its rubbery lips and tossed its head in pleasure as it closed its teeth around the sugar and bit down. Then she caught up her horses and led them to the stable and brushed them down and checked their feet before saddling up the red mare and filling her saddlebags with the supplies she'd bought earlier.

The parting wasn't easy. She and Farley stood before each other and she tried to find the words to thank him, to express what she felt, but he cut her short. He said there were acts performed out of a pure-ness of feeling and those acts required no thanks for they arose out of desire and desire alone. He told her if she ever needed him she could rely on him and he also asked her to be careful on her journey home because he hoped to see her again and he would feel cheated if that were not the case.

They embraced, and then she mounted the red mare and he handed her the lead rope affixed to the gray and she laid the reins against the mare's neck and put her heels to her and the mare stepped smartly forward and the gray followed. She headed out in the morning light without once looking back until she reached the slough at the far edge of town, where the dead animals rotted in the emerald water, and there she stopped and stood in the stirrups and turned and looked back from where she had just come and she saw him standing there still, looking after her, a big man in a smooth-domed hat with a beard darkening his face, and she lifted her hand and waved to him and he waved back, his arm moving slowly through the air as if in a dream, and then she turned the mare to the north and clucked to her and gave the rope a tug and setting her haunches deep against the cantle, she rode away at a rolling canter.

The land before her glowed yellow beneath the gold of the sun. She imagined that in this world there were sins so great they could never be forgotten nor forgiven, and she wondered if these were the same sins men pondered over and for which they sent forth their punishments or if these evident evils were not in fact the lesser crimes and that what lay in the hearts of men, the blackness undetected there and therefore overlooked and indulged, was not the stuff of greater malignance. She had known the goodness in the world and she had also known the depravity, often resident within the same man, and she knew that what could live in one man could easily live within another, given a small turn of fate.

When the editor had said to her, How long since you last saw your husband? she had been startled by the word because she had long since ceased thinking of him as such.

Long ago, she'd replied.

Long, long ago.

He had sat in the kitchen that day, wearing a defeated look, his face unshaven and drawn and his clothes filthy from his long journey, worn down by the night he'd spent sleeping in the wagon drawn up before his mansion where his older wives had locked their doors against him, a broken man, cut off from the church he loved, shunned by the Prophet he revered, fearful for his future.

I done the best I can here, he said, sitting at the table, looking so wounded, glancing first at her, standing there at the window, feeling sick from the child growing within her, and then he'd turned toward Emma who seemed almost as anguished as he. And all she could say was, I don't know how I got into this. I don't think I got a lick of sense. I just don't know how I got in this.

All things pass. That's what Emma used to say when things got bad. This too shall pass. And it had. And it always would.

She set herself a northerly course as the sun disappeared behind clouds that blew in suddenly, turning the day gray and overcast and cool. She felt some pressure in the world, as if the leaden sky were too large and heavy for what lay beneath it, a vast darkening dome, lowery and weighted with heavy flat-bottomed clouds lined up over the mountains like frigates on a nonexistent sea. In the distance she could see the wispy curtains of walking rain pushing across the snow-laden ridges and darkening the sloping gray foothills. It is here, then, she thought, as the storm moved toward her. And yet she did not even mind the thought of rain. The dog trotted ahead, its square white rump traveling slightly sideways, its head low to the ground, as the first drops began to fall.

PART FOUR

Rachel

Moenabba, Arizona Territory, July 1, 1877. Morning clear, windy. My first day back here at the farm. This morning I planted some beets, onions, radish, lettuce, peas. About midday the Indian named Shew came in search of a cow but did not find her. Where is Yawgatts? he asked, and it fell to me to give him the news. He is gone, I said, they have killed him. When? he asked. Four months ago I told him. It has taken me that long to return. He put his hand to my shoulder, meaning to console me, then invited me to the villages to one of their Cocheenas, a performance according to their tradition and kind of worship. I declined, but thanked him anyway. Evening I read to the children and caught up my journal while they were in bed. I am as forlorn as I have ever been. But the spirits have manifest themselves to me this evening and I believe it will only be a matter of time before he, too, comes. Behind this shanty the cliffs rise like red walls, and in the rocks I sometimes see angels. I see the crucified form of Jesus and I behold the patriarchs and prophets of old. There are spirits all around me, I know. I feel their presence most acutely at the end of day, when the setting sun casts its light against the red cliffs, giving the shadows the shapes and forms of wingless angels and floating heads. Sometimes I see my mother in the stones. Or my sister Aggatha. Or the profile of the Prophet Joseph. And sometimes I see nothing but the cliffs, crumbling and being eaten away, stone by stone.

JULY 3. Hot and windy. I planted some more peas and by the help of Frank and a Piede passing by I made a shade on the N.W. side of the shanty to keep the sun off us. Belle and Joe are quite unwell, both down with the gripe. I gave them each a dose of the pills and wrote in my journal in the evening. Frank is a great help to me but manifests a much troubled spirit, the result, I know, of the loss of his father.

JULY 4. This morning about 9 a.m. we had a visit from a man of the Oraibi tribe named Tow-wow-we-win and his squaw, She-ma. They had heard the news about Father. Very solemnly they laid a fine melon at my feet and said, Kiwi avut, and motioned toward the children, pointing at Frank and Belle and Joe, and then brought their fingers to their mouths, encouraging them to eat. Lolomy, lolomy, they cried as they rode away, good, good. What do they mean, good?

JULY 6. The dam has washed out in our absence and Mr. Winburn made no effort to save it. Thus I can no longer rely on the ditches to bring us water. We need several men to help us rebuild the dam. Mr. Winburn, who is old and shows little inclination toward hard labor, is largely useless. I said to Frank, now what are we to do, without the dam? We will water with buckets, Frank said, and that is what we have done today. We arose before dawn to escape the heat. Shew arrived to help us. Frank and Shew and Mahala carried the buckets. Belle and little Joseph and I refilled them. After Mr. Lee's death, Nancy and Alnora said to me, you must come and live with one of us now that Father's gone. You cannot expect to manage that farm by yourself. But I have no wish to live with my married daughters, nor do I care to return to the upper settlements where so much bitterness still exists and where my children would surely be made to suffer insults. This is my land, this farm here in Moenabba—mine and Mr. Winburn's. Mr. Lee deeded me his share, just as he left the ferry and Lonely Dell to Emma, and the house in Panguitch to Sarah Caroline. But he told me I'd have to keep proving the land out or they'd take it from me. So that's what I am doing. Proving it out. Without the dam, and in spite of our late planting. We hand-water only the strongest trees now. The three pear trees and the row of apples and the grape vines Mr. Lee set out himself when he was free on bail last summer.

JULY 20. Morning clear, hot. I hoed up a devil out of the garden this morning. What will become of us now, I wonder. I do know that Jesus is coming and that the blood is flowing and the iniquity is running high and there is no end to man's sinning. Do they know that they have destroyed not only a man but an entire family? And, if they knew, would they care?

JULY 24. No one to celebrate with today and so Pioneer Day goes unmarked by us. We are the only whites for miles around. The red men hereabouts have always been Mr. Lee's friends, and I am trusting they will continue to be ours as well. Yet I am often afraid in the night. I have come to feel the fear as a sickness in my brain, one that can only be cured by the light of dawn, when the sun rises and strikes the cliffs and the spirits again emerge from the stones and take their shapes anew. These red hills are called the Echo Cliffs and they are well named, for I often feel them seconding my existence, returning the ring of a hammer, or a child's voice. The climate here this time of year is most intolerable. It's so hot by midday that the eggs curdle in the coop if I don't collect them early. We spend the afternoons in the root cellar, resting from our morning labors. I have kept the squash and melons alive, but the wind has took the corn, all except that which Mr. Winburn planted early. He is a trial to me. Yesterday he said, Don't think that your troubles have ended with your husband's death. His ignominy will dog you all the days of your life, and all the days of your children's. I am not looking for rewards here on earth, I told him, nor have I ever expected an easy passage. I have set my sights on High and the Paradise I know awaits me there. That's a good thing, he replied and laughed, looking around at the shanty and hills of burning sand, cause you sure ain't agoing to find it here.

JULY 30. Hot, no wind to speak of. My health is still enfeebled by the harsh conditions I endured in prison. At first the warden said, no, Mr. Lee, you may not have your wife with you. What do you think this is, an inn? A house of pleasure? But Mr. Lee proved my worth to him. She can wash, he said. She can clean and sweep and wash the other prisoners' clothes—for a small fee, of course—and she can help madam in the kitchen—she takes no extra space. We can share my bed if only we might have the storeroom to ourselves—it locks, no chance of an escape. And think of the savings to you—in work, I mean. Thus I was permitted to spend much of the last year with him in prison, though at a great cost. My health suffered dearly. I have not been able to rid my hands of the shaking, nor can I sleep fully through a night, and I continue to be plagued by troubling dreams.

AUG. 2. Morning still and lowery. A bow in the wind, indications of rain. At daybreak I attended to the watering, then weeded awhile. I rested all afternoon. In the evening an Oraibi named Taltee came and was very friendly. He asked about Father and I gave him the news and invited him to stay. Packee, I said, kot-taite-nashi—come in and sit down and eat. Mr. Lee taught me to be friendly to these natives, for what we do not give freely they will steal. Taltee ate most of the melon I had picked and wrapped in burlap and set in the cellar to chill. What now will I give my children for supper? We are sorely short of food until our crops come on.

AUG. 3. Evening cloudy and windy. I had troubling dreams. Just before daybreak I was aroused from sleep by the barking of a wolf about twenty steps away from the shanty. He evidently saw the cat and was trying to catch her. I jumped out with Mr. Lee's Henry rifle and met the cat bristled up in fear. I fired into the darkness and at the sound, the barking ceased.

AUG. 4. This morning Belle and Mahala and I gave the trees a good watering. Mahala, my Lamanite girl, is now nineteen. Shew returned and brought me part of a deer. He touched his belly and said, Pow-ah, and through signs made it known that Yawgatt's wo-a-tah would not go hungry. And so I am to be beholden to this Remnant of Israel for the sustenance of the day. Fixed a mess of green beans for dinner and a venison stew. Belle retched hers up, being unused to such rich food. She is a frail child, a condition I attribute to the weakness of her mother, Ann. At times she asks for her mother, and I am forced to say, Forget her, child. She is lost to us, she has gone beyond our reach. The child then looks at me with such wondering eyes I must avert my own. She says she misses her aunt Emma and her brother Sam, and asks if she might be allowed to return to the river to be with them but I tell her she is to live with me now, and Frank and Joe and Mahala. It was not easy for me to gain Emma's consent to take the child but now that I have her, I have no intention of giving her up. I need all the help I can get here, and even a pair of small hands is better than none at all.

AUG. 5. Morning pleasant. This morning, as yesterday, we cut some corn old Mr. Winburn had thought to plant early and we put it out to dry, then went to irrigating turnips and sowed some more. It commenced raining a little while I wrote in my journal. Soon Chief Tuba arrived with his wife, Telly, and an elderly Oraibi and two squaws, one of them a sister to Tuba's wife. They came to mourn my husband. Said he was a friend to the Indians. Said the men that kilt him would be punished and offered to strike the blow themselves. Too late, I said, too late. They embraced me, one by one, and said, henega, which means friend. Finally I got them on their animals and they left but not before inviting us to visit them soon and eat melons and green corn. The blackbirds and wolves have been very destructive on the corn. I follow them and shoot them with the Henry rifle. This forenoon I repaired some fences and then wrote a letter to Emma at the ferry which I hope to send to her with the next traveler passing by.

AUG. 14. Morning cool. Chasing birds off the corn, then boiling and drying corn. Evening a light shower, a blessing to these crops. About 1 p.m. a Mr. De Freeze, agent for the Oraibis, and three of his associates arrived. They felt to warn me the Navajos had conducted raids to the south of here and advised I watch my stock at night. These Gentile men take me for a fool. For my part, I wish to see the backs of them. They said they were agoing to establish an agency at the Moencroppa and take the waters of the five streams and bring it to this valley and bring different bands of natives to this point and let them farm here. I pointed to the creek and said, You'll not be taking my water. They said they had heard that I was intending to remove my family and make another place for them and they thought it was a wise choice for this was no place for a widow. I told them they had heard it wrong. As they rode away I heard one of them mutter, Poor old crone, she looks like she's been through it, don't she? I have had my share of trials, it's true, and no doubt they've left their mark. Once, during our long days in prison, when Mr. Lee was ill and we had no money with which to purchase the needed medicine, in desperation I concluded to attempt to raise the necessary funds. I left him sitting in the sun in our room within the jail and set out on foot for the house of James Carrigan, the husband of my grandniece Henrietta. After walking three miles through the deep snow in the dead of winter, I arrived at their door and knocked. When I told them the purpose of my visit, they turned me out. They said they would give me no money, not one cent. It was my misfortune to have cast my fate with a murderer, and if I chose to stop with him in that damned old penitentiary to care for him, they must drive me from their door, for he was nothing, they said, but an old gut and a disgrace to his family. This was a cold reception to give an aging aunt, but I drew myself up and said that I was glad to learn their feelings and if they would pardon me for intruding on their time, I would see that I never disgraced them again with my presence. This said, I left their house, but I had not got far before they turned their dogs on me. One was a cur, and I was able to subdue it with kind words. But the other was a bulldog, surly and fierce. I turned upon him with a heavy stick that happened to be near, and as he lunged at me, I caught him alongside the head and knocked him down. But he recovered and came at me again, more enraged than ever, and I swung at him again, and again, until the blood of that dog covered my coat and he lay stunned at my feet. When I returned to the prison, Mr. Lee took one look at me and said, Dear Lord, what happened to you? I didn't get the money, I said. And then I took off my coat and set about washing and repairing it.

AUG. 24. This morning the boys and I set off to the upper fields to irrigate and when I returned I found Tuba and Taltee and some other Indians had arrived and suffered their animals to run on my crop and damage it much. Is this how you treat Yawgatt's namattau? I asked. They seemed much chastised and said they would send me a part of a chee vaat, or goat, to make up for their trespass. My Doll Belle mare very uneasy, whinering for her mate, Sir Henry Belle, which Frank has taken on an excursion to the San Francisco Mountains to see if he might procure us some venison. I had to take a dose of pills tonight, a touch of the flux. Earlier I shot us a fine rabbit and we had a mess of first-dug potatoes and the rabbit stewed up together. Tuba and Mrs. Tuba stayed on for dinner, eating up much of the food I had hoped to stretch to several meals for my children.

AUG. 25. Frank met with no luck in the San Franciscos and returned without venison. So Mr. Winburn took the boys and started for the river this morning to see if they might not get some beeves from Emma to see us through our shortage. I am now left alone to take care of the crop and watch over the animals. Belle and little Joe are suffering again from the flux and not much help, but Mahala has worked hard to help me keep the crops watered. My red brethren said today that I looked lonesome and promised they would come often and keep me company till my boys got back. I plucked some melons and

Tuba gathered some green beans. Mrs. Tuba fixed a dinner as I went to irrigating. She served up a respectable meal of succotash of beans and corn and bacon cooked together. I was hungry and the food was tasty and well got. After dinner Mrs. Tuba washed up the dishes while I put the children to bed. Then they left saying, we'll come back tomorrow. And so I am left without even the Remnant of Israel to provide me company through this long night. Mr. Lee left me his diaries, however, and I read in them some tonight to bring his spirit close.

AUG. 28. Quite unwell throughout the night with more flux. Mixed ground charcoal with warmed milk and drank it down which helped some. Today I again hired Shew to irrigate and a native boy to help me cut and shuck the corn. I made a stew of blackbirds that I shot in the corn, some of them fat as butter.

AUG. 30. Awoke with my mind much possessed by night visions. I dreamed I had a visit from Mr. Lee. He told me to be happy and to do the best I could. Wept with joy at our reunion. About 10 a.m. a Pah-Ute and his squaw named Pocky came from Moencroppa with a buck-skin to trade. I gave him twenty rounds of cartridges and took the skin to make the girls some shoes. Evening showery, light here but heavy toward the Kaibabs. A party of Saints arrived about sunset, all immigrant families called to settle the Little Colorado, among them some of Mr. Lee's bitterest enemies, including Bros. Dalton, Blackburn, and Riddle. They had the gall to ask of me if there was anything they might do to improve upon my welfare, and I said, You can shew me your backs and be gone. Such men disgrace the faith and the names of their fathers. Before they left they gave me the news that Brigham has died. He expired two days ago, from unknown causes. Instantly I thought of my husband's prophecy. Before his death, he predicated that Brigham would not outlast him six months. And now his word has come true.

SEPT. 1. Quite cool through the past night. Before sunrise I was hurried out of bed by shouts of alarm from Old Bremer and his tribe that their foe was near. Your foe is not my foe, I said, and held up a poyoo to warn them off. It is not that I am brave, I thought, as I watched them ride away. Rather, I do not mind the thought of death if it will join me to Mr. Lee again. Looking out later, I discovered a hawk perched on top of a dead cottonwood tree some fifty paces distant from my chickens. Seizing the Henry I brought the intruder lifeless to the ground. Then I put the corn to boil while I irrigated some turnips, potatoes, and melons.

SEPT. 2. Today with the help of Belle I picked, strung, and scalded about one and one-half bushels of green snap beans and put them out to dry. Worked all day at it. Sat up with Belle and little Joe stringing beans by moonlight till about 10 p.m. Once again Belle wanted to know about her mother. She understands her father has gone to the Celestial Kingdom and she will not see him again until the Day of Reckoning, but what about her mother? she asked. When will she see her again? I could not lie to the child. I cannot promise you will meet her here on earth before the Second Coming, I said, nor do I know whether she will be raised up in the fullness of time to take her place among us. When is the Second Coming? she asked. I told her that before the century ended the Lord would come again and sweep away the iniquitous and restore his reign on earth. How old will I be then? she wanted to know. I said, well, you are nine now, and there are twenty-three years left until the end of the century, so I reckon you will be thirty-two when the Lord arrives. This seemed to satisfy her and she fell off her questioning and went to bed.

SEPT. 6. A little after sunrise, as I was turning out the water, who should I see but Taltee the Oraibi and his son, Alcalda, from Moencroppa. Taltee seemed chapfallen. I asked him what tidings he had. Not good, he said. He informed me that all the Oraibis had left Moencroppa except Tuba and Telly, and himself and his son, and gone to the villages on the mesas and that Tuba wanted for me and my children to move up with them for safety because the Navajoes were not to be trusted. They had stole a band of horses from the She'beets and killed several men in the ensuing skirmish and if they saw me in an unprotected condition they might make a raid upon my farm. I told him I would not run away but stay here and tend my crops and wait for Frank and Joe and Mr. Winburn to return from the river. And thus said, I returned to work in the fields. The Indian Shew stayed on to help me. I gave him dinner and a half bar of soap and made him wash.

SEPT. 7. Lowery. About eight my Belle mare set to whinering and I looked up to see the approach of my sons Frank and Joe along with Mr. Winburn and Heber Dalton, my son-in-law. We wept at our reunion and rejoiced together that my prayers had been answered and my family almost miraculously preserved and brought through their journey safely. I acknowledge the hand of the Lord in the affair. One ox was lost in the crossing of the Colorado, swept away by the current, but the boys and the wagon came through fine as well as the two beeves they brought with them. They also brought me news of Emma. As I feared, she is being much influenced by forces to sell her part of the ferry. The church wishes to acquire it from her to facilitate the building up of the kingdom in the Arizona Territory. Mr. Winburn tells me she is often seen with a Gentile miner named Frank French. And this with Mr. Lee not yet six months gone. She has a history of seeking the solace of men, whether it be Matt Carney, or the photographer, Mr. Fennemore, or Wells Spicer, who once got her to part with supplies and horses for a misbegotten mining adventure, a move that much upset Mr. Lee. This happened while we were away in prison. I fear that she is making a shipwreck of her faith, just like Ann did. About the two of them there always hovered an element of the unnatural. I am much comforted to have Mr. Winburn and the boys with me again. For the past nights the fear has burned so unceasingly in my brain and now, with their return, I feel I shall be able to drive it away. We will look to God if the Navajoes remain hostile. Before he was taken to the meadow for his execution, Mr. Lee said to me, Fear not, Rachel, for my spirit will be with you in the morn and in the eve and attend you throughout all your days. He said nothing about the nights, however. And it is in the darkness that I feel him so utterly lost to me, and my own welfare so precarious. I would trade all my meager worldly goods to lay one more night with him.

SEPT. 13. Today I fortified the chicken house and made arrangements with my son-in-law, Heber Dalton, to travel with him by horseback to the Black Falls to gather saleratus, leaving Belle and little Joe in the care of old Mr. Winburn. Frank and Mahala are not about, having gone to Moencroppa for wood. Heber and I traveled all day over a barren land of sand and rugged rocks to reach the Little Colorado, a distance of twenty-five miles, where we camped. The river was up and running red. Here we gathered saleratus the next morning and found an encampment where the Arizona missionaries had stayed and left behind items to lighten their load. We got about seventy-five pounds coarse salt and a jar of nails and some other useful things. On our return we discovered a herd of antelope playing in the valley. While we stood looking at them, one approached and came within a hundred yards of us. We both fired at it and it fell. Gutted it and loaded it in on Heber's mule. Traveled five miles down a valley and camped among a cedar grove. Good grass. Tied up at dark lest our animals would leave for water. Heber was curious to know more about the time I spent with Mr. Lee in the territorial prison. How did you endure such close quarters with that most profane, vile, low, vulgar, filthy element of society? he asked. I told him of the trials we endured, and the abuse, not only from the other prisoners but from our warders. The warden's wife, Mrs. Burgher, took delight in humiliating me by reporting what the other prisoners said about my relations with Mr. Lee. Once she even took away a blanket I'd received in payment for washing and mending I'd done. Another time, when a box of apples arrived and the warden encouraged me to help myself to one or two, his wife had snatched my hand away and instead thrust a half-eaten apple into my palm and said, This will do for you. Is it true, Heber asked, that people came from far and wide to gain an interview with Father? 'Twas so, I said, remembering the learned gentlemen and ladies of the East who had arrived, anxious to meet the notorious man who all the papers called The Great Terror of the West, only to remark after their interview with him that they could find nothing fearful or terrific about him, only a kindly man. Even a Dr. Winslow from Boston, who took a phrenological observation of Mr. Lee's head at the conclusion of his visit, could find nothing amiss. He has not the head of a murderer, he said.

SEPT. 16. At daylight we were on the move and after traveling down a smooth wash to the distance of fifteen miles we nooned and baked bread, then started for home. Traveled to the Moencroppa and let our animals rest some two hours. Directly we started out again it began to rain and continued with us home, drenching us to the skin. Through the night we had a thunderstorm, the heaviest of the season.

SEPT. 19. Today I righted and bound up my shucks of corn. An Indian came about 10 a.m. and reported the official in charge of the agency, a Professor Thompson, is trying to persuade the Oraibis and Pah-Utes to drive the Mormons—meaning myself and my family— off this land and not suffer us to settle here, for the Gentiles are said to want to build houses near the springs, but Tuba replied that he wanted Yawgatt's widow to live there and would not drive me off. Thus do I owe thanks to the Lord's Battle Axes, these dark-skinned Remnants of Israel, for my continued occupation of these poor lands.

SEPT. 21. This morning animals on my crops again. Heber's mules almost ruined my squashes and I gave him such a load of chin candy as to make his ears turn red. Last night I dreamed of Mr. Lee again. He appeared much diminished to me. Fencing continued in earnest in an attempt to keep off the animals. Today put up a barrel of pickles.

SEPT. 25. All hands again put to fencing. Killed an old hen that no longer laid and stewed it with potatoes for supper. Heber assisted me today with the work. Full of more questions about our life at the penitentiary. I drew a picture for him of our extreme poverty and deprivation during those long months, and told him how that dirty blackhound guard named Griffin abused me and tricked me into doing his washing and never paid a cent for it. How the warden's wife talked insulting to me every chance she got. And how, when they took the stove from our room, we could not leave our bed for the cold. What I did not tell him was that we often awoke in the night to tell each other our dreams, and in those sweet hours, how Mr. Lee would call me his truest friend, his kind nurse, and his nearest and dearest wife.

SEPT. 27. Weather fine, rather warm. About 7 a.m. Lehi Smithson rode up, having swam his horse over the Colorado and traveled from the ferry here in twenty-four hours. He reported Pres. Young's death. I told him I'd already received the news, and that I could mourn the loss of the Prophet, but not the man. He said he had been in St. George for the dedication of the new temple several months ago. Said the Prophet was ailing badly from gout even then. He had grown so stout and so stove up that he could no longer walk about much. A special chair had to be constructed to hold his bulk for the dedication ceremony and he was carried in this chair from room to room by four strong men, like a prince of India. Upon hearing this I said to Smithson, Enough, I wished to hear no more of Brigham, whose last words to me were that I should not fear for my husband's life, for as long as he had any say, he would not let him die. But die he has, and all know it was Brigham's wish to make my husband the goat and be done with the affair. If only

Mr. Lee had made good on his threat to put the saddle on the right horse, perhaps he would be alive today. Still, the Old Blackheart Brig is the one lying deep down in the ground now, while I feel sure my husband has already ascended to his throne on high.

SEPT. 29. Working on the fencing. Nothing of consequence happened today.

OCT. 5. Light front, heavier toward the Moencroppa. Before breakfast, Frank killed three chicken hawks, which has reduced their number further as he killed some fifteen over the last month. Am I as good a shot as Father? he asked. Very near, I said. Heber took little Joe and rode up to Tuba's to borrow a hand stone to grind some corn native-style in order to make mush while I done some writing. Mr. Winburn cut his foot badly with the ax this morning, which will disable him from working for some time. He is an ill-tempered old man whose presence I tolerate only until I can see a way to buy him out and assume his portion of this farm. Telly and Shew came on a visit. Brought us some melons on a jack. Wind blew a tornado. They helped us winnow up the beans.

OCT. 9. Gathering in beans. Shew and family gone on a visit to Navajo settlements to trade baskets made of skunkbrush for some blankets. Mr. Winburn's foot has begun to inflame. I dressed it and applied axle grease and carbolic acid, which seemed to allay the inflammation some. Weather very cool and uncomfortable. About sunset I looked up to see the cliffs aflame with light. And there in the rocks I beheld the face of our Lord Jesus, gazing down at me.

OCT. 16. A killing frost. The first frost of note. Belle is the strangest child. She wanted to know today if Jesus was a woman. Why he has such long hair. He is not a woman, I assured her, for women cannot be gods. But Aunt Emma read me stories from her book of myths and in them there were woman gods, she answered. That is a mistake, I said. All gods are men. But we can be their helpers. She frowned at me and said that when she prayed she hoped a woman god would hear her prayers. Don't be a ninny, I said, and with that our discussion of godhood ended. I fear Emma has implanted the worst notions in this child's head.

OCT. 17. We hauled in our squashes and native pumpkins, seven loads in all. All hands at this work. About noon, Levi Smithson returned from the Little Colorado and handed me a letter from Emma. Said he forgot to give it to me on his way through earlier in the week. I am suspicious of this statement. The letter looks to me to have been opened and resealed. It is my suspicion that he purposely carried the letter to the elders at the settlements on the Little Colorado and it was opened there and perused by all in an effort to learn Emma's intentions with regard to the ferry. I copy its contents here:

Sept. 21, 1877
Lonely Dell, Colorado River

My dear Rachel,

I am writing to inquire after your well-being and the health and welfare of your family, especially Little Belle who, as you well know, holds a special place in my affections. Many times I have thought of the day when you and Father left for Moenabba, taking Belle with you. I agreed to let you take her that day because you pressed your case so hard and managed to convince me that since I had four girls and you had none left at home that Belle could be of great use and a comfort to you. Yet not a day has passed since that time that I haven't longed for her company and wished she were with me to remind me of her dear mother. I have had no word of Ann. Have you? I pray that wherever she is, she is happy, and in good health.

As the boys may have told you, I am being pressed hard by certain agents (meaning Brigham's boys) to relinquish control of the ferry to the Church in order that they may use it to further the buildup of the King-

dom in the Arizona and New Mexico Territories. I have been offered a
hundred head of prime beef cattle if I will turn over title to the property
within thirty days. This I am considering doing, for I am worn out from
the effort of sustaining my family in this remote outpost. I once thought life
in Harmony was difficult but it seems a lark now compared to the hardships I have suffered during these last seven years at Lonely Dell. If I am
willing to sell, I am told the cattle can be collected at Willow Springs and
it requires only my signature to effect the transaction. I have made the
acquaintance of a proper gentleman miner named Frank French who has
offered to help me remove my effects and the children from here across the
river and to assist me in collecting the cattle due me. From there we intend
to make our way into New Mexico where I am told the Valley of Taos presents a most attractive prospect for ranching. In any event, should all this
come to pass, I would hope to see you in no more than a few weeks. At that
time I would hope to make a request of you, and that is that you allow
Belle to join me in my new life. She would thrive, I think, in the company
of the twins and the boys and her brother who wishes to be reunited with
her. Most truthfully, Rachel, I feel an obligation to her mother to raise this
child who for all the world feels like one of my very own. As you know, I
nursed her at my own breast from the time she was born. To have her with
me again would help make up for the sadness I feel at not knowing what
has become of her mother.

I hope this letter finds you well and at peace in your heart and mind.

Most respectfully,
Emma

I have no doubt that Brigham's spies have by now telegraphed the contents of this letter and with it the news that Emma intends to sell the
ferry. It is her affair, however, not mine. But if she thinks I will be easily parted from Belle, she is wrong. A woman needs youth about her in
old age, and I am not as young as Emma. Not by a mile. Nor do I forget the name by which I was once known to her and Ann. We will see
who is The Mouse now—who is timid, and who is not.

OCT. 19. Morning more pleasant. Light wind, south. Through the week, heavy wind. Principally from the N.W. and S.E. Frost every night. Mr. Winburn's foot much worse.

OCT. 25. Storm of wind and snow from N.W. Snowed nearly all day but melted almost as fast as it fell. By evening the ground all clear. Belle has been moody and sulky with me. Complains of loneliness and asks again how old she'll be when Jesus comes. Will I be married? she wanted to know. And will my husband also be raised up in the fullness of time? We shall just have to see what sort of a husband you choose, I said. If you marry in the temple and take out your endowments and wear the holy garments of our faith and in every other way live according to Christ's principles during these last days, then perhaps you and your husband will be raised up in exaltation, but if not— Before I could finish my sentence Belle piped up and said, I'd like to marry a blackguard just like Daddy! Who taught you such a term, I asked, and although she was loath to tell me, she finally confessed she'd overheard Levi Smithson talking to Mr. Winburn. Poor child. I instantly disabused her of the notion a blackguard is a good thing to be. Surely this earth is ripening for destruction and men and women are fast turning to idolatry and are substituting man's wisdom for godliness and familiar spirits when such falsehoods are told. I live in dread of the evils that are coming upon the earth but I can do nothing but stand still and seek the salvation of God and trust in Him.

OCT. 26. Clear and calm. Indication of pleasanter weather. Through the week we succeeded in getting nearly all our potatoes in, about fifty bushels. We have eighteen young Bremmer chickens, though it is very cold for them. The Navajos are said to be again conducting raids to the south. Nevertheless we are in the hands of the Lord and all things are promised to work together for the good of those who love and fear God, though why this did not save my husband's life, I do not know.

NOV. 2. Today Frank and Heber finished off the walls of the stone granary and covered about half of it. Several natives brought an ass load of timber from the grove in the canyon above the fields. This is the only oak grove known for a hundred miles. I have promised them ammunition in return for the wood. Later Taltee and four Oraibis came on a visit. I traded them for two well-dressed buckskins. They expressed a desire to have me visit Mrs. Tuba, who is ailing. They also asked when Yawgatt's widow would take another man to her bed and I said I would never marry again. Taltee patted me on the haunches and said, Hovee lolomy cho a vah, meaning I am still good to have connection with, and then grabbed at his pwashe and grinned. I raised the ax and chased them off the place for their impudence. Mr. Winburn still unable to do any labor. His left foot much inflamed from where he cut it with the ax. He's had three bad agues in the last few days. The old man is suffering much. I hope the Lord will have mercy upon him and spare his foot but I fear it may have to come off, though where we would find a doctor to perform such an operation, I do not know.

NOV. 3. Today a cold raw wind. Sent the boy to look for the horses that have wandered off but they were not to be found.

NOV. 4. I borrowed a horse of Tuba's to look for my Doll Belle mare and her mate, Sir Henry Belle. Frank and I doubled up on Tuba's little pony and set off. About noon we struck the tracks where my horses had been lost. We overtook them some eight miles from home, near Tuba's village. A little after dark we reached the village to return the borrowed horse to Tuba who had just reached home. He and his wife embraced me. Had us come in and eat some melons. One of his sons claimed the honor of holding Doll and Sir Henry while Frank and I ate melon. After feasting as long as we could, we prepared to leave. Noticing that I was without a coat, Tuba pulled off his blanket and gave it to me. On the ride home, Frank expressed his sorrow that our name has become such a hiss and a byword throughout the territory. You hold your head up, boy, I said. Be proud to be a Lee. Those others who suffer from stiff-neckedness, don't listen to them. On the Day of Reckoning, you'll see. Our glory will be greater than all the others put together. Reached home about nine in the evening, much tired from the journeying.

NOV. 5. A regular cloudburst at dawn. This morning we moved such things into the shanty as would damage from rain. Cut some wood for kindling. Traded twenty-five pounds of prime Red Top Alfalfa seed to Bro. Lot Smith who stopped here en route to settlements. He gave me a camp kettle, a brace, an auger, and some hinges and screws in return. Where had I come by such top-grade seed, he asked? I told him the story of how Mr. Lee had salvaged the seed from the hay he had been privileged to feed the horse and cow belonging to the penitentiary. You mean your husband worked during his confinement? Oh yes, I said. He was given charge of the cow and the horse, and he also had the privilege of blacking the warden's boots, and in the spring he over-saw the planting of the prison's garden. Bro. Smith shook his head and said, I always did believe that John D. Lee was one of the hardest-working men that ever lived. Now I know that it's true, for what other man would work for his jailers for free? After he had gone, I set to thinking about Mr. Lee. How he had spent so many afternoons sitting in that cold barn, sifting the seed from the hay and carefully filling up the discarded grain sacks with the results of his labor. He believed it would be only a matter of time before he was free again and he could return to this farm and set out his crops. Of the seed he salvaged he said, We'll have us the finest crop of alfalfa in the land—we'll get two, maybe three cuttings a season. But he had never lived to farm again. Instead they tried him a second time and then took him back to the meadow and shot him, like some common criminal. Before they removed him from the prison, Deputy Marshal Stokes had inquired of Mr. Lee if he still wore his endowment robes, and Mr. Lee had answered yes, for he had never ceased believing in the One True Church, even if he had come to despise its leaders.

NOV. 9. Repaired the children's clothes and schooled Belle and little Joe for several hours in the afternoon. Belle a bright child, unquestionably, but possessed of a strange turn of mind. She said to me at bedtime, This is a blasted country where a person can't get anything decent to drink. Who says so? I asked. Why Mr. Winburn, she replied. I'll thank you to ignore that old fool, said I. He smells bad, she said. It's true. His foot gives off a frightful odor. It's the odor of the devil, I told her, and you'd better stay clear of it.

NOV. 11. One of my herefords has gone missing, also a keg of white lead. I suspect the Navajos of stealing both in the night. They are exceedingly stealthy and can come and go in the twinkling of an eye with no one the wiser. Unlike the Pah-Utes and Oraibis, who have largely accepted our presence, the Navajos resent the whites settling in this country and for their part take the attitude that since we have occupied their lands, they can take from us freely in return. Mr. Winburn is worse than ever. Reduced to a mere skeleton. The skin over his foot has broken and now runs a green matter. I have washed and dressed his wound every day, though it smelt so miserable as to turn my stomach. He is a great burden to me now, and his delirium keeps us all awake at night.

NOV. 12. Rain and snow all day. Put up my little cast mill and ground some corn and as I did so reflected on happier days, during those first years in Harmony when all our relations and our lives in general were marked by the sentiments suggested by the name we had chosen for our little settlement. It was Emma, I believe, who introduced the first strains of discord. She was not meant to live the Principle, no matter what she professed, but wished to draw to herself all Mr. Lee's attentions. And yet it is true that she remained loyal to him to the end, if you discount her dalliance with Wells Spicer. During the time of our confinement in prison, when she was left to attend to matters at the ferry, we received news of her imminent defection. Mr. Lee was much troubled by reports that she had permitted the Gentile Spicer to slaughter a beef and had outfitted him with horses so that he might conduct a prospecting expedition to the San Juan Mountains. In return, Spicer had promised her one-quarter of all the profits the venture might generate. Mr. Lee wrote to her immediately, informing her that on no account should she allow Spicer or any other man the use of animals that rightfully belonged to him, and he chastised her in the strongest language for her recklessness. In reply he received a letter filled with the sweetest language in which she professed to have acted only on his behalf in an attempt to raise funds for his bail. And, as always, he believed her. But I knew better. She is a woman who has always been vulnerable to the attentions of men, whether it be the hired men she boarded or a passing stranger. I love the company of men, she once told me, and I replied, You do not have to convince me of that. And now she has taken up with another Gentile, this miner named Frank French. I fear the fire of the Gospel has died in her bones and the beastliness of carnal nature is prevailing over her senses.

NOV. 12. Found one of my cows dead today in the bog near the pond, the margins of which are overgrown by a coarse strong grass whose roots mat together and gradually encroach upon the surface, forming a floating edge that appears solid to a man or unsuspecting animal. However, it is easy to overweight it and cattle coming to drink have been known to drown. This is what happened to my cow. I found her badly mired, her eyes rolled back in her head, dead several days and the meat so badly spoilt there was no chance of salvage. Thus I am left with two cows to see me through the winter. Mr. Winburn is now pleading with me to remove his foot. I told him I am not a surgeon. But I see that he will surely die unless something is done. If Emma were here, I know she would perform the operation with little hesitation. I thought long and hard tonight about whether I am capable of undertaking such a procedure, using the crude tools available to me, meaning the handsaw and butcher knife, and I decided I am not.

Were he a brother, perhaps I would try, but what do I owe a Gentile? Even if he did continue to prove out this farm in our absence. If I should let him die, I am sure there will be those who accuse me of wanting him out of the way in order to lay full claim to this place. But I say, let them talk. Every tub must stand on its own bottom.

NOV. 13. Showery this morning, a desperate wind. As I returned from hunting cows and entered the shanty, I had the misfortune to encounter Mr. Winburn hacking at his leg with the saw. He was in a terrible delirium. The Indian Shew had arrived in my absence and was crying, Arick oom cot too soot—Stop you fool!—but old Winburn seemed possessed of a supernatural strength and all attempts by Shew to wrest the saw from him met with failure. Little Belle cowered wide-eyed in the corner of the room, while Mahala stood dumb as an oyster before the fire, her dark Indian features as unreadable as ever. Get out, all of you, I said, and ushered Shew and the girls outside. Then I went to Mr. Winburn's side and quietly said, Give me the saw. He looked up at me with wild and reddened eyes and began to weep like a baby. I took the saw from him and put the water to boil on the fire and began to tear lengths of cloth from an old bedsheet. He had made a bad mess of his leg. Gore obscured his cut and I could not tell how deep it was. Take it off, he pleaded with me, just take it off, begging me to remove his gangrenous foot. I laid out the India-rubber poncho beneath the foot and leg and then I went to work. As I did so I thought of Emma. If she could do this, I thought, then so could I. I gave him a piece of wood to bite down on, yet he seemed to shrink from me as he looked into my eyes, as if he found something there to be frightened of. Bite down, I ordered, and he did as I said. At that moment, I felt a great confidence and strength come into me. Who was The Mouse now? I thought. Where was that timid woman who had endured all those whispered taunts? The two of them always conspiring to reduce me to a spineless creature as though they were the only ones capable of fierceness. Mr. Winburn was shaking badly and he began to sob, emitting small choking sounds from between his clenched teeth. I imagined Emma's strength leaking away and becoming my own as I lifted the saw and grasped the old man's leg with my left hand. With my right I set myself to the hard work of sawing through flesh and bone. The flesh gave easily, but the bone was another matter. At first, Mr. Winburn screamed, spitting the wood from his mouth, and then his eyes rolled back and he passed out. By the time I had finished, he appeared quite lifeless, though his pulse still beat. Yet so far gone was he that I do not imagine he could feel the scalding water I applied to the stump after tying if off with twine. Not long after, Frank came into the shanty, having returned from hunting up the horses, and when he took in the scene, he whispered, Oh, Ma, what have you done? Only what Emma would have done in my place, I said, and then I gave him the gangrenous foot and told him to bury it where the wolves wouldn't dig it up. About 8 o'clock in the evening Mr. Winburn give up the ghost, from the loss of blood, I think. He never regained consciousness. I wept at his passing, not so much for the loss of him but because all my work was for naught. Still, I believe I done the best I could for him.

NOV. 15. Unwell for several days. Feverish, and dreaming off and on, the bitterest visions of gore. We buried old Winburn at the edge of the cornfield in a grave marked by a wooden cross and the effort seemed to expend all my remaining strength. I have not left my bed for two days. The boys have been good to me. Frank cooks and little Joe feeds me by hand. Belle is her usual fractious, high-strung self. It is Mahala who worries me most. She has been exceedingly wooden and cold with me. I feel she blames me for Mr. Winburn's death. She is at an age where I feel she should start a family of her own. What she needs is a husband and I have told her so. But here's the difficulty. I don't believe a white would have her, and it would be nigh impossible for her to return to her tribe, even if we could ascertain at this late date where she had come from. I broached the subject with Shew a while ago and offered her in marriage but he only laughed. Wahkish, he said, meaning if I gave him a cow he might take her. But I have no cow to give, and so the subject was dropped.

NOV. 16. Still confined to bed with weak nerves. My hands shaking worse than ever. The sky outside is a monstrous black. All I do is stare out the window, where one storm after another brews up. The shanty has a canvas ceiling laid over with lodgepole and grass. The walls are made of whitewashed log. I have a rag carpet over a rough board floor, and a wide chimney place. My old white curtains are trimmed in lace but gray from soot. A patchwork counterpane covers this bed. On a shelf sits my Bible, a Book of Mormon, my Deseret Reader, a looking glass, a sewing basket, and a photograph of Mr. Lee sitting on his coffin, given to me by Mr. Fennemore. These are my worldly goods. And that is the nose and tail of it.

NOV. 17. Somewhat better today. Several of the natives helped me fortify the corral to keep the stock from getting loose and I traded them a length of calico I'd been saving and a little beef. Through the night it commenced storming. Snow two inches deep this morning.

NOV. 18. Snow and rain all day. Snow three inches by noon, but by evening the ground bare in spots. This storm has wet the ground more than all put together since July. My mind is much harried by worry for our welfare. We have no flour left, and our supplies of sugar, coffee, and tea have long since been depleted. One of the cows is down with an infected bag and looks very poor. We would be sore put to lose her.

NOV. 20. Storm continues unabated. Found five of my Bremmer chicks froze in their nests.

NOV. 21. Day cloudy. Some snow still on the ground. About noon Mr. Henry Echoles, a Virginian by birth, drove in with a horse team en route to the mines. He concluded to stop with me a few days. I have no objection to this as he seems to be a frank, free, open, and unsuspecting man, ready to take hold and help in any way he can, and I readily admit to welcoming the sight of another white face. Mahala continues in her sullenness. Apparently old Mr. Windburn, unbeknownst to me, had made her an offer of marriage and she had formed an attachment to him. She reported this to Frank rather than me. Now that he is gone, she has become listless and more uncommunicative than ever. She told Frank that she no longer has any wish to live. She thinks her prospects for gaining a husband and home have disappeared with the death of Mr. Winburn. What will become of her now, I do not know. Nor can I imagine how we will make it through this bitter winter.

NOV. 23. By the assistance of the Pah-Utes and Mr. Echoles, we are within one day of curing all the corn and finishing the roof over the stone cellar. Telly, Tuba's lady, arrived in the afternoon for a visit. I put the problem of Mahala to her. Is there not some brave in your village who would add her to his harem? I asked. She acknowledged the prospects were dim, for Mahala is no longer Indian and yet not prized as white but is rather viewed by the natives as an unfortunate amalgam of the two. There is also the problem of her appearance. She is, I'm afraid, most unattractive by any standards. Telly inquired as to why I had taken such an ugly child into my fold in the first place. I had some difficulty explaining that my motive was to save her soul, for I am not sure such a concept even exists within the native worldview, where everything seems to exist in an already saved state. Thinking of Jesus, I attempted to teach by parable. What if you had a cow, I said to Telly, that in every way was a good and fine cow except it lacked one leg and therefore was rendered unable to prosper in the world and yet through a powerful medicine you were able to restore its lost leg, just as the Saints through the power of baptism are able to restore a soul to the godless Lamanite who lost his way so long ago. Would you not strive

288 · RED WATER

to do so? She shook her head. No, she said, patting her pow-ah, I would kill it and eat it. It is at times like this that I despair of my ability to dwell much longer among these ignorant Remnants of Israel. Mr. Echoles, who overheard this exchange, was much amused by Telly's response until I shot him a look that silenced his laughter. Later in the evening he made bold by referring to Mr. Lee and our marriage arrangements. He said he had been told before leaving the upper settlements that he would find one of John D. Lee's widows living at Moenabba, a woman whose sister and mother had also been married to Lee, and he wondered if I could confirm or deny the truth of this report. I explained to him that indeed my beloved older sister, Aggatha, had been Mr. Lee's first wife, and that I had been married to him later, and, subsequent to that, my aged mother had also been sealed to him for the sake of her soul. Ah, he said, with a mischievous grin, so it was as with the three-legged cow! Mr. Lee married your mother in order to make the animal whole again! I found his comment to be most impudent and removed myself from his presence at once. I fear I misjudged him, assigning to him a more noble nature that he actually possesses. I intend to make it clear to him in the morning that I expect him to be gone by nightfall.

NOV. 24. Still cloudy and somewhat cold. Mr. Echoles much subdued with me this morning and I concluded to give him a reprieve for his earlier offense since he agreed to ride out with me to hunt up the cows which somehow got out and have strayed again in search of feed. Each time they go missing I fear I shall find them dead and I darst not let them range far. As we saddled up my Doll Belle mare and Sir Henry Belle, Mr. Echoles made to sympathize with the unfair treatment of my husband. Surely there were others more to blame for that unfortunate affair at the meadow, he ventured. Was it not true that my husband was simply following orders when he led the attack on the emigrants that day? The first thing I did was to disabuse him of the notion that my husband had in any way been a leader of the attack.

But didn't he ride into the encampment with a white flag of truce and persuade the emigrants to lay down their arms and march out, promising them safe conduct, and then, shortly later, when they were all out in the open, give the signal to open fire upon those hapless souls? Without an understanding of context, I informed him, it's impossible to explain these events. I meant to continue in my defense of Mr. Lee but I found myself so overcome by weariness with the subject that I simply mounted up and rode away, leaving him to follow. For much of the morning we kept our distance from each other. He combed the ravines while I kept to the ridges where I had a view of the land. About noon we encountered a desperate windstorm and met up and took shelter by the high side of a cliff where we could be reasonably comfortable. We amused ourselves by attempting to decipher the drawings left on the rocks by some ancient primitive people, figures of horned animals and men with strangely humped backs and long sticks issuing from their mouths. Mr. Echoles guessed the sticks were meant to portray some kind of musical instrument, such as a flute, while I insisted they represented pipes for smoking as I did not think the making of such music instruments lay within the scope of primitives. The truth is we shall never know what these things are for, he said after a while. Their import is as lost to us as their makers, just as we will likely never know who was really responsible for the tragedy that occurred at Mountain Meadows. I felt he had stretched the thing too far in his eagerness, perhaps, to lead back to a subject in which he apparently has a great interest and, as the wind had died down some, I suggested we resume our search for the cows. A wise head knows to keep a closed mouth, I thought, and I decided it best to seal my lips to him. As we set off, we found the footing poor. Ice had formed on the slopes and poor Doll Belle and Sir Henry Belle skidded on their hocks with every step. I began to despair of ever finding my animals but then we crested a ridge and I spied my brindled cow, standing against the wind with her head down and an arrow protruding from her side. When we reached her, we found her in a sorry state with a reddish foam issuing from her nostrils and her sides heaving heavily. I dismounted, and with some effort managed to break off the arrow. I made no attempt to withdraw it as I knew this would result in a greater loss of blood. I then looked up to see three natives emerge from a stand of tall willows. I took them to be Navajos, judging from their attire. They commenced to raise their bows and whoop and holler and cause their horses to prance and spin, at which time I returned to my horse and removed the Henry rifle from the scabbard and took aim. My hands were shaking badly, and this I hoped they could not see, for in truth it is unlikely I could have hit my mark even if I had intended to. I raised the barrel slightly and fired two shots into the air above their heads, at which time they turned and fled, disappearing into the thicket of willows. Mr. Echoles seemed visibly shaken by this encounter and pleaded with me to leave the scene at once but I told him I would not go without my cow. By setting a loop of rope around her horns I managed to coax her into movement and by means of prodding and pulling the wounded animal we were able to retrace our steps and reached home just before nightfall. Frank helped me to treat the wound with saltpeter and gunpowder and we put the cow in the small corral for the night, hoping to find her still alive in the morning.

NOV. 27. Cold. Frost flying all day. Butchered the cow who expired in the night. Hauled willow in the afternoon and hung the salted meat in the cellar. I am now down to one cow, and she is still missing. Mr. Echoles repaired my grinding mill; he is quite handy. Belle has taken a liking to him and follows him wherever he goes. As the afternoon fared away, several Oraibis arrived with the news they had spotted my remaining missing cow in the river bottoms to the north of here, and I dispatched Frank and Mr. Echoles to fetch her. Then I set about schooling Belle and Joe for an hour or two, using the lessons Mr. Lee had written out for his pupils in the penitentiary. I took the opportunity to explain to Belle how even in his most fallen circumstances, her father had seen fit to establish a school within the prison walls for the purpose of attempting to educate the murderers and thieves among whom he found himself. He was a prince among men, I informed Belle, and here is the proof, for who else would think of attempting to better the minds of the lowest elements of society, even as his own life was being threatened? If he was so good, she said, why'd they kill him? Because they weren't half his measure, I informed her, and did not possess his vision. What vision is that? she asked. They did not understand the oaths and covenants that bound him to his duty and nor did they— When I grow up, she said, interrupting me and showing scant interest in my subject, I am going to have twin girls, just like Aunt Emma, and I'm going to name them Orpha Ora and Aura Ola. Such is the strange turn of her poor little mind. Tonight the wind is whistling all around this shanty. The children are all now asleep. I feel rather lonesome and blue and think I, too, shall go to bed. Sometimes I wish I had never seen this old windy land.

NOV. 28. Mr. Echoles departed today, but not before laying out a strange proposal before me. After he had readied his animals, he returned to the shanty where I was engaged with the task of mending and sat beside me and delivered a little speech he had obviously prepared in advance. I am a bachelor, he said, and you a widow woman, and neither of us young anymore. And it seems to me we might be of some use to each other. I propose to return this way in the spring and take you and your children from this harsh life. And where would you take us? I inquired. To California, where my sister and brother are living, and where a man can make a fortune, I'm told, if he's willing to work at it. It's not a fortune I desire, I replied. My riches are already laid up in Heaven where my good husband waits for me. I am sealed to him for Time and All Eternity, and this bond prevents me from entering another union, now and forever. I think he was expecting my rejection for he seemed not surprised a whit by my answer. I proposed that God speed his way, and turned back to my sewing, and without further words, he rose and left.

NOV. 30. Lowery and cool. Nothing of importance occurred today. The place seems quiet with Mr. Echoles gone.

DEC. 1. Found Mahala sitting in the cellar today, making small incisions on her arms with the kitchen knife. What are you doing! I cried, taking the knife from her. Without answering she got up and walked off into the fields and did not return until after dark.

DEC. 3. Day more mild, clear. My sons Frank and little Joe went to Moencroppa with a two-horse team and got a load of wood. I took advantage of the warmer weather and heated water and washed our clothes outside in the big tin tub and hung them on the rails to dry. About 3 o'clock I took the cow to Shew's place and left her to be bred. Around 8 p.m. the Oraibi chief's son, Alcalda, arrived from a trading trip to the settlements and brought me a letter from Emma. He reported the snow two feet deep on the Kaibab Mountains and near the Bitter Springs. Said that six men were at the ferry and that Emma was preparing to remove herself and her children from that place. Apparently Mr. Johnson is to take over the management of the ferry for the church. I waited until I got the children to bed to read Emma's letter in full. It covered three pages, and I could see, from the changes in the quality of the ink, that it had been written over a period of time. In the first part of the letter she inquired, as usual, about my state of health and the welfare of the children. The remainder of the letter was devoted to her true subject, which is her desire to have Belle with her. She claims to have had a letter from Ann who is apparently living in Idaho with an Irishman named Beezer McGee, and in this letter she reports Ann expressed the wish that she, Emma, be given charge of her daughter. It is not that Ann holds anything against me or doubts my fitness to mother her child, Emma explained, but rather that she desires her children raised together. Little Sam pines for the company of his sister, Emma wrote, and given that it is the wish of the child's mother for them to be reunited, she feels we must honor her request. She added that she intends to leave Lonely Dell just after Christmas and that I should look for her to arrive before the New Year, snow and weather permitting. Her letter has left me deeply vexed.

DEC. 1. Cold, light weather. Awoke to find my Doll Belle mare missing. Toward evening the Pah-Ute Cuck-e-bur rode in on his pony leading my mare. Said he found her fifteen miles distant. I think he expected some reward for bringing her back but I could think of nothing I could part with. Then I spied my old Deseret Reader, containing the keys to the Deseret Alphabet, and this I presented to him. He looked perplexed by my gift, but I told him that if he studied it carefully, he could learn to read and write.

DEC. 2. Cloudy and cold. Wind north. Frank has concluded he should undertake a journey to the upper settlements in an effort to procure us flour and other much needed supplies. I am against him attempting to cross the Kaibabs with so much snow and the prospect of more to come. I find the unfavorable appearance of the weather rather discouraging, and after a long discussion, he agreed to defer his trip, for the present at least. We have plenty of corn and beans and potatoes in the cellar, plus the meat from the cow we were forced to butcher. This will last us for a while, though it makes for a tedious diet. What I would not give for a cup of tea, or a slice of bread, or some sugary sweet. In the last few days, I have felt my courage draining away. My body remains willing, if somewhat enfeebled, but my spirit grows increasingly weak. We have nothing to do here except try to keep warm and make our own amusements yet I feel not a shred of joy in this house and no will to make merry. I tried a little singing and step-dancing last night but could not rouse the children to join me. Mahala spends her days I know not where. She leaves the shanty at dawn, wrapped in her heavy blanket, and does not return until dusk. When I ask her where she has been, my inquiry is met with silence or else she utters native words, unintelligible to me, that she has picked up from Taltee and Shew. I believe she often visits them in her daily wanderings, walking the distance to their village, and I fear she may be engaged in unnatural activities. This evening I helped her overcome her reluctance to kneel and made her pray with me. I felt I called forth the Spirit most forcefully but when I opened my eyes and gazed at her, I saw that she was unmoved. She had dropped to her haunches and sat picking at the sores on her arms, her eyes glazed and unfocused. Joe and Frank also seemed unmoved. At the conclusion of my prayer, I caught them arm-wrestling before the fire, attempting to stifle their giggles. How am I to instill godliness in my children without the priesthood here to help me? I looked at my fatherless boys, at my dark-skinned adopted daughter, and at the little raven-haired child who is not my own, and I wished ever so deeply that we could all be transported to that Better Place.

DEC. 13. Weather still unfavorable. About noon commenced snowing heavy. A while later a company came down the road and stopped in front of the shanty. The leader of the company, a man who gave his name as Sailor Jack, asked permission to spend the night as their animals were much wearied and he felt the storm would be best waited out. They have one mule-drawn wagon and a number of riding horses and pack animals and are all Gentile men en route to New Mexico. Their names, as reported to me: A. B. Fergussen, Oregon; Joseph W. Edwards, Missouri; Charles Sylvester, Maine; Charles Martin, Vermont; Edward Ducket, Missouri; John Moody, Maine (also known as Handy Bacon); R. E. Trask, Pennsylvania; and Sailor Jack, the leader, who is an Englishman from Bristol. They all hope to make their fortunes in mining. I gave the company use of the large corral to shelter their stock. In the evening, several of the men, including Handy Bacon and Sailor Jack, came to the shanty and brought me a packet of tea, for which I thanked them. They cannot know what a luxury this is to me. They then inquired if I had vegetables I'd be willing to sell and produced a bag of coins. I told them coins were of little use to me here, but if they were willing to part with a sack of flour I could let them have some potatoes and dried corn from the cellar, and we agreed to effect the transaction in the morning. Before retiring, they proceeded to nose about my shanty, making inquiries about my Book of Mormon and the picture of Mr. Lee, whom they recognized, having seen his likeness in the newspapers. Mr. Edwards and Mr. Ducket, both from Missouri and therefore naturally ill-disposed toward the Saints, said, Why do you have a picture of this butcher sitting on your shelf? And then it dawned on them that I was his widow, and yet instead of apologizing, they began to laugh and, summoning my dignity, I informed them that I wished them to leave as it was time for us to retire.

DEC. 14. Awoke to a scene of mayhem. The company of Gentiles stole away in the night but not before laying waste to my stores. The wind that raged all night covered their departure and I had no premonition of what had transpired until I awoke and went outside. My chicken coop has been emptied, with many of the chickens left dead. Sir Henry Belle is missing. And worst of all, the beef I had laid aside and a good half of my store of potatoes and corn have been stolen. I found my toolshed ransacked and many items taken and what was not carried off had been left strewn about on the ground. I felt so disconsolate I broke down in tears, and Frank was so enraged he pleaded with me to let him take the old Henry rifle and track the company down and reclaim our goods, but I could not let him set off on such a foolhardy mission for he could be no match for such blackguards and I darst not risk injury to my eldest son on whom I depend so heavily. And so I am left more destitute than before, and more filled with certainty that the end must surely be nigh when such iniquitous men walk the earth so freely, preying on the likes of a widow like me.

DEC. 15. Today I repaired a bridle which I hope to trade to Taltee and read some in Mr. Lee's journals. I turned to a page dated Sept. 6, 1875, Utah Penitentiary, the day of Mr. Lee's birth: "Sixty-four years ago today I came struggling into existence and have been struggling and battling with the Tide and Element of opposition ever since. My path, for causes unknown to me, has been a thorny one. A great portion of the Human Race, even many thousands whose Faces I have never beheld, now know my name and have taken an interest in my welfare here on earth. All the powers of Earth and Hell seemingly have been brought into requisition and arrayed ready to call to account every Act of my Life and to expose every weakness of my nature. I have been made to atone for the wrongs and follies that my accusers suppose I may have done and some have gone further even and tried to hold me responsible for something that I might possibly have thought of saying or doing that was evil. The day that gave me birth finds me within the walls of a Prison, associated with Felons of every grade and character. I have tried as a matter of policy to frame my conversation and demeanor to suit the circumstances and surroundings of my associates, that my stay among them might be agreeable and productive of good rather than evil. As the wise man said, there is a time to do all things. I have tried to amuse my fellow inmates by telling anecdotes and jocular sayings and yet in spite of all my collected witticisms and humorous sayings, I have failed to please all. While I humor some, I offend others. Is this not the story of my life? As the Apostle Paul said, So have I tried to be all things to all people. When durst I have tried to instruct the minds of my fellow inmates and improve their morals, in this duty I have made little progress. I am a prisoner for the Gospel's sake. Sometimes I try to lift up my heart and rejoice, believing my reward to be great in Heaven. I pray that my faith may not fail, but that I may stand firm to the end. Better to die like a man than live like a dog. I still live in hopes that I shall yet see the day when these Prison walls will no longer keep me from my Family Dear and Loved Ones at Home." Having read this much, I was overcome by grief and closed his journal until another day.

DEC. 16. Weather uncommonly mild. Frank and I have determined to take the Doll Belle mare and a pony lent by Shew to the Blue

Mountains on a hunting expedition in an attempt to procure venison to replace the beef that was stolen by the miners. Though it leaves me uneasy, given her poor state of mind, I am entrusting Belle and little Joe to the care of Mahala until we return. I do not think we will be gone more than three days and in any case Tuba and his wife, Telly, who arrived last night for a visit, have promised to return and check on my family in my absence. The prospect of this journey leaves me slightly uneasy as we will be entering unfamiliar lands, but I am relying on a map made by Mr. Lee several years ago upon returning from a successful hunting expedition, which lays out these directions: "From Tuba's camp travel north and up the Pah-Ute Creek to Navajo Camp, a distance of eighteen miles, thence northerly to main Navajo and Pah-Ute Trail to Piñon Canyon, thence take trail down through canyon and follow same through Main Valley to Four Needles, a large island of rock standing alone by the side of a big dry gulch. Follow Gulch Valley northerly to cane patch to the head of Canyon Bonito, thence take to the left upon the mesa north course and across the low saddle of burnt range when you will intersect the trail to the Blue Mountains. Game abundant here." I have memorized these instructions with the hope of being able to follow them. We set off in the morning, dragging a travois which we hope to load with game. This is to be the last entry in this journal until our return. May God speed our way.

DEC. 20. I know not where to begin in reporting the tragic events that have transpired since I last sat down to record my thoughts in this journal. I have endured a journey the likes of which I hope never to encounter again, and yet what I discovered upon my return made my own trials seem inconsequential. We were out four days, two of which were spent huddled in a cave against the ravages of a storm that blew up suddenly. The weather was so intense we were trapped without the possibility of even checking on the welfare of our animals which we had turned loose in the hopes they could find feed. At night, the temperatures dropped below zero and we were unable to sustain a fire till morning. When the storm finally abated, Frank and I set off in search of the horses who had taken the backtrack for home. After wandering in knee-deep snow for most of a day, we finally came upon Doll Belle and Shew's pony, both half frozen and in a much reduced state. My own feet were in danger of succumbing to frostbite and I was most anxious to thaw them out. As darkness came on we managed to start a fire beneath an overhang of rock and here we sheltered with the horses till dawn broke gray and cold and full of intimation of yet another storm. After breakfasting on hot cornmeal mush, we felt somewhat revived and set off for home, dispirited to have found no game. At Four Needles Frank shot a hare and this we roasted for a midday meal before mounting up again and pushing on. The climb up through Piñon Canyon left my Belle mare so winded I was forced to dismount and walk the last section on foot. By then Shew's pony had been rendered weak and Frank was also forced to go it afoot. We camped that night along the Navajo Trail and in the morning struck out with the first light, hoping to reach home before dark. We had not yet reached Pah-Ute Creek when Frank's pony slipped climbing a draw and went down with him, breaking his leg badly. As Frank lay in agony, I set about splinting the leg the best I could with branches I cut from willow and strips of cloth torn from his shirt. Throughout it all Frank did his best to be brave but his pain was so great at times I felt him slipping from me. Finally, with great effort, I got him onto the travois fastened to the pony and riding my Belle mare and leading the pony I made my way to Tuba's village, arriving after dark. That night Tuba helped me set the bone in Frank's leg and we cauterized the wound where the bone had broken the skin in the hope of preventing any festering. Then, on the verge of collapse, I gave over the care of my son to Telly, who sat up with him all night while I fell into a deep sleep. In the morning, when I awoke, I found that Tuba and Telly and some of the other villagers were keeping watch over Frank. They had made him a broth of herbs and tallow and this they were attempting to get him to drink. I determined to leave him in their care as I was anxious to make my way to Moenabba and see to my children whom Tuba and Telly had been prevented from visiting due to the intensity of the storm which had also struck this region. After breakfasting on corn mush and dried melon, I bid my poor son goodbye, promising him I would return the next day with a wagon and bring him home soon as he was strong enough to make the journey. I took the shortcut over the hills, keeping my Doll Belle moving at a steady trot, and still the trip seemed to take such a long time. An uneasiness weighed on me, and I was anxious to be home. The closer I came to the farm, the greater my anxiety became, and yet when I crested the last knoll and looked down on my homestead and the peaceful scene it presented, I felt all my worries had been for naught. There was my cow, still in the corral, and there was my little shanty and rock cellar and the mounds of corn fodder piled neatly beside the sheds. Only as I drew nearer to the sheds did I notice something unusual hanging from the big cottonwood tree growing in the yard. At first I thought perhaps Joe and Belle had strung up the Indian poncho as part of one of their games. The dark object twisted and turned in the brisk wind and I made for it, thinking to chastise the children later for having climbed the tree to tie the thing in place and thereby risking a fall in my absence. And then, with a sudden and most horrible feeling, I realized it wasn't the poncho hanging there at all. It was Mahala, shrouded in her dark blanket, hanging there from the limb of the cottonwood with a rope affixed to her neck. I rode up to the body, which was stiff and frozen to the touch. Belle and Joe were nowhere to be seen. I began calling out their names even before I dismounted, and once on the ground I ran for the shanty. I found them inside, huddled in bed beneath several blankets. The shanty was freezing, no fire in the hearth, and the children seemed more alarmed than relieved to see me. It came to me that they were seized by a fear so deep it was as if they had taken leave of their senses and did not even recognize me. Only when I had gained their side and bent over them, pulling each to my breast, did they make any sound, and then it was to let forth such heartrending cries it seemed to me they would both sob their hearts out. I built a fire and managed to coax the story of what had happened out of them and only then did I climb the tree and cut Mahala's body down. I drug it to the cellar where I left it for the night. According to what the children told me, she climbed the tree and hung herself the day after Frank and I left for the Blue Mountains. When they discovered her body hanging there, they had been so frightened they took to bed, which is where I found them three days later. I am so reduced by the events of these past days I have not the strength to add more to this account. May God help me in this darkest hour.

DEC. 22. Buried Mahala today. It took all the strength I could muster to dig the grave in this frozen ground, but by means of a pickax and shovel I was able to open up a shallow recess and lay her body to rest. I grieve that I could offer her no coffin, but I wrapped her securely in her blanket and laid over the grave with rocks. Then I heated water to boiling and poured it over the rocks so that when the temperature dropped at dusk they would freeze in place, thus denying the wolves an easy access to the shallow grave. By then the day was spent and I fixed the children their supper. They appear much vexed and upset by Mahala's death. We must not grieve too deeply, I told them, for Mahala has gone to a better place. To comfort them I pointed to the stars that were just then beginning to emerge in the night sky. She is there, I said, indicating one of the brightest stars. Already she has ascended to a throne on high. How do you know she has gone to Heaven? little Joseph asked. What if she weren't good enough? I know because she was baptized into the True and Everlasting Covenant when she was but yet a child and all who are baptized for the remission of their sins will ascend to the throne and dwell there in peace and everlasting happiness. I want to dwell in everlasting happiness, too, Belle said, and such a sad look came over her face as to break your heart. I drew her to me and said, Oh you shall, Belle, you shall, and we shall all be there together, you'll see. Once I had put the children to bed I sat before the fire, thinking of Mahala. I had never known her true birthday of course and instead celebrated the day of her naming and blessing as such. She was given a name and blessing by Mr. Lee on April 27, 1856, during the Great Reformation when all the Saints were called to undergo rebaptism due to the iniquity abroad in our land. Many Indian children were blessed that Sunday, including a three-year-old boy purchased by Brother Moroni Ingram, and little nine-year-old Sarah Littlefield. Ira Groves, aged thirteen months, was also blessed, though he died four days later, being in a poor condition when purchased. The high priests had sung "How Glorious Will Be the Morning" after which the entire congregation retired to Ash Creek for the purpose of being rebaptized, one by one. President Haight and Elders Higbee and Morris and Roundy and Dalton went first, followed by the other brethren, and then the sisters submitted to the icy waters and the children over the age of eight. We all rejoiced together and spoke our resolve to be better men and women. Never since our little colony was settled had there been such feelings of patience and contrition and joy and thankfulness to God for his mercies and loving kindness toward us through all our wickedness and the hardness of heart that had grown up toward one another. Everyone melted down in a flood of tears with thankfulness to their God for giving us a chance before it was gone too late for us to repent of our ways. Mr. Lee spoke to great effect and said that this was not a revival like had been sometimes of short duration but one that would continue until the dividing line should be drawn between the righteous and wicked and the End Struggle commence between the Two Kingdoms of Good and Evil. Then, pointing to the little red babe I held in my arms, my newly named Mahala, he prophesized that the red souls would also be blessed in the great revival and enjoy the good spirit having come for our mercies and kindness toward them. Now, twenty years after that day and many heartworn times later, I have laid the child I held that day into a cold grave. With no member of the priesthood here to say even a few meager words over her poor ravaged body, I offered up my own. I did the best I could for you, I told her. May God now receive your soul.

DEC. 23. Weather mild. About noon Tuby and Telly arrived bringing Frank with them on the travois, having become worried when I did not return to the village as I said I would. I delayed giving them the news of Mahala's death as Frank appeared so weak and frail. Tuba brought us three melons which will be a nice treat for Christmas. They elected to stay overnight and I fixed a good supper. It was during the meal that little Joe informed the company that Mahala had gone to live in the stars and I was forced to explain her demise. Tuba was much upset by the news and Frank reduced to tears. I felt I could not let my family succumb to grief since our reserves of spirit are so low to begin with and so I expounded on the glories of the next world but Tuba worked against my purpose by claiming that a person who takes her own life in such a manner becomes a walking ghost, unable to settle fully in this world or the next one. He promised to conduct a purifying ritual on her behalf once he had returned to his village and could assemble the elders for such purpose. I concluded to let him have his way, saying, Do as you wish, since I know she is saved through the power of baptism. After dinner I attempted to lift the somber mood by making music with my tambourine. We also sang hymns and thus we passed off the evening. Before leaving the next day Tuba said he had heard that I was going to move back to the settlements in the spring and that if I did they would all cry and be lonesome. Who told you such a thing? I inquired. He said that Jacob Hamblin had passed through the village while I had been away at the Blue Mountains and given them this news. Do not believe old Dirty-Fingered Jake, I told them. He only wishes me gone so he can claim my land, just as Emma is being pushed from the ferry so others can occupy the farm at Lonely Dell. When I mentioned Emma's name, Telly's face brightened. She come here soon? Telly asked, and added that she missed the woman who had once healed her of a bad sickness with her strong medicine. Apparently Hamblin gave them the news that Emma is already packing up her belongings and intends to make her way to Moenabba within the week. When Belle heard this news she began to dance with joy. Aunt Emma is coming, Aunt Emma is coming! she chanted until I told her to cease making such a commotion and we bid Telly and Tuba goodbye. I find myself dreading the prospect of Emma's visit. For one thing, I have so little food here with which to welcome her properly and I despise the idea she might find my circumstances so pitiful that she might feel compelled to treat me to her stores. Why is it that of all the wives it is Emma whom I have always felt to be my true nemesis? Her abundant and obvious strengths point up my weaknesses, her beauty shows up my plainness, and her cheerful manner has always stood in stark contrast to my own sober ways. I must see if I cannot come by a wild turkey or even some fat hares and lay by a few supplies for her visit so it will not be so starkly evident to her that we live little better than the poor suffering natives. Just as I must see if I cannot improve Belle's mood before she arrives for I would hate for her to see the child so troubled. She has not yet recovered from Mahala's death, and has adopted a sullen and largely silent manner with me which in its own haunting way reminds me of nothing so much as Mahala's own behavior toward the end, as if the darkness of the deceased child had somehow entered the living one.

DEC. 25. Christmas dawned upon without a storm, though partially cloudy. I got up a good breakfast of corn cakes and the last of the molasses which I had saved for the occasion. We also ate one of the melons Tuba had brought. Then I laid out the gifts I had worked on for the past weeks. Belle was much pleased with the new dress I made for her doll, and Frank accepted the trousers I sewed for him, using material I picked from Mr. Lee's old coat, though he will not be able to get them on over his splint until his leg heals. Little Joe gave thanks for the buckskin suit I fashioned out of the skins I traded Shew for, though I could sense his disappointment with the gift. I suppose he is too old now at eleven to be much taken with the prospect of playing Indian, especially as he has no other boys for playmates here. The children surprised me by presenting me with a beaded bag they had procured from one of the natives. It is a curious thing to me, an ornament I have no use for, but nonetheless a pretty object and I let them believe it greatly pleased me. In the afternoon Joe and I took the rifle and walked into the hills, leaving Frank and Belle secure before the fire, and I managed to bring down two mourning doves which made us a fine stew for supper. That, and the pot of tea I brewed using the last of the packet given me by the miners, left us with full stomachs at the close of this day, Our Savior's day of birth.

DEC. 26. Weather moderate. Nothing of consequence happened today.

DEC. 27. About 8 in the morning Joe and I took the Doll Belle mare and riding double made our way to Taltee's village to see if we might trade a bridle for two turkeys from his flock. The Oraibis do not keep chickens but they have domesticated turkeys and I hoped to procure a mating pair to breed and establish a flock of my own. It took us most of the day to reach the village which sits atop a mesa with a far view out over the land. It is the custom of these natives to build their adobe houses stacked atop each other, with no windows or doors but rather openings in the roofs through which, by means of ladders, they ascend and descend from one chamber to the next. When we at last arrived at the mesa, I found the villagers busy preparing for one of the dances which they hold frequently this time of year. On the open plazas some of the natives were carving and painting little effigies while others were engaged in making masks. The effigies are wooden images about six inches high meant to represent various gods, some to help them prosper in hunting, others to make rain and snow, and still others to oversee the growing of corn. From what Taltee has told me in the past, they consider the sun or some Great Spirit who dwells therein to be the Supreme God who rules over everything and these images they make are of the lesser gods. Our arrival in the village caused a mild stir for these natives are unused to seeing a white woman traveling alone, with only a child for a companion, buy they soon recognized me as the wife of Yawgatts and I felt no hostility from them. On the contrary they made to welcome me and dispatched one of their numbers to take me to Taltee while others attended to my horse and took charge of Joseph. I found Taltee in one of the underground chambers, arranging pots of sprouted beans before a fire. I recognized Tow-wow-wewin, an Oraibi elder, and his wife, She-ma, sitting in the corner of the chamber. The room smelled heavily of smoke and sweat and other odors I could not define and the heat was quite intolerable to me, dressed as I was for the winter cold. Seeing my evident discomfort, Taltee led the way up the ladder and I followed and to my relief found myself on one of the rooftop plazas where several women were spinning and weaving and mending their moccasins. One woman was engaged in the business of arranging her daughter's hair in the elaborate style worn by the unmarried Oraibi maidens in which the thick coarse hair is twisted into great rounds and affixed on either side of the head. The women giggled when they saw me and averted their eyes while I explained to Taltee the purpose of my visit, using the words for turkey and hunger and barter. I produced the bridle I had brought for trade. He took the bridle from me and examined it and then held up one finger, indicating he would give me one turkey for the bridle. I shook my head and held up two fingers. Thus it went, back and forth, for some time until we heard the sound of a conch shell being blown on the plaza directly below us, indicating the dance was about to begin. Suddenly, from all parts of the village, people began to pour forth from the houses and assemble in the central plaza. Taltee indicated we should follow suit. With my bargaining interrupted, I could do nothing but join the others and hope to resume the negotiation later. Several Indians had painted and rigged themselves out with rattle boxes made of turtle shells with sheep hooves attached to them so that they rattled scandalously with every step they took. Many wore frightful attire. As I made my way to the plaza, I found myself gazing at four Indians with masks on and jaws attached to them about a foot long with two rows of savage teeth. They made their way from dwelling to dwelling, snapping their long teeth and stamping and rattling their turtle shell rattles. I will not attempt to describe fully the ensuing ceremonies as they lasted many hours and involved much frenzied dancing and costume, all the fancy rigging and jumping about that their wild nature and ingenuity can invent. At one point we removed ourselves to one of the underground chambers called kivas and several of the masked Indian dancers came down the ladder headfirst. They were naked except for a breechcloth. They yelled and danced and sang and hopped about until out of breath and then moved about the room, upsetting the pots of sprouted beans. Then they went back up the ladder feet foremost which they seemed to consider quite an exploit. Little Joe was most taken with this display and in fact seemed fully attentive to all the proceedings. When the ceremonies had finally concluded a feast was laid out consisting of the flat corn bread they call peek and stewed peaches and boiled mutton with red peppers and raw onions—more food than I had seen in many months, and I had to control myself in order not to eat so much as to make myself sick but Joe showed no such restraint, gorging especially on the sweet peaches. By then it was too late to set off for home. Darkness had already long since fallen. Taltee made it known to me that I could sleep in his room with him and his wife and baby daughter, and so Joe and I passed the night in an airless chamber, wrapped up in a single blanket, lying on the packed dirt floor. In the morning we breakfasted on boiled corn mush and a soup made from the meat of a panther and I commenced bargaining once again with Taltee for the turkeys, finally striking a bargain for a tom and hen by promising to add an old shirt to the deal. The turkeys were tied up by the feet for the journey home and I set off with the noisy fowl draped in front of me over the saddle and Joe

behind, reaching Tuba's village at Moencroppa by late afternoon. Here
we stopped to rest and ate a melon. Before departing, Tuba made me a
present of a buckskin robe. He said he knew it was the time of year
when whites give presents and since my husband was not here to make
me a present, he would offer one instead. I tried to give him bullets in
return but he said when he made his friend a gift he did not want anything in return. Such are the glimpses of nobility that occasionally
show themselves in the red man's soul. Arrived home at sunset to find
my corrals filled with cattle and two wagons drawn up before my
shanty. Emma and her brood were settled before my fire, having
arrived in my absence. My excitement at seeing her was less than complete, knowing as I do that we will surely face a struggle over Belle
before we are through. Nevertheless, I made as if I was most happy to
see her.

DEC. 28. Snowing like mischief. Felt low-spirited all day. I am trying
to put a good face on the thing but the presence of Emma and her six
children and her new beau, Mr. French, has only pointed up the differences in my welfare and hers in the wake of the loss of our husband.
She appears in her prime and boasts of weighing 165 pounds and her
children also reflect a state of well-being, as if they have suffered little
in the way of deprivation. She complains only of having been cheated
by the Church Authorities, having been unable to collect the one hundred head of cattle she had been promised for signing over the deed
to the farm at Lonely Dell and her interest in the ferry. After making
the journey from the river, stopping at established watering spots at
Navajo Springs, Bitter Springs, and Limestone Tank, she arrived at
the church farm at Willow Springs and attempted to claim her cattle
from Lot Smith who, instead of turning over the hundred as agreed,
allowed her to collect only fourteen head, and those grudgingly given.
She is full of venom for the church and its emissaries and speaks such
invective against it I was wont to usher the children outside to prevent
them from hearing such talk. Mr. French seems a nice enough man, as

Gentiles go, but he is much possessed by the mining fever and makes this his favorite subject. He feels sure there is gold to be found in the Paria Canyon and is sorry to have left the ferry before he could discover it but hopes to resume his prospecting when they reach New Mexico. For her part, Emma favors settling in the new town of Snowflake near the Little Colorado, where she hears there is money to be made in setting up a lodging and dining establishment. Already I can sense a discord between them as to which location they will settle on for their new home—New Mexico or Snowflake. I am only curious to know how long they plan to stop here but it is not a question I can easily ask without risking offense. Still, I feel the old resentment lying between us and I am anxious for her to be gone before it erupts into open hostility. So far, the subject of Belle has not come up. But we had a most unpleasant exchange tonight on the topic of Mahala, whose suicide, when reported, set Emma off on a tirade against the Saints for ever having interfered in the lives of the native children. This led to our first disagreement. What would you have had us do? I asked. Let the babes be sold to the Mexican traders for use as slaves in the mines? Or watch as their captors dashed their brains out against wagon wheels when we refused to buy them? It's a damned bad business any way you look at it, she replied. A damned bad business. Why she has taken to using this kind of language mystifies me for it does nothing to elevate the feminine spirit. In fact, I detect a general coarsening in her behavior, as if she has lost the light of the Gospel to guide her.

DEC. 29. A cold northeaster. Snowing and blowing so hard almost impossible to see from the shanty to the cellar. All forced to pass the day indoors crowded into these small rooms. The children are much excited by their reunion and making such commotion so as to wear badly on my nerves. And Emma full of chatter, reminiscing on earlier times. Remember the storm of '61, she said, when it snowed in Harmony for forty days and Sarah Caroline's poor babes were crushed by the walls falling in on them? As if I could have forgotten that most desperate time. All she accomplished was to remind me of her own heroic actions when, as the rest of us lay sick and despairing, she toiled night and day to keep us fed and raise our spirits. Where she comes by such strength I do not know, but I see that it has not abandoned her over the years but grown in proportion to her trials, while I feel reduced to a shrunken version of my former self. Even to stand next to her is to be reminded of our difference, for her girth and height dwarf my own, and so do our fortunes differ. When she took to complaining tonight about her meager herd of cattle I could not help feeling churlish and remarked that at least she had thirty fine head, with what she drove from the ferry combined with those she gathered from Lot Smith, while I have a single cow left to me, and a skinny one at that. This evoked not a shred of sympathy from her, however. She simply remarked that it was clear to her that I must remove myself from this place as soon as possible and relocate among whites where there might be a chance of making another marriage and bettering my chances for a decent life. I informed her it was my intention never to marry again but bide my time here on earth until I could be reunited with Mr. Lee in the Celestial Kingdom. Well, I would do your biding in a place with a few more creature comforts, she said, lest you find yourself so destitute you are reduced to begging from the natives. It has always been her manner to talk in such a saucy fashion to me and it is no more appreciated now than it was in the past. Before retiring for the night, she added that at least she can take Belle from me, giving me one less mouth to feed and offering the child the possibility of a life among people of her own kind. And what kind is that? I said. Gentiles and whore-mongering miners? No, she replied, just the usual collection of blackguards who go by the name of Mormons. So we parted for the night, with a bad feeling between us.

DEC. 29. Cold, cloudy, windy, gloomy. Emma and her party show no signs of moving on even though the storm has abated, affording them decent weather for travel. I am attempting to get on with life and demonstrate to all that in spite of our penurious circumstances the children are well provided for. During the morning I cut letters out of leather to help the children with their alphabet and gave Frank and Emma's boys a spelling quiz. Several Navajos passed by in the afternoon, driving a band of horses. Mr. French attempted to parlay with them but they showed no inclination to friendliness. These Indians are a very saucy bunch and given to stealing whatever is not closely guarded and I warned Mr. French that he would have to watch his herd of cattle closely once he takes to the trail, now that they have been spotted. I am accustomed to Indian habits, he replied haughtily, as if to say he needed no advice from a woman. His mild rebuke freed me to make my own improper inquiry and I asked when he proposed to set off on the journey to their new home. Now that is up to Emma, he said. She is the one running this show. And so she is. I have observed the way she commands his attention and gets him to do her bidding. In truth she is surrounded by helpful hands. Her eldest boy, Billy, who is now eighteen, appears devoted to her welfare and shows none of the sadness of spirit that afflicts my own Frank. Ike, at sixteen, is a large, well-formed boy. The twins, Annie and Emmie, are now thirteen and poised on the brink of womanhood. Dellie, at seven, is a bright and happy child, as is her sister Vicki, just one year younger. The only odd one in the bunch is Sam, Ann's boy and Belle's older brother, who at twelve has the countenance of an old worried man. I ventured the opinion this afternoon, as Emma and I sat doing our needlework before the fire, that both Belle and Sam seemed to have inherited their mother's troubled nature. As I might have expected, Emma came to Ann's defense. It wasn't that her nature was so troubled but rather she just wasn't happy with her life with Father, Emma said. 'Tis a pity girls like her were married off to such old men. I didn't notice you objecting to such an arrangement for yourself, I said. But I was twenty-one, not thirteen, she replied, and I married for love, and therein lies the difference. She then looked around the room and pointed to her twins playing in the corner with Belle. Can you imagine Annie or Emmie being wed, for instance, to Mr. French? For they are now the same age as Ann was when she was sealed to Father, who was very near Frank's age. Mr. French, who was near enough to hear these remarks, looked momentarily discomfited. I did not say what I was thinking, which was, Mr. French is not the man Mr. Lee was and therefore any comparison is rendered impossible. As if to change the subject, Emma began talking of the recent attempts by Washington to outlaw polygamy in the territory. Many Saints were choosing to flee to Mexico, she said, rather than risk prosecution, and she feels it will only be a matter of time before multiple marriages are abolished. How can they be abolished when polygamy is a Divine Principle given to men by God, and which only God has the power to rescind? I asked her. She simply chuckled and said, Well, perhaps God will change His mind once he sees it's expedient to do so, for the assets of the church might well be confiscated and should that appear imminent, I have no doubt a revelation will be forthcoming, for when it comes to money or God's laws, the Saints are generally shrewd enough to protect their purses first. Such blasphemy, I muttered, and she smiled and laid a hand on my arm and said, I can see, Rachel, that we are no closer of a mind than we ever were but let's not argue for at least there's one thing that binds us, and that is it is we two who stood by Father to the end when all his other wives abandoned him. Aren't you forgetting Sarah Caroline? I said. No, she replied. You and I both know she had no feeling left for him. She simply couldn't be bothered to break the bond since she knew death would do that for her. I fell silent then and affected to be vexed by a problem with my sewing. Poor Mr. Lee, I thought. He had nineteen wives on whom he begat sixty-three children, and this is what it has come to. I am the only one left to protect his name and honor.

DEC. 30. Spent a most troubled night. In the dark the fear descended most forcefully like the fever on my brain. I could not rid my mind of

Emma's words, that she had married Mr. Lee for love. And what did I marry him for? This question plagued me all through the night and kept me from sleeping. Never before had I felt such a need to question my motives. When I first came to know him, he was already my sister's husband and I entered their household during the troubled times in Missouri when the Saints were being much persecuted by the mobs. At once I felt myself enfolded in the safety of their home, with Mr. Lee as my protector. I had always admired my elder sister Aggatha more than anyone else on earth and, from the time I was a small child, I wished for nothing more than to be like her. When her husband began to shower me with flattery, it seemed I was finally becoming her equal in some way. I believe in truth I loved her more than I did him in the beginning, and when the rumors began to circulate that the Prophet and some of the leading members of the priesthood were being sealed to multiple wives, I saw the possibility of being joined to my sister forever through marriage to the same man. And so I began returning Mr. Lee's attentions, careful in the beginning to gauge the effect of my actions upon Aggatha. If she was troubled by the notion of Mr. Lee courting me, she didn't show it. I think we all knew it would be an honor for our household if Mr. Lee was permitted to join the inner circle of elders who were allowed to practice the Divine Principle. On the day of my sealing to him, Mr. Lee stood on the right side of me, and my sister on the left, and truly I felt as if I were being married to both of them, and this filled me with the deepest happiness. I had to admit to myself last night that I did not marry him for love, but to fulfill God's holy ordinance and to assure the progression of our souls and, most especially, to remain close to my sister forever. Does this diminish the sense of connectedness that built up between us over the years? I think not, for I have never been a believer in romantic love, which is of this earth and therefore comes and goes and often leads to nothing but carnal ends. What Mr. Lee and I enjoyed was a rapturous entwinement of souls which spun a weave that nothing could undo and no one could cut. When he passed the nights with Emma or one of the others, when he spent the evenings card-playing and drinking with the hired men and then led Ann off to lay with her, I understood his lust and possession for when the devil comes and offers you your heart's desire, beware! He promises you false rewards when he promises the boat to the fisherman and proffers the horse to a man who hopes to ride, and to the man who lusts for the pleasures of the flesh, he brings not one fresh young wife but two. But perhaps God, in His wisdom, understood that this was what the superior man was due. Because Mr. Lee was a superior man, a man of many talents—a trader and a salesman, a farmer and factory man, a miller and a healer, a leader and interpreter, a ferryman and a builder of houses and of the Kingdom of God. Such men do not go by ordinary rules. Even during those darkest months I spent with him in prison, when all manner of horrible things were said of us, I saw him rise above the misery and never had I felt so closely joined to him. I was his one true wife, the only one willing to share his confinement, and if this is not proof of love of the highest order, what other name can it have? When I rose this morning, my spirit, nevertheless, still felt weighted by jealousy and doubt and, as it was growing light, I took myself into the canyon, to the grove of oak trees, and here I prayed and tried to find the will of the Lord concerning my remaining purpose here on earth. I returned somewhat calmer of mind only to find Emma packing up her wagons and making preparations as if to soon depart. Are you setting out then today? I inquired. I believe we shall, she said. The weather looks good for travel. It will be a pity to see you go, I said. She stopped what she was doing and turned and looked at me and said, Oh Rachel, you do not have to feign an affection for me that you do not really feel. If nothing else we have earned the right to be honest with each other. I felt my face redden and said, So we have. I only meant that the children have prospered in each other's company and I shall hate to see that end. You are not going to let me take Belle with me, are you? she asked. No, I said, I am not. I need her with me, as you can see. Emma said, And do her desires mean nothing to you? Because you know she wants to join us in our new life. Children often want things they cannot have, I said. She'll accept her disappointment once you are gone and we have settled back into our old life again. I could tell Emma was not yet prepared to give up. It is the wish of the child's mother that she be raised by me, she said, in the company of her elder brother. I have never cared a whit about Ann or her wishes and I do not know why I should do so now, I replied. After all, she abandoned her children and with them the right to control their destinies. Besides, I said, you must forgive me, but how do I know that Ann has really expressed such a wish to you? I have not known anyone to hear a word from her since she disappeared. Emma turned away, without a word, and ascended the step of her wagon. I could hear her moving things about though she was hidden from sight behind the canvas. Very soon she reappeared holding a letter in her hand. I take it you can still read in the Deseret Alphabet, she said, handing me the letter, for it's all the poor child ever learned. Under no other circumstances would I ever share this letter with you, but I do not like being called a liar. She then returned to her packing, leaving me to peruse the letter. It was dated October 12, 1877, and began

My Dear Emma,

You will no doubt be surprised to hear from me after all these years. I can offer no excuse for the silence, but then I know none is needed with you, as our spirits have always operated as one. I find myself feeling so low tonight and in need of a friend, and who but you should I think of? My companion of these last years, Beezer McGee, died yesterday, the result of a bad fall from a horse. He was the kindest man I ever knew and he treated me like a queen. I cannot yet think how I will go on without him. But then I remember thinking that about you at the time we parted. Have you always wondered why I did not join you at the river, given my promise to come? I feel I owe you an explanation, even at this late date, not because I think you expect one but because I want you to know the truth of what happened. As you might have guessed, I had come to the realization that I

could not live with that man anymore. You see, I had seen him kill someone in the most coldhearted way, or I believe I did. You may well ask how
I can be so uncertain of such a thing, but here are the circumstances.

Do you remember old Uncle John, the Gentile who came to work for
us for a season and who, after a terrible argument with Lee, decided to
leave Harmony and join some drovers headed to California with a herd?
Lee was much angered by his leaving, especially as Uncle John insisted on
collecting all his wages due, which Lee paid out grudgingly, half in cash
and half in horses. The drovers departed with their cattle but Uncle John
elected to stay an extra day and head out the next afternoon, planning on
catching up with the herd later. He saddled up about four the next day
and said he would make it to Pinto, driving his loose horses before him,
and Lee, affecting a contrite manner as he often did, offered to saddle his
horse and accompany Uncle John to help him with the horses and show
him a good camping ground for the night. Uncle John said all right, and
that, as you know, was the last any of us saw of him. I remember before
they left you asked Lee if he intended to return that night and he assured
you he did but told you not to wait up. He did return, about nine o'clock,
to find you and me and Sarah Caroline still sitting up and talking in her
parlor. He said we had better go home for it was late, and we did, assum-
ing he intended to pass the night with Sarah Caroline. Before we left,
however, I saw him get out his buckskin suit, and this troubled me. As you
know, when he had that on and darkened his face he looked more like an
Indian than old Moquetus. I felt sure there was something wrong when I
saw he was going to disguise himself. I went to bed and must have gone to
sleep for I knew nothing until the next morning. When I got up, I saw
blood on my feet and on the lower part of my nightdress, and I remembered a terrible dream. Then all that had happened came back to me in a
flash. That morning I went out to look for the cows. I ran across the dead
body of Uncle John about three miles up Pinto Canyon. I also found Lee's
Indian suit where he had hid it in some rocks. All this deeply unsettled my
mind, for in what I thought was my dream I had followed Lee into a
canyon and I saw him stoop and cut Uncle John's throat from ear to ear.

Everything that passed the night before was so vividly impressed upon my mind I could have told him every movement he made. And now I found Uncle John's body, with his throat slit, just as I had seen it. Was it a dream, then, or had I really followed Lee into the canyon and witnessed the murder? And if I hadn't, where had the blood on my nightdress come from, and who had murdered Uncle John? I began to doubt my own sanity that day. As you know, I had been in a distressed state for some time, unable to accept that I was with child yet again, and now I felt my mind beginning to unravel further. I could not sleep. I began having terrifying thoughts. I grew afraid of Lee, afraid of what he might do to those who crossed his purposes. A few days later, when he confronted us in the kitchen and demanded to know if we intended to go to the river with him, I felt myself coming apart. Until that moment I had not been sure I believed he was capable of cold-blooded murder, in spite of all that had been whispered about him in relation to the massacre, but that day, I tell you, I knew the truth. I understood that he was most capable of taking another man's life. Or even murdering young girls, as he had been accused of doing at the meadow. He had the wagons already loaded that morning, as you know, with everything he needed to move out of the country, and he left with Rachel and her family shortly afterward. What is more, he had, as part of his herd of loose stock, the horses he had given to Uncle John. When the boys came back for us a few months later, I knew I could not go, so I sent the children with you, promising to follow. But I did not follow, did I? Instead, a few days later, I packed my few belongings and made a fire in the kitchen for the purpose of burning down the house. This should give you an indication of my state of mind. Taking Albert with me on my black mare, I rode into the hills. I stayed a while there in the neighborhood and watched to see how the fire would work. The flames made me giddy. I saw the house all ablaze on the inside, then the rafters and roof caught, and I rode away and never looked back.

Well, Emma, that is the story of my departure from that life we shared. You may think it the evidence of an unsound mind and in truth I have never been able to assure myself that I did not dream the events I have related, except I know I did find the dead man, and I did find the blood on my nightclothes. Some time ago I returned to the vicinity in search of a horse that had been stolen from me. This was not long after Lee's execution, so I know he is gone now and with him a dark past. Still, I feel I will never entirely free myself of his influence, nor erase the memories of him.

I have heard from my brother that you are raising Sam but that Belle has gone to live with Rachel at Moenabba. Though I realize I have little right to make this request of you, I am hoping you will collect Belle as soon as it might be convenient for you to do so and bring her up yourself. It is not that I hold a grudge against The Mouse, but I am anxious that my child not be raised by one possessed by such a religious turn of mind, for I have seen the results of such fanaticism. Poor old Lee, I believe it was the cause of his undoing. Who knows what deeds were committed by him, and those like him, for the sake of such fanatical beliefs? We both know of instances where people were blood-atoned for their defections or presumed sins. Yet I have always felt Lee's actions at the meadow must have been motivated by the prospect of material gain as much as any desire to avenge the Prophet's blood, for who was it, after all, that ended up with most of the emigrants' cattle and at least a share of their goods? I never knew a man to love a dollar as much as he did, or to make himself more a slave to a master, for there was nothing he wouldn't do for Brigham, including murdering innocent souls. It used to turn my stomach to see them together. I hated to see a man grovel so and get caught up in another man's power. And you can see where it got him. When I learned of his death, I almost felt sorry for him, to have been so betrayed by the one he loved most in this world—a man who had been like his father. Now I suppose we have all been freed of the past, except I worry that his children will forever bear his shame, and his children's children, right down through generations, and this gives me all the more reason to hope that you might take Belle and instill in her some of your own fierceness, for I fear she will need it if she is to prosper in this world.

For myself, I am thinking of claiming Albert from my brother. I *believe I am capable now of managing one child, and Albert is young enough he may be able to forgive me and adapt to a life with me, which will surely involve some wandering. I am considering making my way up to the Gallatin Valley in Montana. A man named Stewart has offered me a ranch of 160 acres in return for half of the herd of blooded horses that Beezer and I built up together. Or maybe I will go to Oregon, or even back to Mexico. Wherever I end up, I don't imagine I will be there for long. I am infected by a wandering spirit. I always want to be where I am not, and for this I blame this country, whose big spaces call to me, and whose grand vistas demand that they be seen. I cannot know what your plans are, Emma, or what the future might hold for you, but I will always consider myself the most fortunate of persons to have had such a friend as you. I live in the hope that one day our paths will cross again. Until then, I remain always, your devoted friend,*

Ann

When I finished the letter I put it back in its worn envelope and stood looking out at the red hills, dusted with snow. Emma came to me silently and took the letter from my hand. Tears were coming from my eyes. Why are you crying? she asked. I do not know, I said. I durst not tell her the true reason, that I wept out of pity for myself. The letter had left me with the deepest realization that I had never been loved in such a selfless way, not even by my sister, from whom I had always hoped to receive such affection. Perhaps you can see your way now to letting Belle come live with me, she said. I'm afraid not, I replied, and I raised my head and looked her in the eye so that she might see my resolve and be humbled by it. As I did so, I felt myself growing large with the power I held over her, which was the power to finally deny her something, the very thing she desired most. The shoe was on the other foot now. I felt myself awash with strength, as if I had drawn unto myself a mighty invincible force, an army of souls who stood with me for the sake of the good and the righteous. I didn't think it would make any difference, she said, stuffing the letter into the pocket of her coat. But at least you cannot call me a liar now, can you? You mean the way you call me The Mouse? I said. That was an old game, she replied, one long since given up. Ann is wrong about Mr. Lee, I said. He didn't kill anyone, least of all that poor old Uncle John who we all know was murdered by the natives. She is nothing more than a demented woman, possessed of the most unnatural proclivities, and I thank the Lord above that at least two of her children have been spared a life with such a creature for a mother. She is not only a fool but a liar and I expect she'll come to a bad end. When it comes down to it, we'll all come to a bad end, Emma said, laughing. It's called death. I'm just hoping it gets waylaid and doesn't show up too soon for we've all got a bit of living we want to do yet, don't we? I intend to raise Belle in the faith, I said, just as her father would have wished, so that she might have the reward of being reunited with him in the hereafter. Her reward will be to make it to spring without starving, Emma muttered, and you, too. She then turned away from me and called out to Mr. French, inquiring if he was finished readying the cattle and was prepared to set off. I fetched all the children from the house so that we might bid them a proper goodbye. Frank came out, hobbling on the crutch Tuba had made for him, followed by little Joseph who had donned his buckskin suit for the occasion. Only Belle was reluctant to emerge. I found her hiding beneath the bed, weeping. I clasped her firmly by the hand and ordered her to act the brave part, as her father would have her do, and we joined the others outside. Ike and Mr. French were already mounted up and circling their herd of loose cattle, and Emma and Billy each commanded a team and wagon. One by one the children embraced one another then climbed up to kiss Emma goodbye, all except Belle, who refused any display of emotion. I had expected her to create a scene of extreme distress, but in this I was mistaken, for she stood wooden and silent. At last Emma descended the wagon and went to her and held her for a long while whispering something in her ear. Whatever she said to the child made her laugh. Then Emma crossed to where I stood and took my hand. Goodbye, Rachel, she said. I don't know when we will meet again, but I hope there's a better feeling between us when we do else one of us could end up dead. I could tell she meant it as a joke, but I didn't laugh. You've left two cows in the corral, I said, ignoring her foolery. You won't want to forget them. I didn't forget them, she answered. They're my gift to you—you and the children. I wanted to strike her then, because once again I felt indebted to her, and overpowered by the generosity of her gift. I felt myself shrinking before her while she seemed to grow larger and larger right before my eyes. I realized at that moment that our whole lives are composed of such interplays, and that the only true subject of men's intercourse is the subject of power—not love, not hate, but power, which in the end always prevails. As for this place, she said, looking around her, don't mind what I said. It isn't really so bad. After all, think where I spent the last seven years. She laughed heartily and then smacked me on the back and yelled to Frank and Joe and Belle, Now you children be good and mind your ma else I'll be back to give you all a fine licking, you hear? With that she hefted herself up into the wagon and her children scrambled up after her and amid our waves and shouts of good luck and goodbye, the outfits pulled out, with the wagons taking the lead and Mr. French and Ike heading the herd to the side of the trail. As Mr. French passed by he tipped his hat to me and called out a thanks and said he expected he'd see me by and by as he intended to return to the Paria one day and come away with its gold. No doubt you will, I said, and added that I would always be pleased to see him.

———

DUSK IS falling now. I sit at the table before the window, writing in the last evening light. I have almost filled this notebook and since I have no other, this will perhaps be my last entry. The cliffs are suffused with a rosy glow, as if lit from within, and all the world is cast in a reddish hue. Tomorrow begins a New Year. I am satisfied we have turned a corner and better times await us. I have two turkeys. I have three cows. And I have a sack of flour, which I discovered Emma had left for me in the cellar. And so I begin the New Year with more than I had at the end of the last. I wish I could say I am grateful to her. I suppose a part of me is. But I know that in bestowing these gifts upon me she has reestablished our old relations and the stronger has once again chosen to shower mercies on the weaker, as if I needed a final reminder of our differences. Yet it matters not to me now. Our husband is gone. All the old ties have been dissolved. What was once a great, strong family, overseen by a prince of a man, is now but a vessel broken into its separate parts, never to be reunited until the Day of Judgment comes. My mind has turned back now to the life before me. I believe I will bake bread tonight, as a treat for the children, and then perhaps we'll sing a few hymns and play the tambourine to welcome the New Year. How good is God to have brought us through this first year on our own. How great are his mercies. Just now the sun reddened the walls of this room with an unearthly glow, as if His spirit wished to inform me it is near. I see the faces are beginning to appear in the stones. The cliffs have turned to fire. The sky is molten with color. It is all red tonight, all red and glorious. I feel my sister is here, and my mother, and the Prophet Joseph and the patriarchs of old. I see them beginning to take shape before me. Their countenance is writ there in the stones. The cliffs are aflame with all the hosts of Heaven, and I feel sure that soon he, too, will come and show me his face. He will come now, I know it.

He will come.

And I will be here waiting, his one true wife.

Author's Note

A FEW YEARS after the death of John D. Lee, Emma Batchelor Lee married Frank French and settled down in Winslow, Arizona, where she devoted herself full-time to the practice of medicine and became known as Dr. French. Emma died on November 16, 1897, and is buried in the cemetery in Winslow. The fate of Ann remains uncertain. Sam, her eldest son, was raised by Emma. Rachel kept Belle, Ann's daughter, as part of her family until Belle married and started a life of her own. There exists a notice of Ann's marriage, in 1894, to a man named Frank Kennedy. The date of her death is not known, nor is the place. Rachel spent the last years of her life in the Gila Valley in Arizona, surrounded by her children, grandchildren, and great-grandchildren. She remained a devout believer, and a defender of her husband and her faith. She passed away in 1912 at the age of eighty-seven. She never remarried.

While many of the characters and incidents portrayed in this book are based on actual lives and historical events, this book is a work of the imagination. It should be read as a work of fiction, not as a version of history.

I wish to thank the John Simon Guggenheim Foundation for a fellowship that enabled the research and writing of this novel. The deepest debt of gratitude is owed to the late Juanita Brooks, whose book *The Mountain Meadows Massacre* led to an interest in the topic at the heart of my story. My thanks go also to my earliest readers and trusted advisers: Dr. Gregory C. Thompson, Director of Special Collections at the J. Willard Marriott Library, University of Utah; Dr. Floyd A. O'Neil, Director Emeritus, the American West Center, University of Utah; the staffs of the Huntington Library and the Utah State Historical Society; and Rae Lewis, Sonja Bolle, Francis Geffard, Joy Harris, Dan Frank, and especially the historian Will Bagley, author of *Blood of the Prophets*, a forthcoming study of Mountain Meadows: without his help and endless generosity, I could not have written this book. Finally, to my husband, Anthony Hernandez, who brought me through many a dark night of doubt with such loving kindness, I owe thanks beyond words.